SPARROWHAWK

Book Five
REVOLUTION

A novel by
EDWARD CLINE

Lawson Library
A division of MacAdam/Cage Publishing
155 Sansome Street, Suite 550
San Francisco, CA 94104
www.macadamcage.com

Library of Congress Cataloging-in-Publication Data

Cline, Edward.
Sparrowhawk. Book V, Revolution / by Edward Cline.
p. cm. — (Sparrowhawk series ; bk. 5)
ISBN 1-59692-154-4 (alk. paper)
1. United States—History—Colonial period, ca. 1600–1775—Fiction.
2. United States—History—Revolution, 1775–1783—Fiction.
I. Title: Revolution. II. Title.
PS3553.L544S6273 2005
813'.54—dc22
2005020087

Paperback Edition: December 2006
ISBN 13: 978-1-59692-109-2
ISBN 10: 1-59692-109-9
Manufactured in the United States of America.

10 9 8 7 6 5 4 3 2 1

Book and jacket design by Dorothy Carico Smith

Cover painting: The Evacuation of Charleston, from "The Story of the Revolution" by Henry Cabot Lodge (1850-1924), published in *Scribner's Magazine*, September 1898 (oil on canvas) by Pyle, Howard (1853-1911)

SPARROWHAWK

Book Five
REVOLUTION

A novel by
EDWARD CLINE

"To hold an unchanging youth is to reach, at the end, the vision with which one started."

Ayn Rand, in *Atlas Shrugged* (1957)

CONTENTS

Chapter 1: The Pens

In June of 1765, what became known as the Virginia Resolves were first published in Rhode Island, in the *Newport Gazette*, all but the third Resolve, whose curious omission went unnoticed by anyone reading them for the first time. Subsequently, the seven Resolves — often only the first five — were reprinted in virtually every colonial newspaper.

The *Virginia Gazette* was not one of them. Its editor, an ardent Tory, refused to publish them, either from repugnance or at the behest of Lieutenant-Governor Francis Fauquier. Unless they procured copies of other colonial newspapers, Virginians gained knowledge of the Resolves and details of the dramatic session that produced them from letters, in taverns and coffeehouses, at weddings and balls, from merchants and tradesmen. Governor Francis Bernard of Massachusetts pronounced the Resolves an "alarm bell to the disaffected." Commander-in-Chief General Thomas Gage in New York wrote to George the Third that the Resolves "gave the signal for a general outcry over the continent."

The Resolves became the subject of earnest conversation among merchants, planters, farmers, and artisans, and a topic of heated debate in various colonial legislatures. These men were already fearful, sullen, and disaffected. The Resolves spurred their hopes that the Stamp Act could be successfully resisted, and caused them to adopt their own resolutions to defy and openly criticize Parliament. The Resolves acted as a linchpin that set their minds free to work; they were an example that certain words and actions were possible and necessary.

Throughout the colonies, even before the Resolves were broadcast, pens and tongues were busy assailing the Stamp Act. In Annapolis, Daniel Dulany, a lawyer and a member of the Maryland Assembly, was taking notes for a vigorous reply to two pamphlets whose arguments he took grave exception to. One, written by Soame Jenyns of the Board of Trade and a member for Cambridge Borough, lightly dismissed the principle of consensual taxation by representation. The second, written, suspected Dulany, by Thomas Whateley, secretary to George Grenville and a member for Ludgershall, implicitly upheld the opposite view, contending that, like nine-tenths of other Englishmen, the colonies were "virtually represented" in Parliament, and therefore subject to Parliament's authority in all matters, especially taxation. Dulany argued that the notion of virtual representation was as covinous in England, and for more Englishmen, as it was in the colonies and for all colonials.

In Boston, another lawyer, John Adams, was taking notes for a "Dissertation" on the origins of and obstacles to English liberty, and in time devoted some pages of his paper to a learned reminder to his fellow citizens that ignorance of the history of liberty was as great a danger to them as tyranny itself. "Liberty cannot be preserved without a general knowledge among the people." A second cousin, Samuel Adams, Harvard graduate, brewer, man of action, and member of the Massachusetts Assembly, was busy writing pamphlets that assailed the Stamp Act. Josiah Quincy, Jr., a lawyer and recent Harvard graduate, was penning anonymous letters to the *Boston Gazette* that questioned the legality of the Stamp Act and other Parliamentary legislation. Still another Bostonian, Jonathan Mayhew, a popular dissenting minister already renowned for his opposition to an Anglican episcopate in the colonies, preached to his congregation that no distinction should be made between an episcopate and the stamps, both being infringements on English liberty. These and numerous other correspondents, writers, and pamphleteers all agreed on one thing: That the Stamp Act was a violation of the British Constitution, *prima facie* null and void, and could be defied and flouted with impunity.

True to their promises, two Virginia ministers, Reverends William Robinson and Albert Acland, wrote to their superior in England, Richard Terrick, Bishop of London, who was also a staunch supporter of Grenville. Robinson reported that Patrick Henry, who first spoke treason while arguing against the Parson's Cause two years ago, "blazed out in a violent speech against the authority of Parliament," that he had proposed "several outrageous resolves, some of which passed, and were again erased as soon as his back was turned," and that the culprit had "gone quietly into the upper parts of the country to recommend himself to his constituents by spreading treason, and enforcing firm resolution against the authority of the British Parliament."

Acland had not attended the session in Williamsburg, but learned much of what was said and done in its last three days from Reece Vishonn, who imparted his observations in casual and worried conversation after services on the Sunday following the General Assembly's adjournment; and from Edgar Cullis, who related his version of the events over tea the following Monday in the manner of a confession. The burgess also provided his minister with a copy of the Resolves.

What Acland learned served to increase his resentment toward Hugh Kenrick and his enmity for Jack Frake. "Parties residing in my own parish," he wrote to the Bishop, "are active in fomenting treasonous defiance of the Crown amongst the plain people here, and behave in the matter little better than pranksterish, gin-sodden university students. It is hoped by many dutiful subjects in my parish that such behavior be rewarded with a noose or two, or at the very least with an introduction to the lash. It is also my own firm hope that your lordship, upon receiving this intelligence, employs his not insignificant influence to persuade the ministry to quell such obstinate words and actions with forthright words and actions of their own, in order to exact universal deference to the Crown and its gloried authority. Your lordship has the ear of His Majesty, and the collective ear of the noble upper House, and I am confident that you will speak with grave concern to these parties about the alarming, rebellious developments in these His Majesty's dominions."

The "pranksterish" behavior to which Acland alluded (but did not describe to the Bishop of London) comprised a host of matters. The first was Reece Vishonn's decision not to hold a ball at Enderly in honor of the king's birthday. This was an annual occasion to which the pastor was usually invited to lead the planter's guests in a prayer for and the first toast to their sovereign's health. This year, so soon after the dissolution of the General Assembly in remarkably acrid circumstances, the master of Enderly did not expect many of his guests would care to celebrate. Acland had heard also that the same event, held at the Governor's Palace in Williamsburg, was a dismal affair, attended by barely a dozen guests instead of the usual throngs. Acland knew that Hugh Kenrick had in the past attended that ball, but he was not certain whether his non-attendance this year was a consequence of ill will between the planter and Fauquier or disrespect on the part of the burgess. It did not matter to him which it was; there was the latter's role in the passage of the Resolves, which Acland regarded as bordering on criminality. There was, too, the overall surly mood of the reverend's parishioners. His recent sermon on the virtue of humility was met by the congregation with an almost tangible indifference, while the collection plate that Sunday returned to him nearly empty. Acland penned his letter to the Bishop with narrowed eyes and a wry grin; he derived more satisfaction from composing the missive than he ever had from drafting an exhortation.

Ironically, Reverend James Maury, the parson whose cause two years before won him an award of one penny, wrote in glowing terms of the rising colonial uproar sparked by the very same lawyer who had once referred to him and his colleagues of the cloth as "rapacious harpies." Maury was among those who first heard accusations of treason flung at Henry in the Hanover courthouse, yet he said in a letter to a friend in London, after a long disputation on the evils of the Stamp Act, that the widespread defiance of Parliament authority would likely cause some notable men to "brand us with the odious name of rebels, and others may applaud us for that generous love of liberty which we inherit from our fore-fathers."

In 1739, "Prime Minister" Robert Walpole, still smarting from the defeat of his excise tax proposals six years earlier, and casting about for ways and means to reduce the government's debts, replied to a query about why he did not propose to tax the American colonies directly: "I have old England set against me; do you think I will have *new* England likewise?" His successors in office and in Parliament were not imbued with such practical wisdom. They were arrogant enough to be idealists; they wished to assert Parliamentary authority in all they surveyed.

Early in July, a coastal sloop called on Caxton. While the crew unloaded some of its ballast — French molasses and Portuguese salt smuggled past the customs and naval tenders at the mouth of the York River near the Bay, nearly a hundred sacks of the salt cleverly overlaid with sand — its wiry captain strode up the hill and onto Queen Anne Street. After stopping in Mr. Rittles's store to purchase some tobacco, he walked up to the *Courier*'s office and dropped off a bundle of mail.

Among the letters he left with Wendel Barret was a brief note to Hugh Kenrick from Otis Talbot in Philadelphia: "Sir: I have dispatched, on your request, the several copies of the Resolves of your legislature to corresponding merchants of my acquaintance in various towns on the seaboard, with urgings appended by me to invite their printers to broadcast them to whoever they believe would be receptive and friendly to them." Talbot also reported that the Massachusetts Assembly, "on the suggestion of James Otis, has posted a letter to all colonial legislatures inviting them to choose delegates to a congress in New York October next to discuss measures and actions concerning the Stamp Act. Surely, Virginia will oblige him in that regard, and you will be one of those delegates." There were also letters for Reece Vishonn, Thomas Reisdale, Jack Frake, and Wendel Barret himself, all of them postage-paid, except for the penny charged by the sloop captain for having carried them. Barret paid the captain the pence, then sent one of his apprentices out with the letters to deliver them and collect the cost.

Hugh Kenrick was in the middle of the fields, sitting on a stool before an easel, sketching in red crayon a vista of the property, when Spears came out and handed him the single letter. Hugh opened it, then grinned and exclaimed to his valet, "Ah! The mischief has been done, Spears! The fuse has been lit!" But as Spears hiked back to the great house of Meum Hall, Hugh sat and brooded over the news of the colonial congress. He did not think it odd, though, that he had been kept in ignorance of the proposed congress. Peyton Randolph, John Robinson, George Wythe, and other powers in the House of Burgesses no doubt had knowledge of the circular letter, which would have been addressed to Speaker Robinson. Opposed as those men had been to the Resolves, they would not be keen on sending even informal observers to the congress. And, thought Hugh, informal they must be: The General Assembly would not convene again until October or November, after the congress in New York. Lieutenant-Governor Fauquier would not even need to prorogue the Assembly to prevent the burgesses from choosing official delegates. What unfortunate timing!

Later that afternoon, he rode over to Morland, and found Jack Frake, John Proudlocks, and about half of the plantation's tenants busy with shovels and pick-axes in the construction of a ditch. Two weeks earlier, over supper at Meum Hall, Jack revealed his plan to dig a "canal" through his fields from Hove Stream.

"My fields table a few feet above the stream," Jack had explained, "then level off about sixty yards from the great house. A conduit such as you devised would be impractical, because it would require some kind of pump to pressure the water up and over the rise. So, what I've decided on is a narrow canal or channel that will cut through the fields, one wide enough to accommodate a bucket, but no more than half a man's stride. At the stream, where the ground is at least twice the height of my fields, I will build a sluice to let in the water and to stop it before it overflows the channel." He showed Hugh a diagram of his plan. "This way, my people needn't go so far for water, and this ought to eliminate the salt from the river I've had to water the fields with."

"Excellent plan," remarked Hugh then. He volunteered to donate a mound of flat stones his own tenants had removed over the years from Meum Hall's fields. "You'll need those to brace the walls of your ditch, and perhaps even to pave the bottom of it. How deep will you dig it?"

"About a foot and a half."

Today, as he rode his mount through stands of tobacco and corn stalks under the hot July sun, Hugh saw that the canal was about half finished. Jack Frake saw him approach, and paused to drop his shovel and take a drink from a flask. Hugh walked his mount up to him and tipped his hat. Jack smiled up at him as he ran a bare wrist over his sweaty brow. "Nothing could bring you here today but news," he said.

Hugh nodded. "Yes. I've had word that Mr. Talbot has relayed the Resolves."

"I've had a note from Captain Ramshaw, who delivered his own bundle of them in New York. He reports that the merchants and gentry there regret they did not think of the Resolves first." Jack picked up his shovel, then plunged it upright into the ground and rested his forearms over the handle. He asked, "What was that phrase your friend Jones wrote that Colonel Barré used in the Commons? 'Sons of liberty'?"

"Yes," replied Hugh. "'Sons of liberty.' Why do you ask?"

Jack's mouth bent in a smile that was half mischievous, half serious. "It would be an interesting name for an organization."

Hugh sat back in his saddle and gave it some thought. "Yes," he said, "it would be an interesting name. But what would be the purpose of this organization?"

The smile disappeared from Jack's mouth. "To oppose the landing of stamps here, in November, if the opportunity favors us."

"I see," said Hugh. After another moment, he asked, "By 'oppose,' do you imply that their landing should be physically prevented?"

Jack nodded. "I mean that, exactly. With arms, if necessary."

Hugh raised his riding crop and scratched his forehead with the end of it. At length, he remarked, "This wants thought, Jack. And discussion. The Attic Society meets this Saturday at Mr. Safford's place. Will you propose the creation of such an organization as a subject of discussion?"

"I will propose that the Society adopt that name."

Hugh frowned. "The Society's purpose would be altered."

Jack shook his head. "Not necessarily," he answered. "Our purpose would be consistent and extended, from talk of principles of liberty, to practicing them."

Hugh's eyebrows went up, and he sighed. "This, too, wants thought." He glanced down at his friend. "I must consult my law books." He tipped his hat again, reined his mount around, and rode out of the fields back to Meum Hall.

Jack watched his friend ride away, then turned to rejoin the line of men busy at the ditch.

* * *

The private room in Steven Safford's King's Arms Tavern on Queen Anne Street, in which the Attic Society of Caxton usually met, had been dubbed, at Hugh Kenrick's request, the "Olympus Room." What distinguished it from the tavern's other, nameless rooms was the stenciled name on the door and a framed print of Mount Etna in Sicily on an otherwise bare wall just inside the room.

Safford, a tall, lean, steely eyed, blondish man born and raised in Massachusetts, had been one of the nearly three thousand colonial volunteers who helped to take French Louisbourg twenty years earlier. He was missing his left ear; it had been removed by a French musket ball during that campaign. He found the print in a miscellaneous goods shop in Williamsburg, and put it up on his own advice. "But, it is not Olympus," protested Hugh when he first saw it a year ago. "Olympus is in Greece."

"So it is," replied Safford. "But, Etna is in Italy, which was ancient Rome. We are the citizens of a new Rome, and this Etna rumbles with eruptions. When did Olympus last rumble?"

Hugh could not answer the question, and conceded the publican's observation. He searched among his own books and periodicals for a representation of Olympus, but could not find one.

The room also featured a large round oaken table that occupied nearly a quarter of the room's space. It could accommodate ten patrons. Other chairs and a serving table were the only other furniture. Wall sconces lit the room, as did a pewter candelabrum that sat in the center of the round table.

Among the few souvenirs Safford brought back from Louisbourg — Commodore Warren of the Royal Navy squadron there having forbidden the colonial army from sharing in the prizes of the town's capture — was a pair of Arabian ivory combs and an old jack of the Honorable East India Company, given to him by a drunken British marine in exchange for a half-

gallon of Jamaican rum. Safford supposed that the combs, which he later
bartered for provisions with the colonel of another New England company,
and the flag were taken from a French warehouse in the town, and that
they were the forgotten booty of a past engagement between armed merchantmen of the French and English East India Companies off the west
coast of India.

The jack now served as a tablecloth. Safford, who was a member of the
Society, decided that his learned colleagues deserved a more gentlemanly
surface on which to sup, imbibe, and conduct their business. He removed it
from his trunk, paid the town's best seamstress to repair it, and presented it
to the Society as its exclusive property. At the conclusion of each meeting,
the flag was folded up and put away until the next synod of savants.

It was nearly the size of an army ensign, and draped neatly over the
round table, its four points touched the bare wooden floor. It was composed
of seven red and six white alternating stripes, and a white canton with the
red cross of St. George. It had been struck several times by French ball and
grape during that long-ago duel over mercantilist domination of those faraway waters, but the seamstress, Lydia Heathcoate, had skillfully mended
those places to near invisibility.

The Society met twice a month, planting and harvesting permitting. Its
only permanent office was that of recording secretary; this was held by a
non-member, usually one of the planters' business agents who could take
rough stenographic notes of what was said and done in the course of a
meeting. The "chair" rotated among the fifteen members every two or three
months; this person had the privilege of resting his elbows and tankard on
a portion of St. George's cross and of maintaining civil order during what
at times became acrid debates.

The Attic Society had been Hugh Kenrick's idea, and although it was a
less formal version of the Society of the Pippin in London, he was happy that
it existed and was welcomed by many of his neighbors with an eagerness and
literacy that matched his own. Jack Frake, normally a man who preferred
solitude and his own company, also welcomed meetings of the Society, for
they seemed to echo, at least in spirit, his life with the Skelly gang in the
Marvel caves of Cornwall long ago, and gave him a chance to measure his
neighbors' capacity for the liberty he was determined to preserve.

Tonight the meeting was attended by nearly the full membership: Jack
Frake, Hugh Kenrick, Thomas Reisdale, the attorney and present
chairman, Wendel Barret, the printer; Edgar and Ralph Cullis; Henry

Otway; and Carver Gramatan, of the rival Gramatan Inn and Tavern further up Queen Anne. Other members sat at the table or around the room. At Reisdale's left was Obedience Robins, Jack Frake's business agent, in the role of recording secretary, ready with a letter book, inkpot, and a brace of quills.

After a supper of beef and ale, Steven Safford treated the company to one round of his best Madeira; more could be had at three pence per glass. Toasts were made to the king, to Lieutenant-Governor Fauquier, and to Safford himself. A last toast was made by Hugh Kenrick; he had introduced it to the Society and it became popular: "Long live Lady Liberty!" Reisdale then asked Robins to read the notes from the last meeting of three weeks past. The subject then was the Stamp Act and the Resolves passed by the House of Burgesses in May. The Society's own resolution, adopted by a vote of hands following hours of debate, was that the Stamp Act was unconstitutional in principle, extortionate in practice, and likely to "provoke invidious and vigorous sentiments against Parliament and the Crown."

When Robins was finished, Jack Frake indicated a desire to speak. Reisdale recognized him. Jack rose to face the company. "In light of our resolution, I propose for discussion this evening two points: That this Society adopt the name 'Sons of Liberty,' and that whether or not that name is adopted, we discuss what actions may be taken to prevent the landing and employment of stamps in this county." Then he sat down.

The company, for a long moment, sat silent and stunned. Everyone stared at Jack Frake, some in horror, others in bewilderment, and still others with genuine interest. Edgar Cullis looked away and muttered under his breath, "Oh, this is too much!" Only Hugh Kenrick, sitting next to his friend, did not stare at him; his gaze seemed to be fixed on Mount Etna on the wall across the room.

Thomas Reisdale was the first to recover. He looked stern now, and full of reproof. He rose and to the dozen men said, in a warning tone that was almost menacing and nearly condescending, "Allow me, sirs, to reply to that proposal with an entertaining procession of *laws* as much in effect here as in England." He raised a finger in emphasis. "First, three or more persons who perform an 'unlawful act of violence' for *private purposes* — and opposition to any act of Parliament, which sits by leave and in the name of the king — is deemed a *riot*. Secondly, an uncompleted, failed, or foiled act of violence for a private purpose, is a *rout*. Thirdly, an act of violence *contemplated* by three or more persons, for the express private purpose of harassing a Crown officer or interrupting him in the performance of his duties, is *ipso facto*, an *unlawful assembly*."

Reisdale paused to glance pointedly at the face of every man in the room. "Lastly," he said gravely, "and however, here is a saving grace of an unlawful act by any number of us, either performed or contemplated: If that act is public, that is, if it is sanctioned by a large group of citizens who share the legitimate, unredressed, unacknowledged complaint of the actors, if their act is undertaken for a recognized *public good*, then that act may be deemed *treason* against the Crown and the king's writ, that is, a crime of presumption for acting in the name and place of the king." He shook his head. "The simple act of obstructing a Crown officer is fraught with insidious intricacies, sirs. Why, that unlawful act could be construed as an act against liberty itself!" He paused to raise his hands. "I have cited variously the findings of our most eminent jurists: Blackstone, Hawkins, and, of course, Coke. And, I must remind you, sirs, that at this very moment, *we are all sitting in unlawful assembly!*" Reisdale glanced around the room again in hopes of seeing that each man before him realized the sobering jeopardy of resistance to the law. He saw faces as grave as he felt his own to be. He sat down and rested his arms on a bar of St. George's cross.

Hugh Kenrick, who with Jack Frake was unmoved by the attorney's litany of legal terror, signaled a wish to speak. Reisdale nodded to him.

Hugh rose, stepped away from the table to face the company, and said, "Everything our esteemed chairman said is true, sirs. He neglected to mention, however, because it is so obvious to us all, that conviction of any one of his charges would earn the severest and *most final* of penalties."

Reisdale held up a hand. "I beg Mr. Kenrick's pardon, but I also neglected to mention that I have received not three days ago letters from correspondents in New York, Philadelphia, New London, Newport, and Boston. Not a single author of them approves of the Resolves. These men are merchants and men of parts and wide experience. They view the Resolves as a whole as an incitation to rebellion, as provoking treason, as criminally reckless and irresponsible." He snorted once. "As *premature!*"

Jack Frake asked, "If the Resolves are all that, sir, how else can one protest a deliberate reduction of our liberties? Surely, it is not by obsequious submission to tyranny."

Reisdale frowned, unsure of the object of his friend's contempt. "Excuse me, sir," he replied, "but I did not say I agreed with my correspondents. I agree with you about the futility of submitting to tyranny." He looked to Hugh Kenrick. "But, let us hear what the gentleman has to say."

Hugh, amused by the exchange, nodded to both men, then continued. "However, *violence* may not be necessary. Here is my reasoning, sirs. I doubt that the stamps will arrive here in the company of soldiers or special magistrates charged with enforcing their distribution, purchase, or employment. Appointed distributors may arrive with the stamps, or the stamps may be met and secured by distributors appointed from among applicants here." He paused and smiled easily at the company. "Of course, if planters and merchants and lawyers here united in a refusal to use the stamps, there would be a stoppage of trade and court business. Mr. Ivy here and Mr. Ambler in Yorktown at the customs house there would refuse to clear vessels and their cargoes without them. Should these gentlemen, however, be persuaded to risk penalties by issuing clearance papers to vessels here or in Yorktown without stamps, then the customs packets and naval tenders at the mouths of all our rivers to the Bay would deny them passage, and perhaps even seize them, unless their captains are granted special indemnification and dispensation by our governor or surveyor general to permit ships and cargoes to pass *sans* a single stamp. Governor Fauquier, as you all know, has commanding authority over all naval and customs vessels in these waters." Hugh turned to Reisdale. "Is this not true, sir?"

Reisdale nodded. "Yes, this is true. He could do that, were he willing to risk censure by the Board of Trade and, perhaps, even his removal from office."

Hugh turned and smiled at Jack Frake. "Perhaps, but that would be at his own risk. His Honor professes love of this colony. Let him demonstrate it," he remarked. He continued. "Now, undoubtedly, suits against merchants and ship captains and masters and customs officials and inspectors would follow, should all that come about. But these, I believe, would be futile, for I am certain that our courts would either refuse to sit — for stamps would be required to bring suit against anyone in any matter — or our courts would sit and hear all cases brought before them without benefit of stamps, as they always have, and as they always must, in either instance, declining to uphold a law which our own magistrates must deem unconstitutional. And no suit over the failure to purchase or employ stamps would be recognized by those courts."

Hugh paused to smile again. "And so, with all respect due to our chairman and his procession of definitions, I contend here and now that little risk would attend a refusal to allow passage of stamps from ship to shore in this county." He pointed to Jack Frake. "Further, sirs, come what may by the end of this meeting, and regardless of what actions we may resolve to take on this matter, you may be sure that when the moment comes, I, for one, will assist this gentleman in the execution of his proposal!"

Hugh returned to his chair and sat down. Jack Frake nodded in acknowledgement of his statement. The chairman, however, looked alarmed. He rose and said, "I disagree, sir, that violence may not be necessary! I believe it is *imperative*. If the Crown is as determined to introduce the stamps as we are to stop their introduction, well, logic requires that it must come to a show of force, and one side must yield."

Hugh rose and replied, "You exaggerate the power of the Gorgon Grenville, good sir. One man will appear with a cargo of paper — hardly a formidable enemy. Oppose this man, promise him grief, and the paper will become mere paper."

"You are proposing *rebellion!*" exclaimed Carver Gramatan.

"Raising our hands against the king!" echoed Ralph Cullis.

"No, sir," countered Wendel Barret, "against Parliament, who are the true rebels, serpents of a Medusa-like creature playing at king!"

"Mr. Barret is correct, sirs!" said Henry Otway. "His Majesty is the sole proprietor of this colony, not Parliament! Our charter says so!"

"His Majesty will protect us from Parliament's avarice," insisted another member, "once he realizes he has been gulled by ministers and sly counsel!"

"This is true!" protested another. "Why, I read in *Gentleman's Magazine* that His Majesty spurned a petition by peruke makers to enact a law that would require all men to wear wigs! He himself is reluctant to wear one! Now, *I* say, *there* is a revealing side of his benign character, one on which we may depend!"

Jack Frake frowned in amazement and shook his head. He rose and said, "You all forget that the king who spurned a wig also signed the Proclamation of '63, sirs! That villainy is as much a seizure of our lives and property as will be the stamps!"

"I, too, have read that particular number of *Gentleman's Magazine*," said Hugh Kenrick with a shrug. "In that same number, it was reported that Queen Charlotte's elephant is daily exercised by its *mahout* in St. James's Park."

The other men looked at him in confusion. "Your meaning, sir?" queried the member who mentioned the petition of the peruke makers.

"That the outings of Her Majesty's elephant have as little to do with the Stamp Act as has His Majesty's snubbing of the peruke makers." He paused. "More connected to our dilemma, and by way of a clue to the efficacy of action, are the disturbances and commotions by the silk weavers and glovers in London, who are feeling the pinch of the nonimportation agreements of our northern cousins to reduce their purchase of mourning blacks." Before anyone else could speak, Hugh turned to Edgar Cullis. "Sir," he asked, "have you received information about a congress of delegates from all the colonies to meet in New York in October?"

Hugh's fellow burgess seemed genuinely surprised. "No," he said. "Why do you ask?"

"You are a member of Mr. Randolph's committee of correspondence."

"I was, sir," replied Cullis. "I may be reappointed to it in the next session. Mr. Randolph does not privilege me with communications from other colonies when the Assembly is not in session." He shook his head. "Like you, sir, I am but a 'junior' burgess."

"I see." Hugh did not pursue the subject, but other members expressed interest in the news. He explained the purpose of the proposed congress and briefly outlined his own thoughts on it. He had already told Jack Frake, who did not join in the animated speculation about the congress's aims or the ramifications of holding such a conclave.

Abruptly, Carver Gramatan silenced the hubbub of talk when he rose and proclaimed angrily, "I have sullied my loyalty to His Majesty by remaining here amongst this...*unlawful assembly*!" The room remained quiet. Gramatan, a man some years older than Safford and who, besides owning the Gramatan Inn, also owned a handful of tenanted farms up and down the length of the York River, claimed to be a distant relative of the Duke of Marlborough. He picked up his hat and cane and announced, "You may take my departure as a resignation from the Society, which I see is becoming a clutch of traitors and conspirators, a cursed bevy of Guy Fawkes' and Gunpowder men!" The aristocratic publican turned and walked to the door. There he turned again and with a disdainful glance at Safford, added, "The Cumberland Room at my establishment will be made available to any of you who wish to partake of civil, learned, and *untreasonous* discussion, to men whose loyalty and allegiance to His Majesty and our mother country are beyond testing and above doubt. Good night to you, sirs!" He opened the door and stalked out.

Steven Safford rose and addressed the company. "Until now, gentlemen,

I did not begrudge the late member his good fortune or the quality of his fare. As you all know, he has recently returned from England, where a deceased brother left him a substantial estate in annuities, consols, and income from a shipbuilding concern near Portsmouth. Submission to stamps will not much affect his station, here or in England." He paused. "Do any of you gentlemen wish to accept his invitation?"

No one else in the room spoke or moved.

"Very well," said Safford. "Mr. Reisdale, let us debate Mr. Frake's proposals."

Two hours later, after votes of hands had been taken, both proposals were defeated by small majorities. Jack Frake was not discouraged. Nor was Hugh Kenrick. They rode back to their plantations together that evening in silence, until Jack said, "I am not surprised by the outcome, Hugh. It is too early for most men to think in my and your terms." He sighed wistfully. "I think this time other men, in other colonies, will raise the hue and cry. Virginia lit the torch and held it aloft for all to see. Other men will carry it, for now."

Hugh smiled. "It is a rare treat, Jack, to hear you utter such poetical sentiments." He added, after a moment, "I believe that what troubles our friends is that they don't yet know how the stamps will arrive. Nor are they certain how the Crown will behave if some combination of the colonies is accomplished."

"An unreasoning fear of an enemy can inflate his size and power," remarked Jack.

Hugh nodded in agreement. "Well, we have both faced small enemies, and large, my friend. Now, we shall face one together."

* * *

Chapter 2: The Paladin

While men in the colonies talked and wrote about the Resolves, Patrick Henry, and the ominous nature of the Stamp Act, and allowed their fears, outrage, and disaffection to guide their thoughts and actions, the mood in London was quite the opposite. Grenville's ministry was doomed, and as the prime minister was being maneuvered into resignation in July, men were jockeying for the right to form a new government or for a place in it. The colonials passed the days, weeks, and months of the summer of 1765 in grim anticipation of their own actions and the Crown's; their cousins in England passed them in a frustrating stalemate of ambitious obstinacy. In the corridors and closets of power, there was much bickering, posturing, and conniving; much activity, but little action.

The Duke of Cumberland, burdened with a variety of uncomfortable maladies and a discreet reluctance to embroil himself in affairs that would rob him of his diversions, served on Grenville's departure as prime minister *pro tempore*, and worked closely if unsuccessfully with the aging Duke of Newcastle to assemble a ministry acceptable to both George the Third and the King of Commoners, William Pitt. Pitt, emerging from his disabling melancholia lucid enough to manage for a time the direction of his career and ambition, twice overcame his painful gout to be taken by sedan chair to see the king, but refused to form a ministry unless he could bring into it his brother-in-law, Lord Temple. The king could not sanction any ministry that counted among its principals a man who had so openly supported the loathsome John Wilkes, who had suggested that the king was a fool and a liar. The two monarchs could not agree on other terms of *rapprochement*, leaving the kingmakers, power-brokers, and hopefuls for preferments muttering imprecations and scurrying to find a willing substitute for Pitt.

Baron Garnet Kenrick and Sir Dogmael Jones remained aloof from the imbroglio over who was to succeed Grenville. The Kenricks departed London to spend the season in Danvers, while Jones divided his time between Danvers and London. In the city, he performed his tutorial duties at Serjeants' Inn, argued a number of cases at the King's Bench during Trinity term — representing clients prosecuted under statutory censorship — and monitored the contest for ministerial succession.

In early July, after Grenville had gone, Jones journeyed to Danvers to report developments in London to his patron.

"Domestic relations are in a furtive dither, milord," he said as he and Garnet Kenrick rode leisurely on horseback through the Danvers estate on an inspection tour. "Cumberland is lumbering — Ah! There's the germ of a scandalously picturesque doggerel! I must complete it and submit it to the newspapers! — lumbering, as I said, between Richmond and Windsor Great Lodges, between all the baiting, hooting parties like a blindfolded bear at the Southwark Fair, shackled to the wishes of his nephew the king, taunted with morsels by his friends, nipped at his heels by mongrels from the Grenville and Bedford kennels. What a thankless task! Mr. Pitt interviewed twice with the king, but formally declined to head a new government unless Lord Temple could be brought into it without His Majesty making a face, and Lord Bute banished beyond influence to the Hebrides, and Bedford and anyone who supported the Treaty of Paris he negotiated absolutely barred from a place in administration. Temple, in any event, rebuffed his own sponsors and refused the Treasury, for many reasons to be sure, but chief among them his unwillingness to become his brother-in-law's mute valet in policy. What a conundrum of siblings!" laughed Jones.

He took a puff on his pipe, then continued. "Everyone but Mr. Pitt labors under the suspicion that His Majesty continues to seek the devilish advice of Lord Bute. To allay that suspicion, he has graciously agreed to remove from their places a number of Scottish lords, including Bute's brother. A very *plaid* promise, that!" Jones shook his head. "And, everyone wishes Mr. Pitt to succeed Mr. Grenville, milord, even His Majesty, but his terms are either too offensive or too strenuous. It is common knowledge that he is not open to concession. Nonetheless, it is tried. To appease him, Justice Pratt may be elevated to Lords. Newcastle is willing to follow Marlborough as Lord Privy Seal. A program was drawn up, I understand, designed to seduce Mr. Pitt: An alliance with Prussia, repeal of the cider and American stamp taxes, nullification of general warrants by the Commons, restitution or reinstatement of army officers who did not vote to Mr. Grenville's liking — in short, a deliberate and thorough repudiation of the whole of Mr. Grenville's program, which, I needn't point out to you, milord," added Jones with dark humor, "was endorsed by His Majesty, except for the Regency Bill, of course."

Jones glanced over at his patron. "There is more, milord. Shall I wait until we have had dinner to continue?"

Garnet Kenrick grimaced. "Thank you for asking, Mr. Jones. But, go on. My appetite can endure it."

"Very well. Charles Townshend will very likely agree to gild his fingers as the new Paymaster. His cousin of the same name may find a place on the Admiralty Board. Mr. Dowdeswell is to be the new Chancellor of the Exchequer, although he is keen only to see repeal of the cider tax. Grafton has accepted appointment as Secretary of State for the North, provided Mr. Pitt can be lured into the government. General Conway will be Secretary for the South. Charles Yorke is playing the demure maiden over becoming Attorney-General. He is especially desired by the king for his declamatory skills in the Commons." Jones paused. "As for Lord Rockingham, his sole political experience as Lord of the Bedchamber cannot help but be reflected in his role as First Lord of the Treasury." He sighed. "I would grieve for my country, milord, but only after a long, hearty laugh. All in all, it has been a very amusing entertainment, a circus of decorous turpitude."

The Baron frowned. "I have not made his acquaintance. How old is Lord Rockingham?"

"Thirty-five, milord," answered Jones. "Much older than your son, who is so much wiser." He tapped his forehead with the stem of his pipe. "He is without a program, in a manner of speaking, quite saddleless in his principles. Wealthy, of course, a member of the Jockey Club. Well, I have spoken with him — made his acquaintance at a congress of anti-Grenvillites — and am of the opinion that as prime minister, he will be good for only one-half turn around the Ascot course before he winds himself and is tumbled by the headlong imperatives of empire and ineptitude. I expect to compose many letters to the newspapers about his anxious term, and refer to it as the 'Rocking-Horse Ministry.'"

"You would make a cruelly just satirist, Mr. Jones," remarked the Baron with a chuckle. Then he was silent for a while as they rode on, except to comment on the neatness of the fields. At length, he asked, "What is my brother up to? He must be in the thick of things."

Jones spoke freely about the Earl of Danvers, as he knew he could to the man's brother. "I have heard that he is circulating the notion that Mr. Pitt ought to be awarded a peerage, too. His minions, Sir Henoch and Mr.

Hillier, in the meantime, are busy advancing the notion among members of the Commons that should Mr. Pitt accept a peerage, it would be a gross betrayal of his friends and of liberty." Jones scoffed. "The devil's advocate for chastity and modesty at work there, I should say!"

The Baron frowned in perplexity for a moment. Then his face brightened. "Ah! I see what they are up to! Mr. Pitt as Earl Something-or-other in Lords would remove him from the Commons, where he is most effective and feared. And, his party there would become rudderless and embittered. What an insidious ruse!"

"Insidious, milord? Agreed," said Jones. "And effective, if it can be accomplished. However, unless he is also afflicted with the vanity of omnipotence, I don't see Mr. Pitt falling for it."

Soon after he returned to London a week later, Jones was visited in his new rooms near the Serjeants' Inn by two messengers. The first, from Benjamin Worley at Lion Key, brought him a thick parcel from Captain John Ramshaw of the *Sparrowhawk*, now waiting in queue in the Pool of London. Jones opened it immediately and found in it a printed copy of the Virginia Resolves and Hugh Kenrick's long letter describing their passage in the House of Burgesses.

The Resolves caused Jones to gasp in happy shock, the letter caused him to chuckle in grim admiration of the frankness of the Resolves' advocates. He frowned, though, when he read that part of Hugh's narrative that briefly mentioned the assault on him by John Chiswell, another burgess.

"That was, I contend," wrote Hugh, "a measure of the last argument Parliament and the Loyalists here have in their arsenal of persuasion on this or any other legislative matter. I beg this favor of you, my honorable friend, that you do not mention this incident to my parents. (I have sent my father copies of everything now in your hands, even a copy of this letter, from which I have omitted mention of it.) I do not wish them to become alarmed about my safety. I relate the incident to you so that you may properly gauge the level of feeling in these parts about Crown authority. As you will deduce from the addresses of Mr. Randolph and his party, there exist here sundry and numerous allies of those in the Commons who will become your opponents when this matter arrests the attention of the House when it reconvenes in December, as surely it must. Undoubtedly, repeal of this act, or at least consideration of its mitigation, will occupy much of your and their time and energy, leading to sittings late at night and early in the morning…. *Manus hæc infensa tyrannis….*"

"This hand is also hostile to tyranny," mused Jones to himself. He turned to read the transcripts that had accompanied the letter and the Resolves. An hour later, he finished reading and turned over the last page. Then he pounded the page with a fist. *My God!* he thought. *These men put the best of us to shame!* "If this be treason, then make the most of it!" he said out loud, and laughed quietly at the ease with which he pronounced those words. "May George the Third profit by their example!" *What a sublime insult,* he thought, *and a well-deserved one! Mr. Henry,* he thought, *you have my salute! Such sentiments, uttered here by you or me, would see either of us clapped in irons within five minutes of a motion to censure and expel! For what offense? For having made an address to the throne of right and reason!*

Jones put the papers aside on his desk and sat to gaze out his window at London. He loved the city. He doubted he could ever be persuaded to exchange living here for a chance to settle in America. But, he thought: *Though I love my country, I am willing to help midwife the birth of another, for another country…another kingdom…is the only logical consequence of these speeches, and of the Resolves, and of the spirit that made them….*

The second messenger, a haughty, liveried creature, called on Jones near dusk, and presented him with an invitation to a levee the next afternoon at the Bloomsbury residence of John Russell, the Duke of Bedford.

A levee was an 18th-century social occasion, one of whose purposes, especially in politics, was the nose-counting of friends and allies. It could be as formal or informal as the host wished. He could circulate among his nervous, smiling, expectant guests and confer his approval or disapproval with a kind word or pointed inattention. Or, he could allow his guests to group themselves in their own familiar circles of colleagues, associates, and cronies, letting them chat away until any one or number of them were summoned to briefly converse with him. At royal and aristocratic levees, an attendee insolent enough to approach the host was sure to be rebuffed. Even prime ministers and lord chancellors could not speak to a king or a member of the royal peerage unless spoken to. Ladies and gentlemen of the lower strata often held levees in the morning, in their bedchambers, and served coffee and repartee while their servants flitted about preparing their employers for public appearance. Royal and aristocratic levees rarely stooped to that level of discriminating intimacy.

Jones audited the servant who stood in the study of his new rooms by the Inns of Court. He had just moved here and wondered how the Duke of

Bedford had learned so quickly of his new residence. His servant was a tall, rough-looking fellow sporting an immaculate white wig, white stockings, silver-buckled shoes, green breeches, and a belaced green frock coat. He did not seem to be comfortable in the garb. He had been instructed, he said, to wait for a reply and stood patiently at a distance from Jones's writing desk. Jones imagined that he had seen this man somewhere before, but put the thought out of his head because not even he paid much attention to the faces of lackeys. He opened and read the invitation, which had been sealed with the wax arms of the Duke of Bedford. He looked up from the invitation, crossed his legs, and asked, "Am I to be entertained at this midday soiree of caitiffs, or to provide the entertainment?"

The servant frowned, uncertain how to reply. Jones perceived a sly, offended intelligence in the blank blue eyes. "I do not know, sir," replied the man. "His lordship did not enlighten me about the purpose of the invitation."

Jones narrowed his eyes and hummed in thought. "Well, no matter. I have braved the entire House. I see no reason why I should endure a conclave of soused louts." He held out the invitation. "Please inform *his grace* that I cannot oblige him, as I have a previous engagement with the Duchess of Britannia." When the servant blinked in surprise, he added, "It is to a masque, you see. My hostess is to appear as Lady Liberty, and I shall go in the raiment of Algernon Sydney." He smiled and waved the invitation once again. "*His grace* will understand the import of my regrets, and excuse it, if you do not."

The messenger made an oddly pained face. "As you wish, sir." He stepped forward, took the invitation, stepped back, bowed slightly, and said, "Good day to you, sir." He turned smartly and left the room.

When he heard his foyer door close, Jones rose and went to his window, which faced Chancery Lane. He saw the man emerge from the apartments and step into a waiting sedan chair. Jones grabbed his cane and hat and rushed from his rooms and down the stairs to the street. Another sedan chair and two lounging porters were across the way. He handed the lead porter half a crown and instructed the pair to follow the chair that had just left. The porters lifted the conveyance before he could close its door and were off in a trot that jolted him against the backrest.

When he recovered, he observed from the window that the messenger's chair was headed for Fleet Street, when its porters should have gone north on Chancery to Holborn, which led to the Duke's residence. On Fleet, the porters turned right onto the Strand, and jogged straight up the darkening thoroughfare towards Charing Cross and Whitehall. Jones's own porters pursued at a discreet distance.

Some twenty minutes later, the messenger's chair came to a halt at the gate of Windridge Court, the walled residence of the Earl of Danvers. When his chair had been set down, the messenger stepped out, paid the lead porter, and strode through the open gate into the courtyard. He saw the man remove his hat and wig and stuff the wig into a coat pocket. Jones's porters had slowed to a walk. Before they could come abreast of the first sedan chair, the barrister leaned out the window and ordered them to return him to Chancery Lane.

As the porters toted him back down the noisy Strand, the member for Swansditch thought it odd that he should be invited into the enemy's camp — and falsely invited, no less. His presence at the levee would have been as flagrantly incongruous as would John Wilkes's. During the degrading squabble over who was to follow Grenville, the Duke of Bedford and his family let it be known what kind of policy they would follow in office, one that moved beyond the status quo to become actively hostile to liberty both in England and in the colonies. Jones was certain that Bedford knew his positions on the Stamp Act, on Wilkes, on general warrants, and a host of other issues. The Earl of Danvers was in the Duke's camp, as were his men in the Commons, Sir Henoch Pannell and Crispin Hillier. Grenville himself would likely be at the affair, and even some men who had been asked to join Rockingham's ministry, such as Charles Yorke.

Jones tapped his chin with the cane handle in thought. He wondered what had been the purpose of the false invitation. What had the Earl in mind for him? Compromise, or humiliation? Had it become known by his allies in the Commons that he, Sir Dogmael Jones, had attended the Duke's levee, he would have been compromised, for it would be assumed that some sort of voting arrangement would have been sought by him between him and the Duke's party, with a promised reward of some kind. Further, he would surely have been humiliated, for the Duke would have had him escorted to the door, and perhaps none too gently tossed from that regal portal of preference.

The ruse had failed for a single reason, thought Jones, at least to the messenger's mind: He had referred to his putative employer as *his lordship*, rather than *his grace*. Jones suspected that the man would keep that *faux pas* to himself. It had been a clever, carefully plotted prank, enacted for some devilishly important end. Its failure would greatly upset the Earl; he would be outraged if he ever learned that it had failed because his servant had had a slip of mind.

Jones shrugged as the sedan chair dipped and swayed from the porters' exertions. He would have declined the invitation even had the Duke sent his carriage around for him. What a quaint adventure! He was so pleased with this bit of detective work that he had the porters stop outside the Lovely Ducks Tavern while he dashed inside and bought them each a flask of rum, and rewarded them at the end of their labors with another half crown.

Jones pondered the paradox of Charles Yorke. There was a man, he thought, whose commitment to liberty was skewed by ambition. He had exchanged some letters with the former and perhaps future Attorney-General since the recess on the legality of general warrants and other constitutional matters. The spare, academic, but cordial exchange convinced him that Yorke, whom he conceded possessed a fine mind and an enviable stock of legal knowledge, harbored an ambivalence on constitutional questions rooted in an ambition dependent on precedent, not principle, on the status quo in law and government, a status quo in which he had risen steadily for thirty years and which he was obsessed with preserving. Yorke, he concluded, wished to be a part of that status quo. Yorke so detested Wilkes that he had been willing to endorse the alleged legality of general warrants, when Jones knew that Yorke did not much credit his own arguments for them.

Absent a rigorous system of the principles of liberty, Jones reflected — and he for one believed that the colonials were on the trail of one — Yorke was like so many other men in the Commons and the courts, engorged with rancorous fear when Parliamentary or Crown authority was questioned or challenged. And in Yorke's character Jones had observed, in both the man's letters and his speeches in the House, that the fear had spawned a curious, habitual style of malice, one that assaulted its object in the vagaries of legal circumspection. His official opinion on Wilkes's alleged libel two years ago was that it was not treasonable, but rather a "misdemeanor of the highest nature." Last March, in the Commons, he had defended the legality of general warrants in Wilkes's case on the premise that the issue of libel was a matter of abstract law, not one of political or judicial weight.

Jones sighed in tired disgust. And now, he reflected, that constitutional chimera was being courted to hold again the great seal of Attorney-General.

Dusk had already slipped to darkness by the time Jones paid the porters and ascended to his rooms. In his study, he lit two pump lamps —

gifts from his elector, Garnet Kenrick — and completed a task interrupted by the messengers. It was a letter to Sir Charles Pratt, chief justice of the Common Pleas, congratulating him on his recent elevation to the peerage. Pratt was now Baron Camden of Camden Place in Kent; Jones had heard the news a day after his return from Danvers. The news disturbed him, for Pratt was one of the few sitting justices he admired. As tactfully as he could, he expressed hope that his elevation to Lords would not dilute Pratt's devotion to the principles of liberty. "Forgive me the presumption," he ended the letter, "but I am certain that the honor conferred upon you by His Majesty will not for an instant cause your lordship to doubt the wisdom, efficacy, and necessity of upholding the Constitution." In other words, thought Jones with a wry twist of his mouth, I hope you have not been bought. He dipped a quill into an inkpot, signed the letter with a flourish, and set it aside to be copied and sealed later. If his new lordship took offense at the hypothetical imputation of corruption, so be it.

During the Parliamentary recess, and in between appearances at the King's Bench, Jones immersed himself in as many forays for freedom and liberty as he could manage. He offered *pro bono* counseling to John Bingly, who had continued to publish John Wilkes's *North Briton* at great risk to his freedom and solvency. Bingly's partner, John Williams, had been pilloried in the Palace Yard; Jones had contributed to the fund established by Williams's supporters to defray his legal expenses. Jones had represented John Entick, whose *Monitor* publications were being censured by the courts and who was suing the Secretaries of State over general warrants. He had followed closely in the newspapers the course of victories and setbacks of Pascal Paoli and the Corsicans in their fight for freedom from Genoese domination, and wrote letters to the papers inquiring why the government did not lend assistance to the rebels, "if only for practical reasons of strategy," he pointed out in one published letter, "for if Paoli is crushed, and the Genoese sell their rights to the island to France, British ease of sail in the Mediterranean may in future be had for an extraordinary *toll*, or perhaps denied altogether."

At the King's Bench he had accepted the briefs of two important cases. Richard Hogue, a notorious producer of "interludes" in a variety of unlicensed theater-taverns in London, had in the spring staged a play that incorporated the libretti of sections of Handel's *Dettingen Te Deum,* an oratorio that celebrated George the Second's victory during the War of the Austrian Succession. Hogue regarded the piece, which he himself wrote, as

an "interlude," even though it used speaking actors and actresses to
advance a vaguely lewd story. He consequently had not bothered to submit
the work to the Lord Chamberlain's office for approval and a license to
stage it, as the Dramatic Licensing Act of 1737, enacted to protect political
figures from devastating caricature, required of all plays. At its first staging,
someone in the audience took exception to the dialogue and lyrics, filed
informations with the Lord Chamberlain, and Hogue's play was closed by
bailiffs and Hogue himself arrested and imprisoned.

After he had agreed to represent Hogue, Jones visited Philip Dormer
Stanhope, the Earl of Chesterfield, at his residence in Greenwich, to solicit
his advice on how to argue this particular case. The Earl had spoken against
the Act in debate in Lords, asserting without qualification the right of the-
atrical satire to immunity from government regulation and suppression.
Ridicule, he had argued, was an elemental aspect of the theater, and the bill
then before the House represented an infringement not only on liberty but
on property, "wit being the property of those who have it." Jones was
inspired to seek the notorious Francophile's advice because in his private
library was a pamphlet containing the Earl's speech, which he found years
before in a St. Paul's Churchyard bookstall. It had been printed in Dublin,
Ireland, and professed to be something found in the closet of a "deceased
gentleman" — a standard ruse contrived by pamphleteers to avoid prosecution for having reported a Parliamentary speech.

"Dear me!" the aged statesman had exclaimed after Jones explained the
purpose of his call. "I did not think any young person had even heard of
that episode!"

Jones smiled and replied, "I am a barrister, your lordship, and laws and
their fulminatory origins are my natural interest and obsession."

Chesterfield had laughed. "Have you seen this circumventing 'interlude,' sir, or read the playbook? What is its title?"

Jones looked ironic. "It is called 'The Beaux's Pestle,' your lordship. I
have not seen a staging of it, but read the book. It is quite a slender con-
coction, even though it filches generously from Farquhar and Marlowe,
albeit my client admits only to a judicious adaptation of Mr. Handel."

Chesterfield laughed again. "The advancement of liberty so often is
mandated by the freedom of scoundrels!" He studied his caller for a
moment. "You do not come to me as a stranger, Sir Dogmael," he said. "I
have read your letters in the *Post* and *Evening Signal*, and could not more
agree with your points if I had made them myself." He paused. "I have

heard of you, as well. Were you not defending counsel at the trial of those freethinkers some years ago? The 'Pippins,' I recollect they were called."

Jones nodded. "Yes, your lordship. I was their counselor."

"And you lost that matter."

"Yes." Jones's features darkened with bitter memories. "They were found guilty of seditious libel, but, in truth, they were neither guilty nor scoundrels." He paused. "Lord Wooten presided."

"Oh? Grainger the Groundless? Yes, that is correct. I have met him. Rather a cow's bladder of a man. Well, then I am not surprised that you lost, if *he* presided. The Crown made an excellent choice in that matter." Chesterfield glanced for a moment out the study window to his garden. "Then, be prepared to lose again, my good man. I possess no arcane insight into the nature of the Dramatic Licensing Act, which is plainly clear in its wording and allows no leave for interpretation. I cannot imagine any justice who would risk contradicting it, except for Pratt. I agree with you that the Act deserves repeal, for it is contrary to the Constitution, and because it condemns genius to the sponger before it has even set pen to paper. Your Mr. Hogue, apparently, is no genius, but he has been denied his right and opportunity to prove it. And if there are any new Shakespeares among us, I bristle at the thought that they must wait on mediocrity for permission and approval before they might make their presence known to us." The Earl sighed. "Until the Act is repealed, we must all remain captives of Drury Lane and Covent Garden. I am sorry, but I have no special advice to offer you." He smiled then. "Sir, your visit is timely. In another day or so, I am to Bath to bathe my physical complaints. However, would you stay to supper? What are your views on this Stamp Act we have so carelessly thrust upon the colonies?" He picked up an ear trumpet and brandished it. "I have not attended Lords in years, sir, for I can no longer hear what is being said in the chamber." Then he grunted in contempt. "There, I am missed for my wit, though not for my wisdom."

Jones lost the case, as Chesterfield had predicted. "Words were spoken, not sung," read the decision of the three judges at the King's Bench, "in between tasteless renditions of dollops of Mr. Handel's works, and these words, having been spoken in conjunction with actions by the players, communicated a story, one only occasionally interposed by singing accompanied by musicians, though not so frequently or of any duration that the work could be called an *opera*. Therefore, the work in question is a *play*, for the exhibition of which to the public for fees or other recompense its author and manager has neglected to apply to the Lord Chamberlain's office for a reading and license." The court recommended to the jury that it find Hogue in violation of the Licensing Act, fine him five hundred pounds, and commit him to the King's Bench Prison for one year. The jury complied.

Jones also lost a second case, that of a young law student from another Inn who had managed to report, verbatim, many of the important speeches made in the Commons the last session. The student secretly sold them to other law students as study aids in contemporary rhetoric. He, too, was served with a general warrant for having violated the ban on public reporting of Parliamentary business. He was found guilty as well of violating Parliamentary privilege, fined one hundred pounds, required to apologize in person to the House when it next sat, and prohibited from pursuing a career in law.

Jones had persuaded Garnet Kenrick to pay most of the student's fine to keep him out of debtor's prison — the youth's tobacconist-shop parents being in no position to pay it themselves — and frequently employed the youth as secretary and amanuensis. And, because the youth had a penchant for law, Jones was making progress in convincing him to emigrate to the colonies, where he could practice it beyond the court's jurisdiction.

When he could budget the time, Jones attended the intellectual *soirées* of Elizabeth Montagu and Mrs. Macaulay. He found these tea table discussions less stimulating than the time he spent thinking and writing in the Purgatory, Mitre, and Turk's Head Taverns. In these busy, smoky environments he had composed most of his anonymously written pamphlets on a variety of subjects, mostly political.

One, entitled "The True Colonial Monarch," caused a minor sensation among those who worried about the effects of the Stamp Act. In it Jones attacked the Act, and posed the paradox: "By the Revolution of '89 and the Act of Settlement, Parliament wrested monarchial power from the monarch. If the colonists appeal to His Majesty for protection, for their rights and liberties are guaranteed by his hand in their various charters, is it not implied that they wish His Majesty to reassert and reclaim powers ceded to Parliament? Would they not then be asking him to become again a true sovereign, and not an executive? To subvert the Constitution? To rule them, and in time, us, with the same unmindful recklessness with which Parliament now presumes to rule? If we cannot entrust either the king or Parliament with the shield of liberty, then what might be the solution…?"

Tonight, Jones turned to another chore, that of writing to Garnet Kenrick and his son Hugh, informing them of the change in ministry and the events leading up to it.

He wrote: "...I am suspicious of Mr. Pitt's devotion to our liberty and that of the colonies. Without casting aspersions on his character, I can only wonder, were he not so distracted by afflictions of the mind and foot, would he not be a worse taskmaster than Mr. Grenville, a greater enemy of the colonists than a friend? You must recall that some time ago, when he was in better health (I believe at the outset of the late war), he stated in the House that he was opposed to encouraging the colonies to manufacture necessities and luxuries for themselves and the mother country, and would sooner blast their every factory and furnace than cause misery and starvation in England...."

He also discussed the nascent efforts of British merchants and employers to petition the Board of Trade and Parliament to repeal or relax the Stamp Act, for they were anxious that the Act would depress an already reduced trade with the colonies.

Jones brought back with him from Danvers copies of several colonial newspapers forwarded to the Baron by Otis Talbot, the family's agent in Philadelphia. In one of them, the *New York Journal*, was a reprint of Paoli's "Corsican Manifesto," in which the rebels pledged themselves to die "rather than submit ourselves and posterity to the insupportable yoke of Genoese tyranny and slavery." The "Manifesto" was accompanied by remarks by the paper's publisher, who praised the Corsicans as models of virtue for mankind: "Not as you are, but what you ought to be."

Jones was touched by that sentiment. He carefully underlined it, clipped the item from the paper, and pinned it to the wall over his desk. It both consoled him, and warned him, for while he was endeavoring to be "what he ought to be," he felt alienated from most men with whom he allied himself in championing liberty, and knew that they were flailing approximations of what they ought to be, unable or unwilling to capture the greater vista of things. He glanced up at the clipping now, then concluded his report on the merchants. "Depend on *them* to sunder their principles from their purses."

Under the steady, constant light of the pump lamps, Jones wrote on, not permitting himself to think of a person many leagues away, of Alice Kenrick, his patron's daughter, who was now seventeen, and with whom he was in love. His discipline faltered, but then he remembered something only after he had finished the letters and put them aside for the law student to copy into his letter book. In a brief postscript to each of them, he reported the adventure of the second messenger.

* * *

It was "Mr. Hunt" — Jared Turley, Basil Kenrick's reclaimed bastard son, now in his father's service — who, at his father's request, laboriously penned the false invitation, sealed it with the wax lifted from the Earl's own invitation to the Bedford levee, then donned a footman's livery and delivered it to Jones's chambers.

When he returned to Windridge Court, Turley first stopped in the kitchen to fortify himself with a dram of whisky before reporting to the Earl in his study. He took the wig from his coat pocket and tossed it contemptuously on the servants' table; he hated wearing the things, and hated having to don the livery, for he considered a menial's job beneath him. He longed to change back into his own fine clothes. But he gathered his courage and marched upstairs.

Turley presented himself in an almost military manner, hat removed and tucked under his arm, and stood stiffly at attention, more from fear than from respect. "I regret to report that the...ruse...was not a success, sir," he said in a dry voice. He produced the spurned invitation from inside his coat and laid it on the Earl's desk. "The gentleman declined the hospitality."

One eyebrow of the Earl's rose in question. "I am sure he declined in so many words, Mr. Hunt. What were they?"

"Rude and cryptic, sir." Turley repeated from memory Jones's precise words, omitting his error in address.

"I see. He did not question the authenticity of the invitation?"

"No, sir."

With a grimace, the Earl took the invitation and methodically tore it to pieces. "Based on your own reports of his arrogant and heated temperament, I was certain the fellow would be foolishly bold enough to accept. Or at least be curious enough to attend." He tossed the pieces over his shoulder, then thoughtfully drummed the fingers of his hands on the velvet blotter. "Had he accepted, and appeared at the levee, he would have acquired more enemies than he now has — among his own party. And his grace the Duke would have been stung by his rudeness — good word, Mr.

Hunt — and indeed entertained the company with Sir Dogmael's abrupt and deservedly vulgar ejection from the premises on the belief that he was spying on his grace with a forged invitation. He would have been as welcome there as one of the mob of silk-weavers who recently besieged his grace's residence, but were bloodied and trampled by the Guards and Lord Ancram's cavalry. Well, you were there with me, Mr. Hunt."

Turley winced at the Earl's use of the proper address, but disguised it with a nod of agreement. "Yes, sir, and had the privilege of tossing a few stones at the scoundrels before they were dispersed by the authorities." He paused. "I am afraid, though, that it will take more than stones to disperse Sir Dogmael. His patron is your brother, the good Baron."

The Earl sighed in disappointment. "Well, there will be other occasions. " He opened a desk drawer, removed five guineas from a box, closed the drawer, and put the coins on the blotter in front of him. "It is not your fault that the jest failed, Mr. Hunt. It was to have been a birthday gift to Sir Henoch, who celebrates his debut in the world tomorrow, and who will accompany me to the levee. He would enjoy the spectacle, and, had we succeeded, Sir Dogmael's humiliation would have been repayment of some kind for that caricature of Sir Henoch he broadcast. Now, I must settle for some common bauble to present him." He paused. "I promised you a bonus to carry it out, Mr. Hunt. The jest was only half successful, so you have earned only half the bonus." The Earl looked away with disdain, and waited.

"Thank you, sir, " said Turley softly. He took a step closer, picked up the golden coins as quietly as he could, and quickly pocketed them. He stepped back to await dismissal.

The Earl ended the audience with instructions to his son that he begin packing his things for the journey to Danvers, where they would spend the balance of the summer until the fall, when Parliament would prepare to reconvene.

* * *

Chapter 3: The Informer

Edgar Cullis carefully brushed the dust from his attire, braced himself, and strode resolutely past the open gates of the Governor's Palace in Williamsburg. He was not happy about coming here, but he was determined to complete his mission as quickly and coldly as possible.

It was a sultry, humid afternoon in late July. The ride from Caxton yesterday morning had been a miserable journey aggravated by the swirling dust from roads that had not been dampened by rain in over a month, and by the cicadas, wood beetles, and other noisy insects that clicked and hummed incessantly from the trees above. The combination of the heat, dust, and insects was mentally suffocating. His head still throbbed.

And although he did not dwell on this aspect of his purpose here, it was made more distasteful by the suspicion that he had been approached and requested to perform this task for a reason he did not allow to congeal into a certainty. He tried not to imagine the faces of the persons who summoned him to Williamsburg and explained the mission to him, nor the reward promised him should he accept the task. He tried not to remember the promises he had made to the men who reelected him this month as burgess for the county. And he refused to think of Hugh Kenrick, who had also been reelected.

Inside, beneath the great wheel of weapons on the ceiling in the grand foyer of the Palace, he was intercepted by the housekeeper and asked his business. Rather abruptly and officiously, he replied that he wished an interview with the Governor concerning urgent Assembly matters. With meek, patronizing authority the housekeeper asked him to wait in the well-appointed room to his right. He entered the room but did not sit down. A colored paper fan had been placed on a side table for the benefit of guests and visitors. Cullis swept it up and impatiently waved the fan to cool his face in the moist warm air as he paced back and forth. To his side he clutched a leather portfolio. In it was the reason he was here.

Half an hour later he was escorted by a footman back outside the Palace to the Governor's other office, in an eastern wing building within the Palace walls. He was asked to wait in a larger, more sumptuously decorated room. Another half-hour passed, and then a secretary appeared to show him upstairs to the Governor's office. Francis Fauquier received him graciously, and offered him some refreshment from a decanter of punch. Not so much thirsty as desperate to wet his throat in order to speak with the boldness he knew was required, he accepted. When Fauquier had finished the courtesy, he sat down behind his desk and exchanged some pleasantries and complaints with his visitor, using a fan to cool his brow. At one point he asked briskly, as though remembering that his time was valuable, "Well, Mr. Cullis! To what do I owe this call?"

Cullis assumed an air of relaxation, sat back in his chair, and crossed his legs. Over one knee he balanced the portfolio. He spoke now with some confidence. "No doubt, your honor, you are aware of the ferment and commotion caused by the resolutions passed in the Assembly this late spring."

The Lieutenant-Governor chuckled morosely. "Oh, how could I not be?" he exclaimed. "Why, I receive correspondence about it every other day, it seems, from the three points, and even from the west." He shook his head. "Poor Governor Bernard in Boston is most to be pitied. That is where much of the commotion occurs, you see. And I fear it will grow worse." He turned in his regal chair to glance out the open window, and nodded to the town beyond. "The people are not well here, either. They are unhappy, uneasy, and a madness grips them." He grinned in self-effacement. "I am unhappy, uneasy, but not mad."

"Yes, your honor," replied Cullis. "I fear that more serious commotion is in the making."

"How so, sir?"

Cullis cleared his throat. "I represent a group of burgesses who are mindful of the mood of His Majesty's subjects here, and who have observed the commotions and madness of those in other of his colonies." He pursed his lips and sped on. "Some weeks ago the House received a missive which we construe is a measure of the imminent peril of anarchy and lawlessness. The group I represent are properly concerned and dismayed, and wish only to apprise you and the Crown of our thoughts." He paused. "I have here a document to show you, your honor, one which I believe you will find equally dismaying." He opened the portfolio and took out a one-page letter. "If you would be kind enough to read it, your honor, I hope you will understand why I presume to encroach upon your time." Cullis rose and handed the Lieutenant-Governor the paper over the desk, then resumed his seat.

Fauquier stuck out his lower lip and read the letter. It was dated June 8th, and was an invitation from the Massachusetts Assembly to the twelve other colonial assemblies to select delegates to a congress in New York "to consider of a general and united, dutiful, loyal, and humble representation of their condition to His Majesty and Parliament; and to implore relief."

When he was finished, Fauquier put the letter down on his paper-strewn desk. "Disturbing mischief, indeed, sir. I had heard some rumor of such a congress, but was not certain it could be true. This document proves it." He paused to finish his punch. "Well, presumably your group of disinterested burgesses have some recommendations or advice for me." He smiled expectantly with patient benevolence at his visitor.

Cullis smiled in apology. "Forgive us *our* presuming to advise you, your honor, but you are correct that we do. News of the congress has already spread throughout the colony here. Most certainly the call for such a congress was precipitated in no little way by the illegal broadcasting of the Assembly's resolves shortly after they were passed, and also by the agitations of similarly reckless persons in Massachusetts and New York. A great deal of pamphleteering is being indulged in now by wags in most of the colonies, much of it calling the Act unconstitutional, or a breach of royal charters, or a design to enslave the colonies and make them absolutely dependent on the Crown." The burgess for Queen Anne County made a face and sighed. "I have read some of this seditious literature, out of duty, of course, and my head grows dizzy with the menagerie of arguments that now circulate among His Majesty's subjects here, like the distemper that has plagued our livestock."

"I have heard some of them myself, sir," remarked the Lieutenant-Governor, "and even debated them with some of your colleagues in private. And I agree with you, that they can dull one's clarity."

"Now, your honor, come the next Assembly here in November, the members of our House will doubtless demand to make the choosing of delegates to this congress their first order of business, in or out of session, within or without the Capitol, with or without your approval or that of the Council, or even of the Speaker."

Fauquier looked thoughtful for a moment, then said, "But, good sir, the gentlemen in this letter call for a congress in October, weeks before an Assembly here could convene."

Cullis added with irony, hoping he did not give the impression that he was contradicting the Lieutenant-Governor, "I would not be surprised, your honor, if many of them arrived far ahead of time to convene a private assembly of their own. Their elections would be doubtless assured, and they would act with the confidence that they were entitled to act for the Assembly." He paused. "I am told that many members of the Assembly, who have been alerted to the congress in their own private correspondence with other colonies, plan to do exactly that, your honor."

"I see," said Fauquier. After a moment, he asked, "What *is* your recommendation, sir?"

Cullis cocked his head in feigned innocence. "I do not presume to recommend anything myself, your honor, although my group wish to take the liberty of pointing out that the House could not choose delegates if an Assembly...had not been called." Although the worst of his mission was over — now that the words had been spoken — he could not control the gulp that caused him to pause. He added, "We fear that, if given the opportunity, the House would select delegates who were most responsible for the resolves, and who could attend the congress in New York and perhaps return here in time to attend the Assembly, as well, and very likely introduce more mischief."

Fauquier hummed in thought. "Yes, yes...I see what you mean. That Henry fellow, the one who made so much fuss, I could see him going to this congress and calling for my head!" He chuckled. "No, no, that wouldn't do at all!"

Cullis said, "Of course, your honor, it is for you to decide whether or not to prorogue the new session. But, as I am sure the Attorney-General himself would advise you, an official delegation of gentlemen from this colony to the congress could not be named and dispatched by a non-existent Assembly. We have consulted the law, and judge that any burgess who appointed himself, or was appointed a delegate by an ad hoc committee of burgesses acting outside the Assembly, but still representing himself as a delegate of the Assembly, would naturally run afoul of the law, and could be removed from his office, or expelled, or penalized in some manner." Cullis paused again. "It is a delicate and disagreeable conundrum, your honor, one which we are sure would have undoubtedly occurred to you, as well, without our presumptuous advice."

"Please, Mr. Cullis," grimaced the Lieutenant-Governor, with a wave of his hand, "I am not as wise as you wish me to be." He reached for the decanter and poured himself another glass of punch, then gestured to his visitor's empty glass. Cullis shook his head. The Lieutenant-Governor sipped the beverage, then said, "A moment ago you referred to the 'illegal' broadcasting of the House's resolutions, Mr. Cullis. I do not understand that disapprobation. They were bound to be made public in some manner."

"It was their manner of promulgation that my group object to, your honor, and believe violates the House's privilege," replied Cullis, who was embarking on the most delicate part of his mission. "May I point out that the populaces of other colonies are under the false impression that all seven of Mr. Henry's resolves were adopted by the Assembly, when in truth only four were. Mr. Henry doubtlessly conspired to have all seven printed on a broadside, and, without care for fact or House privilege, advertised them as official actions of the Assembly. Other newspapers have reprinted the four, in addition to the ones that were not adopted."

Fauquier shrugged. "It was not Mr. Royle of the *Gazette* who printed the falsity, sir. I have it from him that he would have first broken his press before he would print a single word of those resolves."

Cullis smiled. "A very patriotic man, Mr. Royle," he remarked. "But, it was Mr. Wendel Barret, proprietor of the *Caxton Courier*, who printed large numbers of sheets containing the seven resolves. He obtained a license to publish his paper and operate a press by special leave of Governor Din-widdie, your predecessor. By that license, he is permitted to reprint news and intelligence from other papers, in addition to advertisements and announcements of a local character, but never news of a general nature that has not first been reported elsewhere. That stipulation is made clear in the license, a copy of which must be in your files. Further, other than printing account books, blank legal documents, and the like for sale, he is forbidden to print instruments of any...political nature."

"I see. Well, I did not know that." The Lieutenant-Governor's eyes were round with shock.

"In fact, your honor, by printing the resolves, in addition to overstep ping the strictures of his license, he further violated the privilege of the House and Council of the privacy of their deliberations and resolutions." Cullis paused. "Mr. Barret's guilt in this matter can be proven by a simple comparison of a number of the *Courier* and one of the illegal broadsides. I am certain that Mr. Royle, upon consultation, could point out the recurring styles, anomalies, and consistencies in them." He looked into the space above the Lieutenant-Governor's head. "A royal governor granted him the license by his leave and privilege, your honor, and one may revoke it, as well."

Fauquier's brow wrinkled in annoyance. "I am conscious of my pre-rogatives, sir," he replied in mild rebuke. He noted the red flush of embarrassment in his visitor's face. What a knowledgeable man, he thought. He did not wonder now why none of his three closest friends in the House had approached him with this information and advice. Young Mr. Cullis could accomplish this task without incriminating any of them. The Lieutenant-Governor's mouth flattened in transient disgust with this political business. "Well, Mr. Cullis, I thank you for your visit. I will give your group's thoughts some consideration." He rose and picked up the circular letter. "With your permission, I would like to have copies of this made so that I may forward them to the Board in London. You may wait downstairs. The task should not take long."

Edgar Cullis rose, stepped back once, and inclined his head. "Thank you, your honor, for the opportunity to render some service to the Crown and colony."

Cullis left the Palace, gave the footman at the gate a penny for having watched his mount, and rode up the Green to Duke of Gloucester Street. Some minutes later he dismounted again outside the Edinburgh Coffeehouse near the Capitol. Peyton Randolph and George Wythe, also recently reelected burgesses, sat at a table in the rear of the near-empty establishment. Without greeting, he sat down at the table, took out the circular letter, and laid it on the table. "It is done, sirs. He had copies made of it."

Randolph asked, "Will he prorogue the fall Assembly, Mr. Cullis?"

Cullis grimaced. "He did not say, Mr. Randolph. He was very much disturbed by the letter and my arguments." He paused. "I adhered to your instructions, sir, and pointed out to him the advantage of not calling an Assembly. He seemed to agree, but did not actually say so."

"I see," said Randolph. "Well, we must simply wait on his decision." He reached for the letter and put it into his own portfolio. "What did he say about Mr. Barret and the broadsides?"

"Only that he was conscious of his prerogatives, sir. I do not think he was aware that there was another press in these parts. He seemed truly surprised, and no doubt has by now instructed a clerk to find Governor Dinwiddie's license. However, I had no hint in word or manner what he may do about it."

Wythe sighed and remarked, "His excellency is a first-class card player."

Randolph observed the restrained sour look on Cullis's features. He said, "At the risk of repeating myself, good sir, you must appreciate why we have resorted to so...sly a method of communicating with the Governor. It would seem indecorous for any one of us to urge him to postpone our own Assembly."

Cullis could not quite suppress the contempt and bitterness in his words. He replied, "I fully appreciate *your* predicament, sir."

But, it was with a cloying nausea of shame that he later that day rode back to Caxton. He was glad that the road would not take him past Wendel Barret's shop, nor anywhere near Meum Hall.

* * *

Lieutenant-Governor Fauquier spoke the truth about himself. He was not as wise as others wished him to be. But he was wily. In the next issue of the *Virginia Gazette*, over his signature, there appeared three proclamations. The first read:

"Whereas I find no urgent occasion for the General Assembly to meet in the Fall of this year, I have therefore thought fit, by and with the advice of His Majesty's Council, by this Proclamation, in His Majesty's name, to prorogue the Assembly until the first Tuesday of March, 1766."

The second proclamation dryly announced that the General Court would sit in November. The third proclamation read:

"Whereas the contentions and distemper of these times over recent, troubling actions of His Majesty's Government are conveyed in so many diverse and provocative forms that endanger the lives of His Majesty's subjects and the peace of his dominion here, I have thought it fit, by and with the advice of His Majesty's Council, by this Proclamation, in His Majesty's name, to suspend temporarily the publication of this Gazette, commencing after its next number, until such time as this His Majesty's colony is adjudged by me to have returned to a state of harmony and tranquility."

"We did not ask for *that!*" exclaimed a stunned Peyton Randolph when he read the proclamation.

"How are we to know what goes on elsewhere?" asked a panicked Wythe.

Randolph muttered an inaudible curse and tossed the *Gazette* down on Wythe's desk. It was a sour victory, as sour as his qualified triumph over the Resolves. Having succeeded in scotching further complicity of Virginia in expressing insolent sentiments and sanctioning the unwarrantable combination that was to take place in New York in October, he, Wythe, and the most responsible House leaders had unintentionally provoked the Lieutenant-Governor to impose a reign of ignorance on the colony. The *Gazette* was the sole official source of news. "It is unprecedented," he remarked to the room at large.

A thought flitted through his mind that this was, perhaps, a species of tyranny that was being protested. After all, what was the difference between the Lieutenant-Governor's actions, a prorogation of the right of assembly, on one hand, and his prorogation of the accumulation of knowledge! He could hear the flaming rhetoric now! And what was the difference between those actions and a tax that would all but smother trade and legal business because most people would not be able to pay the tax, a tax levied over and above all the taxes and fees charged and which more often than not went to support the whole apparatus of royal governance? A tax over and above all those already charged by the Assembly itself! He wondered about the hubris of a man who would decree that His Majesty's loyal and dutiful subjects should remain ignorant of events and happenings beyond the colony's borders, who would deny them the means to express their own dissatisfaction or even satisfaction with present conditions.

But Randolph's mind swerved away from focusing too long on that thought. He did not wish now to pursue that line of reasoning. The unbidden cogitation swept into his mind, and he let it plummet into the depths of his other concerns, such as how to reward Edgar Cullis. Perhaps a permanent appointment to one of the permanent committees.

He stopped pacing and turned to address Wythe, whose dour expression seemed to reflect similar remorseful thoughts. "It seems that murdered Cherokees and the Augusta Boys and other pressing business have addled the good sense of our friend down the way," he said.

"We cannot now advise him to rescind the suspension, Mr. Randolph," replied Wythe.

"No, that would be testing his patience." Randolph paused. "We have both observed him when he is possessed by anger. To question his action would seem like challenging his lawful prerogative, even though that is not what we would do." He chuckled once in ironic amusement. "And, of course, he must have guessed who sent Mr. Cullis."

"Do you think the citizenry will be possessed by anger?" asked Wythe. "Now no one will have the means to advertise wares, or property, or runaways, or any of the mundane business we are accustomed to. Many legitimate announcements must now remain...unannounced. It is, as you say, unprecedented."

"I cannot imagine how the citizenry will swallow it," said Randolph. "It seems that while we have persuaded him to thwart intemperate actions and words, we have also invited him to fix a pair of blinders over our eyes."

Wythe nodded. "It smacks of Romish politics," he remarked. "People may think he is practicing the powers of the Pope. Or the Prussian king. 'Look straight ahead to your business, and never mind what other unpatriotic fools do or say.'" Wythe's face seemed then to explode in horrified realization. "Why, his action will lend credence to Mr. Henry's most incongruous and absurd fears!"

The two veterans of Virginia politics looked at each other in surprise at their tacit agreement with a man and an idea with which they did not wish to agree. The logic of events, however, was compelling them to. They did not like it.

* * *

Chapter 4: The Duel

Israel Beck, manservant and assistant bookkeeper at Morland Hall, late one morning in early August drove a sulky into Caxton to purchase some new ledger books, writing paper, and a pattern book for Ruth Dakin. He stopped when he saw a small crowd of townspeople gathered around a wagon outside of Wendel Barret's shop, his first destination. He saw two men in fine clothes mounted on horses, and several liveried Negroes carrying out the wide wooden type cases of Barret's press and loading them onto the wagon bed.

Just then Travis Barret, the printer's twelve-year-old grandson, flew from the crowd and ran toward Beck. Beck signaled to him with his crop. When the boy stopped at the sulky, he asked, "What goes on here, young Barret?"

"The Council's shutting us down, sir! Orders from the Governor! Grandpa's all a fury! Got to tell Mr. Kenrick!"

"Oh, my!" exclaimed Beck. "Well, go ahead, and be sure to alert Mr. Frake, too!"

"Yes, sir!" Travis Barret sped off again in the direction of Meum Hall as though the devil were chasing him.

At Meum hall, Hugh Kenrick was in his study, taking a respite from the heat, reading a volume of Tacitus, when a breathless Travis Barret was shown in by Spears. When the boy told him the news, he sent the valet to Morland to inform Jack Frake.

"Who are these men?" Hugh asked the boy.

"Never saw 'em before, sir! I think the one's name is Waldo, or something like that, and the other is John Chiswell. Mean lookin' cuss, he is! He shoved Grandpa aside and threatened him with his boot!"

Hugh paused long enough to wonder if he should wear his sword. He wore it occasionally as a mere formality, when he thought of it. He decided to err on the side of caution. Chiswell, who was not reelected to represent Williamsburg because of the incident in the town in May, might cause trouble again. He snapped on his tricorn, and strapped on his sword, but in his hurry and outrage left his frock coat behind.

He rode into town with the boy riding double behind him. The entourage was just about to leave the front of Barret's shop. The boy slid to the ground and ran to join his grandfather in the watching crowd.

Hugh recognized both of the mounted men: the monkish face of Nathaniel Walthoe, Clerk of the Council, and the pinched, sour face of John Chiswell, former burgess for Williamsburg and father-in-law of Speaker John Robinson. Their presence here was odd. The liveried servants he recognized as staff from the Capitol. He glanced at the crowd and saw Wendel Barret glaring at the horsemen. Sheriff Cabal Tippet and under-sheriff George Roane, standing with Mayor Moses Corbin, were also in the crowd, looking helpless and resigned.

Hugh rode directly in the path of Walthoe and stopped. He pointed to the wagon. "What means this, sir?" he demanded.

Walthoe frowned, halted, and held up a hand. His entourage stopped. "Mr. Kenrick," he said pleasantly, "good day to you."

Hugh again pointed at the wagon. "I recognize Mr. Barret's livelihood there, sir. What means this?"

Nathaniel Walthoe was reluctant to reply to such a question, but felt he must. He had heard this man speak in the Assembly, and also felt obliged because the man hailed from nobility. An answer was required of him. He said, "Mr. Barret was found to be in violation of the terms of his license, in addition to having violated the sanctity of the House by printing the resolves of the late Assembly."

Hugh grimaced. "In what capacity do you act, sir?"

"There being no appointed deputy King's Attorney for this county — the worthy Mr. Reisdale having declined that office a number of times — I have been temporarily deputized to that office by Mr. Randolph, the Attorney-General, with the approval of the Council and his honor the Governor."

"I see." Hugh glanced at John Chiswell, who sat in his saddle regarding him with an ominously seething patience.

Walthoe only now remembered what had happened last May in Williamsburg, when Chiswell attacked this man with his cane on Duke of Gloucester Street, and had even attempted an assault in the House chamber. The man was already in a funk over having lost reelection as burgess for Williamsburg. He realized that perhaps Chiswell was the wrong man to have brought here. He said, "Mr. Chiswell is my own deputized bailiff, sir, the House bailiff being indisposed with a stomach ailment and there being no other man of authority available."

"An authority by virtue of marriage," remarked Hugh with contempt. He nodded to the wagon again and the three liveried servants who sat on the riding board. "You are employing Capitol hands to effect a wrong that doubtless Mr. Randolph was loath to commit himself."

Walthoe frowned. "Think what you wish of it, sir, but I have the Council's leave to employ them. Now, Mr. Kenrick, if you would kindly allow us to pass....?"

Hugh may as well not have heard the request. "What proof have you that Mr. Barret printed the resolves?" he insisted.

Walthoe sighed. "The proof was provided by a patriotic subject of this very county, sir, and has been authenticated by an authority whose veracity can hardly be questioned, Mr. Royle of the *Gazette*." Walthoe paused. "Mr. Barret's property will be returned to him at the leave of his honor the Governor. He will be officially charged in the General Court in November, but no further action will be taken against him, providing he does not repeat the offense. His honor judged that removal of the means of repeating that offense will secure that particular end. In the meantime, Mr. Barret is permitted his liberty. He may continue to receive mail and conduct such business as he may."

"How generous of his honor. Have you a warrant for Mr. Barret's arrest?"

"No, sir. It was the prerogative of his honor to order one drawn up, but his honor has decided it would serve no purpose. A writ for the seizure of the press was deemed sufficient penalty."

"And Mr. Barret was found guilty by the Council?"

"The Council presented its evidence, sir, and it was his honor's decision to take this action. All the legal niceties were observed."

"I am sure they were," replied Hugh. He put on a challenging grin. "I paid for the printing of those resolves, Mr. Walthoe," he said. "Perhaps his honor might wish to serve me with a legal nicety, as well. I, too, violated a House rule by effecting the promulgation of the resolves."

Walthoe looked genuinely surprised, but said, "It was assumed that someone paid to have the offence committed, sir, but that is not the matter at hand."

"And when will his honor see his way to returning Mr. Barret's property?"

"When he sees fit," replied Walthoe.

"When he permits the *Gazette* to resume publication, perhaps?" asked Hugh in mock speculation. "We here in Caxton did not place much importance on the *Gazette*'s suspension, given that it is so much influenced by his honor the Governor. We had the *Courier*. And now we are to be denied it, as well."

Walthoe fiddled with his reins and sat straight in his saddle. "That is not my affair, sir. Now, we wish to return to Williamsburg before dusk, if you please, and must be on our way."

Hugh said, "I shall speak with the Governor myself, sir, and you and Mr. Chiswell may find yourselves sued for damages."

"No, you will not speak to anyone — regicide!!" bellowed John Chiswell, who drew his sword in time with his words.

Walthoe's jaw dropped and he glanced in panic at his deputy bailiff. But Hugh, having sensed Chiswell's intent, had already reined his mount around and galloped a few strides away from the men, but heard Walthoe demand that Chiswell sheathe his sword and turn about.

Without stopping, Hugh tugged on one rein and brought his mount around smartly as he drew out his own sword. Chiswell hurtled directly at him, cursing wildly, digging his heels repeatedly into the flanks of his horse.

Hugh urged his mount into a gallop.

Chiswell's sword was raised to strike at Hugh's head. As it came down, Hugh deftly parried it with a clang of steel as he sped past the ex-burgess.

Hugh quickly reined about and charged again. Chiswell had barely enough time to urge his horse to recover and move to meet Hugh. With a flick of his blade, Hugh connected with the guard of Chiswell's raised weapon, wrested it from the man's grip, and sent it wheeling through the air over Chiswell's head. In the same deft, liquid movement, he whipped the flat of the blade down and struck the rump of his opponent's passing horse.

Chiswell's horse screamed in surprise, bucked once in mid-stride, causing the man to lose hold of his reins, then bolted off, throwing its unbalanced rider to the ground with a thud and a cloud of dust.

Cheers, laughter, and applause burst from the watching crowd. It was the first time anyone in it had ever seen such combat.

Hugh turned and walked his mount up to the toppled ex-burgess, his sword blade resting lightly on a shoulder. He looked contemptuously down at the sputtering, shocked older man. "Shall we continue this, sir?" he asked.

"You may go to hell!" replied the wild-eyed Chiswell, now hatless, his wig askew, and his scabbard bent in half. He looked very foolish, and knew it. He searched for his hat, and found that he was sitting on it.

Nathaniel Walthoe, scandalized and angry, trotted up to the pair. He offered his bailiff a hand to help him up, but the man slapped it away with his crumpled hat. Walthoe then commanded, "Sir, please recover your horse and sword! You have besmirched the lawfulness of our purpose here!"

"You can go to hell, as well, sir!" spat Chiswell.

Sheriff Tippet and George Roane quickly strode up to the group. Tippet addressed Hugh. "Sir, do you wish to charge this gentleman with assault? Witnesses to his action there are aplenty!"

Hugh narrowed his eyes and smiled. "Yes, this time, and I — "

Walthoe interjected hastily, "You cannot charge Mr. Chiswell with any offense, sirs! He is on Crown business! But, I will vouch for the wrongness of his action, and promise that he will be reprimanded." He paused, then added, reluctantly, "I, too, was a witness."

"This *regicide* was obstructing our way!" shouted Chiswell, picking himself up from the ground and waving his hat at Hugh. "It was my duty as bailiff to move him out of it!"

"That is not what we saw — " began Tippet.

"Never mind what *you* saw! It's what *I* saw that counts!" He turned and looked up at Walthoe. "You, sir, must vouch for *me* that this…creature was obstructing our way! He was obstructing officers of the law in the performance of their duty!"

"No, sir," answered Hugh. "I was questioning the propriety of tyranny."

Chiswell cursed again and shook a fist at Hugh.

Walthoe laid his riding crop on the man's shoulder and spoke with angry impatience. "Mr. Chiswell, I am a moment away from remanding you to the mercies of this county's justice! You have already forfeited your fee for this service! Kindly reclaim your horse and accompany me back to Williamsburg!"

Chiswell looked up at the deputy King's Attorney and saw that Walthoe meant it. He straightened his wig, put on his hat, and retrieved first his sword, then his horse, which had stopped to water itself at a trough outside the King's Arms Tavern a way down the street. He mounted it and trotted past Walthoe and the waiting wagon in the direction of the Hove Stream bridge and the road back to Williamsburg.

Walthoe motioned the wagon to follow him and rode on.

Tippet chuckled and remarked to him as he passed, "Next time, Mr. Walthoe, choose an abler bailiff!"

The deputy King's Attorney said nothing and passed by.

Hugh turned his mount around to watch the party leave. He saw Jack Frake and John Proudlocks, also mounted, staring at him from across the street. Jack Frake then saluted him with his tricorn, as did Proudlocks. Hugh smiled, returned the salute, and without flourish sheathed his sword.

Sheriff Tippet shook his head and said to Hugh, "Pardon me for saying this, Mr. Kenrick, but you had no authority to interrogate Mr. Walthoe. I already asked him some of those questions."

"Yes, I had, Mr. Tippet," replied Hugh. "This gave me the authority." He tapped his forehead with a finger.

"Well," conceded Tippet, "*I* could not stand in the way of the Crown."

Hugh dismounted, hitched his horse to the post outside of Barret's shop, and entered the place. He found Wendel Barret railing in a fit of boiling rage at Jack Frake, Proudlocks, and the other men who crowded into the shop. The printer's face was red, his eyes flashed, and his hands shook uncontrollably. "They have robbed me of my joy!" he proclaimed. "I am nothing without my press!" He patted one side of the press. "Now my machine of knowledge is…gutless! They have left me a brain without words!" Travis Barret stood in a corner of the cramped room with Cletus, the apprentice slave.

Jack Frake asked with genuine perplexity, "Why did they not take the press?"

"They could not have stolen it without breaking it up, Mr. Frake! Assembled, it will not fit through the door! Besides, his honor the Governor could not be accused of *censoring* the press when he has left it intact! But, the thing is useless without *words*, sir, and those are now gone!"

Lucas Rittles, Barret's neighboring grocer, volunteered to Jack Frake, "Mr. Walthoe's warrant stated that he had the authority to remove all the type cases, even the ones used for printing account book pages and such."

Jack Frake scoffed. "But, he *can* be accused of censorship," he said. "He has suspended the *Gazette*, as well."

"Bosh!" exclaimed Barret. "I'll wager that Mr. Royle is well compensated for *his* inconvenience, and that he still has his type cases! He won't mind the suspension! Saves him the bother of courage to say what's on his mind!" Barret waved a hand around the shop. "Half my revenue came from the county's advertisements. Royle is on the same budget!"

Reverend Albert Acland, who had joined the crowd in the shop, said, "I don't see the injustice, sir. You were granted a license to operate a press.

There were conditions. You violated them. Your license has been suspended, that is all."

Barret glared at his pastor. "I should not require a license to operate a press, sir, no more than you should require a license to shovel food into your hasty maw!"

Jack Frake turned to the minister and remarked, "Or to offer an unsolicited opinion."

Acland, offended, turned and left the shop.

Jack turned to Hugh. "This must be protested. I will ride to Williamsburg tomorrow and demand to see the Governor."

"My thought, too. We will go together."

Jack Frake and Hugh Kenrick approached Barret. "Sir," said Jack, "Hugh and I will ride to Williamsburg tomorrow and accost the Governor for an explanation of this outrage. Will you come with us?"

"Yes," replied the printer without hesitation, "if you trust me enough not to call him out for pistols at twenty feet!"

"We trust you. I'll lend you my sulky," said Hugh. Then he asked, "Where are the rest of the broadsides?"

"They took those, too!" roared Barret, but he paused to chuckle. "But, I have a bundle of them stashed under my bed next door. Not many, but some." He glanced at his two apprentices. "You there, son!" he said to Travis. "You be sure when I die, one of those is buried with me!"

Travis Barret nodded solemnly.

"And you, Cletus," said the printer to the black boy, "you be sure to remind him!"

"Yes, sir," answered the boy.

Jack looked around and saw Israel Beck in the back of the crowd. "Well, Mr. Beck here has some purchases to make. We'll talk later in the day, Mr. Barret."

Outside, Jack, Hugh, and Proudlocks rode down to the King's Arms and went inside. When they were seated at a table, Jack asked, "Who do you think told the Governor?"

"Mr. Cullis," answered Hugh immediately. "He was the only one of our party last May who doubted the wisdom of printing Mr. Henry's resolves. And he opposed the last resolves, and refused to vote again for any of the ones that had already passed." He paused. "And I believe he helped persuade some of the others to change their votes, as well."

"Do you think he has been bought?"

"No," answered Hugh. "I believe he is afraid."

"Frightened men can be bought with security against that which frightens them."

"True. We must call on Mr. Cullis."

An hour later, after making arrangements with Wendel Barret for the journey the next morning, Jack, Hugh, and Proudlocks rode to Cullis Hall, the easternmost plantation in the county. But Hetty Cullis informed them that her husband Ralph and son Edgar had gone hunting for wolves west of the Falls. "I understand that the House has raised the bounty on the beasts, sirs. From there, they may take the waters at Warm Springs. My husband has been complaining about a painful stiffness in his limbs. They will not return for some weeks."

Hugh thanked the woman and the trio left.

"Wolves!" scoffed Jack as they rode back to Caxton. "There are packs of them at large right here!"

"And they do not all emanate from the lair of the Palace and the Council chambers," remarked Hugh.

"You are referring to Robinson and the Randolphs, of course?"

"Of course. The circular letter would have been addressed to the Speaker. And the Governor would have had no reason to prorogue the Assembly except to prevent delegates from being chosen to attend the congress in New York. Much House business was to be carried over to the next session, but Robinson and Randolph and the Governor would gladly have postponed it." He paused. "I received letters recently from Mr. Henry and Mr. Washington. They plan to come to Williamsburg in October."

Jack said, "The Governor is determined to preserve the peace in Virginia."

Hugh shook his head. "It is the peace of a cemetery," he said. "But they shall all learn that many of its intended occupants are not willing to be interred in that peace."

John Proudlocks remarked, "The Governor? He is a man who wishes to be a governor."

*　*　*

Lieutenant-Governor Francis Fauquier was afraid, as well. When the trio called on the Palace late the next morning, he agreed to see Hugh Kenrick, but refused admittance to his office of Jack Frake and Wendel Barret. They waited in the visitor's parlor near the marble-floored foyer while Hugh was escorted across the courtyard to the Lieutenant-Governor's other office.

The interview was brief, cordial, and nearly acrid. Fauquier said, "I cannot help you in this matter, Mr. Kenrick. Mr. Barret overstepped his license, and I cannot condone the action."

"It was a right action, on two counts," replied Hugh. "As burgess for his county, and because he agreed with the resolves I supported, I had a right to communicate them to him, and he to his fellow...subjects. You must remember that the public space was occupied to the limit when the resolves were introduced, debated, and voted on. And the *Courier* is his livelihood, and he subsists on the revenue from subscriptions and advertisements, as well as from his other printing business. You have denied him both the right to speak and the right to practice his trade."

"Mr. Walthoe explained your position to me, and Mr. Barret's interpretation, as well, sir," replied the Governor. "He was of the opinion that these arguments are irrelevant. I must concur with him." He paused to rub his eyes with the palms of his hands. "Now, Reverend Robinson of the Council has already written to the Board of Trade and the Privy Council about the broadsides. Also, I understand from him that your own Reverend Acland has written the Board and the Bishop of London. You must appreciate that I must prove I have taken the appropriate and lawful actions, for otherwise I would be reprimanded and perhaps even removed from this office. My successor may not be as tolerant as I am, nor acquire any love for the colony and its people as I have." He shook his head, wondering why he said such a thing. "This is a very serious matter, sir."

"I agree, your honor," said Hugh. "It is a very serious matter."

"However," sighed Fauquier, "considering that public notice revenues comprise such a goodly portion of your friend's livelihood, I will contemplate lifting the suspension in a month's time, and return his property. He is fortunate that I did not endorse a permanent revocation of the license. Some on the Council and in the Assembly have pressed me to take that action."

"I have also violated the House rule, your honor, in the best spirit of Mr. John Wilkes in the Commons," said Hugh. "What punishment is in store for me?"

Fauquier cleared his throat, and looked away. "That is for the House to decide, when it reconvenes, and if it wishes to make it an issue." Before Hugh could raise the subject of Fauquier's proclamation proroguing the

Assembly until March of the following year, the governor waved a hand and said, "About Mr. Chiswell. Mr. Walthoe related to me that unfortunate incident." He picked up a string of white beads that lay on his desk. "See these? They are a present from the Little Carpenter, an envoy of the Cherokees who called on me here last month about what the Crown planned to do about the murders of his brothers in Augusta. A very interesting fellow, that Indian. Anyway, Mr. Chiswell is a colonel in the Augusta militia, and I requested that he give the Little Carpenter and his companions a safe escort back to his parts under the protection of this colony. Mr. Chiswell has only recently returned from that journey. Fatigue must account in part for his behavior in Caxton toward you. I must grant him some leniency in that respect."

"But the larger part of his behavior, your honor, is his enmity for me. That was his third attempt to harm me."

"So I have been informed," said the Governor. He sighed. "I speak now as the chief justice of the General Court, sir. All I can do in the way of justice in that particular matter is assure you that he will not collect his bailiff's fee. He was acting as a Crown officer, and, as much as I sympathize with you and condemn his action, he is indemnified against a private suit. It must be decided whether or not he acted in his capacity of bailiff, or from private vengeance. Should he behave again in that manner as a private citizen, then the full scope of the law will encompass him."

Hugh asked, "And suppose he had injured me, or even succeeded in murdering me, your honor? Would he still have been indemnified?"

"I think not, sir, but that would be for the full General Court to decide." Fauquier waved a hand again in front of his face, as though to clear some cobwebs that had gathered there. Then he rose to end the interview. "I am sorry I cannot be of more help to you and Mr. Barret, Mr. Kenrick. At the moment, I am striving to prevent a war between the settlers and the Six Nations along the frontiers of our own colony, and the frontiers of others as well, a war that could spread out of control. I have mountains of correspondence to read and answer on the subject. Also, there is the usual nasty business the Navy and customs men at Norfolk bring me to settle. Please forgive me for allotting so little time to your complaints."

Hugh Kenrick rose also. "Thank you, your honor," he said brusquely. "Just one question more, if it please you," he added. "When Mr. Cullis informed you of Mr. Barret's transgression, did he also alert you to the congress in New York in October?"

Fauquier frowned, but wanted to smile. What a simple trap the young man had set for him, one so easily avoided. "I would not say I was *informed*, sir, for that would asperse the patriotic character of the gentleman who came to me with the information. Nor will I confirm that it was Mr. Cullis."

Hugh grimaced. The disappointment must have shown in his features, for the Governor blinked once in surprise. "Your honor," said Hugh, "more and more, you are becoming a stranger to me."

When he rejoined his friends in the Palace foyer, he shook his head at them and motioned them to the grand double doors of the entrance, and they left.

* * *

Wendel Barret expressed his gratitude to his friends.

He continued to rail against the injustice, the Governor, the Council, and John Chiswell. Two afternoons after his return from Williamsburg, he addressed his apprentices, Travis and Cletus, as he paced furiously back and forth in front of them in the quiet shop, shaking his fists in the air, his eyes coals of fire. "I cannot say when his Officiousness will deign to unshackle my *words*, young sirs!" he said, his face and manner becoming as agitated as they were the day Walthoe and Chiswell had burst into his shop to seize the type cases. "And I cannot support either or both of you without the requisite revenue! Now, you know I have a sister in Fredericksburg, and she has a thriving millinery shop there, as nice as Widow Heathcoate's here! And her scoundrel of a husband is an ironmonger. Fashions anchors and tackle and parts for the Navy and merchants. You shall both stay with them until my press has been permitted to speak again! I have already sent my sister a request to come and collect you."

"But, what is to become of *you*, Grandpa?" asked Travis Barret with genuine concern.

Barret paused to smile at his grandson. Then an odd look abruptly changed his features. He opened his mouth to speak, but a strange sound came from it. Then he looked surprised, and clutched the cloth over his heart. He slowly collapsed, and his other hand shot out to grasp a column of the press. Travis and Cletus rushed to him. The printer slumped against the side of the press, and made awful gagging sounds that frightened the boys. They had never before witnessed such an affliction. Travis sent Cletus to fetch the apothecary down the street.

But before that man arrived, Wendel Barret, publisher of the *Caxton Courier*, and first printer of the Stamp Act Resolves, died of a stroke.

* * *

Chapter 5: The Gazette

He was buried two days later in the Stepney Parish Church grave-yard. The funeral service was attended by half the population of Caxton. At the request of Travis Barret, copies of the *Courier* and a copy of his Stamp Act Resolves broadside were sealed in an oilskin pouch and placed on his chest in the coffin. Jack Frake and Hugh Kenrick shared the costs of the coffin, headstone, and the funeral.

Reverend Albert Acland performed the service, and delivered a sermon on the transient nature of life, managing to slip into his pious oratory a few critical asides on the wages of sin, alluding to the late printer's often delin-quent attendance of services in the church and especially to his role in broadcasting the Resolves. He felt duty-bound to mention these offenses, but did not dwell on them, for he knew that there were more friends of Mr. Barret in the congregation than there were adherents to the litany of pre-ferred religious and public virtues.

Hugh Kenrick sat with Etáin, Thomas Reisdale, and Sheriff Cabal Tippet and his wife in a front pew. Etáin was surprised that Hugh deigned to enter the place. It was the first time she had seen him in it. She knew that he disliked both the minister and the institution as much as did her husband, Jack. Hugh confided to her that he was present out of curiosity, not because he expected to be comforted or solaced by anything Acland might say.

Jack Frake refused to enter the church; he sat on a bench outside and waited. When the service was over, John Proudlocks came out to fetch him, for he had volunteered to act as pallbearer with Hugh, Proudlocks, and William Hurry, Jack's overlooker and steward. It was a short walk around the side of the church, down Queen Anne Street to an unnamed road, and into the graveyard that was enclosed on all sides by a fieldstone wall. At the gravesite, Acland performed the usual ritual, then looked around and said to the throng gathered around the grave and the coffin in it, "I have said enough in praise and commendation of Mr. Barret. Has anyone here kind words for him that he wishes to speak on behalf of the deceased's bereaved friends?'

Jack Frake looked up and around at the throng. "Ladies and gentlemen," he said, "we have just bid farewell to a portion of our liberty, as well as to a patriot who championed it."

A gasp shot through the crowd. Curiously, though, no one objected to the words. Almost everyone present had felt, if not thought, the same thing.

"Amen," added Hugh Kenrick.

Several of the men in the crowd exchanged glances, then answered almost in unison, "Amen."

Reverend Acland frowned, then sniffed in dismissal of the demonstration. He closed his prayer book and walked away, signaling the end of the funeral.

As the parishioners followed him and dispersed from the graveyard, Reece Vishonn left his wife's side and caught up with Jack Frake to remark, "I did not know he had a condition, Mr. Frake. He seemed always moved by an impish vigor."

"It was not happiness that killed him," replied Jack. "It was an oppressive grief, caused by a mortal blow to his life and livelihood, delivered by the Governor."

Vishonn scoffed. "Oh, come now, sir! That is over-sentimentality. Our dear Governor cannot be blamed for Mr. Barret's demise!"

"Yes, he can, sir," answered Jack with finality.

Arthur Stannard, the resident tobacco agent, had been trailing the group of men leaving the graveyard. He interjected with some heat, "Mr. Vishonn is correct, sirs!" he said to the group. "The Governor is a fellow of the most excellent character! He cannot be held accountable for every consequence of performing his duty!"

"Yes," chimed in Henry Otway, a planter and neighbor of Hugh Kenrick, "this is true! If any blame is to be assigned, it must be to Mr. Barret himself, whom the Governor held accountable for a flagrant abuse of his Crown-sanctioned privilege!"

Jack stopped in his tracks and faced the trailing group. "Then the duty ought to be abolished, so that men of such excellent character may remain blameless and powerless to dispense or withhold such a privilege, and so author no further consequences." He turned and walked on.

"Pish!" muttered Stannard, who said no more.

Hugh Kenrick grinned in contemptuous irony. "*That* sentiment, sir, is one I imagine is regularly expressed in the Commons, though in so many more words."

Stannard merely snorted in reply, but noted that Vishonn, Otway, and a few other men who had nodded in agreement with him, chuckled silently.

The funeral party broke up on a note of muted acrimony.

Later that day, after consulting with Thomas Reisdale about the status of Wendel Barret's property — "He left his will with me," said the attorney, "and his house and most of his effects are assigned to his sister, who is expected here shortly, but who will need to auction much of that property to pay some of his debts" — Jack and Hugh agreed to go into partnership and purchase the idle press, the two bills of Caslon type, which weighed nearly a thousand pounds and had been confiscated by the Governor, the stock of paper, and all the tools associated with the printing trade. Reisdale cautioned them to wait until Barret's sister or brother-in-law had decided on what course of action to take. That evening, at Morland Hall, Jack and Hugh put their signatures under a letter of inquiry to Lieutenant-Governor Fauquier about Barret's printing license.

A week later, Hugh's valet, Spears, returned to Meum Hall from his errands in town, bearing a letter that carried the Governor's seal, which had been left at Safford's King's Arms Tavern, which now replaced the *Courier*'s shop as the informal mail drop or post office for Caxton and the county.

Although the letter was addressed solely to Hugh and not to Jack, it mentioned both of them. "I have been instructed to inform you gentlemen," wrote the Governor's secretary in an elegant hand, "that the license to own and operate a press in this colony to which you refer, owned by the late Mr. Wendel Barret, regrettably expired with him, and may not be renewed or purchased. Furthermore, it is the opinion and conclusion of his honor the Lieutenant-Governor, without casting aspersions or doubt on the wisdom of his predecessor, that a renewal of such a license would contribute to a redundancy of purpose and intelligence in these parts."

"*A redundancy*??" barked Hugh in anger when he read that sentence. He immediately rode to Morland Hall and showed the letter to Jack. When the latter had put it down, Hugh commented, "Well, now we know it would be futile of me to introduce a bill to permit the continuance of the *Courier*. It would likely be rejected by the Committee on Propositions."

Jack added, "And that would save the Council and the Governor the excuse of vetoing it, even were it to survive your committee and a House vote."

"Even were there a House to vote on it," remarked Hugh. "I fear that the Governor has not finished proroguing the Assembly, even though it often behaves like a Roman lictor, clearing the way for his honor's pleasure and peace of mind."

"Why do you think so?" asked Jack. He reached for a pipe and began packing it with tobacco.

Hugh shrugged. "Because I do not believe he knows otherwise how to address the crisis, than to prohibit other men from addressing it, or at least to make it inconvenient — perhaps even unlawful — for them to assemble to discuss it."

Jack chuckled. "He is afraid the patriots will move long before the politicians, and out-distance them through the gauntlet of revolution, to liberty." He paused to study his friend's incredulous expression. "It *is* a gauntlet we will face, my friend," he added, "and the cruelest part of it will be manned, not by our obvious enemies, but by our friends."

Hugh had stopped pacing and stood facing his friend at the desk. "Have you ever thought of standing for burgess again?"

Jack lit his pipe with a match. "Once, years ago, and was not elected. That was soon after I came into possession of Morland." He shook his head. "I don't mind being elected an officer of the county militia, but burgess? No, thank you." He chuckled again. "I saw what you endured in the last Assembly. Perhaps I'm not as strong as you are in that regard. I can argue a matter up to a certain point, but no further. I haven't the patience. No, I've always preferred to stay far ahead of the politician."

Hugh sat down in a chair across from Jack. "That's a pity, Jack. You see, I don't believe that Mr. Cullis will be reelected, come the next call for an Assembly, whenever that may be. Rightly or wrongly, most everyone in town 'does not believe that the closing of the *Courier* and Mr. Cullis's absence are coincidence. Mr. Reisdale, for instance, suspected that he contributed to the reduction of Mr. Henry's Resolves in May, and reached that conclusion without my assistance. I merely confirmed it for him." He wagged a finger of confidence at Jack. "*You*, however, would not need to expend money wooing votes. *You* would not need to swill the farmers and planters here with bumpo or solicit inebriated loyalty or mount the gasconade."

Jack shook his head again. "Neither would Mr. Reisdale," he answered. "There's your partner in the Assembly, Hugh. He's a respected man. I would go so far as to endorse him. But I will not offer myself as a candidate, should you be right about Mr. Cullis's prospects for reelection."

Hugh sighed. "I will speak with him about it." He grinned. "You know, it has taken me some time to accustom myself to our society's new name. 'The Sons of Liberty.'" A week ago, he and Jack had persuaded the Attic Society's membership to change its name. The change was agreed upon by a margin of one vote.

Jack grinned in answer. "It is partly your own fault, Hugh. You introduced our toast, 'Long live Lady Liberty.' But you may share the blame with Colonel Barré."

* * *

Thomas Reisdale's plantation, simply named "Freehold," lay across the Hove Stream from Meum and Morland Halls, surrounded on three sides of its irregular rectangle by a dozen smaller freeholds. The attorney-planter's great house was a mongrel composite of additions and alterations built over the course of more than a century. Most of its fertile fields were once swamp land, patiently but ruthlessly drained and reclaimed by Reisdale's father and grandfather. Freehold owed its steady prosperity to its rich soil and the efforts of a capable overlooker and business agent retained by Reisdale after he inherited the place. The scholarly attorney kept a critical eye on the management of the plantation, and made some suggestions to his managers on minor matters, but otherwise did not interfere in the running of the place. This policy allowed him to pursue a law practice, sit on the county court as its chief and oldest justice during county court days — which were usually held every three months but especially a week before the General Court convened in Williamsburg and before the opening of a General Assembly — and ensconce himself in his well-stocked, disorderly library and bury himself in his books in search of clarity, justice, and truth.

He was a shy man in social occasions. He had never married, and never bothered to apply his energies to the daunting and ticklish project of finding himself a wife. He addressed a statute with more confidence than he could a widow or any available lady. As a youth, he had studied law at Gray's Inn in London, and had permitted himself some dalliances then, but now, at the age of fifty-one, those days and that particular confidence were fading memories. He was more likely to recall an obscure lecture from those years than he was the name or face of any woman he might have squired in that metropolis's pleasure gardens. Occasionally he felt a loneliness, and in a dry,

wistful manner contemplated the advantages of a companion. But this
malady's corrective was a distracted search for a certain turn of phrase or
point of legal reasoning in an ancient tome.

It was raining the day Hugh Kenrick called on him. He welcomed the
interruption and the respite from his present labors. He was struggling to
compose an address for the next meeting of the Sons of Liberty in two
weeks, an address he planned to develop into an "inquiry" as a pamphlet
he hoped he could find a printer for. He was attempting to establish a solid
argument that the Stamp Act was legally and morally unconstitutional, and
that colonial courts could, without risk of censure, and in conformity with
colonial charters, sit within the bounds of the Constitution without
employing or requiring stamps in any action or document presented to
those courts for adjudication, and retain the legal force of those actions and
documents.

At the moment, his address was a confused, unruly *mélange* of ideas
and theories. Since the stamps were in fact and in effect a new duty or tax,
and an internal one at that, he felt comfortable in resorting to the Parliamentary Petition of Right from Charles the First's time, for although Parliament had authored the act, the act remained a nullity until endorsed by
the king as executive. One of the points of the Petition of Right was that the
king could impose no loans or taxes without Parliamentary leave or consent.

George the Third had indeed endorsed the Stamp Act, authored by Parliament in violation of most colonial charters that stipulated that no taxes,
imposts, or levies could be introduced in the internal affairs of the colonies.
George the Third was ostensibly the guardian of those charters, but instead
of exercising his veto on a patently unconstitutional law, had endorsed the
Act, and in so doing abdicated his constitutional role as a check against Parliamentary caprice and avarice. Reisdale did not accuse His Majesty of
indifference, neglect, or wickedness — God forbid — but insinuated in his
argument that His Majesty was the victim of evil counsel. The king had
joined in unfortunate accord with Parliament, and consequently made a
mockery of his oft-expressed desire to be a "patriot king" and his concern
for *summum bonum,* or the supreme good, which was the preservation of
the liberty and happiness of his subjects, wherever they might reside.

This end, stressed Reisdale on paper, was demonstrably not served by
the Stamp Act.

Following that notion, he wished to dwell on the corruption and con-

fiscation of wealth caused by the customs and regulatory machinery, and in
great detail to illustrate the destruction caused by ancient Roman sump-
tuary laws, which taxed or punished luxuries. Then he would argue that
the Stamp Act would render colonial courts a luxury and in time put them
beyond the means of most of His Majesty's subjects in North America, as
well as so many articles of British manufacture upon which the colonials
had become dependent as necessities. The Act would thus reduce most
industrious and thrifty colonials to a state of rightless, voiceless, and hopeless beggary, and foster an altogether different breed of lawlessness and dis-
honesty.

Next, he planned to rail in decent terms against the provisions in the
Act that empowered vice-admiralty courts exclusively to try offenses concerning stamps. The number and convenience of those courts, he asserted,
was not irrelevant; their "generous" multiplication from one to four simply
multiplied the opportunities to try Englishmen without benefit of jury or
justice.

Next, he wished to weave into his argument the reasoning of John
Locke, Hugo Grotius, and other proponents of natural rights and natural
law, and delve into the moral legitimacy of protesting and even flouting
Crown authority concerning the noxious Stamp Act.

He wished to conclude his address with the assertion that the Act represented a declaration of pecuniary war against the colonies, and that it
was no less a precedent than when Roman Emperor Sulla, for the first time
in that republic's history, lead an army of Romans against fellow Romans.
The Stamp Act contained in its presumption of power all the violence of a
siege and the wastage of a perpetual tribute paid to a besieging army. He
would assert that destruction of liberty and property under the Act was as
certain and guaranteed as if Parliament had chosen to employ engines of
war to collect revenue by means of fire and sword instead of by the
innocuous stamps, the minor difference being the subtlety versus the
immediacy of that destruction.

But what confounded Reisdale was his desire to couch his argument in
"modest" language, certainly more modest language than that of the
Resolves of last May. Like many men in that critical time, he was emboldened by the Resolves, yet frightened or intimidated by them, as well. What
perplexed him was that no matter how gently he composed and arranged
his arguments, there was in them an element of violence and implacable,
offensive certitude that he could neither tame nor eradicate.

When his servant announced the arrival of Hugh Kenrick, Reisdale reluctantly, but with a sigh of relief, put his pen and draft aside and made his guest welcome in the library, and ordered that a pitcher of lemon punch be brought in. After an exchange of pleasantries and comments on the much-needed rain that fell in rivulets down his library windowpanes, he asked Hugh the purpose of his visit.

Hugh queried him on the idea of standing for burgess in opposition to Edgar Cullis.

Reisdale rose and paced back and forth before his guest for a moment, then retired to his commodious armchair. He shook his head and said that he declined even to weigh the possibility of a more public role in the county's affairs. "I should need to surrender my place as chief magistrate here, Mr. Kenrick," he said, "and that I am not prepared to do." He shook his head again. "You must, of course, know that you are not the first to solicit my candidacy. It has been necessary for me to request my past erstwhile sponsors to withdraw my name, and on numerous occasions."

"Why are you so unwilling?" asked Hugh.

Reisdale cocked his head. "For many reasons, sir. First, six men, including myself, sit on this county's court. Now, the other five, although otherwise upstanding and well-meaning men, are not persons of sound legal knowledge or fairness of judgment. I have guided them in the administration of justice for close to twenty years. Please excuse my vanity, but I fear that if I resigned that task to represent the county in the Assembly, for I must quit one bench to claim another, no one could replace me, and our court here would undoubtedly fall into miserable confusion."

Hugh sighed in concession of this truth. Reece Vishonn was one of those justices and the next senior, but he, too, required Reisdale's direction and knowledge. The other justices were smaller freeholders who had studied law but had never practiced it or made it a profession, except in Caxton's diminutive courthouse. He grimaced in irony and related his conversation with Jack Frake from the day before, and wondered out loud who in Queen Anne County could oppose Cullis in the next election. He remarked, "I do not relish the prospect of sharing a seat with him."

Reisdale did not immediately reply to his guest's plaintive musing. "Besides," he said at length, "I am too well associated now with you and Mr. Frake and the Sons." He paused. "Now, sir, you must have observed," he continued in a more serious tone, "that this county is more patriotic than it might appear. My election, should I relent and stand for burgess,

would in no sense be guaranteed, no matter how disliked or mistrusted Mr.
Cullis might be — and I agree with you that he is one or the other among
the freemen here. For the nonce, my good man, you and he, so far as the
county's electorate are concerned, comprise a safe, perfect, representational
balance in the Assembly. I am certain they would want to continue that balance. Lacking another candidate of Mr. Cullis's character, they would, I am
afraid, merely reelect him."

Hugh's eyebrows went up. "I did not know that my own character was
so feared."

Reisdale frowned. "Not at all, sir. You and Mr. Cullis act as curatives
on each other, in the electoral eye. Mr. Cullis is more congenial and accom-
modating, while you are a...model of principle." The attorney stopped
speaking then, because he suddenly realized that his guest was a key to the
best way to compose his address and inquiry, and also an obstacle to it.
There was something ingenuous about the young man that was also fundamentally right. His whole character and person exuded that odd quality.
This posed a paradox to Reisdale, for his guest's person and character were
both attractive and repellent, at the same time.

HIs other neighbor, Jack Frake, presented the same paradox, but in
more severe terms. He thought of the frank gray eyes, and the scar on that
man's forehead, and then remembered that this man, too, was his friend.

The subject of Reisdale's candidacy being exhausted, Hugh and his host
chatted for a while about their properties. Hugh spoke about the progress his
tenants were making in topping his tobacco. "My wheat, corn, and oats are
about ready for harvesting. I am almost glad that the Governor has prorogued the Assembly this fall. My crops will exceed last year's gross."

When his guest departed, Thomas Reisdale turned back to his labors,
but soon gave up the effort. Hugh Kenrick had gone, but somehow an aura
of him remained in the room. Reisdale glanced over the words in his draft,
and judged his prose to be not only inadequate, but abhorrent, given its purpose. It read like the bluff words of a coward. The absolutes he wished to
communicate did not wear well the garb of abnegation. This thought
caused the attorney to blush in anger, anger with himself and with the
conundrum. Abruptly, he felt the throbbing of a tremendous headache. He
rose and retired to his bedchamber to take a nap.

When he had made himself comfortable, he listened to the rain. It
helped him slip into a sound sleep, and the sudden headache receded. But
even then, he was troubled by an exchange that he and Hugh Kenrick had

had weeks ago. It kept repeating itself in his mind, and would not go away.

"You are our resident legal scholar, sir, and we shall rely on your mental archives in our quest for greater liberty."

"But, sir!" he had protested with humor, "do not mistake me for a Schoolman, I beg of you!"

"Oh, no! Never that!" Hugh Kenrick had replied with a laugh. "Thank God you are not one of *those*, wherever He may be!"

It had been the jocular end of another conversation, but it seemed to Reisdale to contain the careless regard for propriety that colored so many of his remarks. A careless, and dangerous, regard.

* * *

It was a half-hour's ride from Freehold to Meum Hall. In the same rain, Hugh Kenrick rode down the tree-lined boulevard in between long worm fences that bordered Reisdale's spacious crop fields to the Hove Stream, then across the log bridge into his own plantation and well-tended fields.

The rain had become heavier and he noted that his tenants had retreated to their homes on the far eastern part of the fields. He rode parallel to the bamboo conduit he had designed and built years ago; in the downpour it looked superfluous. He smiled in thought: not so superfluous. The water it had carried from the Hove Stream to his crops recently when there was no rain had allowed him to prosper while other planters struggled to salvage their thirsty crops. Reece Vishonn at Enderly had tried to copy the idea, using iron pipes fashioned from his mine in the Piedmont, but it was a patchy network that could not properly water the uneven areas of Enderly's fields. Jack Frake had built a trench that served the same purpose as the conduit, and no longer had to rely on his oxen-pulled "water wagons" to nourish his fields during dry spells.

Arriving at his own great house, Hugh handed his mount to the stable boy, asked his cook, Fiona Chance, to fix him a light dinner, then changed into some dry clothes. The desk in his own study was cluttered with books, newspapers, and letters.

One letter was from Dogmael Jones, dated mid-July, in which his friend in the Commons reported the king's dismissal of George Grenville. "This came not as a surprise to the gentleman," wrote Jones, "but the expected flick of His Majesty's handkerchief cannot have been a less bitter snub. He had such great ambitions, and they proved to be in mortal conflict with St.

James's Palace. As if to augur the fate of the late minister's government, Mr. Williams, who has continued Mr. Wilkes's *North Briton* in a like style, was this last February, before the Stamp Act debates, put on a pillory in the Palace Yard for the offense of perpetuating the miscreant publication. A mob soon constructed a gallows opposite him in support of the fellow, and suspended from its bar a boot stuffed and decorated with straw. Some two hundred pounds were also collected by the mob to defray Mr. Williams's legal expenses, to which I contributed a small sum. It was certainly a distinct species of creature, that mob, from the one that greeted you and the Pippins at Charing Cross so many years ago...."

A letter from his father reported that "the work on the Blackfriars Bridge has recommenced, the fourth arch to the north side of the center nearly completed.... Those old hazards, the overhanging shop signs, are fast disappearing in London, as a result of the law passed some years ago. Oddly, I shall miss them.... Mr. Jones reports that there is some talk among persons connected to the Board of Trade that your royal governors may be relieved of their colonial appropriated salaries by naming them to His Majesty's annual civil list, thus making them independent of your various legislatures' approval or censure. Methinks the proposal, if the rumor can be credited, augurs ill for any future ministry, for it would be breaking windows with guineas in a tantrum of spite. It will be interesting to observe how Mr. Grenville's successor will address the matter.... The *Evening Signal* carried an item about Mr. Wilkes, whose lodgings in Naples were broken into and papers of his stolen. He reportedly has accused his enemies here of conspiring in the theft.... The *Post* carried an item from *L'Orient*, by way of our Indiaman *Ajax*, concerning a French Indiaman *Duc de Praslin*, which sailed from here last year for Bengal, employing a machine on board for making sea-water fresh and potable, according to a method conceived by a Mr. Poissannier. The Indiaman was at sea some five months, and the machine produced sixty barrels of sweet water for two months."

His father's letter had accompanied a crate of books and some housewares and clothing. Among the books were Charles Perrault's *Parallels of the Ancients and the Moderns* and Voltaire's *Letters Concerning the English Nation*. Weeks ago he had written Otis Talbot and Novus Easley in Philadelphia about the closing of the *Courier* and the suspension of the *Gazette*. They had responded by sending him back issues of the Pennsylvania and Maryland *Gazettes*.

He was amused with his divided attention: Otis Talbot in a letter

described some of the turmoil over the Stamp Act in Rhode Island and Massachusetts Bay — colonial gunners at Fort George in Newport Harbor had
even fired on a naval schooner over the impressment of some Rhode
Islanders and the theft by British sailors of pigs and chickens — and a
mental itch to know how the French Indiaman could purify water without
burning prodigious amounts of wood or coal. There were many persons who
lived close to the Bay here, he thought, whose livelihoods centered on puri-
fying and selling sweet water to farms, naval vessels, and merchantmen.

Rachel, the black servant who worked with Miss Chance in the
kitchen, appeared and set before him on the desk the serving tray with his
dinner. Hugh ate idly, brimming with quiet pride as he studied a copy of the
Maryland Gazette, dated July 4, that he had fixed to the wall opposite him,
beneath the long series of sketches he had done of his friends the Pippins.
It contained all seven of Patrick Henry's Resolves from last May, sent to the
paper, noted the editor in a brief preface, "by an anonymous gentleman."

Hugh could only grin and chuckle to himself. He thought, *I had a hand in
that, it went out into the world, and now the world is about to be set afire again.*

*   *   *

As Hugh Kenrick had only an inkling of the growing ferocity of that fire,
Jack Frake and his wife, Etáin, could only suspect the turmoil that was
occurring in the northern colonies. They sat together over their own
dinner that afternoon, in the supper room of Morland Hall, reading colonial newspapers of last month that had arrived yesterday by post-rider and
merchantman. They did not yet know that in Boston, the appointed stamp
distributor's house had been sacked, and that only a few days ago, the
house of the lieutenant-governor and chief justice of Massachusetts had
been similarly sacked and all but destroyed, including the official's fine
library, by mobs that threatened retribution for anyone who sympathized
with, submitted to, or attempted to enforce the Stamp Act. They had not
yet received a copy of the *Pennsylvania Gazette*, in which were printed the
names of all the appointed stamp distributors in all twenty-three British
colonies in North America and the Caribbean, although they and everyone
else in Virginia by now knew the name of the appointed distributor for the
colony: George Mercer, the son of an old, respected Virginia family.

One of the newspapers reported what Hugh Kenrick's father had
written to his son about, that a French Indiaman had successfully tested a

sweet-water machine. Etáin noted it and read the item for her husband, knowing his near-obsession with the best way to water his crops.

Jack Frake thought alike enough with his friend and neighbor that he, too, was intrigued by the question of how sixty barrels of sweet water could be produced without burning enough wood to fill one of the enormous Indiaman's profitable holds. His only reply to his wife was accompanied by a pensive frown: "It can't have been better than brackish," he said, then added, almost dreamily, "the brackish language of remonstrances and memorials." He smiled at Etáin cross the table. "But, the language of the Resolves — *that* is the language of men."

Etáin was neither confused by her husband's state of mind, nor of a mind to reproach him for it. She knew what was demanding his attention of late, and had demanded it ever since last May: how to prevent the introduction of stamps in Queen Anne County.

Jack had set aside the newspapers, and another periodical sat before him, Number Forty-five of *The North Briton*, which he had recently borrowed from Hugh. He had read and heard so much lately about the Constitution and the rights of Englishmen, that he was curious to know what difference existed, if any, between what caused the reported clamors in England and the closer disturbances in the colonies. He was certain that a difference existed and could be identified, and his intellectual appetite would not be satisfied until he knew it.

Reading the text of John Wilkes's alleged insult to the king was what had moved him to make his "brackish" comment to Etáin. It was that very criticism that had angered the king, led to Wilkes's expulsion from Parliament, and moved the courts to declare him an outlaw. "A well-read and literate rogue," was how Hugh had characterized the renegade.

Jack read the article with a qualified admiration. It was reminiscent of the style of expression of his dear friend Redmagne from his Cornwall smuggling days, when that late hero set his sights on politics and wrote with a fiery, biting pen. But something was lacking in the piece, an animate spirit of some kind; and at the same time, something was there that nullified the power of the criticism.

He had narrowed it down to a solitary thing, and that thing explained the absence. It resided in Wilkes's closing remark: "I hope the fine words of Dryden will be engraven in our hearts, *Freedom is the English subject's prerogative.*"

The culprit was the term *subject*.

Jack's only answer to that term was: *I am no one's 'subject.' I am a free man.* More than that, he could not now say. But he felt that he was closer now to finding the words that Augustus Skelly had said long ago he would find.

His eyes narrowed, and then he read the sentence to Etáin, and asked her, "There is something wrong about that notion. What do you think it is?"

Etáin sipped some tea while she considered an answer. Her eyes never left Jack. Then she put down her cup, and smiled. "Freedom and subjection are not possible in the same nation, at the same time." She paused to study her husband for a moment. Her eyes were lit up with a new discovery. "It is curious," she said, "but until now, I never thought of you as an English *subject.*"

Jack grinned. "Do you now?"

Etáin shook her head and said quietly, "No. The notion is preposterous." After a moment, she added, "Nearly offensive."

Jack looked as if a question had been answered. He smiled at his wife, reached over to take one of her hands, and raised it to his lips in thanks.

There was a commotion outside the supper room. The doors opened and William Hurry came in. He was returning from a trip to Williamsburg to purchase supplies. The man removed his hat and shook the raindrops from it, then held out something to his employer.

Jack had never seen the man so agitated. He took the thing from Hurry's hand. It was a copy of the *Virginia Gazette*. He frowned and glanced up at Hurry.

"On the first page, sir!" said the steward. "Another proclamation! He changed his mind!"

Jack opened the damp, folded paper and read the boxed block of print on the first page, in the first column:

"A concern for the happiness of this colony, together with considered apprehensions about recent events, had caused this office to take the extraordinary measure of suspending publication of this Gazette. Said suspension, which has distressed and inconvenienced the people, has now been rescinded, beginning with this number of the Gazette, as this office has judged that the tranquility of His Majesty's colony has been preserved. Given under my hand, and the seal of the colony, Francis Fauquier."

* * *

Chapter 6: The Taverns

In June 1765, a month before a bitter George Grenville would surrender the seals of the First Lord of the Treasury and go into opposition as merely a member for Buckingham Borough, the man responsible for his imminent departure wrote to his uncle, the Duke of Cumberland: "They are men who have principles and therefore cannot see the Crown being dictated to by low men."

George the Third very likely was referring to Grenville as one of those "low men." That commoner had attempted to usurp His Majesty's privilege of choosing who should serve as regent in the event His Majesty was incapacitated and unable to perform his royal duties. That commoner had also demonstrated an unforgivable and annoying lack of gratitude, manners, and deference by complaining repeatedly that his own favorites and friends were passed over for places and sinecures, which were instead awarded to His Majesty's favorites and friends. That commoner was subsequently made to feel unwelcome, and soon would be gone.

George the Third was now warming to his uncle's suggestion that Charles Watson-Wentworth, the second Marquis of Rockingham, would with his allies perhaps form a ministry more amenable to the Court. To so high-minded a Court as George the Third wished to create, manipulate, and reward during his reign, a friendly, unobstructive, and grateful ministry, agreeable to the means and ends of a patriot king, implied a wealth of principles and virtues among its office-holders.

George Grenville and his fellow architects of the Stamp Act, however, had unwittingly set the stage for "low men" of another caliber not only to dictate to the Crown, but to compel it to repeal that Act, or else lose their trade, revenue, friendship, and possibly even sovereignty over them. It was not coincidence that all but one of the newly appointed stamp distributors were American colonials.

This was thought a cunning stroke of practical statecraft by Grenville and his party, for the premise was that while the colonials might detest the stamps that were to be affixed to virtually every printed document required in trade, law, and even amusement and edification, the pain of paying for those stamps would be somewhat ameliorated if the payment were made to fellow colonials. After all, the majority of resident customs men and their superiors in the colonies were Americans; stamp distributors and their assistants could become, in time and from necessity, just as much a fixture in the courts, customs houses, and seaports. And, anyway, the architects presumed, that money was never to cross the Atlantic to fill royal or Treasury coffers, but would remain in the colonies to defray the costs of their military and civil administration.

Few in London that summer had yet fully grasped that the colonials' repugnance for the extortionate stamps was a measurable expression of the odium they felt as well for being militarily and civilly administered by a callously ignorant power three thousand miles across an ocean.

Two of those few sat at a table in the Ram's Head Tavern on the Strand in London. It was early September. Before them were tankards of port and a plate of sweetmeats. One of them was saying, "You must have observed, on our tour, milord, the difference between English and French clocks. An analogy may be credibly drawn here on our styles of timepieces and our styles of polity. The French are enamored of a fantastic mechanism of government, while the English mechanism boasts the supreme virtue of utility. The French deem utility of lesser importance than appearance; the English judge appearance subordinate to utility."

"You have endured the depredations of the Commons, sir, and suffered a multitude of defeats in your natural realm of the courtroom, yet you speak more and more like a child." The speaker paused. "Please, sir, accept that as a compliment."

"I do, milord, and thank you. I have read somewhere — in Thomas Traherne's work, I believe — that a child is the best idealist, or visionary. Well, if I am to emerge from this career hale and hearty, then I must adopt the mien of informed innocence, and the hide of a rhinoceros."

Baron Garnet Kenrick laughed. Sir Dogmael Jones busied himself with lighting a pipe. The Baron took a sip from his tankard, then remarked, "But it seems we are adopting the vices of the French now, Mr. Jones. This scheme of the American Stamp Office is quite fantastic, gilded with a hundred heads and hands. It will oversee nine colonial stamp districts, headed by nine inspectors, who will in turn oversee twenty-three stamp distributors. Supporting them all must be a vast army of supernumeraries, including secretaries and clerks and warehousemen and such. And their recompense in fixed salaries and percentages of collected revenues and the pittance paid to watchmen and packers and printers and the like.... Why, did not Mr. Grenville imagine the great pump works necessary to implement his plan? Was this subject never debated or discussed in the Commons?"

Jones shook his head. "Details, milord! Mere details! He left the working out of that malevolent mathematics to Mr. Whateley. Mr. Grenville had grander matters on his mind. Why would you expect him to bother himself with the utility or justice of a thing? 'Tis beneath him!" Jones exhaled a burst of smoke with a scoffing sound. "Pshaw! By the time all the human sieves, pipes, channels, and gutters have been paid in that great pump works, milord, a soldier in the colonies will be fortunate to see a shilling of his promised wage with any regularity. Complaints will subsequently be made, and unrest detected, and a new act proposed to amend that oversight. A new act for the laying of new taxes."

The Baron had come up to London from Danvers on business, and at Jones's suggestion had accompanied the member for Swansditch on a week's tour of the commercial districts of the metropolis. Jones's purpose was to poll the owners of various enterprises on their willingness to sign a petition to the Commons concerning real or projected harm to those enterprises as a consequence of a reduction of trade caused by the Stamp Act. A partial non-importation movement in the colonies over the Sugar Act was already contributing to that reduction. Worry was also expressed about rumors of a greater non-importation movement if and when the Stamp Act was enforced. They had canvassed the printmakers and booksellers of Pall Mall, the wine merchants of Wapping, the carpenters, carriage makers, and furniture factors of Swallow Lane and Southwark, the shoemakers, hat factors and glovers on Maiden Lane, and the clockmakers and watchmakers on Fleet Street.

The fear of damage to trade in exports and raw material imports had already been voiced by Benjamin Worley, the Kenricks' business agent at Lion Key in the Pool of London. Jones had persuaded his patron that it would be worthwhile to determine whether other merchants shared this fear. They had encountered a mixture of positions: agreement that trade would be affected, indifference, resignation, and, in some instances, hostility towards the colonies for opposing a tax that was already paid in Britain. It had been an arduous, disappointing venture, their tour; only a handful of merchants were willing to sign a petition of remonstrance to the Commons, or to appear as witnesses to testify in possible hearings that the Commons was sure to schedule in its business if resistance to the Stamp

Act could not be purchased with moderation.

They had just returned from a day's rounds to a number of clock-makers and watchmakers on Fleet Street, where many of the artisans were either French Huguenots or German religious refugees who did not under-stand British politics, or did not wish to arouse enmity against themselves by protesting a law they did not completely comprehend.

On their way up the Strand in a hackney, Jones had espied the Ram's Head, and mentioned to his patron that it was once the Fruit Wench, where his patron's son had regularly met with the persecuted Society of the Pippin. "I do not imagine the new proprietor has much changed the place, milord," he said. "Mrs. Petty confided in me that she sold it all to a fellow who was returned from India with a chest of gold and silver. Shall we stop in before returning to Windridge Court?"

The Baron expressed an eagerness to see the place where his son Hugh had cut so many of his intellectual teeth. Jones had long ago told him the true story of why Sir James Parrot, King's Counsel during the Pippin trial, had been unwilling to submit to the court descriptions of the three missing Pippins he claimed to have, and which Mabel Petty, the proprietress of the Fruit Wench, claimed to Jones before the trial she had given the prosecutor. Some time after the sale of her establishment and her removal to Bristol, she wrote Jones and informed him that while she could do nothing for the five Pippins already in custody, she refused to give descriptions to Parrot of the other three. She managed to back her refusal with the threat of informing Parrot's wife that she had observed her husband, whose identity she did not know until she was subpoenaed to give evidence, often frequent the Fruit Wench in the company of a succession of ladies of various ages and stations, and on almost every occasion reserve a private room on the third floor of the establishment. Her daughter, Agnes, and her ward, Tim Doody, could also attest to this business.

Her threatened blackmail, unfortunately, while it allowed her to defy the Crown and protect some of her favorite clients, did not protect her from zealous municipal authorities, who revoked her publican's license and imposed a fine. Parrot, she wrote, had secretly paid that fine in a gesture of mutual good riddance, but could not save her license without enmeshing himself in further costly bribery and risky subterfuge, which he refused to do. Widow Petty acquiesced to this, feeling at the time fortunate not to have been summarily sentenced to Bridewell or the Clink.

Through Jones, the Baron had anonymously bestowed on Mabel Petty a purchased annuity as a reward for her loyalty.

Jones had just finished commenting on the likely fate of the Stamp Act when a group of men came through the smoky haze of the front parlor and sat at a table across the room. "What propinquity!" the barrister exclaimed.

Garnet Kenrick glanced inquiringly at his friend.

Jones nodded to the group. "Of course, you are acquainted with Sir Henoch, and know Mr. Whateley by sight. The other gentlemen, sitting opposite Mr. Whateley, is Mr. Edward Montagu, a lawyer at the Middle Temple, and agent for your son's General Assembly — the Council, I believe. A diligent but ineffectual fellow. Next to him is Mr. George Mercer, a colonel in the Virginia militia and a veteran of the late war. He is here on Ohio Company business, but in truth he has been treading water here and in Ireland for nigh on two years, waiting to be rewarded for his war services with lucrative employment with the Crown in the colonies. He is about to take ship home with his distributor's commission. I have met him. He is a modest, unpompous chap, and I could not decide from my brief encounter with him whether he wished to celebrate his appointment, or commiserate with the other two Americans who happened to be here to receive their own commissions in person." Jones paused to sip his port. "Three hundred pounds a year in salary, in addition to eight percent of his colony's stamp revenues, are to be his remuneration. From that, however, he must hire and pay twenty or so under-distributors and other factotums. The other distributors are appointed on more or less the same terms." Jones chuckled. "Mr. Mercer was not particularly pleased with the appointment — I believe he was pining for something more prestigious and less larcenous — for he knows his fellow Virginians well enough to suspect that he will have fewer friends among them when he assumes his office. But he believes they will resign themselves to the inevitable."

"Who were the other Americans?"

"They have already departed for America, and the greetings that await them there are a matter of speculation. There was Mr. Jared Ingersoll, former agent for Connecticut, and a close personal friend of Mr. Whateley there, the master of details. Mr. Ingersoll doubted the practicality of the stamps, but supplied Mr. Whateley with invaluable advice on those details. His reservations over the Act's goodness notwithstanding, he accepted a distributor's commission, believing that he has done his countrymen a great service by recommending that the shackles refined by Mr. Whateley be lined with fur, so that they are pleasanter to wear. And Mr. George Meserve, of New Hampshire. I have also met him. A plain, timid fellow, a friend of John Thomlinson, agent for that colony and a bashaw from Antigua. Thomlinson's son, John, is a victualling contractor and a member for Steyning."

"Sir," chuckled the Baron, "you are yourself a wealth of detail!"

"It is part and parcel of the career, milord," said Jones, "to attend innumerable meetings and levees to audit the thoughts and assertions of friend and enemies alike. Now," he said, gesturing with the stem of his pipe to the men across the room, "every one of those distributor chaps owes his appointment to connections in the Commons, connections leading from Mr. Grenville to Mr. Whateley and from him to the Board of Trade to hither and yon in our own bureaucratic mechanism. Quite an insidious, complicated pump works, indeed."

The Baron looked thoughtful for a moment, then frowned. "In truth, sir, I cannot blame them, if they resign themselves to such a fate. The power of the Crown seems to all of us not a part of it like a great, unstoppable wave. Defy it, and it will crush you. Ride with it, and it may spare you." Garnet Kenrick looked melancholy, and said wistfully, "I have been reading Mr. Hume, you know. He claims it is possible for a falling pebble to extinguish the sun, or a man's fervent wish to alter the orbits of the planets around it. That we cannot be certain of immutable laws in man or nature. However, I do not think he ascribed that fanciful metaphysics to the tax farmer." He shook his head sadly. "Even Mr. Hume did not believe that his mutable skepticism applied to the Treasury or Customs Board. Those institutions seem to be unalterable absolutes as is death."

Jones grinned, pleased to hear the comment. "Milord, what a delightfully dark thought! I beg permission to use it in a letter, or in a speech. Mr. Hume may be proven wrong, after all, if the colonials succeed in defying the Crown! Oh, damn!" he said abruptly. "The great straw-shoe of the Commons has seen us, and advances rapidly!"

He nodded in the direction of Sir Henoch Pannell, who crossed the room and approached their table wearing a jaunty smile. The member for Canovan stopped and nodded to the Baron and Jones. "Good afternoon, your lordship, Sir Dogmael. You are looking cheerful in spite of your travails. May I sit for a moment?"

"Briefly, Sir Henoch," answered Garnet Kenrick in the manner of a warning.

Pannell looked genuinely stung by this reply. "Not a second more than is necessary, your lordship," he said. "I would not be so rude to my own company," he added suavely. He pulled out the table's only vacant chair and plumped down into it.

"What is the purpose of this intrusion, Sir Henoch?" asked Jones, relighting his pipe.

"It is in the way of a farewell, sir. Shortly I am to leave to join my wife in Marsden for the remainder of the season, and will return late fall to prepare for the session." Pannell was Baronet of Marsden, in Essex, a property and title he had been awarded years before for his successful capture of the Skelly gang in Cornwall.

"Fare thee well, sir," said Jones, lazily waving his pipe.

"Thank you, Sir Dogmael. By the bye, have you heard about your other stout friend, Mr. Benjamin Franklin?"

"We have heard many things about him, Sir Henoch," said the Baron.

"Then perhaps you already know that, in his capacity as deputy postmaster for the northern colonies, he has accepted the appointment of collector of stamp revenues."

"We knew that, sir," said Jones. "What significance do you assign to the fact?"

"Not a significance, to be sure, but rather an irony. You know, of course, that he has been pestering the devil out of the Board of Trade and anyone else's ear he can bend, to effect a change in the status of Pennsylvania from a proprietary to a royal colony, to better tax the Penns by the legislature there in order to raise funds for arms and men to combat the savages on the western frontier." Pannell shook his head in feigned wonder. "Not dissimilar to the predicament the Crown finds itself in. It is one of the reasons we passed the Stamp Act. I almost sympathize with Mr. Franklin."

"Surely, you have a reason for repeating this information, sir," said Garnet Kenrick.

"I do, your lordship, and it is this: Without the least effort on Mr. Franklin's part, and in fact quite contrary to his own known sentiments on the subject — and, between ourselves, quite tepid sentiments, if I may say so — he has been handed the profitable place of collecting all the stamp revenue he inveighed against." Pannell chuckled. "Why, I know that he even criticized those Virginia resolves that seem to have been broadcast throughout the colonies. 'Premature,' I believe he called them."

"Have you read them?" asked Jones.

"I was privileged to see that document, Sir Dogmael. It is but a fustian of treasonous fallacies! Well, why am I so surprised?" remarked Pannell with feigned insouciance. "It was composed by an alliance of lawyers and hard-scrabble planters!"

Jones shook his head. "I, too, have seen them, Sir Henoch. That document is an assertion of uncontestable truths."

"We are obviously not of the same opinion."

"I do not voice opinions, sir. I make observations."

"I may say that, as well, sir. *I* see the makings of treason and sedition."

Jones sighed tiredly. Then he smiled in challenge at his adversary. "Through tattered rags small vices do appear. Robes and furred gowns hide all. Get thee glass eyes, and, like a scurvy politician, seem to see things thou dost not."

Pannell chuckled again, waved a hand at Jones, but addressed the Baron. "There he goes again, your lordship, assailing me with Mr. Shakespeare!"

Jones's eyebrows went up in surprise. "My compliments, Sir Henoch. You properly identified the weapon. But, can you identify the character who spoke those lines?"

"I confess I cannot, sir. Please, enlighten me."

"King Lear, near raving mad, addressing blind Gloucester. Act four, scene five."

Pannell laughed, and again addressed the Baron. "What else can one expect from this gentleman but the regular spoutings of a yearning actor?"

"There you are, sir," said Garnet Kenrick with a wicked, unfriendly smile, "growing old in fraud, past your manly bloom, artfully adopting the ruses by which gay villains rise to reach the heights which honest men despise."

Pannell snorted in surprise. "Mr. Shakespeare again, your lordship?"

The Baron shook his head. "No, sir. The late Mr. Charles Churchill, liberally paraphrased in your honor."

"Well, what a relief! I must say, it is a pleasure to have been assailed by two poets, and in one day!"

"Please, Sir Henoch," said Jones, "come to the purpose of your congeniality."

"As I said," replied the member for Canovan, "it is not so much anything but a farewell of sorts. My own, and to colonial blather. You see, your lordship, Sir Dogmael, I am quite satisfied that our course of action last session was right and proper. If so stalwart a huckster of colonial rights and immunities and privileges as Mr. Franklin is willing not only to concede our authority, but to allow himself a role in it, there cannot be the least credible objection to the tax among those of his countrymen who are far less informed of the matter. That is all I wished to say."

"You are gloating," said Jones, sitting back and puffing on his pipe. "But, oddly, that becomes you." He paused. "Beware, Sir Henoch, and take care what you say, next session. You may find your likeness in the newspapers again."

"Thank you for the warning, sir, and for permitting me some ecstasy, as well." Pannell rose and bowed slightly to the Baron. "Well, the gay villain must take his leave, your lordship, and polish his glass eyes. An American over there needs this scurvy politician's reassurances that we mean him and his countrymen no harm. Sir Dogmael...." He nodded to the barrister, then turned and left.

"That man is impervious to insult, Mr. Jones!" observed the Baron with some astonishment. "He has the hide of a rhinoceros that you mentioned!"

Jones shook his head in regret. "I fear that I have trained him in the art, milord, these few years."

"What hubris! Why is he so certain he is right?"

"Because he has seen strong men falter in the employment of their principles — men such as Mr. Franklin — and this apparently permits him to believe in the practicality of compromise and the foolishness of principled certainty." Jones shook his head. "It saves him the necessity of honor and the inconvenience of upholding it. So, he has no honor to offend or defend. Paradox solved!"

The Baron's brow furled in thought. "That is a more fatal skepticism than Mr. Hume's." He added, a moment later, after watching Sir Henoch talk with his companions across the room, "And a sad vanity."

Sir Henoch Pannell at that moment was consoling George Mercer with some advice: "Feel no shame about your commission, sir. Nor any trepidation. To be employed by the Crown in so vital a post is an honorable entrustment of duty. Do not doubt that. With all modesty, I offer myself as an instance. Long ago, I took a job, commissioner extraordinary of the revenue, on these very shores, and during my tenure I was mocked by my employers, shunned by my fellow countrymen in whose service I labored, and duped by outlaws and smugglers. A humiliating experience that called for iron mettle! Yet I persevered, and here I am today, and that dark and contentious adventure is in the past. My employers recommended me to the Court, where I received more honors, and those outlaws and smugglers perished by steel or hemp! But here is my main point: It was a necessary adventure, to occupy a low, despised place in the scheme of things, in order to advance to higher, envied places!" Pannell put a steadying hand on Mercer's shoulder, and smiled blandly. "You, sir, would be wise to adopt the same view." Then he picked up a tankard of ale and took a long gulp from it.

George Mercer blinked in understanding. But he replied with some worry, "Thank you for the advice, Sir Henoch, however, you have not dealt directly with Virginians. They may choose to risk the bayonet and the rope over submitting to the Act. I even took the liberty of advising Mr. Grenville of that possibility, when he was so gracious as to grant me an interview. The esteem in which they hold me now may not protect me, and my service to my country, for which I have sought only a just reward, may not absolve me, in this circumstance. They may despise me, and accuse me of disgrace, and heap upon my head all kinds of abuse!"

"What an absurdity!" exclaimed Pannell, slamming down his tankard. "Why, I am speaking with a Virginian this very moment! There is no God-given reason why all Virginians cannot, in time, and with the boundless patience of the Crown, example your own upstanding character, sense of expedience, excellent wit, and other fine qualities!"

Edward Montagu opined, "Sir Henoch is correct in his views, Colonel Mercer. Fate is on the side of the Act, and you can only profit from that fate."

Thomas Whateley advised, "You have been entrusted with a patriotic duty, sir, and it is nearly treason to doubt the expediency of it."

In addition to his other fine qualities, George Mercer was appointed on the strength of high praise by Lieutenant-Governor Fauquier and his Council, and by the Committee of Correspondence in the House of Burgesses. These recommendations were ignored by George Grenville for other kinds of appointments, except when he and his party decided to make Americans the cat's paws for enforcing the Act.

George Mercer did not think of himself as anyone's cat's paw. The praise of the Lieutenant-Governor and his fellow countrymen, he thought, must count for something. Then there was his friendship with George Washington, another hero; who could oppose or defame a friend of that noble giant? And what helped to allay his doubts about the expediency and propriety of his commission was his more intimate acquaintance with his fellow colonials, and in particular his fellow Virginians. This knowledge was buttressed by the authority of George Grenville's private assurances to him that, based on ample evidence from the past, in such instances as this one, colonial unity on any issue was a laughable oxymoron, and that, anyway, the Act would necessarily enforce itself if the colonials wished the protection of Crown and colonial law.

Armed with this sad vanity, George Mercer sailed on September 12th from England on the *Leeds* for Virginia. In the hold of that merchantman were sealed crates of stamps and stamped forms of almost every conceivable kind, destined for Maryland and North Carolina, as well as for Virginia.

Following a few days later in the wake of the *Leeds*, also bound for Virginia, was the *Sparrowhawk*.

* * *

Across an ocean, on another river, in another tavern, on the evening of the same day, a man said, "Live free, or die."

Jack Frake stood to one side of the round table in the Olympus Room of Safford's King's Arms, and glanced around at the faces looking up at him in the candlelight, waiting for a response. The room was quiet. He pronounced the words as an ultimatum, even though he was proposing them as a motto for the Sons of Liberty.

This was a meeting of that society. Thomas Reisdale, who chaired the meeting, had already given his address on the evils of the Stamp Act and the best means to understand and oppose it in argument. His speech had caused some desultory debate among the Sons' members, but the few doubters had been persuaded to agree with it.

Jack stood with a yellowed sheet of paper, from which he had read the words. When the agenda for this meeting had been decided on weeks ago, he had gone home to his study and taken out his copy of *Hyperborea*. From between its middle pages, he removed a folded letter that was stained with the sweat of forgotten labor and the blood of remembered battles. The letter was contained on both sides of a single sheet. It was written and signed by Redmagne and Augustus Skelly in the Falmouth prison, days before they were hanged. It was secretly conveyed to Jack by Simon Haslam, a local prosecutor, in a gesture of mercy and contrary to Commissioner Henoch

Pannell's orders that Jack was to have no further communication with his fellow prisoners.

In the letter, among the many things said by Redmagne and Skelly, there was this:

> "We fill our remaining hours with mutual remembrances of great things and small in our individual and shared lives. These things are ours to remember, and you, brave and dear sir, are included in our reveries. We are cruelly parted at the moment, but we are still together, and will always be so, for we are certain that you will understand our new-found maxim: Live free, or die. Perhaps, someday, you will understand it better than we have, and attain a greater liberty than we can now imagine. And never mind that we have lived free, and are about to die. Incidentals are irrelevant to universal principles. Therefore, we bequeath this maxim to you, our heir in spirit...."

Jack knew who had penned that part of the letter — Redmagne. It was in his hand. But both men had signed it. He did not need to read those words from the letter. He brought the paper to the meeting as a gesture of justice, as a mute witness, as though its presence here were a kind of vindication of its authors' lives and actions, to complete some kind of connection between the leagues and years of the faraway past and the present moment.

Hugh Kenrick, sitting at Jack's right at the table, spoke first, in a whisper of reverence. "What a marvelous sentiment!" After a moment, he asked, "Did you compose it?"

"No," answered Jack. "Two very good friends, whose likenesses you were kind enough to preserve for me." He looked down at his friend and saw that he understood. Jack folded the letter and dropped it into his coat pocket. Again, he faced the men in the room. "What say anyone to that as our motto?"

The room remained quiet. No one spoke.

"There is nothing to say to it," said Thomas Reisdale, after a moment. "It is an eternal verity."

All the other members nodded in agreement or voiced their consent.

"Now, to our banner," said Jack. "I propose that we adopt this —" he paused to tap a finger on the East India jack that served as the organization's table cloth "— but alter it so that it properly represents the unity of the colonies against the Stamp Act. With Mr. Safford's permission, the jack can be altered, or we can contribute to the creation of a new one like it, but with significant differences."

Steven Safford spoke up from the back of the room. "I am willing to see it altered, if that is necessary."

Jack nodded in thanks to the publican. "Fine. Mr. Reisdale, if you please."

Reisdale's inkwell, minutes ledger, and elbows were resting on the canton that bore the cross of St. George. The attorney promptly removed them.

Jack picked up a corner of the flag and pointed to the stripes. "There are thirteen stripes here, and each can represent one of the principal colonies, at least the ones that were most on Mr. Grenville's mind when he and his placemen concocted the Stamp Act. I propose that they be left intact, except to have sewn on one of the white stripes the name of our organization." He dropped the corner. "Is this agreed?"

The members said "Aye."

"But why only thirteen stripes?" queried one of the members. "There are over twenty provinces that come under the Stamp Act."

"We will not include the Canadian and Caribbean colonies, nor even the Floridas," answered Jack. "We have had no news of protests from those quarters, so we may rightfully assume they will submit to the stamps." He glanced around in search of disagreement with his reasoning. He saw none. He continued, and pointed to the canton. "I further propose that the cross here be replaced with a plain blue field with our newly adopted motto emblazoned in gold letters."

One man asked, "Do you mean, replace the cross?"

"Yes."

"That is too much, sir!" objected one of the former doubters. "Such a device smacks of…secession!"

Jack said, "Not so, sir. This is to be a private device of a private association. It is no more provocative than the Masons' use of the compass in their own device."

"This is true," concurred Hugh. He continued. "Besides, the adopted motto does not agree with the canton as it is now. It needs a proper background, an agreeable field." He paused. His face lit up, and his eyes became bright. "*Cobalt*, sirs," he said. "A field of *cobalt*. The richest blue. A proper background for gold."

No one, not even Jack Frake, knew that Hugh was prompted by the sudden recollection of the words of his dying friend, Glorious Swain, on the Charing Cross pillory: *The sky is growing more blue…a royal cobalt…the canopy of Olympus….* Hugh said, in the manner of a dedication, "The canton must be cobalt."

Jack sensed that this color was for some reason important to his friend. He said, "Then the gold shall sit in a field of cobalt. Is this agreed?"

The membership assented.

"Who would alter the jack, or sew a new one?" asked one of the members.

Jack said, "Lydia Heathcoate." The woman was Caxton's finest seamstress and owned the town's sole millinery. She often repaired the jacks and pennants of the merchantmen that called on the town. "Each of us will contribute something to pay her for the task. Is this agreed?"

It was agreed.

Later, as they rode together in the dark back to their plantations, Jack asked Hugh why he had insisted on cobalt.

With some emotion, Hugh explained the moment on the Charing Cross pillory.

When Hugh had finished, Jack smiled in fondness for the gesture and for his friend.

* * *

Chapter 7: The "Madness"

One day in late September, news arrived in Caxton, from the captains and sailors of some merchantmen anchored there and at Yorktown, that the stamp distributors for New York and New Jersey had resigned in the face of threats to their property. That same day, Edgar Cullis returned with his father from their outing in the Piedmont. The next afternoon, Edgar Cullis rode to Meum Hall to call on Hugh Kenrick.

Hugh was in the hot fields, supervising the topping of his tobacco and appraising his other crops, when Spears came out and informed him of his visitor. He accompanied the valet back to the great house. He did not bother changing into more formal garb, as he might have for other gentleman visitors, but merely freshened his face with handfuls of water, and ordered some tea brought into his study. He found Cullis leafing through one of his books, Le Sage's *The Bachelor of Salamanca*. Hugh nodded in silent greeting, and waved his fellow burgess to a chair in front of his desk. Cullis nodded in answer, then gently returned the novel and took a seat.

"I trust that your expedition was a success, Mr. Cullis," said Hugh, sitting in his chair behind the desk. His hand rested on his brass top, which was always there, and toyed with it during the interview.

"Yes," replied Cullis, who looked tan and leaner now. "We bagged five wolves and two litters of them. Also, we shot one great cat that had been stalking us, and accompanied a party of shirtmen as they tracked some bison." He paused, feeling uncomfortable under Hugh's steady scrutiny. "Yes, thank you. It was a success, our expedition. Then we repaired to Warm Springs, where my father took the waters for his rheumatism. He is better now."

"I am pleased to hear it," remarked Hugh.

Cullis smiled nervously. "We encountered rain," he added, in reference to the drought that had baked many of the Tidewater's crop fields this year. "I must say that it was a relief to be soaked by it, even for the inconvenience it caused us."

"It rained some here, as well," said Hugh. He paused. "I trust you have been informed of Mr. Barret's death."

"We learned of it upon our return home," said Cullis with a sigh. "We were saddened by the news." Before Hugh could query him further on that subject, which he expected but nonetheless dreaded, he cleared his throat and rushed to say, "Before returning home, however, we stopped briefly in Williamsburg. I was unexpectedly summoned by Mr. Robinson and Mr. Randolph on House business."

"There is no House to do business, sir," said Hugh.

Cullis flashed a brief smile. "No Assembly has been called, it is true. But it is known that many members will ignore the Governor's announcement of a delay of the first session of the new Assembly, and come to the Capitol, before the General Court sits, chiefly to attend the theater, for private business, and for other purposes."

"There is a question of whether or not the General Court will be able to sit," replied Hugh.

"Why would you doubt it?" asked the visiting burgess. His host's manner was curt. He had expected that, too, but still did not like it.

Hugh shrugged. "If no lawyers or stamps arrive to facilitate court business, then there will be no General Court. There is also a question of whether or not our county court will sit before that, for the same reasons."

There was a knock on the study door and Fiona Chance, the cook, came in with the tea. Hugh smiled in amusement. Usually it was Rachel, the cook's black kitchen assistant, who brought refreshments into the study. But he assumed that Fiona knew about his dislike of Cullis, and wanted to see for herself how the visit was progressing. When she had arranged the tray on Hugh's desk, served the men the tea, and had gone, Hugh said, "But enough about the Court. What other business did you conduct in the Capitol?"

Cullis sipped his beverage before answering. Then he put down the cup and said, "Although there can be no formal session, in view of the Governor's proroguement, the Speaker and Attorney-General believe it would be an opportunity for those who do come to Williamsburg to participate in the formal passage of some bills left over from last December, and their entry into the House journal." He paused. "It is hoped that you will attend, even though you negatived virtually all the bills outstanding. Mr. Randolph and Mr. Robinson expect there will be enough members present in town to form a scratch quorum."

Hugh's brow creased in perplexity. "But, if no session of the Assembly sits next month, Mr. Cullis, how can laws be credited to it?"

This time Cullis shrugged. "It is a mere formality. The Speaker, Attorney-General, and Council all feel that to wait to carry them over to the next actual sitting would be inconvenient and overly tardy."

Hugh sampled his own tea. "It is irregular and flirts with fraud, sir," he said. "Posterity will believe that a session occurred, when in truth none had."

"Irregular, but necessary, from an administrative perspective," answered Cullis. "The commutation of bills from one session to its successor is certainly no precedent. I believe I instructed you in that practice some time ago."

Hugh nodded. "Yes, you did, but then you spoke of sessions that had not been prorogued. Well, that is the risk of Mr. Robinson and Mr. Randolph. Still, I would not attend this ghostly Assembly, for the reasons I have just cited. And a true assembly is to sit in New York next month. I will be there to observe it."

Cullis frowned and sat up. "On whose authority?"

Hugh scoffed. "My own, sir. I need none from the House to go in a private capacity."

Cullis put down his cup and saucer thoughtfully, and rose from his chair. "I beg your pardon, sir, but you are a member of the House, and need to be selected as a delegate by it. This so-called 'congress' is irregular, and your action will be irregular. Why, you could be censured by the House, or even expelled by it!"

Hugh smiled. "These are irregular times, sir, that call for irregular actions." He paused. "And who would make a motion to censure or expel me? You, perhaps?"

Cullis stiffened. "It will be my duty to inform the House of your intentions."

"But there is no House to inform, sir," replied Hugh, rising from his chair. With a hand, he moved his cup and saucer aside on the desktop. "Just as there was no House to inform the Governor of the danger of choosing delegates to that congress, or about Mr. Barret's role in disseminating Mr. Henry's resolves." He shook his head. "You were party to some very grave and ramifying irregularities, Mr. Cullis, and you have not been forthright about it. Neither have Mr. Randolph, Mr. Robinson, and very likely Mr. Wythe."

Cullis could only manage to reply, "I...deny it! And, you impugn dishonor not only to me, but also to those...fine men! His honor the Governor prorogued the Assembly on his own initiative, to prevent just the kind of foolishness and recklessness you plan to commit! And your presence in New York will be misinterpreted, sir! Surely, you must introduce yourself to those...renegades as a member of our House!"

"Surely, but as a private person and a patriot," answered Hugh. "It is the view of more thoughtful men in this county that it would be a disgrace if Virginia were not represented in some form at the congress. I have agreed to go, to maintain our country's honor."

"*Our country's honor!*" spat Cullis. "Again, I beg your pardon, sir, but you will only dishonor the House, and Virginia, and impute treason to them into the bargain!"

Hugh's congenial visage hardened now. "I can only repeat Mr. Henry's words, sir: If this be treason, let us make the most of it." He added with a contempt of whose object Cullis could not be certain, himself or Parliament, "It is not the prey who proposes treason here, sir, but the prowler." He nodded to the study door, and folded his arms. "Good day to you, Mr. Cullis."

Edgar Cullis glared at his host with lips pressed hard together in angry restraint. Then he snatched up his hat and put it on. "Why was not I consulted about this matter, this...seditious gambol to New York? We are this county's burgesses, and ought to act in concert!"

Hugh shook his head. "You were away, sir, hunting wolves in the hills, while we were preparing to trap some in this very county, come November."

Cullis's curiosity, whetted by this last reply, was greater than his desire to escape. Hugh seemed to know this, and simply stared at him with a subtle dare in his expression to ask him questions he would not answer. Cullis steeled himself and grimaced in disgust at his defeat. "Good day to you, as well, sir," he said. He turned on his heel and left.

From his study window, Hugh watched his fellow burgess mount his horse in the yard and ride away.

* * *

"I have essayed a project that Mr. Barlow Trecothick, a former American here in London, and an alderman of the city to boot, is rumored to be contemplating, which is to solicit the views of merchants far and wide, concerning the Stamp Tax, and to perhaps persuade them to act in a body to recommend to the Commons its relaxation or modification, if not its repeal," wrote Dogmael Jones in another letter to Hugh. "If the Commons last sitting would not receive American petitions, protests, and advice over the likely consequences of the Act, then perhaps my colleagues will listen to and heed the remonstrances of the merchants and factors here. The newspapers, coffeehouses, and Royal Exchange are all abuzz with worry and trepidation. As the merchants' purses become lighter and their account books painful to peruse, their complaints grow louder over the present reduced trade and the likely mischief of the Act. But I believe they are blind to the nub. The question for the colonials is ever more not so much one of ruined trade or the effects of a concerted abstinence from it, as one of proper authority over trade on the whole. The arguments must advance even further, on your side of the ocean, to the true distinction between the kinds of unrest arising here and there from this conflict. You and your fellow British-Americans are closer to it, I believe, and in it will find your unassailable argument, leaving us poor benighted souls far behind, westering with tattered sails beneath a smoky sky for an elusive sun we have yet to glimpse."

It was late September. Hugh's desk was piled up with more letters from his father and Jones, together with newspapers and pamphlets from other colonies. There were also letters from Otis Talbot and Novus Easley in Philadelphia reporting events in the northern colonies and closer to Virginia.

Riots had occurred all over Rhode Island. The stamp distributor for Connecticut resigned after he was threatened with lynching. The distributor for Maryland fled to New York after his house was destroyed by a mob. The distributor for New Hampshire resigned at the request of his countrymen before he even stepped off the vessel that brought him from England to Boston Harbor. The distributor for New Jersey resigned without prompting. The distributor for New York resigned from fear of the consequences to his property if he did not.

Merchants, artisans, farmers, planters, and lawyers in Virginia all remarked to their friends, families, and associates: George Grenville, author of the Act, had surrendered the seals of office. Would Mr. Mercer have the decency to surrender his appointment? Ominously, in Westmoreland County in northern Virginia, George Mercer and George Grenville were hanged in effigy.

Hugh could hardly contain himself for all the news that seemed to arrive each day. Buried under the pile somewhere was even a pathetic note from Lieutenant-Governor Fauquier, who apologized in it for his "transparent and unforgivable rudeness" to Hugh "when you last called here on the *Courier* matter," and went on to express his "desperate misgivings" for the "madness of the people in these times," and concluded with a plea for understanding. "In confidence, and as a measure of my own sincere sorrow for the current troubles, you should know that some years ago, during the late war, and not long after my own arrival here, Mr. Pitt himself queried me on the best way to pay for the war and the maintenance of the colonies, and proposed just such a tax as that which now distresses schooled and unschooled people alike. I answered him with the most delicate apprehension as that such a measure would occasion great uproars and disturbances...."

Hugh read that letter, and could feel only a twinge of pity for the man.

This afternoon he sat with Jack Frake in Safford's King's Arms Tavern, over tankards of port at a table by the window in the main room. He would leave for Hampton in two days, driven in the sulky by Spears, and there find a billet on a coastal vessel bound for New York. He hoped to reach the town a few days before the opening of the congress in early October, then return. "I want to be here when the General Court opens," he said to Jack. "It will be interesting to see what happens, with or without stamps."

"Etáin has joined Widow Heathcoate in fashioning our banner," said Jack. "It should be ready by the time you return."

Hugh chuckled in mild amusement. "I did not know Etáin could sew."

Jack shook his head, also amused. "Not so finely as Widow Heathcoate, who has apprenticed her to the art."

Steven Safford, owner of the tavern, approached them with fresh tankards of port, and in the bargain brought them news of another incident, relayed to him earlier by the master of a lumber boat from the Northern Neck. An effigy of Mercer had been tied to a horse and paraded through the river port town of Dumfries on the Potomac, then taken to a tree and hanged. Safford took their coins and walked way to serve other patrons.

"It has always astounded me," remarked Hugh in a low voice, "the volume of intelligence that man can collect with his one ear." A musket ball had removed the publican's left ear during the Louisbourg campaign.

Almost directly across Queen Anne Street from the tavern was the former residence and shop of Wendel Barret and the *Courier*. Sitting in front of it now was a wide, oxen-teamed wagon. William Fletcher, the late printer's brother-in-law, had come down from Fredericksburg to collect his nephew, Travis Barret, and the shop's contents. The boy and the apprentice slave, Cletus, had been staying with Sheriff Cabal Tippet until they could be claimed by nearest kin. Fletcher met with Thomas Reisdale, Barret's attorney, and learned that he would need to either sell or auction off much of the property, including the house and shop, to pay the late printer's debts. Reisdale, who had Barret's account books, however, assured him that sale of the land and the building on it would more than satisfy the printer's creditors.

Jack and Hugh watched Fletcher, his own grown son, John, Travis Barret, and Cletus carry furniture and other household items from the building and load them onto the wagon. To their amazement, they witnessed Fletcher and his son remove pieces of the dismantled press and none too gently toss them onto the bed of the wagon.

"What a waste!" sighed Hugh. "I myself arranged to have that press loaded onto Mr. Ramshaw's *Sparrowhawk*, in the Pool of London, together with many of the bills of type seized by the Governor."

"Mr. Barret deserved to live long enough to see what that press has wrought," said Jack.

"Agreed."

Hugh showed his friend some of the letters he had received by postrider and merchantmen over the last week.

To Jones's letter, Jack remarked, "He *knows* what is in store. I hope to meet this friend of yours some day." To Fauquier's letter, he said, in reference to his marriage to Etáin, "I am sorry that it was necessary to choose between Reverend Acland and him." He handed back the letters. "What do you expect the congress to accomplish?"

Hugh shrugged. "Undoubtedly, compose a number of protests, the chief one adopting the form of Mr. Henry's resolves. I can picture it now. They will address the Board of Trade and the Commons thusly: Repeat the remonstrance of last December, and assure the Crown of our loyalty. Assert the rights of Englishmen here, as guaranteed by the various charters, and contest any Parliamentary authority over our internal governance. Trumpet the mutual dependency of Britain and ourselves for the prosperity and good fortune it facilitates, and warn of a harsh reduction of both our fortunes if the Act is enforced. And, of course, protest the powers of the vice-admiralty courts as unconstitutional incursions on the right to trial by jury."

"Why are you so glum about the force of a protest?"

"I suspect that the forces of moderation will wish to be gentle so as not to frighten our legislative cousins in London."

Jack took a draught of his port. "Do not gainsay them before the fact, Hugh. Only time can teach them that civility will only invite more abuse. Your friend Jones is not the only one who has not yet glimpsed the sun, though he is right about our being closer to it."

Hugh grinned in astonishment. "Why, Jack, I have never before heard you counsel patience!"

* * *

A few days after Hugh had departed for New York, Thomas Reisdale reported to Jack over supper at Morland Hall that the Governor had returned the cases of the *Courier*'s type. "They are of no use to anyone here," he remarked, "and I am reluctant to offer them to Mr. Royle at the *Gazette*. I shall query the printers in Maryland and Carolina."

After a moment, Jack said, "I'll buy them."

Reisdale frowned in surprise. "What on earth for?"

Jack only smiled. "So that Mr. Barret may perhaps someday speak again, in future."

That October, the cases of lead type were delivered to Morland Hall. Jack Frake stored them in the basement of the great house.

* * *

Chapter 8: The Justices

On the day that Hugh Kenrick journeyed to Hampton and found passage on the *Skate*, a sloop bound for New York with a cargo of tar, shingles, oats, and Jamaican rum, Thomas Reisdale sent a servant around to the five other justices of Queen Anne County with an invitation to Freehold the next evening to meet over supper and a Michaelmas roast goose. The county court was scheduled to sit two weeks before the General Court sat in Williamsburg, the same day the Stamp Act was to come into effect. He wished to discuss with his fellow magistrates whether or not to open the court. The court sat for a few days each month, when the number of cases on the docket, usually civil matters, justified it.

He also sent an invitation to Jack Frake. He wished to have that man there, for his presence among any group of men exerted an inexplicable persuasion on them. He was not certain what it was or how it worked. Jack Frake was somehow like a rock of certitude.

That very evening, he was surprised when a servant showed into his study John Proudlocks, who offered his employer's thanks and regrets. Reisdale asked the Indian, to whom he gave occasional instructions in law, why his employer could not come.

Proudlocks looked courteously informal, and almost sorry that he had to answer the question. "Mr. Frake asked me to convey this answer to you, should you chance to ask that, sir: This is something you must do yourself, on your own." With that, he nodded his head, took a step back, turned, and left.

Reisdale did not fully comprehend the meaning of that answer, until after the Michaelmas supper the following evening.

It was a happy, convivial gathering of justices at his table, and in the course of the feast they traded news about their harvests, staff problems, the Indian war in the west, and rumors and news about the unrest in the northern colonies. When the subject of Ralph Cullis's trip in the Piedmont was disposed of, Reisdale steered the conversation to the purpose of the supper. "As you know, sirs, the Stamp Act does not affect criminal matters.

Writs and other legal documents necessary to the hearing and prosecution of simple larceny and other petty felonies may be employed without the requisite stamps."

"What a benevolent exception to our persecution," remarked Jock Frazer, whose plantation neighbored Freehold. "We may judge our fellow slaveys without fear of feeling the sting of a whip."

Reisdale's other guests grumbled in agreement.

Reisdale continued. "For this reason, and because there are three men languishing in Sheriff Tippet's jail" — they all knew about the sailor who was caught stealing pullets from Lucas Rittles's yard, and the two ship-wrights who had absconded with lumber from Henry Nault's warehouse on the river front — "I propose that the court open to try these cases this month, and after November first."

"That is an ironic distinction," ventured Reece Vishonn, "considering that the Act itself can be construed as an instance of *grand* larceny."

The men around the table, including Reisdale, laughed without humor.

"That is the opinion of many thoughtful friends of mine in Maryland," said Ira Granby, whose plantation neighbored Vishonn's Enderly. "Curiously enough, they, too, have called the Act one of legalized theft!"

Moses Corbin, the mayor of Caxton and also a justice, said, "My friends in Pennsylvania write me that many courts in all the colonies may close in protest of it, or never open. The question is furiously and often violently argued everywhere."

"I'll wager there will be much rejoicing among debtors should that come to pass," said Granby.

Reisdale said, "Our court needn't be closed to criminal cases, sirs. We may sit without risk of censure, penalty, or nullification."

"That is not a *protest*," opined Granby with scorn.

Ralph Cullis said, "Indeed, that would be sitting by leave of Parliament, or by its neglect or oversight."

All the men at the table glanced at Cullis. That man noted the attention, and rushed to add, "I disagree with my son on many matters, sirs, and that is one of them."

Reisdale commented, "Very good point, Mr. Cullis." He smiled in gratitude. "I shall work your observation into my pamphlet."

Reece Vishonn mused, "Boston is a rowdy, dissolute town, ruled by mobs, malcontents, and idle sailors. Not at all a civil place. We would not want to emulate that den of iniquity in any protest."

"Quite true," agreed Reisdale. "We want no drunken rioting or pillaging to occur here. The question, then, is this: In future, after November first, will we convene for civil cases, as well, and risk Crown action, if we proceed without stamps? Now, the citizens of our fair county are not so litigious as are those in other counties, so our docket is not overflowing. Still, we would want to see justice done and our docket kept spare."

"If the stamps are not here to use, then we cannot do business," said Cullis with a shrug. "Why, we must needs tender our resignations to the Governor in protest. I have heard that the justices of Westmoreland County are contemplating such an action."

Granby shook his head vigorously. "If the stamps are not available, then we cannot *but* proceed with business, sirs, and let the Governor do what he may about it!"

"He may relieve us of our seats, sirs, but we will have made our point," said Corbin.

Vishonn snorted and said, "Let us not resort to a caitiff's ploy, sirs! We ought to sit regardless of the Crown's pleasure or displeasure! Do we abandon our houses, because we have espied a scamp canvassing our property and planning his burglary?"

"If we sit," said Reisdale, "we must inform the county of our intention, and the Governor, as well." He paused. "We must behave as though no Stamp Act ever threatened us. Here, then, is another question: Are we all agreed that the Act comprises a violation of the Constitution?"

The company muttered agreement.

Jock Frazer said, "If we sit, sirs, we must be frank about it. Perform a zestful Highland fling for them all to notice, not some dainty minuet!" He sat forward and glanced at each of his companions. "We must say that we sit without stamps, now and forever, for we judge the Act null and void for Constitutional reasons!"

"Aye, aye!" agreed the company.

"Who would pen such a statement?" asked Cullis.

Everyone looked at Reisdale.

"Very well," said the host with a modest smile. "It is agreed, then. We will sit the second week of October. I will compose a statement of our intent and purpose." He paused to caution, "It will require all our signatures."

"Of course," chuckled Vishonn. "We would not protest as masked Italian revelers!" He pounded the table once with a fist. "No dominos or funny hats for us! Let us sign our names with fire and fortitude!"

Jock Frazer rose and proposed a round of toasts to celebrate their decision. He picked up his glass of sherry and bid his fellow justices to rise. "To
liberty!" he said.

"To Queen Anne County!" said Granby.

"To Virginia!" said Vishonn.

"To our host and his even-keeled wisdom!" said Corbin.

After his guests left that evening, Thomas Reisdale reflected on the
meaning of courage, and understood what Jack Frake had meant. He had
expected his fellow justices to unanimously agree to wait until George
Mercer and the stamps arrived. It fairly shocked him that they agreed to sit
in defiance of the Act. He had expected to argue himself hoarse in an effort
to persuade them to sit for any reason, and to be defeated in the effort. It
amazed him that it had been so simple and almost effortless a persuasion.
Obviously, he had underestimated the determination of his fellow justices.

And he had secretly harbored the hope that he would be defeated, in
order to save himself the courage to act against what he knew was wrong.
Now, he had a taste of courage, something he had never had reason to call
upon in his whole career. While the servants cleared the supper room, he
found himself moving to his study to sit and compose the announcement.

Two days later, he accompanied a servant in his sulky to the courthouse in Caxton and watched the man nail a notice to the door of that
modest structure. It read:

"To the Honorable Governor and his Council of Virginia, in
Williamsburg:

"We, the undersigned magistrates of Queen Anne County,
wish to inform you of our intention to act in our said capacity, and,
by loyalty to our judicial oaths, and in conformity with and in
steadfast recognition of the intrinsical liberties guaranteed by our
charter and engrossed in our excellent Constitution, to dispense
justice and equity to the inhabitants of said county, whether or no
stamps required by the late Act of Parliament are available after the
first of November next; and, furthermore, we will in future refuse
to permit said stamps to bestow redundant, pretended, and abro-
gated legitimacy and sanctity upon any findings and proceedings
which the undersigned may effect in this venue.

"Thomas Reisdale. Reece Vishonn. Ira Granby. Ralph Cullis.
Moses Corbin. Jock Frazer."

Without fanfare, the attorney rode with his servant back to Freehold. Townsmen gathered at the courthouse door to read the notice. The notice caused them to talk, to speculate, to frown. A few of them turned and saw the sulky halfway down Queen Anne Street, and doffed their hats in salute.

John Proudlocks, in town to have some of Morland Hall's horses reshod at the smithy, noticed the crowd in front of the courthouse. He rode over, dismounted, and read the notice. "Ah!" he said to himself. "The sachem is a Long Knife after all!"

* * *

It was the second letter from county magistrates received by Lieutenant-Governor Fauquier. The first was from Westmoreland County, in which the justices tendered their resignations rather than "become instrumental in the destruction of our country's most essential rights and liberties." The one from Queen Anne County seemed to the Governor to indulge in outright delinquency. "Madness!" he exclaimed, tossing the letter down on his desk. "Sheer, brazen, hare-brained, lop-sided madness!"

"It smacks of rebellion, your honor," suggested the secretary who brought the letter to him. This man then reminded the Governor of the day's schedule, which included meeting some members of the Council at Mrs. Vobe's coffeehouse near the Capitol in one hour. "Will you walk, sir, or shall I order the carriage?"

By now Fauquier's pale features were livid. He rewarded the secretary with a scowl. "I shall walk!" he shouted angrily. "What do you think I am? An invalid? A fop? A macaroni?"

The secretary, startled by this uncharacteristic outburst, withdrew meekly from the office.

At the coffeehouse, Fauquier showed the letters to Councilmen John Blair and Peter Randolph. Blair was president of the Council and Auditor-General, Randolph, Surveyor-General of the Middle District, and brother of the Attorney-General, Peyton. "Madness, sirs!" fumed Fauquier. "Utter madness! What are we to do?" He had requested a meeting with these men to discuss the Westmoreland County letter. Now there were two letters for them to judge.

The Councilmen read the letters in turn and clucked their tongues.

"Let them be," advised Randolph. "The fever will subside, once the stamps have been made necessary to lawful adjudication."

"Yes," said Blair. "Once the people have accustomed themselves to their necessity, this reckless frivolity will cease. 'Tis but puffed-up nit-picking!"

"But they are challenging the constitutionality of the stamps, sirs!" protested Fauquier, "And Parliament's right to legislate for the colonies!" He wagged a finger at the Councilmen. "I tell you, gentlemen, I have lived in London, and know the difference between cankerous, rummaging mobs and rebellion! An ignorant rabble provoked by rogues like that Wilkes fellow is one thing! But a revolt by educated lawyers and justices is quite another! It is unprecedented!" Fauquier paused to catch his breath, then picked up one of the letters and tossed it back down again. "I have the distinct impression that they are *daring* me to act, calling me out to blades on the Palace Green with their effrontery! Every one of them!"

Randolph sighed and shook his head. "Do nothing, your honor. Deny them satisfaction."

Blair urged, "Yes, your honor. Do nothing. Take no notice of it. Wait to see how severe the fever is."

The conversation died for a moment, as it will when such counsel is given.

Blair thoughtfully sipped his coffee and helped himself to some bread that lay cut on a plate. He said, "I find it curious that so light a tax upsets so many bodies, your honor. The Assembly here is every bit as, shall we say, *onerous* in taxation as is Parliament. To me, the grounds for such a fuss as the people are making are muddy and quite shallow."

Randolph nodded in agreement. "My brother Peyton and I discussed this very question the other day, your honor. We concurred that if, by remote and absurd chance, the Act were rendered harmless, very likely attention could be turned to the Assembly itself. Why, we tax everything from carriage wheels to slaves to real property. We regulate taverns and ordinaries and the production and export of our tobacco, and charge the people for the imposition. I, too, am confounded by the distinction that is being trumpeted about! It is unfortunate that we cannot better instruct the people in the imperatives of state and empire. If we could — and it would necessitate another tax to accomplish the thing — we would see better behavior and reasonableness among the people."

Blair said, "I have heard that Mr. Mercer and Mr. Grenville were hanged in effigy in Westmoreland by that rascal Richard Henry Lee, and that he plans a demonstrative parade of some kind in this very town, before the General Court!" He scoffed. "Now, what kind of behavior is that on the part of a responsible, educated man?"

"One must suppose that he is feeling snittish about not having been appointed this colony's stamp distributor," remarked Randolph with smug condemnation. "He has formed an organization called the 'Sons of Liberty.' One must wonder where he got that appellation from."

"Very likely from that other rascal, Henry," speculated Blair. "It is in his style."

Randolph chuckled, "One may wonder, further, if his application for the office had been successful, then he might have formed an organization called the 'Sons of Placemen.'"

The two Councilmen laughed, temporarily oblivious to the Governor, who sat listening to this exchange with widening eyes.

Blair squinted in thought again, and said with more gravity, "It is absolutely imperative that Parliamentary authority in this matter be upheld, acknowledged, and respected. If it is not, we should not rest easy that the Assembly's authority is secure, simply because the people rally to its independence from what they claim is interference. If they succeed, the people may be inflamed by a sense of heady victory over so large a power, in having checked Parliament itself, and campaign to reconstitute the government here, as well, to remove what they may charge as burdensome and intrusive costs."

Fauquier blinked in incomprehension at the revelation, because it was a point that would never have occurred to him. The violence of the notion caused him to study his Councilmen as they talked. Both men were stout, well fed, and comfortable in their state. In fact, he thought, there was not a man on the Council who was not similarly endowed, except, perhaps, Thomas Nelson. There were Mr. Robinson, the Speaker of the House, and Randolph's brother, Peyton, the Attorney-General, and so many of the principal men in the House. All stout, fattened by time, power, and privileged profligacy.

Fauquier shifted in his chair and felt his own light frame, which was delicate and nearly fragile. The contrast caused him to blink again and shake his head in dismissal of the observation.

"Why, they could very well deny us the authority to tax or regulate them in any matter!" Blair was saying to Randolph. "Can you imagine any worse conundrum? In order to raise revenue for worthy projects and the security of the colony — not to mention our salaries and the costs of maintaining the machinery of our government — we would be compelled to *ask* them, hats in hand, like common beggars!"

Randolph frowned in puzzlement, then grinned. "I fear that your beverage has been doctored with some fantasizing herb, sir! Now you have flown out into the realm of comical farce! Pshaw! The day will never dawn when we would be required to *ask* for such a thing! That would be ascribing wisdom and foresight to common men, granting them the power to decide what was or was not a worthy end! It is a foul scenario you belabor, sir, and I will not entertain the prospect a moment more!"

"Banish the thought, sir, and forgive me for having spoken it!" replied Blair with mock humility. "My only excuse is that I have been perusing my stately library, and encountered a similar notion in some tract or other." He stopped to wonder why he had called his library "stately," then remembered the contemptuous oratory of Patrick Henry last May. He wondered why he should recall that particular phrase, and in turn deemed it contemptible and banished the thought from his mind.

Fauquier grimaced and spoke. The Councilmen glanced at him as though remembering he was present. The Governor glanced around furtively at the other patrons in the room. "Speak low when you trade such speculative ramblings, sirs!" he admonished them. He took a last sip of his coffee and rose from the table. Blair and Randolph rose as well. "I must return to my duties now. And if by chance I am beset by nightmares tonight, I shall have two of my Councilmen to blame!" He picked up his cane and made to leave.

"But your honor," asked Randolph, "what will you do about these justices?"

"I shall take your advice, sirs, and do nothing. There is nothing to be done, except to let the fever run its course."

* * *

Some days later, on a cloudless October afternoon, Thomas Reisdale, in one of his infrequent moods to stroll in the sun, wandered through his landscaped back lawn, inspecting the maze of boxwoods that had been planted in concentric crescents and the holly trees that stood in the center of each arc, a copy of Robert Molesworth's *An Account of Denmark as it was in 1692* tucked under his arm. When he heard, then saw, a riding chair and two horsemen come up the road that divided his fields and led to the great house, he walked back to the courtyard in the front of the house to wait for the party to arrive.

Jack Frake and John Proudlocks rode up, followed by Etáin in the riding chair. They exchanged greetings. Proudlocks was holding what looked like a banner fixed to an oaken staff. The banner was furled, secured by a cord.

"We have just come from Widow Heathcoate's shop," said Etáin.

"Is that the banner?" asked Reisdale.

"Yes." Jack nodded to Proudlocks, who reached up, untied the cord, and unfurled the banner. A warm breeze played at the folds, and Reisdale saw the red and white stripes undulate in the wind. In the cobalt canton he saw the motto of the Sons of Liberty, "Live free, or die," while "Sons of Liberty" was stitched in black on one of the middle white stripes.

"Surely," said the attorney, "you did not come here just to show me that. The Sons meet in a week."

Jack Frake shook his head. "We have seen your notice at the courthouse," he said. "I thought you deserved to see it first."

A strange sensation of pride and expectation tingled the attorney's heart and limbs. He did not understand it, at first. He was moved by the gesture. He thought the banner atrocious, gaudy, and crude. He was fascinated by it, and hoped he would have an excuse to carry it someday. The cloth and the colors represented a radical departure from everything he had ever known. They expressed a threat and a promise at the same time.

All these confusing thoughts occurred to him at once. Fighting a frustrating emotion, he stammered a thank you, and somehow managed to invite his callers inside for dinner without tripping over his suddenly hard-to-pronounce words.

Later, after his friends had left, Reisdale wandered again through his boxwood park in helpless elation, a feeling that was not just a feeling, one based on the knowledge that he was no longer merely a legal scholar or a "mental archives," as Hugh Kenrick had once called him. Now he was a man.

He felt dangerous. He did not know he was smiling.

* * *

Chapter 9: The Lacuna

Captain Walter Sterling, aged forty-five, was humming to himself over a glass of French brandy, rapidly signing a batch of clearance documents, when his steward knocked on the cabin door and announced the presence on board of a gentleman who wished to see him on urgent Crown business.

Sterling, captain of the *Rainbow*, a fifth-rate frigate now riding anchor off Old Point Comfort, Hampton, commanded a busy fleet of smaller warships and vessels that policed the waters of Chesapeake Bay, gateway to all of Virginia's rivers. His task was to ensure that all vessels of trade and commerce, British and colonial, that came and went carried the correct papers for their enumerated cargoes, to discourage and capture smugglers, and to collect the Crown's due when a vessel's paperwork contained irregularities and deficiencies. He was also empowered to seize and impound vessels whose captains or masters flagrantly and with criminal intent flouted the navigation laws.

One such was being detained in Norfolk now, fresh from Lisbon with wine, oil, and arrack. Sterling was still awaiting judgment from the admiralty court in Halifax about whether or not Captain Jeremiah Morgan of the *Hornet* had taken it at sea or within the capes on Chesapeake Bay. If taken at sea, then Sterling, Morgan, and their crews would be entitled to half the proceeds from the sale of the vessel and its cargo; if taken on the Bay, one-third of those proceeds could be claimed by Lieutenant-Governor Fauquier. Naturally, Sterling hoped the court would recognize a seizure at sea. He was accustomed to such delays; this kind of jurisdictional spat had arisen before.

"Who is it?" he asked the steward, not looking up.

"Mr. George Mercer, sir," answered the man, a rating assigned to wait upon the captain.

Sterling paused in the middle of a signature in recognition of the name, but finished signing the form, and said, "All right. Show him down."

He knew the name well, and that this person was the appointed stamp distributor for the colony. He knew also that this person had been hanged in effigy in various towns and hamlets throughout the colony, even in Hampton. He had heard the man's name cursed in the taverns and inns in Old Point Comfort, which he often frequented as a relief from the fare of the *Rainbow*'s galley. He wondered how so disliked a man was going to fulfill his duty or keep his place.

The captain was ambivalent about the Stamp Act, no copy of which he had yet received. Enforcing it would simply add a new burden to his job here. It would mean increased vigilance, additional checking and inspections, and even more unpleasantness than usual. If there were any truth to the stories reported by his officers and crews about what was occurring in Virginia and Maryland, enforcing the Act was going to be very difficult, indeed. Or, he reflected, perhaps not. There was also a rumor going about that all commerce itself might cease until the colonials' complaints received some form of redress, or until the colonials submitted to the Act.

Sterling heard footsteps approaching his door. He rose, slipped into his coat and patted his bob-wig to make sure it sat true, then sat back in his chair and waited.

The steward showed in George Mercer, a young man of thirty-one or so. Sterling frowned, startled by the visitor's appearance. There were bruises on the fellow's face, and a large one that was just a hue short of a black eye. The lower lip was cut in two places. There were rips in the man's frock coat, and buttons were missing from it. The hose beneath his breeches was torn on both calves. The man looked like a London beggar. Sterling half expected him to utter a whining plea and hold out his hand.

Mercer removed his hat and tucked it under his arm. "Thank you, sir," he said, "for allowing me to intrude upon your time. Captain Anderson sends his compliments."

Still startled by the man's state, the captain rose and indicated a chair before his desk. "Anderson?" he asked dumbly.

Mercer smiled weakly and sat down. "Of the *Leeds*, sir, my conveyance from England, just now dropped anchor at Point Comfort." He paused, and added, "A few hours ago, that is."

"Oh, yes. Anderson," said Sterling. "I see." He picked up his glass. It was empty. "May I offer you some brandy? No, no, I have just finished the last bottle. Some Chateau Lafite, perhaps? A very good claret. Have a bumper of it, sir, and then you may explain your, er, condition." Without waiting for a reply, he took a key from his coat pocket, went to a cabinet, and unlocked it. He took an open bottle from the cache of liquor inside — most of it "captured" from offending vessels — and found two more glasses. When he had finished serving his visitor and himself, he said, raising his glass, "To your health, sir — or what remains of it."

Mercer smiled weakly again, nodded in thanks, and drank, wincing when the liquor touched his lip.

Sterling took his seat, and said, "But, first, please confirm for me that you are indeed the same Mr. Mercer who is the...expected stamp distributor."

Mercer nodded, and put down his glass on the edge of Sterling's desk. "I am that person, sir."

"How did you come here?"

"On Captain Anderson's skiff, direct from the *Leeds*."

"I see. Well...?" prompted Sterling, gesturing with a hand.

Mercer said, with some bitterness in his words, "I must assure you, sir, that in spite of my experience — nay, perhaps even *because* of it — I am determined to meet the terms of my commission." He saw the captain's expectant look. "It was a frightening experience, sir. I went ashore with the other passengers to await my luggage and also my brother, who is to meet me here with our chaise. I have been away for two years, and naturally my luggage is considerable. I knew I should have to wait until it was retrieved from the hold and assembled. I repaired to a chophouse I had patronized in the past, and someone from my county — from Frederick, that is — happened also to be there, and recognized me. He was John Hite, a fellow I bested in our county elections years ago. He got but one vote, and it was his own! By the time I had finished my plate, a group of men, including that fellow, had gathered outside. Cads, ruffians, and lumpers, they looked like. One of them said, 'There's the king's pick-purse!' and soon I found myself encircled. At first, I was assaulted by taunts and rude names, then by hands and fists. They played a very mortal game of hot cockles with me. I could hardly defend myself and knew I was in great peril. My injuries might have been more severe, had not a group of passing gentlemen come to my rescue and dispersed this mob with canes and swords. I do believe I was intended to be tossed off the dock into the water and dunked until I was drowned!" Mercer paused, unsure about whether to be ashamed or outraged. "My sword and pocket watch were taken during this ambuscade. I returned to the *Leeds* and apprised Captain Anderson of the matter."

"Rough lot, some of those lubbers." Sterling shook his head in sympathy. "I have a surgeon onboard, sir. Will you need his attentions?"

"No, sir. Thank you," replied Mercer bravely.

"Has your brother arrived?"

Mercer nodded. "Shortly after the incident, he came into town. He awaits me there. He brought word of the danger to me, even in the Capitol!"

Sterling put on a puzzled grin. "But, sir, did you not expect such a reception? These parts have been riled for some time, since June. Several of your commissioned colleagues have been obliged to resign their appointments, in fear for their lives and property." He paused to study his visitor. "And, you, sir, have been manikinned, hanged, and burned clear from the Potomac to Norfolk, together with Mr. Grenville and poor Lord Bute!" He chuckled. "Why, one of my officers was in Williamsburg yesterday, and returned to report that one of your fellow burgesses — oh, yes, I know you are in the House, how could I help but know, for all the chatter! — he conducted a parade of manikins down the main street there, consisting of a hangman's cart pulled by Negroes in high boots and red coats. On the cart were you and Mr. Grenville. Several fellows acting as sheriffs, bailiffs, and the like followed, including the instigator of the affair. What is his name, now? Oh, yes! Lee. Richard Henry Lee, of Westmoreland." He paused. "My officer reported that it was quite a novelty, and the crowds were entertained immensely and quite friendly to the spectacle."

"Lee!" spat Mercer. "I understand that he applied for my commission! How waspish of him, to behave in such a manner!"

"Fair is foul, and foul is fair," remarked Sterling. "Well, sir," he said, sitting back in his chair, "what *is* the purpose of your call?"

Mercer made himself comfortable. "It is this, sir: The stamps I must convey to the Capitol are on the *Leeds*. Though they accompanied me on the voyage, I have not officially taken charge of them. Captain Anderson wishes to proceed on his vessel's business, once he has been cleared. In any event, he does not wish the stamps to remain on his vessel. There are three consignments of the stamped paper and stamps in his hold: one for Virginia, and one each for Maryland and North Carolina. Captain Anderson has asked me to speak with you about their security."

"I see." Sterling took another sip of his claret, then gazed out his stern window into the bright late-October afternoon. Something caught his attention. He picked up a spyglass and with it swept the vista beyond. "Ah!" he commented, "there's the *Falmouth*, just coming in. And the

Morag, too, Mr. Kennaway's schooner, brailing her sails, as well. And the *Excelsior*" — he turned with a smile to Mercer, and added with a note of confidentiality, "she needs careful auditing, her Captain Washburn would slip in the King of France if he thought he could wool my eyes —" then turned back to his spyglass, "and there's the *Sparrowhawk*, just tacking to port. What a rush of business of a sudden!" He turned to Mercer again and put the spyglass aside. "Good crossing, Mr. Mercer?"

The Virginian nodded. "Yes, sir. It was a swift and amiable passage. The *Sparrowhawk*? She nearly rode our wake the whole way, sir. We thought she would pass us, a few times."

Sterling said, "Fine ship. I know the captain well." He shook his head. "A damned difficult situation we have here, sir. I cannot assume responsibility for the stamps, not unless I receive a request from Governor Fauquier. That is something you must discuss with him. Of course, should he request it, I will comply. After all, he is vice-admiral of these waters. I am in regular communication with him." He paused. "May I ask how you planned to deliver the articles to Williamsburg?"

Mercer shrugged listlessly. "I had hoped to hire a vessel to take them up the York to Queen's Creek and Capitol Landing, and thence to the Capitol. My brother, father, and I arranged by letter months ago that my brother would meet me here today or tomorrow, to convey me and my baggage by chaise." He paused. "But I did not know how serious the tumult was here, until just a few hours ago. Now is it especially urgent that I get to the Capitol, as soon as possible. The General Court opens in a few days, and the Governor doubtless is relying on me to make the stamps available. I would not wish to compromise him or inconvenience the Court."

Sterling's eyebrows rose. "Of course not. But I have heard that courts throughout the colonies may not even open, come their time, in protest of the Act." He barked once in contempt. "Why, even the justices have chosen to discount the law! You would think they would welcome another law to enforce!"

"That may be, sir," replied Mercer with some testiness. "So, it is of utmost importance that our General Court set an example for other superior courts to follow, and conduct its business in conformance with the law, with the stamps." He reached for his glass of claret and took a gulp. "Can the *Leeds* be detained until I have spoken with the Governor?"

Sterling cocked his head. "I don't see why not," he answered tentatively. "I imagine that now Captain Anderson must regard the stamps as a hex, and will not leave until he is rid of them."

Mercer put his glass down and swallowed his spit. "Until they are employed, sir, may I stress that the stamps are Crown property? I...believe the Navy must at some point act or be asked to ensure their security."

Sterling frowned and turned his head slowly to Mercer. His eyes narrowed, and he replied frigidly, "I am aware of my duties, sir." Then he looked away to stare into space.

Mercer blinked and ploughed on. "The stamps are packed in three sealed crates. Now that I have a truer picture of the ferment here, I believe that the ones marked for Annapolis and Wilmington ought to be taken in hand by the Navy and delivered to those towns. I had intended to arrange for their transportation on a private vessel. In view of the circumstances, I believe that is now a foolhardy plan." He paused, and leaned forward to address the icy profile of the captain. "Sir, I am not presuming to instruct you in your duties. I am certain they have occurred to you. I am merely telling you what I would expect Governor Fauquier will tell me. Forgive me if I sound impertinent."

Sterling's eyes slid in Mercer's direction in acknowledgement of the apology. Then he slapped a hand on the pile of customs forms at his elbow. "Here is what I can do, sir. The stamps must remain on the *Leeds*. I will detain her on some irregularity or other until I hear from you or the Governor. I can arrange to have the *Diligence* take one consignment to Wilmington, and the *Charlotte* another to Annapolis. These are swift, ten-gun sloops, sir, the best chasers on the Bay. However, I will not act on that, either, until have heard from you or the Governor." He smiled at the crestfallen look on his visitor's face. *Presumptuous puppy!* he thought. *No lubber gives me orders and expects me to jump!* Then he said, "I am keen for some mischief to break the routine here, sir. The General Court must sit, and sit it will! I share your ardor in that respect!" He grunted once in happy anger. "By God! Between us, we will show these blustering Boanerges that they can't toy with the Crown and not expect a bellyful of shot in reply!" He paused. "Would the Virginia stamps fit onto your brother's chaise?"

"Hardly, sir," answered Mercer, intrigued. "The crate would likely break the wheels. It would require a suttler's wagon to move it. The paper in it is destined for all the courts here, not just the General Court, and there is enough of it of various kinds to last two years."

"I see. Well, we must think of something else, then. You may have noticed my contingent of marines, sir. They are idle. I was thinking of providing you an escort." Sterling looked wicked, and massaged his chin in thought. "Ah! Here it is, then! You will return to the *Leeds*. Break open the Virginia crate. Remove from it a small amount of what you think the General Court alone will need for its immediate business. Have Anderson repack it into a smaller crate. I'm sure he has spare material in his hold that can accommodate you. The balance of the stamps may be brought in and introduced in due time. Then, this is what I propose...."

When Sterling had finished, Mercer pondered the idea for a moment. Then he said, "It is a rather round-about way to deliver the stamps, sir."

Sterling shrugged. "Of course, the new box could easily be fitted onto your chaise. But would you want to chance another assault by ruffians, this time with the true object of their hatred in your possession? I fear you would risk more permanent damage. It is many miles between here and Williamsburg, and you would likely encounter persecutors every other one of them."

Mercer looked disgusted, and made a face. "For the Crown to need to resort to such sneakish ruses and cowardly circumspection — it is ignoble and humiliating!" he protested.

"I agree," replied the captain with empathy. He added with righteous enthusiasm, "But, together, we shall make them pay for the ploy! You in Williamsburg, and I, here!"

Mercer sighed. "All right, sir. I agree to the plan."

Sterling smiled. "I guarantee that you will be able to supply the General Court with all the stamps it needs, sir, and promise that you will have them a full day before they are required." He rose and filled both their glasses again with the claret, then raised his glass in salute. "To King George, sir!"

Mercer rose also and half-heartedly raised his glass. "Long live the king," he said.

* * *

Hugh Kenrick had never met George Mercer in the House of Burgesses — that representative for Frederick County having been absent the last two years — and so did not recognize him when he observed that man and his brother pass him on the street in a paired chaise on their hurried way out of Old Point Comfort. He had heard that Mercer had arrived and was roughed up by a mob some hours before the *Morag* dropped anchor and her few passengers came ashore. The tavern he had gone to for a hearty dinner was loud with talk of Mercer and the incident, a cacophony of anger, boasting, and jest.

He had left New York before the Congress ended so that he could be in Caxton or Williamsburg on November first, when the Act was to go into effect, and managed to find a berth on the *Morag*, which carried a cargo of salt licks, pickling vinegar, and barrels of oatmeal and English split peas. The speed of the schooner left him in awe; three days from New York harbor to Hampton. He had had lively talks with the captain, Ian Kennaway, who was once a Scottish tobacco factor on Long Island but had decided to strike out on his own. The salt licks would be deposited in Kennaway's Hampton warehouse and sold to local farmers, and the *Morag* would proceed to Norfolk with the rest of the cargo.

What a difference in opposition to the Act, he observed, from the grave convocation of the Stamp Act Congress in New York, roisterous as it sometimes became! There was more reading in his travel bag than he had taken with him to New York: a draft of the Congress resolutions, a *Maryland Gazette* that contained the Maryland Resolves, a copy of Daniel Dulany's pamphlet, *Considerations on the Propriety of Imposing Taxes in British Colonies*, and other pamphlets and broadsides he had collected during his two weeks there.

The Stamp Act Congress's resolutions and the Maryland Resolves had adopted the format of Patrick Henry's Resolves of last May. He had read all the material many times over, and while the protests elated him, something about them disturbed him. Something was missing from them. It made him uneasy, knowing that something was absent in all those brave, defiant words. He could not put his mind's finger on it. There was a glaring lacuna, not in the texts of the literature, but in their spirit.

Hugh had left the chophouse and was walking along the front street, on his way to the hostler's stables, where Spears had left a mount for him to ride back to Caxton. He could pay the hostler and be saddled for the long ride to Caxton in half an hour. He was eager to get back to Meum Hall and share his experiences in New York with Jack Frake and Thomas Reisdale.

He saw a group of people cross the front street to the chophouse from the dock, and only then realized that the *Sparrowhawk* was moored and that these people were probably passengers.

There were seven men and six women in the group. One of the women was tall, graceful, and queenly with ease. There was something attractive and commanding in her haughtiness. Her black eyes matched her black hair, which was pinned up under a straw sun hat secured by a red ribbon.

It was Reverdy Brune.

Hugh stood stunned, unable to move, to think, to react in any way or form.

It was she. Some years older. And magnificently so. Worthy of the statue he had once planned to have made of her, and put on a pedestal in a private Doric temple.

He stood watching the group as it made its way to the chophouse. A man was with her. It was not Alex McDougal, her husband, but James Brune, her brother. Where was her husband? He was not among the men. What was she doing here?

He stood transfixed by the vision, remembering his love for her, and his recriminatory words to her in his last letter, so long ago....

"Mr. Kenrick...?"

Hugh thought he heard a voice, and dreamily shifted his attention to its source. He found himself staring into the concerned eyes of John Ramshaw, captain of the *Sparrowhawk*. "Mr. Ramshaw...hello," he answered, startled by the man's presence, but not yet fully conscious of it.

"Greetings, sir," said the captain. "If you please, I have little time and urgent information for you."

Hugh forced himself to forget what he had seen, and pay attention to the man. "How did you know I would be here, sir?"

"I didn't. I came ashore to hire a fellow to ride like hell to Caxton to deliver a message to you and Mr. Frake. But, here you are!" The captain paused and nodded to the travel bag in Hugh's hand. "Are you embarking on a voyage?"

Hugh shook his head. "No. I have just arrived, on the *Moray*, from the congress in New York."

"What congress?"

Hugh explained the purpose of the congress, and brought the captain up to date on all the events since the *Sparrowhawk*'s last visit.

"Trouble!" exclaimed Ramshaw. "I was certain of it! What did this congress accomplish?"

"More assertions of liberty and appeals to reason," answered Hugh.

"They may as well be appeals to heaven," remarked the captain, "for all the good they will do."

"What message, sir?"

Ramshaw glanced up and down the front street, then took Hugh's elbow and led him to stroll down the length of the waterfront. "Have you heard about Mr. Mercer, the stamp distributor who has just arrived?"

"Yes, and that he was assaulted."

"He has brought stamps with him," said Ramshaw. He nodded to the *Rainbow* sitting offshore. "He and Captain Sterling there have conspired to deliver some of them to your Capitol in two days."

"I don't understand."

"They mean to bring them in through Caxton, Mr. Kenrick, and I have been pressed to assist them in the subterfuge."

"Pressed? How?"

"The good captain promised not to rummage my ship for contraband — and half my cargo is that, as you well know. At least, that was his insinuation." Ramshaw paused. "They are afraid that the stamps will be seized and destroyed by rebels. And if Mr. Mercer's treatment today is any measure of the animosity at large here, that is a certain wager, if care is not taken."

"Did you not protest?" asked Hugh.

"No! How could I? I am a loyal subject of His Majesty and a strict abider by all his laws!" replied Ramshaw with irony. He grinned. "Better the devil you know, than the one you don't. But I am a devil of a different bent." Ramshaw scoffed angrily. "He called on my ship with a crew ready to begin knackering it to pieces. He calls me 'friend.'"

"But why Caxton?" asked Hugh. "And why your vessel? There are other merchantmen here, and the naval vessels, as well."

"My first calls in these waters have always been Hampton, Yorktown, Caxton, and West Point, in that order, and occasionally planters' piers on the York. Sterling knows this." He waved a hand at the Bay. "All the others there are sailing south." Ramshaw paused and took out a pipe. "As for Caxton? He explained his reasoning to me, the trusting soul. The stamps cannot be taken overland, for fear of seizure and altercation. Yorktown he deems a haven of sedition and treason. And Capitol Landing would be too embarrassing to your good Governor, should the ruse be detected. Many of the farmers at Porto Bello there are in debt, he said, and would have a special interest in alerting interested rebels if he attempted to bring the stamps up Queen's Creek. No stamps, you see, so no court, no creditors' suits!" The captain packed his pipe and lit it. "Caxton, however, in his judgment, is peaceful and innocuous."

"And, not half a day's ride from Williamsburg," said Hugh.

"Yes. Mr. Mercer is proceeding to his father's house there. That is where the stamps are to be delivered, the day before the General Court opens, on the first."

"Why not to the Palace?"

"Again, they do not want to risk embarrassing the Governor."

"Delivered by whom?"

"Mr. Sterling will make me a gift of one of his lieutenants and a body of trusted crewmen. They will be aboard the *Sparrowhawk* when it goes to Caxton. Then they will take the stamps to Mr. Mercer."

Hugh frowned. "They will not set foot in Caxton, I can promise you that!" exclaimed Hugh. He told Ramshaw about the Sons of Liberty, and their resolve to prohibit the presence and use of stamps in Queen Anne County.

Ramshaw laughed. "Well, how about that!" But then he looked grave. "Will your Sons be willing to foil this business at any risk, sir? Will they carry arms?"

Hugh frowned in turn. "No. I don't see why arms would be necessary."

"You may think it necessary, sir. You see, the *Sparrowhawk* will be followed at a distance by one of Captain Sterling's tenders. On it will be half a company of marines. They will intervene if there is trouble, and escort the stamps to Williamsburg if it is thought necessary to ensure their safe delivery."

"When do you leave?" asked Hugh.

"Tomorrow morning, at the break of dawn. You ought to see my sails approach Caxton the next morning, the thirty-first." Ramshaw puffed on his pipe. "Sterling confided in me the most curious aspect of this business. He instructed Mr. Mercer not to reveal any of it to the Governor, who would learn of it only when he heard that there was a party of ratings and marines in the Capitol. He fears that if the Governer got wind of it, he might be struck with funk and order the plan abandoned." The captain laughed again. "It seems that the only person willing to marry himself to the stamps is Mr. Mercer. Sterling will not accept responsibility for them, unless ordered to, and the Governor will not, because he would not wish to risk souring the love for him that he believes the people here have. That is how Sterling explained it to me." He shook his head in dark appreciation. "He knows his men, on board and off!"

Hugh scoffed. "Would that the king were so mindful of his prestige! He would save his subjects and himself so much grief that is sure to come, if he had devoted a moment's thought before signing the Act!"

Ramshaw remarked, "Well, kings don't need to think, or so I've heard." He puffed on his pipe thoughtfully, then asked, "So, dear Mr. Barret is gone?"

"Yes," answered Hugh. "That has cost the Governor some love in Caxton."

"Who is accepting mail there now?"

"Mr. Safford."

"Very well." Ramshaw took a sealed sheet of folded paper from inside his coat. He held it out to Hugh. "This contains all the particulars of the ruse, Mr. Kenrick," he said. "I was to entrust it to a stranger. Instead, I give it to a friend."

Hugh took the paper and tucked it inside one of his pockets. "Thank you, sir. You must stay at Meum Hall, when you come to Caxton." He wrestled with a desire to query the captain about his passengers. He wrestled in turn with his desire to get to Caxton as quickly as possible, and with the desire to enter the chophouse and see Reverdy. He smiled at his old friend, then frowned. "And you, sir? If the Act is not repealed or amended, how would you fare?"

Ramshaw shook his head again. "I wouldn't. My man can counterfeit everything but those bloody stamps! And they can't be purchased *sub rosa*. So, I am for repeal. I am also for the freedom to trade without cockets and bills and the likes of Captain Sterling." He sighed. "Well, now I must join my former passengers at the inn up there for a feast of eatables. Even my cook has repaired to the place! Interesting group I brought over, this time. Plumb folks visiting their kin here. Then there is Mr. James Brune, who has come over to survey the possibilities for trade here. I have advised him that Norfolk is the place for him. He is employed by some Scottish firm. His sister accompanied him for the tour."

"How odd," said Hugh reluctantly, thinking his voice was cracking and betraying his interest, "that he would bring his sister on such a rigorous journey."

Ramshaw laughed. "Now, sir, you are insulting my accommodations!" he said in jest. "But not at all odd. Seems she was married to his employer's son. He died in a riding accident, and she wished to expend her grief in the diversion. Her family, I understand, hold stock in her late husband's firm, and her brother has stepped into his place."

Hugh shut his eyes briefly, then said, "Well, I must go to Caxton, and you to fair company." He took the captain's hand and shook it. "Thank you again for the intelligence. Forewarned is forearmed." He paused. "Do not be surprised by what you may see, when you come to Caxton."

"I'll try not to give myself away," said Ramshaw. "'Til we meet again, sir." He turned and strode back down the street in the direction of the chophouse.

For a while, Hugh was conscious only of sounds: the wind blowing in from the Bay, the crying of seagulls, the groans of docked merchantmen pulling on the hawsers that tied them to the land.

Hugh pursed his lips in determination, then turned and walked briskly to the hostler's stables, where he paid the stable boy a crown to saddle his horse. Then he mounted and left the stable.

He could not resist going by the chophouse. He paused. There, through the window glass, he saw Reverdy's profile at a table. She turned and saw him, and her eyes widened in recognition.

Hugh did not see her astonishment. By now he had wrenched his sight away from her, dug his heels into his mount's sides, and struck the rump of the horse with his riding crop. The horse broke into a gallop. Hugh did not rein it in to a slower pace until he was well out of the town, on the road that cut diagonally across the peninsula to Williamsburg.

Some hours later, he cantered past a paired chaise with two men, and left them behind.

* * *

Chapter 10: The Lieutenant

Lieutenant James Harke, aged twenty-two, of the *Rainbow*, did not grasp his dilemma until he was halfway up the York River. He stood on the *Sparrowhawk*'s quarterdeck, watching the opposite bank glide by as the pilot took the merchantman up the middle of the river. It suddenly occurred to him that he had been delegated a responsibility — and possibly even a liability — that he did not want and did not think it was right of Captain Sterling to delegate. His eagerness and impatience to perform a welcome duty soured with his growing suspicion of having been duped.

He knew that he could hardly have protested his orders, which were to deliver a box of stamps and stamped paper to George Mercer's residence in Williamsburg, by way of Caxton, with "the least disturbance of the populace and with utmost discretion." The captain had explained the reasons for the ruse and pointed out the risks. An earlier plan to dispatch a tender with a complement of marines to follow the *Sparrowhawk* and support Harke and his party had been abandoned as "too likely provocative and risky." Harke commanded a party of ten crewmen, each man armed with a cutlass, sword, or pistol. Leading them was Bosun Will Olland. Harke had briefly met Mercer before that man was rowed ashore from the *Rainbow* to begin his journey to his father's house in Williamsburg.

Harke glanced at the object of the conspiracy, which sat on the quarterdeck not three feet away, a brown wooden container, roughly knocked together, about half the size of a sea chest. Carrying poles were fixed to its sides. He and his party were to quick march it to Williamsburg and deliver it. He had been instructed where to find the residence of the stamp distributor's father there. Once the stamps were delivered, he and his party were to find a vessel to transport them back to Hampton. Harke was to hire or commandeer a vessel at Capitol Landing or Yorktown to convey him and his party back to the *Rainbow*.

They were not to dally in Caxton or the Capitol, lest the colonials take exception to their presence or wonder about the purpose of their mission and create an incident.

Sterling assured the lieutenant that he would not encounter any oppo-sition in Caxton — "it is a sedate and loyal hamlet, I have heard that the court there intends to carry on its business nevertheless" — nor on the road to Williamsburg. Sterling gave him strict instructions not to stop in Caxton, but to pass immediately through it and over the Hove Stream bridge. If he were to be asked by anyone what his business was, he was to say only that he and his party were on Crown business, and no more than that.

If pressed for a better answer, he was to say that Captain Sterling was an acquaintance of Mr. Mercer, and that his party was delivering as a favor some of Mr. Mercer's personal property that had been misplaced in the *Leed*'s stowage and found only after Mr. Mercer had departed Hampton. "Above all," cautioned the captain, "avoid communication with anyone in the government there. No one in it must know or suspect the purpose of this plan, especially not the Governor."

The dubious legality of his mission had since dawned on the lieu-tenant. Because he led a party of armed men, whom he would naturally order to defend themselves and their burden if attacked, an admiralty court and a civilian court could easily view the plan as an attempt to "visit vio-lence upon civilians without the leave of a civil magistrate, in an illegal action to suppress without authority rioting and anarchy." Harke and Ster-ling could be cashiered from the Navy and charged with criminal offenses, even though their actions were taken in an effort to enforce Crown law. Perhaps, in that instance, a court might make an exception, together with the consideration that the violence was visited on mere rebellious colonials. It depended on the seriousness of the incident and the political sensitivity of the men charged with judging the circumstances.

But Harke knew that there was no way to predict with any confidence how a court would interpret the intent or execution of the plan. If an inci-dent occurred and the matter were sent for judgment to a court of inquiry, he knew that Captain Sterling had enough influence in the upper strata of the naval establishment to ensure that responsibility would be deflected from him and placed directly on his lieutenant's shoulders.

Harke grinned bitterly as he recalled Sterling's words: *least disturbance to the populace...utmost discretion.* Such caution could be interpreted three-score different ways! And the relationship between the naval and civilian establishments was rife with so many contradictions! Officers could be cashiered for upholding Crown law by bashing the heads of gin-sodden rioters without the Riot Act first having been read, yet he himself had led press gangs in London and Portsmouth to "visit violence" on men who resisted involuntary servitude in His Majesty's Navy, a common "crime" fully sanctioned by the muteness of civilian courts.

Harke stood quietly fuming a few feet away from Captain John Ramshaw, who had said little to him the whole trip except for the usual cordial chat. The man's vessel had been literally commandeered for the mission, so he could not blame the man for his stingy reticence. Harke's men stood below him in a group on the main deck, apart from the vessel's few passengers, silent and apprehensive. He heard the pilot call to the topmen in the masts to give him more canvas to catch more of the slight breeze that propelled them upriver. He thought he heard a church bell ring in the far distance, but his mind was too focused on his dilemma to pay it much attention. He stood stiffly at the rail, almost at attention, rocking on his feet now and then, hands clasped behind his back, one of them gripping a spyglass.

Some time later, Ramshaw returned from some chores in his cabin below, and stood next to him. "Caxton half a league ahead, Mr. Harke."

Harke nodded in silent acknowledgement and turned to look in that direction. Beneath a cloudless blue sky he saw the steeple of Stepney Parish church and the still arms of a miller's windmill on the bluff overlooking a narrow waterfront of wooden and brick structures. There was a crowd on the riverbank at the piers. As the *Sparrowhawk* neared the town, Harke discerned a man on horseback in the throng holding what looked like a flag on a staff. It fluttered in the wind and he recognized the stripes of an East India jack. He brought up his spyglass and trained it on that object. Yes, it was an East India jack, but the red cross and white canton had been replaced with a blue canton, on which was some lettering he could not make out from this distance.

"What the devil...?" he muttered to himself. He ranged the glass over the crowd itself. He saw men in it carrying muskets, and others holding staves or long-handled farming tools. The muskets, he noted, were not brandished in any threatening or challenging manner; their bearers looked at leisure, as though they were waiting their turn at a shooting match. Still, thought Harke, the tableau had the character of a military assembly.

He made up his mind then and there. His mission was hopeless. Sterling was wrong about Caxton: It was as much a venue of resistance to the stamps as Yorktown and Norfolk. He glanced once at Ramshaw. That man was leaning on the railing, seemingly as curious about the tableau as was he.

Harke frowned. Somehow, the colonials had been warned about this expedition.

He resolved to try once to persuade the authorities in that crowd to allow him and his party to pass. Failing that, he would return with his men and the stamps on the first vessel the pilot would take back downriver. He saw two smaller coastal vessels and a sloop secured to the piers.

He felt the eyes of Bosun Olland and the crewmen on him. He turned a blank face in their direction, and they looked away. They saw that it was futile, as well. Harke grimaced and trained his glass again on the jack. The wind played with it enough so that he could read the words in the blue canton: *Live free, or die.*

* * *

An hour before, Reverend Albert Acland of Stepney Parish church was in his vegetable garden at the side of the rectory, fretting over his insect-infested potatoes and cursing the hornworms that had eaten so many leaves in his tobacco patch — that tobacco was a money crop and had sustained him in hard times — when he heard the pounding of hooves approaching the church on Queen Anne Street. The rider seemed to stop directly in front of the church. Then he heard the church door open and someone race through the space to the altar.

He jumped once when the single bell in the modest steeple began ringing with some odd urgency.

"What the devil...?" he exclaimed. He left the garden and rushed inside the church through a back door to see who was committing the outrage. Inside the bellroom, he nearly collided with the culprit, Henry Buckle, Thomas Reisdale's cooper. "What are you doing?" he demanded of the man.

"Ringing the bell, sir," replied Buckle, still pulling on the rope.

"Why?"

"You will soon see, sir!" said Buckle. "Come to the waterfront in an hour!"

"Well," said Acland, "stop this instant! People all over will think something is wrong!"

Buckle grinned at his pastor. "That's the idea, sir! Something is wrong! Just a few tugs more!"

"What are you talking about?" sputtered the minister. "Stop, I say!"

Buckle let go of the bell rope and smiled almost like a lunatic at the red-faced minister. "The stamps are coming!" he exclaimed as the bell above them swung on its timber to peal in diminishing loudness. "We're going to send 'em back where they came from!" Then he rushed out, leaving Acland to wonder what it was all about.

Over the next hour, he watched with growing trepidation as men and women closed their shops along Queen Anne Street and walked singly or in groups toward the waterfront and River Road below the bluff. Soon he noted people from outlying farms and plantations hurrying in the same direction.

But what sent his heart to his mouth was the sight of Jack Frake, Hugh Kenrick, and John Proudlocks riding together on horseback amongst a group of men he knew were members of the Sons of Liberty. Jack Frake carried a banner, the likes of which the minister had never seen before. Following them in a sulky was Thomas Reisdale, and on horseback behind him the five other justices of the county court, lately adjourned after a three-day sitting.

"What do you make of this, Mr. Harke?" asked Ramshaw. "You'd think they were expecting a visit by the king! What a royal reception!"

Harke glanced again at the captain, unsure whether the man was serious or was mocking him.

"I hope it is mere dumb-show and noise, sir," he replied, using a phrase whose origins he only vaguely recollected. He had read *Hamlet* years ago in school, but had forgotten the source of his inaccurate but somehow apt choice of words.

"Well, I know those people a mite," said Ramshaw. "A few stern words will part the ways for you and your men. Invoke the name of the king. That usually does the trick."

Harke did not think it would. He did not communicate this thought to his host.

Ramshaw said, "Sir, allow my passengers to disembark first."

"No," answered the officer. "Someone may alert those people down there."

"I believe they have already been alerted, Mr. Harke." Ramshaw clucked his tongue. "Well, sir. Something of a drama at work here! If you go ahead with Captain Sterling's plan, you may be remembered in history as the man who delivered the stamps over a beach strewn with casualties, in what may be called by some wit the beginning of our second Civil War, or perhaps our second Glorious Revolution!" He paused. "Perhaps you will be available for an interview."

"Enough, Mr. Ramshaw," replied the lieutenant with some tartness. "I see the situation here. I will not press the matter."

They were saved an argument. When the *Sparrowhawk* was secured by hawsers and the gangboard was lowered, and as the anchors were being dropped, several men who looked like gentlemen approached down the pier and stopped to wait at the bottom. One of them was the man whom Harke had first noticed carrying the altered jack. That object was now being held by a dark-complexioned fellow who sat easily in his saddle behind the crowd below.

Ramshaw preceded Harke down the gangboard to face the waiting men. The leader, a tall, flaxen-haired man with impenetrable gray eyes and a grimly set jaw, nodded once to the captain, who silently returned the greeting and stepped aside. The leader turned immediately to face Harke. Before the lieutenant could speak, he asked, "Are you the officer entrusted with delivering a consignment of stamps to Colonel Mercer in Williamsburg?"

Harke frowned in surprise. What brass! "If I am, sir, I don't see that it is any of your business."

"Colonel Mercer sent word to the sheriff of this county with a request that he take custody of them. The sheriff has declined to. He cannot ensure their safety."

"Are you the sheriff?" asked Harke, more intrigued by this change of plan than put out by it.

"No. But I speak for him."

"Then I will speak with that gentleman, sir," replied Harke with all the officiousness he could muster.

The tall man shook his head. "He does not wish to speak with you, sir."

Harke wanted to reply that this was not the arrangement that he, Sterling, and Mercer had agreed upon in the cabin of the *Rainbow*. There was no mention of transferring custody of the stamps to anyone but George Mercer. But he had not been impressed with that man's resolve and was not surprised to hear that he had made other arrangements. Harke stayed his tongue. Instead, he said, addressing the leader and the group of men behind him, "I am on Crown business, sirs, and my best advice to you is to allow me to discharge my duty." He paused. "What are your names?"

The leader replied with matching coolness, "Our names are none of your business."

Harke scrutinized the delegation. These men were too well dressed to be rabble. They were probably planters. But most of the crowd beyond seemed composed of farmers, tradesmen, and artisans, with a sprinkling of women. Children and slaves also stood in the throng. Harke wondered which person in the crowd was the sheriff.

He noticed one solitary figure standing at the head of the road that rose from the waterfront to the top of the bluff, a man dressed in the somber hues of a minister.

Captain Ramshaw, certainly aware of the growing and possibly dangerous tension between the lieutenant and the group, nonetheless with effort repressed a grin. Standing before him was Jack Frake, who was acting as spokesman, and behind him were Hugh Kenrick, Thomas Reisdale, and Jock Frazer. He felt grateful that the first thing Jack Frake had done was deal the lieutenant a false card, thus removing him from any suspicion that he had warned the town of the attempt to smuggle in the stamps.

Jack Frake continued. "And my advice to you, sir, is this: If you attempt to bring the stamps through Caxton here, you will be opposed. The entire county has been alerted to your presence and business. Sentinels have been posted at every possible landing, up and down the river."

Harke narrowed his eyes in defiance of this man. "The Act goes into effect in one day, sir, and if you or any of your companions have any regard for the law, you must recognize that it is imperative that these stamps be delivered to the person who must take final custody of them. You are proposing interference with a Crown officer in the course of his duty. Surely you must know that is a capital offense."

His opponent shook his head. "The stamps interfere with our liberties, sir, and that is a much worse offense."

Harke sighed with impatience, and looked over Jack Frake's shoulder. "Is there a magistrate present with whom I might speak?"

A bespectacled, pale-looking older man, who had the air of a scholar about him, stepped forward. This was Thomas Reisdale, whose name Harke would never learn, either. That man said, "I am a magistrate, sir, and our county court has resolved that since the Act violates our excellent constitution, it is null and void." Harke began to reply, but the gentleman continued, as though he were lecturing a class of law students. "Of course, that is the obverse side of a corollary. The reverse side of it is equally true: If a court upholds the lawfulness of that Act, then it declares the constitution null and void." He paused. "Surely, your honor, that must have occurred to you, as well."

Another man stepped forward to say, "You labor under a misapprehension, sir. The sheriff receives his place by leave of the Crown in the person of our Governor." This was Hugh Kenrick. "The articles in your custody are creatures of Parliament, whose legislative authority cannot extend to governing or altering the internal business of His Majesty's colonies. So the sheriff of our county cannot assume responsibility for the stamps."

A fourth delegate added with a Scots burr, "So you see, your honor, we have a higher regard for the law than do Parliament, and that's a fact!"

Harke could not hold his temper. "The Act was endorsed by His Majesty, may I remind you gentlemen, so it is *his* law that you propose to flout!"

The leader remarked, "Then the king was ill-advised to endorse it."

"And ill at the time, so we have heard," added the magistrate. "We have granted him our doubts concerning the state of his mind when the Act was proffered for his seal. We would not gainsay his wisdom in the matter."

This assault, combined with the presumptuous leniency accorded the sovereign, was too much for the lieutenant to grasp and reply to. Constitutional and legal arguments were beyond his ken. He was trained to lead men, sail ships, guess the weather, and assess military crises, not trade rebuttals and retorts. He managed to stop himself from sputtering in furious frustration.

The leader seemed to sense his impotence to argue or protest, and said, almost with the casual friendliness of conversation, "If you attempt to discharge your duty, sir, we will restrain you and your men, and seize and burn the stamps." He nodded to a small brick house that stood at the end of a tobacco warehouse. "Do you see the pile of ashes yonder, sir? That is where the inspector here destroys trash leaf. I can promise you that that is where the stamps will meet their end, as well."

Harke tried to make himself as tall as his tormentor. "Then *you* will be opposed, sir!"

Again, the leader shrugged. "So be it."

Hugh Kenrick said with disquieting calmness, "If you attempt to board this ship of liberty, sir, you will be repelled."

Harke was beside himself with unchanneled rage. He had continued arguing against his own best advice because he did not like surrendering the issue or the moment to these arrogant colonials. He fixed his sight on the flag that fluttered on the staff held by the horseman beyond the listening crowd. He could read the lettering on one of the white stripes now: *Sons of Liberty*.

So that was it! He was faced with one of these damned "patriotic" vigilance clubs! They seemed to be springing up everywhere, throughout all the colonies, so Captain Sterling had informed him. Harke raised his spyglass and pointed to the flag with it. He bellowed, "How dare you desecrate the king's colors??"

Jack Frake glanced once at the banner that was held by John Proudlocks, and smiled. "We have not desecrated them, sir. We have removed them." He nodded once in courtesy. "Good day to you, sir." Then he turned to address his companions. "Our business here is finished, gentlemen." He led his companions back down the pier, where they joined the silent, waiting crowd.

Ramshaw glanced at the lieutenant in wordless question. Harke replied with a grimace, then turned and strode back up the gangboard. Ramshaw followed him to the quarterdeck.

"Mr. Ramshaw," said Harke, "you may disembark your passengers. I am abandoning the mission. Please ask the pilot to inform me when he plans to depart and on which vessel. We are returning to Hampton. I shall transfer the stamps to that vessel when it is ready."

"And Mr. Mercer?" queried Ramshaw. "Will you want to send him a message?"

Harke exploded. "Damn Mr. Mercer! He may stew in his own funk!"

Ramshaw managed to look innocent. "A wise decision, Mr. Harke," he sighed.

The lieutenant softened the rigid set of his face. "May I have a letter from you to Captain Sterling, one that will exonerate me and my men of the predicament here?"

"Gladly, sir," replied Ramshaw, managing to stifle a chuckle. "I shall credit the good sense of your action."

Ramshaw turned and went down to the main deck to tell his passengers that they could leave the vessel. Lieutenant Harke glanced at Bosun Olland and his men, then looked away and turned his back on them to gaze over the stern in angry shame. If his glance had lingered a moment more, he would have seen in his crewmen's expressions gratitude, relief, and even a dollop of respect for his decision.

Ramshaw returned to the quarterdeck some minutes later and approached the sullen lieutenant. "I have advised the pilot of your request, Mr. Harke, and he will take the *Swiftsure*, the sloop at the next pier, back down to Hampton in a few hours, once it has been made ready. He knows her master and is certain the man will accommodate you and your men."

"Thank you, Mr. Ramshaw."

"Before I retire to my cabin to pen a note to Captain Sterling, may I inform the gentlemen down there of your intention? They won't stand down until they know it. I have business ashore, and they'll press me for an answer."

Harke nodded assent. "But they won't leave, either, will they?"

Ramshaw shook his head. "Not until they see the stamps transferred to the *Swiftsure* and see her round the bend downriver."

"All right," snapped the lieutenant.

"Thank you, Mr. Harke." Ramshaw left the quarterdeck. Harke braced himself and followed. He was in the middle of telling his crewmen what had been decided when a great cheer arose in the crowd at the foot of the pier. Muskets were fired into the air in celebration, and the Navy men heard a chorus of huzzahs. Harke turned briefly. He saw the leader and two of the other men from the delegation sitting on their horses. Many men in the crowd were turned towards them and waving their hats in salute of those men. Other people in the crowd were welcoming the passengers who had disembarked.

One hour later Harke and his men transferred the box of stamps to another pier and up another gangboard to the *Swiftsure*. They quick marched along a short stretch of beach between a cordon of armed colonials. The crowd had thinned out a little, but Harke estimated that he was still outnumbered ten to one.

He said nothing and did not look to his left or right, except when he approached the trio of mounted colonials who had been saluted by the throng. He gave Jack Frake a wicked look. That man merely watched him pass by and step onto the pier.

An hour later the *Swiftsure* weighed anchor, hauled in her hawsers, and slipped away from the pier on an outgoing tide. When the sloop was in the middle of the river, her sails were made taut to catch the wind, and she began to glide back down the green highway of the York River.

The crowd cheered again, and muskets were fired again in triumph.

Jack Frake turned to Hugh Kenrick and grinned. "We did it, Hugh," he said quietly. He turned in his saddle and raised his hat in salute to his companions behind him. And again the group was surrounded by an astonished and jubilant crowd.

Hugh Kenrick felt the elation of triumph, as well, but it was tempered by the knowledge that Reverdy Brune was not one of the passengers who had come down the gangboard.

* * *

Chapter 11: The Victory

When the sails of the *Swiftsure* were no longer in sight, an impromptu meeting of the Sons of Liberty and the magistrates was held in the Olympus Room of Safford's King's Arms. An exuberant Reece Vishonn almost immediately proposed holding a victory ball at Enderly to celebrate the success of the stamp blockade.

Jack Frake, however, cautioned patience. "Let us first see what happens in Williamsburg on Friday," he said.

"How can there be any doubt of what will happen there?" queried Vishonn. "Your own man reported that Mr. Mercer was nearly mobbed today. He will not be able to assure the General Court any stamps, and so the Court must either proceed without them, or will not open."

"Yes," chimed Jock Frazer. "Mr. Crompton said that he heard that many attorneys may not even appear to press their cases, and that the Governor and the Council may find themselves facing an empty bar."

Aymer Crompton, Jack's brickmaker, had been dispatched to the Capitol to observe and report events there, and had returned early in the afternoon with news of George Mercer's reception. Henry Buckle was sent yesterday to Yorktown to spot the *Sparrowhawk* coming upriver on its way to Caxton.

As soon as Hugh Kenrick arrived in town, instead of going first to Meum Hall, he had ridden to Morland to see Jack Frake, and together they devised a plan to foil landing of the stamps: Most of the county's residents, they knew, complained bitterly about the new tax burden, but did not know how to oppose it. Jack hit upon the idea of informing them of the conspiracy and what the Sons planned to do. "We will send some of our tenants around to everyone, and ask the people to pass the word to come to the waterfront when Ramshaw's vessel has been sighted," he said.

"How will they know when to come?" asked Hugh.

"When they hear the bell at the church."

Hugh grimaced in doubt. "Reverend Acland will not ring the bell, nor allow it to be rung."

Jack shrugged. "Then we will not inform him of the plan."

Hugh was quiet for a while. "If the marines are ordered to force their way ashore, there may be a fight."

"Then there will be a fight," remarked Jack. "There are enough veterans here to make it hot for the marines and the Navy men. That must be made clear to everyone who comes, including Captain Sterling's escort." Jack paused. "If we demonstrate that we are prepared to respond with force, his men may have second thoughts, and abandon their plan."

"They may be rash enough not to have second thoughts," said Hugh with irony. "Nor even to think at all."

"Then they must risk that oversight," said Jack.

Hugh recalled their mutual relief when, sitting together on horseback on the waterfront, they saw that the *Sparrowhawk* was not accompanied by a boatload of marines. "I suppose," he remarked to Jack then, "that Captain Sterling decided that moderation was the better part of base bravado." He also recalled their mutual relief when, on the previous evening, they met with Thomas Reisdale, Reece Vishonn, and other leading men in the county, and secured unanimous agreement that the stamps must not be allowed to enter the colony of Virginia and the plan he and Jack had devised received complete endorsement.

Today, Aymer Crompton was asked to describe George Mercer's reception in Williamsburg. He stood in front of the room, hat in hand, and addressed the gathering, at first shyly, then with growing excitement as he saw the intense interest in the faces of his listeners. "I do believe the colonel feared for his life, sirs, and had good cause to! He left his father's house and walked to the Capitol and the General Court to report to Mr. Fauquier, where he'd heard the Governor was having tea nearby at Mrs. Vobe's tavern. And as he went up the street, more and more gentlemen, mostly merchants, and lawyers and tradesmen — all who's in town for the General Court — joined him and buzzed about him surly like, asking what he was to do: Would he resign like a good Virginian, or not? Did he have the stamps? Would the Court open with or without them? Colonel Mercer kept putting them off with answers that ain't answers at all, and was surely relieved when he passed the Capitol and saw the Governor on Mrs. Vobe's porch with some Council members. Mr. Robinson and Mr. Randolph were there, too."

Crompton paused to catch his breath. "Then the colonel nearly ran from the wake of gentlemen behind him and rushed up the steps to join the Governor, and the mob might have, too, and I was sure I'd see some nasty business if they did. But the Governor stood up and faced the mob, and the gentlemen in it would brook no molestation of him, nor of Colonel Mercer. The colonel was pressed for an answer anyway, and he promised them one on Friday, but many of the gentlemen protested, saying that was the day the Act was to start, so the colonel said he'd have a statement for them tomorrow right there at the Capitol at five of the clock.

"The Governor walked with him through the mob, leaving them all behind. Well, sirs, if it weren't for the respect the mob had for Mr. Fauquier, I do believe they would've wrung a resignation from the colonel then and there. The Governor and the colonel walked back to the Palace and went inside. They were in there for the longest time, and not knowing when the colonel would come back out, I mounted up and came back to town here."

"Good work, Mr. Crompton," said Jack.

"Thank you, sir," said Crompton, who put his hat back on and walked to the back of the room.

"Well," said Thomas Reisdale, "that event was almost as exciting as our own!"

The men in the room laughed at the remark. Jack Frake said, "Now we know where the colony stands. Mr. Kenrick and I will ride to Williamsburg to witness Mr. Mercer's statement tomorrow. Who will join us?"

Several of the listeners voiced their intention to go to Williamsburg.

"Very well," said Jack Frake. "It will be interesting to hear how Mr. Mercer justifies his actions."

Hugh Kenrick remarked, "No doubt he and the Governor will concoct a *pièce de théâtre* to quell the commotion."

"Or a litany of lies," added Jack Frake. He said then, "Mr. Kenrick not only brought news of the plot to smuggle in the stamps, but has just returned with news of the congress in New York." He gestured to Hugh to rise and speak.

Hugh Kenrick rose and spoke to the gathering about the Stamp Act Congress. "It is a shame that Virginia could not be represented in an official capacity in this congress, for I believe that if she had sent delegates, the resolutions adopted by the congress would have been less humble and more forceful. However, the resolutions voted by the nearly thirty delegates from the nine colonies comprise a declaration of rights and liberties, resembling in essence our own resolves of last May. They protest not only the Stamp

Act but the power of the admiralty courts to subvert our judicial establishment."

Hugh removed a sheet of paper from a leather pouch and read a draft of the congress's resolutions. When he was finished, he said, "As you can see, the resolutions address a broad field of subjects." He paused to collect his thoughts. "It is not likely that Parliament would grant these resolutions any serious cognizance, even were they more consistent in spirit and intent. They are peculiarly steadfast in their humility and moderation. I would not blame the government for dismissing them out of hand, for while they challenge Parliament's right to legislate the internal polity of the colonies, they also assert the rights of Englishmen but at the same time deny that we can be represented in the Commons, and therefore claim a uniqueness deserving of special, conciliatory consideration. Even Mr. Grenville's lowest placeman could not help but see the contradictions in the resolutions."

"Still," remarked Ralph Cullis, "it is a protest, not merely by one colony, but by a congress of colonies. I cannot imagine how Parliament or His Majesty could ignore such an event."

"Perhaps the new ministry will be more conciliatory," speculated Reisdale.

The meeting ended with a toast to the success of the day. Steven Safford supplied a puncheon of his best port at his own expense to celebrate. Jack Frake, however, attempted to put his listeners in a sober frame of mind. "Gentlemen," he said, "the Act still stands. Mr. Mercer may, tomorrow evening, even tear up his commission before a host of witnesses, and consign the pieces to flames, yet we will still be burdened with the Act. And do not forget that the Crown is determined to collect an extra-legal revenue from us to support our warders. We face an uncertain future. The Proclamation of two years ago still imprisons us, as do a host of other regulations and proscriptions. Our labors have only just begun. Remember that it costs Parliament nothing to pass an unjust law over us, but that the cost of securing its repeal or nullification will always fall on us." He paused and added, "This is not the end, sirs. It is but a beginning."

Later, after the meeting was finished and Hugh, Jack, and Reisdale paused in the main room of the King's Arms for a supper before journeying home, Hugh voiced more critical thoughts of the New York congress. "It was an edifying sojourn, sirs. The experience has convinced me that colonial unity is and always will be a hard-birthed chimera. I had not expected to witness the rivalries and contentions that were evident at the congress that I observed in that town. It is a wonder to me that the gentlemen who were sent by their various assemblies were able to agree on a final draft of the resolutions."

"How so?" queried Reisdale.

"Well, there was Pennsylvania, represented by Mr. Dickinson, Mr. Bryan, and Mr. Morton. Mr. Franklin, the colony's most preeminent citizen, is in London attempting to persuade the Crown to convert his colony into a royal one, so that it may better defend itself against French and Indian incursions in the west and to erase the abuses visited on the colony by the Penns. There is a bitter conflict between his party, led by Quakers, and the party of Presbyterians and Anglicans who wish to preserve the proprietorship. They ceased their squabbling only for the moment in order to unite against the Stamp Act. Mr. Talbot, my family's merchant agent in Philadelphia, also went to New York, and apprised me in detail of the struggle between the factions. Mr. John Hughes, a friend of Mr. Franklin's, apparently was nominated stamp distributor on Mr. Franklin's recommendation, and is being pressed to resign. If he does not, he risks having his house pulled down and his person abused. He is a loyal Tory, however, and I doubt that he will surrender his commission under such threats."

"The colonies will unite, in time," said Jack. "They are largely disunited now over interference by Crown policies." He smiled confidently, almost in defiance of his friend. "In the long view, we must seek to extricate ourselves from the clutches of the navigation and trade laws, which at present yoke us to the designs of British merchants and an avaricious Crown, and penalize those who risk indulging their freedom to trade beyond the proscriptions of the mother country."

Hugh shook his head. "The dissension is too deep, too ill-bred," he remarked. "Inside the congress and without, I saw how they behaved like wolves rivaling over the same hunting territory."

"They will unite, in time," repeated Jack.

Proudlocks glanced at his employer. "You are beginning to sound like Mr. Kenrick here, sir," he said. "Your *manitous* are becoming much alike."

Reisdale said, "Some friends of mine have sent me late *Pennsylvania Gazettes*. In one of them, William Franklin, governor of New Jersey and son of Benjamin in London, protests in a letter the notion that his father encouraged Parliament to pass the Act."

Jack Frake, Hugh Kenrick, and John Proudlocks rode to Williamsburg the next morning. The three men from Queen Anne County stood in the rear of the throng beyond the Capitol gate. Thomas Reisdale had come with Reece Vishonn in the latter's carriage. Other men from Caxton, including Steven Safford, Carver Gramatan, and others, came independently and joined the throng. The last day of October was a pleasantly mild one, with a brilliant blue sky and a slight breeze.

Hugh studied the crowd that had gathered in front of the Capitol to await George Mercer's arrival. In it were merchants, planters, farmers, servants, ministers, slaves, and artisans from all over the colony, here because the General Court required their presence in some matter or other. He noted the presence of many burgesses, as well, mostly the younger ones, with a handful of the older. He saw Edgar Cullis and his father on the other side of the throng. His fellow burgess nodded coldly to him in greeting.

At five o'clock George Mercer arrived on horseback in the company of his brother James. They both dismounted and stepped before the crowd. A delegation from the crowd had thoughtfully provided an empty crate for the burgess from Frederick to stand on so that the crowd could better hear him. His brother stood nearby, hands folded in front of him, eyeing the crowd warily. After a long silence, George Mercer stepped onto the crate and produced some sheets of paper. He read sonorously and convincingly from them, although at times his voice cracked and squeaked, as though he were exerting an effort to speak words he did not wish to speak and did not really mean.

George Mercer claimed that he could not be blamed for accepting an office whose legitimacy could not be questioned. He claimed that when he left England, he had heard of the House's Resolves, but could not credit the truth of them for he said he never saw them in printed form, but had only heard talk of them. He claimed that the "greatly esteemed Mr. Benjamin Franklin," whom he met briefly in London, "deemed the Resolves precipitous and reckless," so he, not so great a man, could hardly be blamed for doubting the legitimacy of the Resolves, as well.

George Mercer claimed that, during the voyage home, he determined to learn for himself the truth of the matter, and learned upon his arrival that he had been hanged in effigy and his good name sullied, "very likely by persons disappointed in their own application for the commission I received."

Hugh remarked to Jack at that point, "He is referring to Mr. Richard Henry Lee." He sighed. "Do you see what I mean about contentiousness?"

George Mercer hoped that he would be permitted to acquit his conduct to date and that his auditors would have patience with him. He claimed that his distributor's commission was a consequence of the praise and recommendation of the House and Council for some kind of Crown reward, and that he could not be blamed for the form in which the Crown deigned to bestow it upon him.

George Mercer claimed that he was told that he had encouraged passage of the Act in question, and that the commission was his reward for his efforts to that end. He assured his listeners that he had no hand in the business, and had no prior knowledge or promise of the appointment, until he returned from a visit to Ireland, which was long after the Act had been passed.

"Gentlemen," concluded George Mercer, "I am thus circumstanced." He wished now to act in such a way that would satisfy his friends and countrymen, but that, on so short a notice on so weighty a matter, he could only promise that he would not execute the Act until he received orders from England, and then only until he received assent from the General Assembly to execute the Act.

Hugh frowned. "But there is no General Assembly to approve or disapprove," he scoffed.

George Mercer ended on a patriotic note, asserting that no man could more ardently wish for the prosperity of the colony, and desire to protect the rights and privileges of its inhabitants, than he.

Someone in the crowd led it in a round of huzzahs, and then George Mercer was hoisted up on the shoulders of two men and cheered. "But he has not resigned," remarked John Proudlocks with disbelief. He glanced at Hugh and Jack, hoping for an explanation for this odd behavior.

But Hugh also blinked in exasperation, and added, "He has only promised to stay his hand, until the House has empowered it to act without risk of maiming."

"What a fog of sophistry he has fled into!" exclaimed Jack with contempt. "Yet look at how they treat his words!"

"As though he had just denounced the Act, and Parliament for having passed it!" added Hugh. "In truth, his speech was worthy of the Bard's most conniving cad!"

Proudlocks watched as the crowd carried Mercer past the Capitol gate and brushed by them in a noisy procession down Duke of Gloucester Street to a tavern. "He does not look very happy about his great deed," he observed.

"He has lied," remarked Jack, "and hopes his renewed friends will never learn that he has."

Hugh nodded in agreement. "A riskier offense than confessing the truth, to be sure. He will watch his tongue until it is safe to wag it again."

The trio stood and let the throng rush by, and watched as it moved down the boulevard in a cacophony of shouts and rejoicing. They saw many from their own county join the crowd. After a moment, they turned and walked together to another tavern.

George Mercer was feted that night. Townsmen appeared with French horns, fiddles, and drums to play in honor of the man who said he would not take advantage of "an office so odious to his country." And on the following evening of the day the Stamp Act was to go into effect, a great ball was held in his honor at the Raleigh Tavern. From Queen Anne County only Reece Vishonn, Henry Otway, and Jock Frazer attended it. They liked a good party, where a good table, good drink, and good cheer were to be had for the mere price of being present.

* * *

George Mercer became a master of the art of duplicity.

When the General Court opened the next morning, presided over by Lieutenant-Governor Fauquier as chief justice and members of his Council as fellow justices, the sumptuous, imposing, well-appointed courtroom beneath the Council chambers in the Capitol was empty but for the justices and the Court's functionaries. No one sat in the public place. Attorneys were not present, nor their clients, nor any defendants. The Governor heard men talking and moving about outside. Twice he ordered the bailiff to ring his bell on the Capitol steps to announce the opening of the Court.

Not a single soul came through the great doors of the courtroom. The chamber remained ominously empty. The Governor asked George Mercer, who sat on the side with the chief clerk, if he could provide stamps in order to proceed with business. Mercer replied that he could not. The Governor next asked the chief clerk if he could proceed with business without stamps. The chief clerk replied that he would not, for he did not wish to risk a penalty by approving such an action. George Mercer then offered his resignation from the office of stamp distributor. Fauquier refused to accept it, replying that he must submit his resignation to those who granted him the commission.

The Lieutenant-Governor sighed and ordered the Court adjourned. He had expected this to happen, but could not quite believe in the possibility until it did happen. "Madness," he muttered to himself as he led a procession of nonplussed Council members out of the courtroom to the chambers upstairs.

The next day, in a written statement to the Governor and the Council, George Mercer "declined acting" as the appointed stamp distributor before he received further orders, and denied that he brought any stamps with him, "or was ever charged by the Commissioners of the Customs in England with the care of any stamps." The stamps just happened to have been on the same vessel that brought him back to Virginia. Fauquier and Mercer arranged for the temporary disposition of the stamps.

A few days later, the Governor ordered the printing of certificates that stated that stamps were not available and sent them to Captain Sterling on the *Rainbow*, saying in his letter that the certificates could be used until the "proper stamps came into the country"; that is, until the stamps that were transferred from the *Leeds* to the warship could be safely landed and transported to Williamsburg and other venues where they could be employed. He took this action on the advice of Peter Randolph, Surveyor-General of the customs for the Middle District and a member of the Council, in order to placate merchants who had vessels waiting to leave for other ports. The stamps intended for North Carolina and Maryland were sent by Captain Sterling on sloops-of-war to Wilmington and Annapolis.

George Mercer lied — to the Lieutenant-Governor, to his family, to his fellow Virginians. Fauquier never learned of the ruse to bring in the stamps, for neither Mercer nor Captain Sterling ever informed him of it. To the Governor, he represented that it was too dangerous to bring the stamps to Williamsburg; to the crowd, he represented that he did not have the stamps and would not introduce them without the approval of the General Assembly.

He neglected to mention to anyone that he had been promised the commission in early April of that year, and that it was dated August 2nd, which commission would not have been made out unless he had tentatively accepted it beforehand. He never really resigned from the office, but signed a power-of-attorney that gave his brother James the responsibility for the stamps. Nor did he mention to the crowd that he had gone to England two years before not only as the Ohio Company's agent to lobby for the salvaging of that enterprise's interests — damaged by the Proclamation of 1763 — but also to seek a reward for his services during the late war, which meant, in those days, a lucrative Crown appointment of one kind or another. He also pleaded ignorance of the constitutional and economic consequences of the Stamp Act, and professed little knowledge of its intent and scope.

The Stamp Act and growing reports of its often violent opposition in the colonies were reported in personal and official correspondence and in the British press months before Mercer boarded the *Leeds* for the voyage home. It occurred to no one, however, that Mercer had possibly accepted the commission in hopes that a grateful ministry would express its gratitude by conceding some of his Ohio Company's claims on land west of the Alleghenies in exception to the Proclamation of 1763.

George Mercer was either clueless and witless, or a liar and dissembler of the second rank. Suspecting that he had permanently blotted his reputation as a loyal Virginian and sullied the esteem in which his fellow Virginians had held him, he left Virginia for England on 28 November 1765, never to return. He continued to represent, in the end fruitlessly, the claims of the Ohio Company, and testified of his experience in Williamsburg before the Commons.

Hugh Kenrick, Jack Frake, and John Proudlocks returned to Caxton the morning after George Mercer's apparent capitulation. Proudlocks that day went to the fields with the other Morland tenants to help bring in the harvest of wheat. Jack Frake met with John Ramshaw to arrange for hogsheads of tobacco to be loaded onto the *Sparrowhawk* and to claim a consignment of farming implements and seeds from England that he wished to experiment with. Hugh also saw to some of his plantation tasks, and made time to write his father, Dogmael Jones, and Otis Talbot about the events of the last few days.

And in the back of his mind for the last forty-eight hours was the woman he had seen in Hampton. The brief glimpse of her skewed his thoughts and scuttled his focus despite his best efforts. He struggled against a tenacious distraction, knowing it was not a distraction at all, but a desperate need.

And he would not know it for months, but the day before, when George Mercer made a show of resigning before a tense and expectant crowd, the man to whom Hugh had neglected to bow so many years ago died. William Augustus, the Duke of Cumberland, now obese, nearly blind, asthmatic, and suffering from leg abscesses, succumbed at his residence of Cumberland House to a heart attack hours before the arrival of Lord Rockingham and his ministers to decide on a policy and plan to deal with the rebellious colonies. Cumberland was a soldier; consequently some of the ministers had wished to persuade the Duke of the necessity of using the Army to enforce submission to the Stamp Act.

Lord Rockingham, Secretary of State Henry Conway, and the Earl of Northington, together with other high ministers were abruptly left without a rock to cling to, and flailed desperately in the roiling waters of impotent vacillation and fulminating indecision until the stark reality of the crisis forced them to think hard and decide quickly, lest they squander a portion of a hard-won empire and lose it.

Hugh Kenrick, some three thousand miles away, exerted his best self-discipline not to succumb to the temptation to return to Hampton, and thence to Norfolk, to regain something he thought he had lost. To his staff he became an austere, tight-lipped, enigmatic presence. They wondered in private about the monkish reticence of their otherwise generous and vivacious master.

* * *

Chapter 12: The Assessment

"The true source of our suffering has been our timidity. We have been afraid to think.... Let us dare to read, think, speak, and write.... Let it be known that British liberties are not the grants of princes or parliaments...."

So wrote Massachusetts lawyer John Adams in a pamphlet Hugh had bought in New York, "A Dissertation on the Canon and the Feudal Law." Hugh bought five copies of it: one each for himself, Jack Frake, Thomas Reisdale, his father, and Dogmael Jones. Adams's call to aggressive colonial self-edification was the leitmotif of all the other literature he bought multiple copies of, including Maryland lawyer Daniel Dulany's *Considerations on the Propriety of imposing Taxes in the British Colonies, for the Purpose of raising a Revenue.* He had to purchase a second travel bag to carry all the literature he found. He had been dumbstruck by the quantity and quality of it available in the bookshops of New York; dumbstruck, and then sated, for he consumed it like a starving man.

Most of it asserted the rights of British-Americans, distinguished between Parliament's regulatory imposts on trade and internal taxation, and disputed the legal and moral power of Parliament to legislate laws within the colonies. He spent many sleepless nights in his New York billet, reading by candlelight, and many more in the company of delegates to the congress, debating the liberties, questioning Parliamentary power, and arguing the pros and cons of colonial representation in the Commons. He talked himself to passionate hoarseness on those occasions, as did his fellow debaters.

He was often asked by gentlemen from Massachusetts, New York, Georgia, and Pennsylvania why the Virginia legislature had not sent official delegates to the congress, since it was that body's Resolves from last May that had largely emboldened other legislatures to approve of the congress. He could only report Lieutenant-Governor Fauquier's proroguement of the General Assembly and speculate on the motive behind the gubernatorial action. "Very likely he has mistaken an assertion of our liberties and resistance to encroachment on them as a declaration of war on Westminster," he replied just as often.

"He may very well be correct on that assessment, in the long view," said one delegate.

Hugh had shrugged. "The assessment is incorrect. We seek only to preserve our rights and liberties from abridgement and eventual erasure. *We* are not guilty of declaring war."

"It is Westminster that seems to have declared war on us, and by that action, on the Constitution itself!" protested another delegate with some worry.

"Perhaps. Perhaps not," replied Hugh. "But Parliament may very well adopt my governor's view, and either recognize our arguments, or dismiss them. They may act out of fear, or from contempt. Time will tell. Perhaps the new ministry will be friendlier to reason."

"I am not acquainted with any politician who is friendly to reason, sir," said another delegate. "That creature is as rare as elves. If we are successful in our redresses, methinks we must credit, not reason, but the influence of British merchants. A friend writes from London that our resistance to several late acts of Parliament has pinched many a purse in London and all the outports there, and tens of thousands of souls are now without employment. The euphoric industry of the late war and of the peace before it has given way to universal despondency, there as well as here. Methinks the Solons of the Commons will hark to the complaints of British traders before our protests are ever given weight."

And while the experience gave him a strange, exhilarating kind of exhaustion, the lacuna also troubled his mind. He could not identify it. When he boarded the *Morag* in New York for the trip home, he slept soundly in his berth that first day out, for the first time in two weeks, oblivious to the noisy efforts of the crew, to the rocking of the schooner, to the sudden heaves as its sails caught wind and propelled the vessel forward — and the first thing he thought of when he awoke was the question of what, for all the reading, thinking, speaking, and writing, was missing.

Perhaps it was not a thing at all, but rather a perception. Or perhaps it was something present in all the rhetoric and grandiloquence.

John Ramshaw brought him mail from his father and Dogmael Jones. With Jones's correspondence were copies of London newspapers that carried items and letters about the colonial troubles. One paper was a number of the *London Weekly Journal*, which carried Jones's latest venture into political caricature, entitled "The Westminster Fair; or, a Summer Divertissement by Ye Extraordinary Salmagundi Touring Troupe for the Claque of the Commons."

It was a larger and more biting caricature than the one Jones and Hugh's father had put into the paper earlier in the year. It depicted some principal figures of the new ministry as members of a traveling troupe of performers in a satire on the Southwark Fair. A throng of dour, sour-faced figures, representing Lords and the Commons, watched five separate acts. Some of the spectators were vaguely recognizable as prominent members of both Houses.

George Grenville was represented as a wizard, bedecked in robes that bore strange symbols and sporting a conical hat. He stood before a pedestal that held a cracked and chipped stone, labeled "America." The figure held a wand labeled "Stamp Act." A balloon over the figure announced, "Watch as I strike the stone and cause it to bleed revenue."

The Duke of Cumberland was represented as a sleeping bear, around whose mangy and scarred hulk swarmed gnats and flies. The bear was also surrounded by a pack of small dogs barking at him to rise and give the spectators a show for their money.

The Marquis of Rockingham was shown sitting astride an overly ornate rocking-horse, labeled "Fortune's Favorite." He wore the silks and long-billed cap of a jockey. Balloons over two spectators remarked, "It is furious action, but he goes nowhere," and "But he is nearing the end of the course!"

Sir Henoch Pannell and Crispin Hillier were represented by two figures identified by a placard as "Mr. and Mrs. Mumpsimus," and also as "The Undertaker of Onyxcombe" and "The Runnion of Canovan." Hillier was portrayed as a dark-dressed undertaker proclaiming the efficacy of his elixir, while Pannell rose out of a coffin, garbed as a disreputable woman. Balloons above them read, "My potion of excises and tariffs will embalm the industry of England forever more," and "I took the elixir twenty years ago and I am as fresh as a maid in her bloom!" Several spectators were shown with expressions of revulsion and horror as they stepped back with gesturing hands from "Mrs. Mumpsimus." Balloons above them read, "No! She is poxed with the plague of preferences!" and "Merciful odium!! Return this fulsome creature to the cemetery!"

The Duke of Bedford was paired with a representation of Britannia.

The latter had dropped her shield and spear and was clinging precariously to a liberty pole, while behind her the Duke had a boot planted on her rump and strained to pull on the strings of a bodice Britannia had been fitted into. A balloon over Bedford remarked, "Liberty must be strung into a tight constraint to foil anarchy! I shall pull the laces of law until she groans in agreement!" The laces in his hands were marked "Stamp Act," "Cider Tax," "General Warrants," and "The Army." A third figure, representing Lord Northington, the Lord Chancellor, as a besotted tailor, observed the contest from the side with a pensive but bleary look. A balloon over that figure read, "But, sir, my new fashion requires the rack to ensure a perfect fit."

Desultory remarks by the spectators expressed disappointment and boredom with the spectacle.

Hugh was amused by the caricature, and showed it over supper an evening soon after to his guests, who included Jack Frake and Etáin, Thomas Reisdale, John Proudlocks, and John Ramshaw. They, too, were amused by it. "Mr. Jones and my father are preparing for the new session in January," said Hugh. "They expect the Stamp Act to be debated on both sides with great liveliness. Mr. Pitt may yet enter the debates. Jones has dubbed the new first minister 'Lord Rocking-horse,' and expects that Pitt will move him to adopt a policy."

*   *   *

Reece Vishonn held his victory ball at Enderly a week after November first. To mark the day, he requested that Sheriff Tippet arrange to fire the old cannon that sat in front of his jail. Tippet agreed with alacrity. As dusk approached, the gun was fired. The field piece, captured by Queen Anne militia from the French two wars ago, had not been drafted into the confrontation between the town and the Navy; it lacked ball. The long, cresset-lit path leading to the great house of Enderly was soon busy with carriages, riding chairs, and sulkies as the evening grew darker.

The ball was as grand an occasion as the ball he held to celebrate Wolfe's victory at Quebec years before. The Great Union flag was again fixed to one ballroom wall. Local musicians played on the side, and the guests participated in many gavottes and country-dances. Etáin played a program of music alone and together with the Kenny brothers.

John Proudlocks helped her set up her harp before the Great Union, and stood deferentially to the side, ready to wait on her. It was his first ball. He arrived with Etáin, her husband, Hugh Kenrick, John Ramshaw, and William Hurry.

Reece Vishonn frowned when Proudlocks followed his friends inside the house, but he could hardly object to the Indian's presence. After all, that man had held the banner of the Sons of Liberty at the pier a week ago. He grimaced and turned to greet another guest. Arthur Stannard remarked to him later, "I didn't know you tolerated such foreigners in your home, sir."

"I tolerate whom I please, sir, in my own home," replied Vishonn, some color rushing to his face. "Any friend of Mr. Frake's is my friend. If you cannot tolerate my friends, then perhaps this is not the affair for you."

The British agent's eyes widened and he stammered, "My apologies, sir, for the presumption."

Later in the evening, many men repaired to Vishonn's game room to rest from the music, light their pipes, and exercise their minds. A lively discussion ensued on the week's events.

"We have distinguished ourselves from those other Sons," said Hugh at one point, "by not resorting to anarchy, destruction, and civil intimidation. We were prepared to trade volleys or grapple hand to hand with the King's men, if they tried to proceed with their plan. We met them on the pier, and turned them away. Words cannot convey my satisfaction with that outcome."

"We are fortunate that the obedient agents of the nascent tyrants in the government have no bottom," remarked Reisdale. "They are confounded by their own doubts about the legitimacy and practicality of their actions."

"Aye, that's the truth of it," said Jock Frazer. "They were hoping that we also are wormed with doubt, and would submit to their authority with nary a whimper."

"I would not call Lord Shelburne a nascent or an actual tyrant," opined Vishonn. "I have read in the papers and in my London friends' letters that while he drew up the Proclamation of '63, that is, all its particulars, he did not expect them to be used as a tool of mischief. But when Grenville became head of the government, Lord Shelburne resigned from the Board of Trade, knowing that man's intentions and overall taste for ruling like a Persian. It is not Lord Shelburne's fault that his plan, which would have allowed gradual settlement and exploitation west of the Alleghenies, was misused by his successors in ministry." He paused. "My information comes from a friend who regularly sups with Lord Shelburne."

Jock Frazer laughed. "My information is that he imbibes more spirits than he consumes substance!"

Jack Frake addressed his host. "Are you defending benevolent despotism, sir?"

"I am not defending any despotism," relied Vishonn. "I simply wish to exonerate Lord Shelburne of evil intentions."

"He gave our 'masters' the means to enslave us, whether or not his intentions were benign," said Jack. "From what I have read myself, and by what Mr. Kenrick's friend in the Commons has written, the policy was to contain us in order to better dun us. The Currency and Sugar Acts were the first overtures of that policy. That policy was moved by as many evil intentions as was Mr. Grenville's."

"Really, sir," replied Vishonn, "you must grant the man some doubt, some rope."

Jack shook his head. "I cannot. The rope I would be unwise enough to grant him may someday be put around my neck." He paused. "I have seen men hang for having been right." He added, "It is immaterial what were Shelburne's intentions. Even were it true that he did not intend the lands west of the Alleghenies to be forever beyond our reach, those lands were destined to be parceled out to the colonies by the Crown itself, on Crown terms, at the Crown's price."

Hugh said, "The northern colonies are especially bitter. The Currency Act hurts us all, but the Sugar Act altered and diminished their trade of molasses and rum, whose smuggled exchange once enabled those colonies to maintain their accounts and purchase British goods. What tobacco, wheat, and corn are to us, molasses, fish, and lumber are to the northern colonies. A more ardent Navy in customs enforcement has not helped them at all."

"I am afraid that Mr. Pitt will soon enter the picture," said Reisdale. "He, too, is a good-intentioned man, but he is for empire by means of proclamations and regulations. He may give us half a loaf, but we must beware of it. It may be a sugar loaf, but no less detrimental to our liberties."

"Such as the half loaf the West Indies sugar growers managed to drive through Parliament?" queried Hugh rhetorically. "To hear the northern delegates at the congress tell it, the difference between six pence and three pence on French and Spanish molasses is poverty and hostility. The reduction in that particular tax was a conscious attempt to collect revenue and subvert what little freedom to trade they had up there. Barring free trade, the old Molasses Act of 1733 was the basis of their prosperity. Now new duties on wine from the Azores and Madeiras, and on white sugar, coffee, pimento, and indigo from islands in the Indies not under British sovereignty are also dutied. The extension of that Act and its more rigorous enforcement have brought many merchants in Boston and Newport and New York to grief, especially now that the Navy has become a more conscientious agent of the customs collectors. And the customs collectors themselves, who once turned a blind eye to illicit cargoes in exchange for illicit emoluments, have now mostly eschewed bribery and become more bellicose in their positions."

"I view the empowered admiralty court as just as pernicious a threat," said Reisdale. "It saves the customs collectors the risk of malfeasance, because the Stamp Act allows them to pillage our trade without the necessity of sly, underhanded avarice."

"And indemnifies them against their errors," added Hugh. "And endorses writs of assistance and the employment and reward of spies."

"What are we revolting against, sirs? Power, or the corruption of that power?" asked Henry Otway. "I confess the issue is muddled in my mind."

"Against the corruption, for the time being," answered Jack. "And, when London attempts to make its empire and policies pure and corruption-proof — and I agree with Mr. Kenrick's assessment that this is the direction London is likely to take — then we must revolt against the power. That is in the cards. An honest tyranny is as much to be feared as a dishonest one."

"We are not *revolting*," objected Vishonn. "We are claiming our liberties. I will not tolerate talk of *revolt* in this house." His companions did not know whether or not their host was jesting.

Reisdale chuckled and said, "Then if you object to such talk, sir, I recommend that you stand for burgess next year."

Henry Otway said, "Yes. I have heard that Mr. Cullis may choose to remove himself from his incumbency."

"Sir," asked Hugh of his host, "did you extend an invitation to the Cullis family?"

Reece Vishonn looked innocent. "Yes, I did, sir. You see them here this evening. The father has appeared with his wife, but they asked me to excuse the son because of an *illness*." He paused to chuckle in doubt. "I understand that you assign as much blame to your fellow burgess for the attempted smuggling of the stamps as to Captain Sterling and Mr. Mercer."

"No, I do not," answered Hugh. "He merely prepared the way, a way that cost Mr. Barret his life, as well. And, in consort with the House leaders, he prompted the Governor to deny us any means to protest."

"That is a grave charge," warned Otway.

"The charge is commensurate with the action and consequences. Mr. Cullis would not have acted alone in the matter."

"I did not observe him cheering Colonel Mercer's dumb show at the Capitol, that is for certain," said Reisdale. "Many other burgesses did, but not he."

Hugh shrugged. "Mr. Mercer? Well, he did not much warm a bench in the chamber when he was elected to it, and I doubt he will have the opportunity to ever warm it, now. As for Mr. Cullis, I cannot predict what he will do. I am not concerned."

Henry Otway picked up a copy of the *Virginia Gazette* that lay on a side table near his chair. "Doubtless you have all read his statement here," he said, waving the newspaper in the air. "There was a serving of kickshaw to compete with the worst plate ever prepared by the cooks at the Raleigh!"

Reisdale nodded in agreement. "Yes. Speaking of kickshaw, his feast of words left me feeling empty. There was far too much piety in them for me to purchase belief in their sincerity."

"A half loaf of another kind," remarked Hugh. He chuckled in contempt, and reached for the *Gazette*, which Otway handed him. He read from the column "'Thus, gentlemen, I am circumstanced.' What villainous blather!" he scoffed, handing the paper back to Otway. "No man journeys all the way to London in a quest for a Crown sinecure without being 'circumstanced.' He seeks such a circumstance."

Reece Vishonn turned in his chair and addressed Arthur Stannard, who stood with a glass of port in the shadow in back of the circle of seated men. "Sir, we know you are full of perspective, yet we have not heard a word from you on any subject. You may speak without risk of censure here."

"We did not see you at the pier last week," said Otway. "Too immersed in your account books?"

Stannard shook his head. "No, sir. Frankly, I disagreed with the action taken on that day by many of you here, and decided I would not lend my presence to the protest. I still object to it. As does Reverend Acland. Even Sheriff Tippet had his reservations, and Mayor Corbin." He paused. "Reverend Acland declined to attend, as you well know." He smiled nervously.

Jock Frazer laughed. "It is the first ball he has ever missed!"

"Well, Mr. Corbin and Mr. Tippet certainly haven't objected to the outcome!" laughed Vishonn. "They're here, lapping up my punch and kickshaw! They're welcome to it!"

"No, they haven't objected to the outcome," agreed Stannard. "What do you think Governor Fauquier will do about it? He is sure to learn of the event."

Hugh shook his head. "Nothing, sir. He failed to ensure employment of the stamps. He will neither do anything about it, nor even mention it to the Board of Trade."

"There's another well-intentioned man," observed Jock Frazer. "I don't envy him his place."

"Trapped in a political purgatory between policy and principle," mused Hugh, "unable to reconcile the requisites of the nation with the tenets of liberty and free trade."

Jack Frake remarked with a nod, "Yes. In the long view, the most benign minister or member of Parliament must choose between reason and force." He smiled at Reisdale. "There is the half loaf we must never accept — the mongrel unity of the two."

Vishonn puffed thoughtfully on his pipe for a moment, then asked, "If you were a wagering man, Mr. Frake, which would you put your money on? Reason or force?"

"Neither, sir," said Jack. "We will see half loaves by the dozen. If the Stamp Act is nullified or even repealed, you may wager on further attempts to subject us. London has won an empire, and is determined to rule it and profit by it. I recollect saying this in this very room, years ago, gentlemen, on the occasion of General Wolfe's triumph at Quebec."

"Do you object to the empire?" asked Vishonn.

"Only if it treats me as its servant," replied Jack. "That would be worth a volume of objections."

* * *

Etáin's last selection was the Welsh melody, "Ash Grove." After taking her final bows for the evening, she spent time with her husband and other guests. But at one point during the ball, she took Hugh Kenrick aside. "Did you meet someone in New York?" she asked.

"Yes," answered Hugh, startled by the question, "many of the delegates." He smiled back at her, and saw in her green eyes that she meant something else.

"Were there many women at the congress?"

"Of course, but not in attendance." Then he understood the import of her question. "Oh. I see. No, Etáin, I did not meet a lady at the congress." He smiled and conceded her powers of observation. "No, not at the congress, but in Hampton." He paused. "But she must have been a ghost, or I had a fever." He chuckled. "How could you guess?"

"You have looked distracted, ever since you returned from the congress."

Hugh grinned. "Don't you mean 'despondent'?"

"All right. 'Despondent.' It darkens your gallantry."

"I did not know I was so transparent."

"You are not to most others, but are to me. That is because I know you too well."

Hugh wished to change the subject. "How are your parents faring? I miss them."

"I, too, miss them. They have settled in Edinburgh. Father is with another tobacco merchant firm, although he often travels to London and Bristol on its business."

* * *

John Ramshaw stayed another week at Meum Hall until his business in West Point and Williamsburg was finished. Hugh did not query him again about Reverdy Brune and her brother.

The captain rode out to the fields with his host to watch the tenants dismantle the conduit and store it for the winter. He did not comfortably ride a horse, but managed to keep up with Hugh. He remarked at one point, as they stopped to rest by the water collection tower by Hove Stream, which was being repaired, "You and Jack and the others have saved me the trouble of retiring early from the sea."

Hugh grinned in amusement, glancing at the captain's crown of silver hair. The shocks of black had vanished now, and he had observed Ramshaw's slight winces when he moved. Arthritis was beginning to claim the man's joints. He guessed that his friend was now somewhere in his sixties. "How so, sir?"

"There was little chance that my artisans could have forged those damned stamps with any success, and in such quantity. And the fates have blessed me all these years, in that no civil or naval limpet has ever rummaged my ship to discover its secret print shop. That can't last. In a few years I shall hang up my sextant." He paused to take a swig of port from a water flask.

Hugh knew about the two men in the captain's crew who worked in a concealed compartment of the *Sparrowhawk* to produce false customs forms and dockets for much of the cargo that Ramshaw brought into the various ports up and down the seaboard. He also took a drink from his flask. "I understand that Jack has decided not to husband the *Sparrowhawk*," he said.

Ramshaw sighed and shook his head. "True. All he would need to do is see to provisioning us for the return voyage. But he won't commit his time or means to such a venture. Offered him generous terms, and he was tempted to accept them. Gave me an odd reason for declining, though."

"What?"

"He said it was too soon, that not enough of us had caught up with him. Said something about his risking a set-to with the customs or Navy, and he would probably be clapped in irons before his time!" Ramshaw paused, then shook his head. "I can't decide whether that is vanity or wisdom."

"Wisdom," answered Hugh. "You should know better, Mr. Ramshaw. Jack is the proudest man in these parts, and the least vain." He added, as an afterthought, "He is the north."

Ramshaw grunted. "Skelly once told me he was the future."

"The future? The future of what?"

"He didn't say, sir. I daresay no one could say. Only Jack." Ramshaw grinned and shook his head. "No, it couldn't be vanity. For as long as I've known him, sir, he's known what he's about."

Ramshaw left Caxton on the *Sparrowhawk* two weeks after the incident at the pier. Hugh, Jack Frake, and Etáin saw him off. They expected to see him again in the spring.

Hugh returned to his routines at Meum Hall. Always in his work was a little ache of memory of Reverdy Brune, one that caused him to wonder where she was now. Was she in Norfolk? Did she and her brother journey to Charleston? To Annapolis? Had she forgotten him? Or was she afraid to see him again?

Then, one morning while he was supervising with his overlooker, William Settle, the plowing of manure and ground clamshells into the cleared tobacco acreage that he had decided to let lie fallow for two years, he thought he heard the rattle of a carriage in the distance. He put the distraction out of his mind. Then Spears rushed over the fields to inform him that he had visitors.

His mind still half on the task at hand, he wondered: Was it Lieutenant-Governor Fauquier calling to enquire about his role in the stoppage of the stamps? Who else in Queen Anne County would visit him in a carriage? And who might have accompanied him? Peyton Randolph? Speaker John Robinson? Had they come to chastise him for having attended the Stamp Act Congress last month? He asked Spears who it was.

"A gentleman, sir," said the valet, "and his sister. Mr. James Brune, and Mrs. Brune-McDougal, fresh from Williamsburg." Spears paused. "They say you are an old friend, sir."

Hugh simply stared at the valet for a moment, speechless, then remembered to instruct him to tell Mrs. Vere, the housekeeper, to make them comfortable, and the cook to prepare some refreshments. "I'll come in after I've seen to some things here," he said. "In a few minutes."

Spears said, "Yes, sir." He paused, then added in confidence, "I do believe they are expecting to stay for a while, sir. A wagon came with them, loaded with baggage, I noted. They did not state what their intentions were, of course."

Hugh blinked once. "Yes. Well, then see that the extra rooms are also prepared, if that is their intention."

"Yes, sir." Spears turned and hurried back to the great house.

* * *

Chapter 13: The Visit

"Gorgeous country here, Hugh," said James Brune. "Reverdy and I quite envy you the place. It is vast and pleasant enough to even stir a bit of ambition in me to perhaps come here and try my hand."

Hugh replied, "You have just missed the summer, James. Summers here can be fatiguing and close. Sometimes, in that season, one feels as though one were struggling inside a vat of butter. Sweat sticks like cloth to one's skin, denying it breath and providing nourishment for countless insects, foreign and familiar."

James Brune laughed. Reverdy's older brother had, of course, matured into reasonable good looks and had developed an amiable manner and perspective on things. The pallor that he, like other travelers, acquired during a first Atlantic crossing, had ebbed. He was a silent partner in the merchant company of McLeod and McDougal of London and Edinburgh. The financial marriage of the Brunes and McDougals had proven to be propitious and profitable for all concerned. In the place of his late brother-in-law, he had come to the colonies to scout out more trade possibilities for his firm.

James Brune and his sister had stayed with some relations of one of his partners in Norfolk. "And, some friends of Mr. McLeod also live there. I have never seen so many Scotsmen together in one place before as in Norfolk, except in Scotland! That area of the James is quite active in trade. I was particularly impressed with the shipbuilding there. It quite rivals any port in the south of England."

They sat together on a bench at the edge of the trim, landscaped lawn that overlooked the York River on the other side of the great house of Meum Hall. The wide expanse below them was a bluish-gray today, dotted with scattered flotillas of waterfowl and ever-busy with craft of numerous sizes and purposes, sailing in the river breezes in both directions on the great commerce way.

Reverdy was in her room, taking a nap after the rigors of traveling from

Williamsburg. She was not yet accustomed to the climate, and was still recovering from the crossing.

"You put the lie to your description of these tropics, Hugh," said James Brune. "You are an advertisement for settling here. Prosperity becomes you."

"My prosperity has required much labor and risk, and some heartbreak," answered Hugh. He could not forget one of the reasons he had decided to stay in the colonies to purchase and revivify the plantation: Reverdy's marriage to Alex McDougal. He still had the letter that broke his heart those many years ago, tucked away at the bottom of forgotten correspondence, but now remembered. He wondered if Reverdy had kept his last letter in answer to her. If she had not, he would certainly understand. He had not kept a copy of it in his letter book, but he could recall its gently embittered reproach:

"Mr. McDougal is, I do not doubt, deserving of your love, as you must be of his. You both will always be what each of you expects the other to be. I feel obliged, however, to caution you that in future, you will find that love *can* be subjected to a most private and honest rational scrutiny. Perhaps, by that time, natural justice will be kind to you, and, having followed its own inexorable course, rendered you insensible to the weight and wisdom of its dutiful verdict...."

And, he did not need to unearth the letter from her that had prompted his gentle condemnation:

"...A cargo of virtues cannot inspire love of its owner. Love springs from the inscrutable but feckful heart, it cannot be analyzed or measured or subjected to rational scrutiny, not without causing it to wither and die. Love can only be felt or observed, never judged or justified. I have tried to love you in the manner you expect me to, and cannot. I have imagined loving you in that manner, and come to know that I have not the strength to sustain that mode without regarding it in time as an unfair, cruel trial that would exhaust my endurance...."

James Brune sat on the other side of the bench, placidly puffing on a pipe. Hugh glanced at him once. He judged the man to be too good-mannered and discreet to raise the subject of his sister's decision to break the engagement. The subject had not come up, nor even been alluded to. He had asked Hugh if it were possible for them to stay a month or so before resuming their travels, saying that they planned to visit Philadelphia, New York and Boston before returning to the mother country.

Ann Vere, the housekeeper, dived into her rare duty of providing for the needs of Meum Hall's houseguests. She was beside herself with delight, for Reverdy Brune and her brother were gentlefolk from England, and apparently in her employer's best graces to be welcomed to stay for some time before resuming their tour of the colonies. Mrs. Vere and her assistant, Rachel, could not wait solely on the guests, so the housekeeper asked Hugh for assistance "from the quarter," she suggested. Hugh subsequently drafted Dilch as servant pro tempore for the duration of the visit. "What do they fancy in the way of table?' she asked Hugh, inquiring about the siblings' preferences in food. "I haven't the slightest idea, Mrs. Vere," replied Hugh. "You will need to ask them."

Hugh himself acted the gracious host, and thought he had succeeded in not staring at Reverdy longer than was necessary. They had not had a moment alone together. He had not yet even had the chance to show them the house. Reverdy retired almost immediately, after an exchange of formal pleasantries, pleading light-headedness and exhaustion from the ride to Meum Hall from Williamsburg. Her brother was made of more robust stuff.

James Brune asked, "I believe that you remarked that your Negroes here are not slaves. I have also learned during my short time here that one can't free them, if one were inclined to. How did you manage that?"

Hugh shrugged. "I sold them to a Quaker friend of mine in Philadelphia, and my father bought them from him in my uncle's name, and freed them subsequently by arrangement. In theory, my uncle owned them, but in fact they are free. Most of them elected to stay in my employ. It is of dubious legality — if one may attach any legality to laws that perpetuate slavery — but no one will challenge it here, for it would raise an issue that few here are either willing to discuss, or could argue for or against with any lasting credence. It was the only way I could see to flout the insidious law that prohibits their manumission." He paused. "Of course, my uncle has no knowledge of the transaction, and I beg you not to communicate to him or to anyone in his coterie his former status as a benevolent slave owner."

James Brune nodded, and thought about this for a moment, then asked, "But, how do you manage in your account books? I am assuming that you pay these people."

"I manage," replied Hugh. His smile did not invite further questions about the means he employed to remain solvent, when so many other planters were technically bankrupt or teetering on the brink of insolvency.

James Brune smiled in answer to the courteous but perfunctory answer. "Have you any news of your friend Roger?"

"Roger has returned to Woolwich as an artillery instructor. He served as attaché on a number of diplomatic missions on the Continent. He wrote me not long ago that he has applied for a position in several regiments." Hugh waited a moment, then asked, "How did Alex McDougal die, James? Captain Ramshaw, who was a guest here, spoke of several of his passengers this last voyage, and happened to mention you and Reverdy."

"Alex?" sighed James Brune. "Very odd incident, Hugh. He and Reverdy and some of his acquaintances were riding together on Pall Mall a year ago. Two or three robbers came out of the bushes to collect their 'toll,' as they put it in their parlance. One of them stood directly in front of Alex's mount, but his pistol went off accidentally, causing Alex's mount to rear up. The hooves caught the fellow on the chin and broke his neck. Alex was thrown and broke his own neck when he tumbled to the ground. The robbers fled. Alex died instantly, and the robber expired not long afterward."

"Tragic," remarked Hugh. "Reverdy must have been beside herself with sorrow."

"She was in mourning for six months, and was morose for some time after she shed her blacks. I proposed that she accompany me on this voyage, and convinced her it might do her some good. I must say I gave good advice. She has emerged from the tomb of bereavement and is quite her gay self again."

At supper that evening, which also included Rupert Beecroft, Meum Hall's business agent, and William Settle, its steward, the Brune siblings were the focus of attention and conversation. They deftly managed a barrage of questions about political and economic conditions in Britain, spicing much serious talk with amusing anecdotes, wistful recollections, and generous compliments for Virginia. Reverdy, to Hugh's qualified amazement and approval, had become a particularly good conversationalist, able to hold her own in any discussion of politics and society matters.

Hugh sat at the head of the table; James and his sister on either side of him. Outwardly, Reverdy behaved more like an old acquaintance than a former fiancée. But her and Hugh's eyes met briefly but often in the course of the supper. He read in her glances little else but a repressed desire to talk with him alone; she saw nothing in his but an intense curiosity coupled with a struggle not to let it be more than that.

It was a terrific struggle, for Reverdy was more beautiful than he could ever have imagined. Her deportment and poise were natural and unaffected, seeming to radiate from her beauty, indelible facets of it and impossible to imagine without it. She was outspoken and well-spoken, able to contradict another's statement or opinion with grace and without malice. She was now the kind of woman that most men desired but still feared.

She turned to Hugh now. "Hugh, James here tells me that you are now a politician of some sort."

Hugh smiled amiably. "I am a burgess for this county in the General Assembly. That is much like a member of the Commons, but without so large a company."

"I dared not imagine that *you* would have the time for politics."

"It was necessary to make the time."

"James also tells me that you have somehow freed the black folk I saw as we came in. Do other planters and burgesses feel the same way?"

Hugh shook his head. "Not all. But many do think as I do. Laws discourage them from contemplating any serious action "

James Brune sighed. "I don't understand why the institution still exists here, Hugh, and on so vast a scale! It is such an unsavory business. Its like is not to be seen in London!"

Hugh shrugged. "The planters and burgesses here have done what they dare to stem the importation of slaves into the colony. Bills are regularly introduced in the House that would tax the sale and import of slaves. There are those within and without the General Assembly who would abolish the institution altogether. However, everyone knows that the Crown, and especially His Majesty, derive a lucrative revenue from the trade, one that will not be relinquished easily, if ever. Even a modest proposal to abolish the institution is met with animosity in London. And the defenders of the trade are insensible to appeals to reason and right. Their ilk are likewise insensible to our own liberties and the Constitution that guarantees them. The Stamp Act is only the latest instance of their moral lethargy."

James Brune looked pensive. "I have the notion that most planters here are slaves themselves in an insidious web. I mean, slavery is the foundation of their fortunes, yet, wish as they might for its end, they would be reduced to paupers if the system were ever corrected."

Hugh smiled. "You express more wisdom than the Privy Council or the Commons, James. My compliments."

William Settle said, "Mr. Kenrick here was instrumental in the passage of the Resolves that have lately roused the colonies. I wish you could both stay long enough to hear him speak in the House, next session. You won't hear its like in the Commons."

Hugh dismissed the compliment with a shake of his head and a sincere smile. "Not at all, sir. It was Mr. Henry's words that roused the colonies. I was merely his factotum."

Settle grinned. "You are second only to Mr. Henry on the floor, sir. Do not deny it!"

Reverdy asked, "Well, why cannot your General Assembly simply pass a law that abolishes slavery? Surely it must esteem itself worthy of such a weighty action."

Hugh shook his head again. "Such a law would most certainly be nullified by the Board of Trade and the Privy Council, with or without a suspending clause in the law itself. Governor Fauquier is continually rebuked by London for neglecting to require a suspending clause in the legislation he signs. And that particular law is one he would never sign. He knows that very likely he would be recalled and replaced with someone not nearly as friendly to the colony as he. But such a law has less chance of passage than a frost felling the sugar cane harvests of Barbados."

James Brune remarked, "We have read some letters in the London papers, from fellows who wonder at the hypocrisy of colonials, who proclaim that their rights are violated by the Stamp Act and other Parliamentary legislation, yet voice nothing about the rights of their slaves."

Hugh shook his head. "Those people have no grounds for making the accusation. We can hardly champion the rights of slaves when we are in a bit of a fog about what our own rights are. Until that matter is clarified, slavery, I am afraid, must remain a pot in the oven."

"Do you know the Governor?" asked Reverdy.

"Well enough to have leave to upbraid him on occasion without risk of censure."

Reverdy stared at him with some secret meaning. "Alex and I often sat in the Commons gallery to listen to the debates. There are many fine speakers to be heard there. Among them, Sir Dogmael Jones. I understand that he is your father's man. Was he not the barrister who defended those freethinking friends of yours, the ones you were arrested for protecting at the Charing Cross pillory?"

Hugh nodded, but said, "Mr. Jones is his own master. He merely acts as my father's proxy." He paused. "And, my own, in a way. We have never disagreed with what the other has said in session on the subject of liberty."

"Liberty!" exclaimed James Brune. "That is a word we have heard from the moment we set foot in Virginia! It seems to be on everyone's lips, and not often as a prayer, but as a curse and an omen, especially in Norfolk."

Hugh smiled. "Here, it is an altar."

"We audited some of the debates in the House on this Stamp Act," said Reverdy, "and heard Sir Dogmael and Colonel Barré speak on the subject. The people here seem to have adopted one of Colonel Barré's expressions, 'sons of liberty.' We saw some of these men put up a 'liberty pole' in Norfolk."

James Brune looked nostalgic. "Do you know that Sir Dogmael was the only member who refused to vote for the Act that people here are so incensed over? Remarkable audacity!"

"Or courage," said Hugh. "Yes, I know. The 'sons of liberty'? We have an organization here in Caxton of the same name. I am one of its founders."

"Mr. Kenrick here warned us about a plot to bring in the stamps," said William Settle, who proceeded to regale the visitors with an account of the incident at the Caxton pier.

The Brune siblings listened with decorous astonishment. But when Settle was finished, the brother said, "If that is a measure of the animosity, then I believe dark times are ahead for the colonies. The Crown means to have a revenue from them, by fair means or foul."

Hugh shrugged. "Then it will need to send troops to collect it." He paused. "I have nightmares, now and then, about what must happen if the Crown persists in collecting a revenue. They can best be cast in Mr. Milton's words, which I remember to the word, for they illustrate those nightmares with a piquancy I cannot forget: 'Peace is despaired, for who can think submission? War, then, war open or understood. Out flew millions of flaming swords, drawn from the thighs of mighty cherubim; the sudden blaze far round illumined Hell. Highly they raged against the Highest, and fierce with grasped arms, clashed on their sounding shields the din of war, hurling defiance toward the vault of Heaven.'" He grinned. "From *Paradise Lost*. I reacquainted myself with some of it some nights ago."

James Brune frowned. "I, too, am acquainted with the work," he said. "However, if I recollect it correctly, you have spoken from the perspective of Lucifer's minions."

Hugh replied with a short laugh. "Then devils we shall be! I own to having a certain fondness for Lucifer. He rebelled against absolute power, as well."

William Settle permitted himself a laugh. "By God, Mr. Kenrick! I'd like to hear you say that to Reverend Acland! Why, he'd spit and sputter like a badly poured candle!"

Hugh grinned. "Perhaps he would, sir. But you know that his own special devil here is Mr. Frake."

Settle nodded. "This is true," he conceded.

"Who are these gentlemen?" asked James Brune.

"Reverend Acland is the pastor of the church here. Mr. Frake is a neighboring planter and a friend of mine, with whom I have much in common. You shall meet him during your stay. I cannot say as much about the reverend. He is a man of the cloth, but his cloth is moldy and exudes the pungence of fear, malice, and intolerance."

"Do you not attend services?" queried Reverdy. "We were told that the law here is strict on attendance."

"Strict, or onerous? No, I do not attend services here. I refuse to be instructed in morality or preached to by my moral inferiors." He laughed once. "Mr. Frake is equally notorious and of the same mind. I have seen him enter the church only once, and that was only to act as a pallbearer."

"But I understand there are penalties," remarked James Brune.

"Yes," said Settle. "A five shilling fine for missing one in four Sundays, or ten lashes if the fine is not handy to the truant."

Rupert Beecroft added, "The law is still on the books, I believe, which allows a fine of fifty pounds of tobacco for neglecting one's church attendance. But I do not recall it ever being collected. Not in this county, at least."

Settle added, "Reverend Acland and Sheriff Tippet don't dare reprove Mr. Kenrick here, nor Mr. Frake. They are, if I may say so, the county's saviors and benefactors, and expecting them to obey church law would be a measure of ingratitude. Reverend Acland does not even dare demand his pence for these gentlemen's tithables."

"Still," said Hugh, "I would like to see the law abolished. Then it could not be used as a weapon or an excuse."

There ensued a lively discussion of the union of church and state in Britain and in the colonies, and of the extortionate injustice to Dissenters who were taxed to support a church to which they did not belong. Hugh described Caxton and talked about some of his friends and enemies here, while the Brunes described the London scene and related some amusing anecdotes about its society and politicians.

* * *

Chapter 14: The Reunion

Later that evening, after the Brunes had retired, Hugh relaxed alone on the spacious riverfront porch, sitting in a cushioned rattan chair, his solitary form lit by an overhead lantern that swayed gently in the light breezes. The sounds of the night always diminished, and nearly vanished, as the fall waned and cooler air gently heralded the coming of winter. The new air sometimes came from the north, sometimes from the south, most often from the west. Soon the only sounds that might fill the nights would be a cricket lingering past its season, an occasional frog, a pair of tardy geese flying south, and the frequent, melancholy singing of the tenants in the quarter. Hugh sat listening, thinking, watching the lanterns of a few vessels on the York, some moving cautiously along the black space of the river, others stationary at anchorages on the opposite bank a mile away. The sky was clear, with countless stars strewn through the black void like the brilliant white grains of a spilled saltcellar.

An idle observation crossed his mind, as he watched the lights: All the river traffic on the busiest day on the Thames west of London Bridge in the busiest season, boasting hundreds of boats — barges, lighters, ferries, yachts — would not begin to crowd this river. That was how wide and deep it was.

On a little table at his side were another lantern, a pewter mug of coffee — he had long since abandoned the custom of drinking that beverage and tea from a bowl — and a book he had selected from his library. He had not yet opened it, his own copy of Blackstone's digest of his Vinerian lectures, which he wanted to peruse to find an answer to a question that had occurred to him over supper tonight, but could not now summon up the interest.

He was waiting.

An hour passed. He listened as the floor clock in the library chimed eleven.

Then, shortly after the last chime, he heard the sound he had expected to hear, the opening of one of the porch doors. He did not rise, but glanced in that direction, knowing what he would see.

Reverdy appeared, her arm partly outstretched with a silver candle-holder. She stepped onto the porch and gently closed the door behind her. She faced him and smiled. Hugh smiled in answer, and gestured to another chair on the other side of the table.

He noticed that she wore her traveling cloak, and beneath it only a chemise. She had unpinned her black hair, which rippled down over her shoulders. She sat in the extra chair and put the candleholder on the table.

He asked, "Could you not sleep?"

She smiled. "No. I napped too long this afternoon, although it seems I only half slept. And I have difficulty resting in a strange place, until I am accustomed to it."

"Would you like some tea, or coffee? Mrs. Vere always leaves a pot of one or the other in the kitchen for me. I keep such irregular hours after staff have bid me good night."

"No, thank you."

He reached over and touched her cloak. He could see her form faintly beneath the light material. "You are quite shameless, Reverdy. You have donned a camisado, to better beguile me."

"Excuse me?'

"A camisado was a kind of tunic that knights once wore over their armor."

"I do not intend to conquer you, Hugh." She paused. "Nor defend myself."

"Perhaps not. But you are making an effective sally, nonetheless."

She looked away in defiance. "The servant or maid you assigned to me looked so peaceful sleeping that I hadn't the heart to waken her to help me dress again."

"Dilch?" Hugh had drafted the woman from the former slave quarter to wait on the Brunes, and had arranged to have an officer's cot he had bought from Ramshaw years ago put in the hallway for her outside Reverdy's door.

"Yes. Dilch." A moment passed. Reverdy asked, "Have you forgiven me?"

"The matter is past forgiveness, Reverdy."

"I did not understand your last letter to me, not until after a year with Alex. But by then, it was too late. You said some cruel things in that letter, but, in time, they became true." Reverdy sighed. "He was a kind and gentle man, Hugh. Not like you at all, of course. I grew fond of him."

Hugh nodded. "But never to love him." He hoped that he had managed to keep the harshness of unbidden jealousy out of his words. He had wanted to say, "In spite of his being those things."

Reverdy nodded her head once in concession to the statement that was not a question.

"Was it your mother's decision, or your own, to marry him?"

Reverdy imagined he had asked, "Whose decision was it to reject me?" After a moment, she said, "A little of both." She paused. "Mother never did approve of you. To her, you were not common enough to be respectable. Or, perhaps, not respectable enough to be common. You often scandalized her by the things you said and did."

"I know."

"Your arrest in London made up her mind."

"Did it yours?"

Reverdy bowed her head and stared at her lap. "Yes," she whispered. "I had always been frightened of you. And, at the same time...thrilled..."

"Which are you now?"

"A little of both," answered Reverdy. "No. Less frightened, and more...thrilled...."

Hugh smiled. "You must know that I am worse than you knew me, when last we met." He paused. "This country coaxes the man out of one-self, if one exists to be coaxed. Completes the circle, so to speak. It demands more of him, or rather something that is not required of him in England, or not solicited there. I know that had I remained in England, I would be only half of what I am now. Yet I am still the same man you knew." He chuckled. "The same man *I* knew."

Reverdy grinned. "If I didn't know you better, Hugh, I would charge you with a vain offense of English manhood."

Hugh shook his head. "*Do* you know me better?"

"I know that had you remained in England, you would still be formidable, half of what you are now, or whole, and in jeopardy because of it."

"Or about to be tried for treason or seditious libel, or already in prison for it."

"When Alex and I were in Paris, we attended many of the *salons*, and at one of them James spoke with the Prussian ambassador. That man told him that he disapproved of all the talk and speculation that is the rage there, much of it that questioned the monarchy. He said to James, 'Argue all you wish, but obey.'"

Hugh scoffed in amusement. "Sounds rather like the summary advice of a philosopher-tyrant, than of an ambassador. And, if that is King Frederick's policy, I imagine that Mr. Voltaire regrets having dubbed him 'the Great.'" Hugh looked at her. "What prompted you to relate that anecdote?"

"You, Hugh. I don't see you fitting into any of the places I've seen. You are too much of a man."

"Virginia tolerates me." Hugh paused, then asked, "Are you making love to me, Reverdy?"

"I confess that I am. I didn't know how I would feel when I saw you again. I didn't expect to see you ever again. Or that you would ever want to see me again. And there you were, staring at me through the window of that inn in Hampton, so soon after we arrived. Then you rode off. I own that I felt slighted."

Hugh smiled. "I was just as startled to see you. Was it your idea to come here?"

"Yes. It fitted James's plans."

"How did you know where I had settled?"

"Your mother wrote me about you," said Reverdy. "It was a courteous note, with nothing recriminating in it. I am ashamed to say that I did not answer her."

Hugh turned in his chair to face her directly. "When you agreed to join your brother on the voyage here, did you hope to find me?"

After a long moment, she whispered, "Yes."

Hugh smiled. "Say it to me."

"I hoped to find you, and break my connection with Alex." Reverdy paused. "The voyage was rigorous, almost a kind of penance for...having abandoned you."

"Why, Reverdy?"

The woman gazed at him, and then at the sky. "For as long as I've known you, Hugh, you have been a kind of Polaris to me, a North Star," she said, nodding upward, "around which all other stars and matters revolve. When I meet other men, and somehow without my even knowing it, I always compare them with you. I even looked at Alex that way, when he would do something, or say something, and I'd ask myself, almost against my will: Would Hugh have done that, or said that? But I persuaded myself that I was not being fair to him, and that he deserved a different measure." She smiled meekly. "I could forget you, for a while, but never what you

were. Sometimes I cursed that measure. I think I called it, in my last letter
to you, a 'cargo of virtues.' It would intrude on my estimates of those other
men. It was an annoying intrusion, until I realized that it was an indelible
measure…and right."

She remembered her last letter, as well, thought Hugh. He sighed once,
reached over and took one of her hands, then raised it to his lips. He let her
hand linger for a moment, then returned it. "Reverdy, I think you should
retire now. We will talk tomorrow. I shall show you and James Meum Hall,
and take you both around for introductions."

"All right." Reverdy rose and picked up the candleholder. "Good night,
Hugh." She made to turn, then paused. "Alex and I took a grand tour of the
Continent, after we were married. Or, rather, a short tour of it. Paris,
Vienna, Rome, Venice, and Naples. We were gone only a year. Alex was also
busy there meeting merchants and correspondents for his firm, as well. I
must tell you about the things we saw, and the people we met, and the
things we heard."

"I would like that. I have yet to set foot on the Continent. I have only
my adventures on this one to relate."

After a pause, she smiled down at him. "You won't mind hearing about
my travels with Alex?"

Hugh shook his head once. "No. Not now."

"Well, good night. Hugh."

"Good night, Reverdy."

He watched her glide away, then open the porch door and disappear
inside. The door closed with a soft click of the latch. He listened to her faint
steps as she went up the stairs to her room. When he could hear no more,
he turned in his chair again and listened to the night. In his thoughts were
questions he could not now answer: Had his first love returned? Or had an
enemy? Or a stranger? He could not decide which question required an
answer.

He knew only that he was elated. He was her north, and always had
been. Etáin had bestowed the same rank, so long ago, it seemed, on another
man. On Jack Frake, his dearest friend. Reverdy would meet them both
tomorrow, he thought, and he wondered whether or not they would think
they had much in common.

But he was her north. He felt vindicated for having predicted the justice that would someday punish her. And punishment was the last thing he
ever wished to visit on her.

* * *

Inevitably, the inhabitants of Caxton expressed curiosity about Meum Hall's visitors. Mid-morning the next day, as Hugh consulted in his library with Mr. Beecroft and William Settle about the day's tasks before he devoted time to "entertaining" his guests, emissaries arrived with invitations to dinner and supper at Enderly, Granby Hall, and Otway's place. Reece Vishonn even proposed a ball. Hugh replied to all the invitations, citing available dates for suppers. He took the time to write Vishonn a brief note of thanks for the honor, declining a ball but relenting to a supper with other guests. When he was finished with those social chores, he donned his "field clothes" — pants, cotton shirt, and straw hat — and took Reverdy and James Brune on a walking tour of the fields, the cooperage area, the brickyard, and the tenant quarter. His visitors were fascinated with the bamboo conduit that Hugh's tenants were still dismantling and carefully storing in a shed near the quarter. "Quite ingenious," remarked James Brune. "That, and the tower there, and the water running from it into the house."

"The conduit has saved me crops, time, and has reduced wastage."

"I suppose other planters have copied your idea," remarked James Brune.

"Some have tried, those who have a stream adjacent to their properties. But, even so, the idea is not adaptable to all fields. Mine has the advantage of a slope, so that the water flows without much effort. My friend, Jack Frake, dug a kind of canal from the stream there to solve his watering problems. I am certain he will want to show you it."

He turned to smile at Reverdy and found her staring at him with more fascination than she had shown for the plantation. Her expression was one of perplexed amusement, as though she were trying to reconcile the intellectual, gentleman, and burgess and his library with the smells, mundane concerns and tasks, and brute labor required to salvage, maintain, and wrest a pound of profit from the earth and the plantation that sat atop it. And in her glance he saw a glimmer of admiration. But he turned to her brother and, with a wave that included the fields they had just traversed, asked in jest, "Still interested in trying your hand here, James?"

James Brune laughed and shook his head. "At this? Gads, no! The merchant's trade for me, ever more, thank you very much, sir!"

When they returned to the great house later in the morning, James Brune elected to take an afternoon nap. "I am afraid our hike has tired me just a bit. May I borrow a book from your library, Hugh?" he asked. "Reading helps put me to sleep."

But Hugh discerned the man's true motive, that James sensed that his sister and host wished to have some time together, alone. "Help yourself, James," he said, waving a hand in the direction of the library. "But, I must warn you: There are no dull books in my library."

James Brune laughed. "I will have you know that any book will put me to sleep, even my own memoirs, if I had enough ambition to write them! I owe many of my slumbers to Mr. Milton's *Paradise Lost*."

Reverdy grinned. "Which took him nearly a year to read, on that account."

James Brune took his leave and headed for Hugh's library. Reverdy and Hugh remained on the porch. Mrs. Vere, ever alert to her employer's and guests' ease, appeared then, and asked Hugh if he required anything. "Tea, Mrs. Vere," answered Hugh. "It is nearly time for it anyway."

Reverdy and Hugh sat in the chairs they had used the night before. She asked, nodding to his work clothes, "Do you dress like that for every guest, Hugh?"

"No," answered Hugh, "only when guests arrive without notice."

"I am having trouble seeing you that way, and remembering your library."

"Then let me help you end your trouble." He turned their conversation to literature and music. Reverdy had read Sterne's *Tristram Shandy*, and Fielding's *Tom Jones*, and asked Hugh what he thought of those and other recent novels.

"I gave up trying to read Mr. Sterne's opus," said Hugh. "It is a monstrously confusing work. And Mr. Fielding's novel is but a bawdy, picaroonish tale, passing for a morality play." He paused. "There are some promising writers about, but nothing I have read to date has surpassed *Hyperborea*. I do not think anything ever will."

"I have not yet read that," replied Reverdy, sounding doubtful.

"I have two copies of the novel. You will have the opportunity to read it."

"In Paris, we attended the Opéra-Comique, and heard Sophie Arnould sing in Rameau's *Les Indes galantes*, an opera-ballet. That was quite a treat! And she has lived quite a fulsome life, as well! We heard that when she tired of her last lover, she sent everything he had ever given her to his wife — jewels, carriage, and even her two children! And that wife was the daughter of a powerful minister at court, and with her father she made such a fuss about all those dubious treasures that appeared on her doorstep, that the luckless fellow was obliged to depart for South America! Why, *that* story was nearly as entertaining as the opera itself!"

Hugh smiled tentatively. "It certainly has the ring of a modern farce. Perhaps, with the right libretto, it could serve as a comic opera, the French managing their stage better than they do their wars."

Reverdy laughed. "Hugh, you are awful!"

They were silent for a while. Then Reverdy announced, with almost childlike enthusiasm, "I can sing! Dare me to name you the parts of an orchestra!"

Hugh turned to her, stunned. *"Sing?"*

Reverdy put on an expression of mock offense. "Yes. I have been taking lessons from an Italian instructor, Silvio Berlusconi, in London. He has coached many of the best opera singers."

"I should like to hear you some time."

"You shall. I was quite honest with Signore Berlusconi when he accepted me as a student. I told him that my goal was not Covent Garden or Drury Lane, but my own drawing room. I still take lessons from him, when I think my voice has grown lazy." Reverdy paused, pleased to see the look of surprise on Hugh's face. "In London, Alex and I gave occasional concerts, with hired musicians. One evening, at our guests' urging, I sang all the lyrics for Rameau's *The Paladins*. It was a great success."

Hugh laughed. "If you are that good, expect to be invited to perform at one of Mr. Vishonn's balls, or perhaps even be invited to the Governor's Palace. Mr. Fauquier holds frequent concerts there, especially when the General Assembly is sitting. He plays the violin, viola, and cello, as well, and often joins with other musicians. He is quite good."

"I hope we can attend one. James and I saw the Governor's residence the day we stopped in Williamsburg. It is grander than any English county seat."

"Of course it is. It is the seat of a dominion, not of a mere county. Of a virtual country, in fact. But there is to be no General Assembly, this fall. The Governor prorogued it until spring of next year, over the Stamp Act Resolves. Still, he may announce a concert." Hugh looked mischievous. "Name the parts of an orchestra."

Reverdy put on an impudent smile. "There are three principal parts: the winds, the strings, and the percussion. In the winds, clarinets, bassoons, and oboes work with flutes, horns, and trumpets for counterpoint. Of the strings, basses, violins, and violas are strategically placed in the pit. Of the percussion, drums and timpani provide rhythm and accent to a score. A harpsichord or pianoforte may either lead, accompany, or comment on a composition."

Hugh regarded Reverdy with newfound respect. "When did you decide that you wanted to sing?"

"I think the notion came to me when you took me to an opera in London."

"I remember how thrilled you were." Hugh smiled. "And with Vivaldi's 'Echo Concerto.'"

Reverdy said, "Yes," then added, "Alex and I spent a week in Vienna. We attended a performance of Gluck's *Orfeo et Eurdice*. Gluck himself conducted the orchestra. I think that is my favorite opera. But in Paris, we accompanied one of Alex's French correspondents to the home of Minister Choiseul, which was a marvelous place. We attended a concert in his Octagon Room, which contains his favorite paintings. That room is lit by a glass dome, the better to appreciate his collection."

"Marvelous idea, that glass dome," said Hugh. "I'm sure that a hundred thousand Paris shopkeepers and country peasants were happy to have contributed so many sous in tax to its cost."

"There you go, talking politics again!"

Hugh cocked his head. "Monsieur Choiseul is our country's most dedicated enemy, Reverdy. He is determined to raise France to greatness again, even on the heads of his own people, or on their empty stomachs. He is rebuilding France's navy, to better oppose our own. Nothing is more dangerous than a humiliated Frenchman bent on restoring his honor."

"I found the French delightful company."

Hugh smiled in concession. "They are delightful, even in war. At least, they are in Europe. Over here, though, they are quite barbaric, even though they think themselves superior in every way."

Reverdy frowned in thought. After a moment she remarked, "I find it amazing that you do not attend services here. Not that *I* am so conscientious about it." She studied him for a moment. "Of course, I am not surprised by your remarks. I remember how you silenced Vicar Faure that evening, when we visited you in London. I know your thoughts on the

Church." She paused. "He married us, in Eckley."

Hugh smiled. "I have read much of the premiere French atheist's works, and found that I had progressed beyond his principled indifference to God and religion — since last we met."

"Who is that? Perhaps we encountered him. We met many clandestine atheists at the *salons* in Paris. They are quite civil and not the monsters churchmen make them out to be. In fact, I found them to be a decenter sort than most churchmen."

Hugh smiled in agreement with her observation. He said, "You will undoubtedly have reason to repeat that sentiment once you have met Reverend Acland." He paused. "Who was that French atheist? Julien Offray de la Mettrie. I have a copy of his book, *Man the Machine*, in my library. He wrote that even if a God existed, there was no moral reason why anyone should worship him. That has been my position for as long as I can recollect. But I don't think you could have met him. He died some years ago. However, there is another fellow, Baron d'Holbach, a chemist who contributes often to Diderot's *Encyclopédie*. I believe he is an advanced atheist." He sighed. "Unfortunately, to openly profess atheism or even freethinking here would invite severe consequences. It is not even an acceptable subject of speculation. Here, religious matters are taken much more seriously than in England."

Reverdy nodded in concession. "And I have observed that people take politics more seriously here than they do in England, as well. James and I have met a number of them who have the same regard for His Majesty as your de la Mettrie had for God."

Hugh chuckled, not at her, but because Reverdy was making some very agreeable observations. He said, "And I expect that number to grow. Your brother James was right, what he said last night over supper. The Crown means to have a revenue from us, by fair means or foul."

They were quiet for a while. Mrs. Vere returned with a tray and a tea service. After she had poured cups, she vanished back inside the house.

Reverdy sipped her tea once, then said, "I was surprised to note my portrait in your library, Hugh. I confess I did not expect to see it."

"Surprised, and pleased?"

"Pleased? Yes." Reverdy took another sip. "Has it always been there?"

"Ever since I moved here, Reverdy." Hugh smiled. "It was one of the first pictures I had put up. I still have your locket, as well, somewhere among my things." He paused. "Do you still have mine?"

Reverdy shook her head. "Mother asked me to remove it, and I did. She took it to a shop in Eckley and sold it". She paused. "But that never could cause me to forget you, Hugh."

"And I could never forget you, Reverdy." Hugh shook his head. "I own that there was someone else for a while, but she was merely the hope of desperation." He smiled. "You were always on the wall of my library of concerns, elevated above all those tomes, as a measure of what I wanted." After a pause, he added, "And you are lovelier than ever, and, I own, more tempting and godly than you were on the afternoon of our moment at the brook on your father's estate."

"Oh, Hugh!" whispered Reverdy. She reached over and touched his hand. "I am so sorry I caused you pain."

Hugh gripped and held the hand over his. "It is past."

"Is it, Hugh?" asked Reverdy. "I know that you are not a forgiving man."

"It must be past. And it is not a matter of forgiveness. You are not afraid of me now, nor of my 'cargo of virtues.'" Hugh looked at her with hungry admiration. "And I have never been afraid of you."

This time it was Reverdy who took his hand and raised it to her lips. The hand in hers turned and traced her lips with a finger, and then the palm caressed her cheek. She breathed once into the palm, then thrust it away and abruptly rose. In a strained, subdued voice, she said, without looking at him, "I think I should take a nap, as well, Hugh."

"Dilch will rouse you when it is time for dinner," said Hugh simply.

Torn between wanting to rush away and preserving her poise, Reverdy walked haltingly to the front door, and went inside.

As she turned to open the door, Hugh noticed a tear rolling down one of Reverdy's cheeks.

He observed the tear and the conflict, and fought the impulse to follow her.

"Not yet," he said out loud to himself. He knew that his emotions were running far ahead of his reason. He said out loud, again, "Not yet. It has been only twenty-four hours, Master Kenrick. Wait."

* * *

Reverdy was a maelstrom of emotions, tossing and turning on the bed, overwhelmed by Hugh's behavior. Cruel tenderness, she thought. That is what he paid me. She had expected anything but that, anything but the noble arrogance of a forgiveness that was not a forgiveness. After all these years, she was still his measure. And he, hers. She wondered, now that she had seen some of the world, as much of it as he had, if she could submit herself to the requisites of his measure. She could not before, but then, looking back over the years, she had only been a girl, alternately frightened and thrilled by the thing she saw in him. His unrequited love, she mused. Could she answer it? Could she be what he expected her to be? Was he something to live up to, to aspire to be worthy of? Had she the strength? She thought she had, now. As did he. What gave him that idea? And what right to think it?

Quietly, into the fabric of her pillow, she cursed Hugh and cried her renewed love for him.

Restless with irresolution, she rose again and left her room. Downstairs, she knocked on the door of Hugh's library, and when there was no answer, opened it and went in. He was not there. She crossed the breezeway, strode through the supper room, went outside to the kitchen and encountered Mrs. Vere in the midst of her chores. "Where is Mr. Kenrick?" she asked.

"I believe Mr. Kenrick is in the fields, milady," answered the woman.

"I see." She noticed Fiona Chance, Rachel, and Dilch preparing some vegetables for dinner. "When will dinner be served?"

"At four of the clock, milady." Mrs. Vere paused. "It is only two now, but I could ask Miss Chance to prepare you something now, if you like."

"No, thank you. I think I shall try to find Mr. Kenrick in the fields." Reverdy turned for the kitchen door. As she left, she felt the eyes of the three women on her, and knew that they recognized her from the picture on the wall of Hugh's library.

Outside, she stood at the edge of the brick courtyard that divided the great house from the beginning of the fields, and scanned the expanse carefully, impatiently, a hand shielding her eyes from the mid-afternoon sun. She saw figures moving far off in the field; none of them was Hugh. She turned and used the brick walkway that skirted the great house. Perhaps he was looking after his landscaped lawn on that side of the house, she thought. But no one was there but one of the black tenants, busy pruning a row of boxwoods and young holly trees with a pair of clippers. She approached this person. "Have you seen Mr. Kenrick about?"

The man rose from his task and doffed his floppy hat. "No, Missy, I haven't. Sometimes, this time of day, he goes into town." He paused. "Want I should look and fetch him for you?"

Reverdy shook her head. "No, thank you. I'll wait until he returns."

The gardener doffed his hat again, then knelt again and returned to his task, trimming the shoots from the trunks of the plants. She wandered away in the direction of the river. She reached the edge of the lawn and the bluff that plummeted down to a narrow bank. Hugh had shown her and her brother the river and the plantation pier earlier in the day. A steep narrow path led from the lawn to the pier. She turned to look back at the great house. It seemed so far away now, and the gardener an indistinct figure half-hidden by the tall boxwoods and holly trees.

Then she heard a noise, a splash, and turned to search for the source.

She saw him swimming in the river below, close to the pier. She watched him stand up in the water, and saw that he was naked. She noticed his clothes piled on the sandy bank. He dived back into the water and swam out a distance from the pier.

Without thinking, almost as though another Reverdy were pushing her to commit the act, she stepped onto the path and hurtled down to the pier, pulled at first almost as much by the momentum of the descent as by a blind, irresistible desire. When she was on the bank, she watched him swim with measured laziness back and forth in the deeper water, some yards from the pier. He did not notice her.

By that time, she understood what had propelled her to the bank: a chance to relive, or recapture, the moment at the brook years ago, on her father's estate, when Hugh had come upon her and paid her an honor she had not since received from another man. Not even from Alex.

Slowly, but deliberately, she removed her garments, all but her chemise.

It was when she stood in only the chemise that he happened to look up and notice her on the bank.

A cool breeze played with the folds of her chemise, making her more aware of her body, and pleasing her more than if she were naked. Reverdy wondered, almost as an afterthought, if she resembled the drawing of her that she had seen at Windridge Court in London, when she happened upon the plans he had drawn of a Doric temple on a secluded part of the Danvers estate. She acknowledged now that it was those plans that had frightened her the most, not their first kiss then, not the violent, possessive way he had held her, not even his outrageous actions and unconventional thinking before then and since, and the trouble those aspects of him would always cause. It was those drawings, and his vision of her, that had planted deep in her consciousness an unreasoning fear of him.

But that is what he is, she thought, and that is what draws you to him. And she felt that other Reverdy take possession of her, and compel her to commit herself to this moment, to be what she was at the side of the brook, even if it meant the demise of everything that had happened after she had written him that last letter. He sees something in me, and it is here now, she thought. She wondered if this was what he meant by justice, as well.

She stepped into the water, not feeling how cold it was. She waded out until the water reached her hips, then immersed herself up to her shoulders.

Hugh swam slowly towards her. She watched him approach for a while, then closed her eyes. In a moment, she felt his hands gripping her shoulders, then one hand was planted firmly in her back, holding her close to him, the other exploring her form beneath the water with wondrous, renewed greed. She answered by moving her hands up to grip his shoulders. Then his mouth was on hers, and they kissed for a long moment.

He picked her up and carried her to the bank. He removed her chemise, then laid her down on her own garments, and knelt over her for a while, drinking in the vision stretched out before him, staring into her half-closed eyes. She reached up, clutched his face, and brought it down to her breasts. A moment later, when he entered her, she whispered into his ear, "I love you, Hugh." His answer was a groan and teeth biting into her neck.

Later, as they lay together in each other's arms, warmed by each other and by the sun, she said into his neck, in the manner of a solemn oath, "I will try to be what you expect me to be, Hugh."

He replied, in a slow cadence, his eyes closed in rapturous exhaustion, "Perhaps, in the effort to be what I expect you to be — or what you imagine I expect you to be — you will become it. Then you will know me better, and I, you."

She pressed her face closer into his neck and inhaled deeply, as though she were trying to breathe some essence of him into her own being.

*　*　*

Chapter 15: The Amazons

It was not until late November, when all the other invitations had been accepted and fulfilled, that Hugh was able to take his guests to visit the Frakes at Morland Hall. On a dreary, overcast afternoon, Hugh rode with Reverdy in the riding chair, while James Brune rode one of Meum Hall's mounts, the short distance to Morland Hall.

The round of dinners and suppers with neighboring planters over the last two weeks had tired them, but Hugh was looking forward to introducing the Brunes especially to his most cherished friends, and assured them that the conversation at Morland Hall would not remain courteously conventional and safely topical. He said little more about the Frakes and their other expected guests, other than giving the Brunes brief backgrounds of Jack and Etáin, of Thomas Reisdale and John Proudlocks.

Hugh and Reverdy met alone when they could. He did not care if their discreet, passionate unions broke all proprieties that governed the relationship between a man of his rank and a gentlewoman of her status.

"It is the end of my Carthusian sojourn," he said to her once as they lay together in his bed one night. "I am almost grateful that Governor Fauquier has prorogued the Assembly, for otherwise I should be in Williamsburg now, engaged in far less joyful matters, and we would only be able to see each other over tea in Mr. Marot's coffeehouse." He pressed some of her disheveled hair to his lips.

Reverdy said lazily into his ear, "Have you been such a monk? You make love, not like a man who has forsaken all earthly ecstasy, but like a master of its arts."

"I have imagined what I would do, how I would be with you, Reverdy, so many times. You were never forgotten, not in any sense." Hugh turned his head to gaze at her. He gently ran the back of a hand from her breasts up to her shoulder, to her neck, then to her face, ears, and hair. "You look magnificently consumed, Reverdy, like a woman who is resting from a violent ride to heaven."

Reverdy blushed with pride, pressed her face into his, while her hand dug cruelly into the muscles of his bare upper arm.

When Etáin met Reverdy Brune-McDougal, she instantly recalled, from so many years ago, during their first meeting at Enderly at the victory ball, Hugh's and her exchange about the woman, whom she recognized from the framed profile of her in Hugh's library.

"Ancient lore has it that a dying Amazon would hold her slayer's eyes, and cause him to fall in love with her, so that after she was gone, he would pine away in regret. Love of her was her cruel retribution." "Has an Amazon gazed into your eyes, Mr. Kenrick?" "I no longer think so. She is not slain, and has married a Boeotian. It is the stuff of one of Mr. Garrick's plays." "One of his tragedies?" "For my role in it, yes. For hers, a farce that was not so amusing. You see, she wrote me a kind letter...."

Etáin now asked herself, as she appraised the regal, elegant woman who was introduced to her by Hugh: Had it been a tragedy, or a farce? Had *this* woman truly married a Boeotian, as Hugh had called the woman's late husband? How could *this* woman have given up Hugh? She glanced at him. He was introducing her brother James to Jack, Thomas Reisdale, and John Proudlocks. He looked happy, and somewhat proud, and at ease as he introduced Reverdy to the men.

And she glanced at Jack. This was one of the rare times that he had decided to hold a supper for purely social reasons. John Proudlocks had brought the news that Meum Hall had visitors, and that they were friends of Hugh's from England. Jack had extended the invitation out of sheer curiosity.

"Except for John Ramshaw, I don't know any of Hugh's other friends," he said when he proposed the supper to her. "For once, I am genuinely intrigued by his past associations."

Etáin had nodded in agreement. "Mr. Proudlocks said that the woman is Hugh's former fiancée, and the man her brother. They grew up together, I understand."

Jack was also appraising the woman, and seemed tentatively to approve of her.

Reverdy Brune-McDougal made her own observations, as well. She could tell by the way Etáin spoke to Hugh, by the way she looked at him, by her manner with him, and by his manner with her, that this woman had been his "hope of desperation." She was not certain she could like her, or her husband. Thomas Reisdale was civil to a fault, while the bronze face of the Indian fascinated her when she knew it should not. She wondered what his place was here. She and James had seen a few Indians in Norfolk, and in Hampton, and they were nothing like this man.

After supper, while Mary Beck, the cook, and Ruth Dakin, her assistant in the kitchen, served tea, coffee, and dessert, Jack Frake announced, "I have decided to use this occasion to allow Mr. Proudlocks there to present his first 'fragment' on politics and law." He glanced at the curious faces of his guests. "He is studying law under Mr. Reisdale. I have not heard yet what he is to read, but I am certain that what he has to say will enliven conversation." He nodded to his friend at the other end of the table.

Reverdy leaned forward a little and addressed her host. "Mr. Kenrick warned us not to expect the usual table talk, Mr. Frake."

Jack Frake nodded in acknowledgement. "Life is too short to spend on the mundane, Madam."

Proudlocks glanced at his tutor. The lawyer motioned to him to rise. Proudlocks stood up, took out a sheet of paper from his coat, and smiled shyly at his audience. "This is my understanding of the Glorious Revolution of late the last century. Please forgive any errors or miscomprehensions I may relate to you." Then he brought up the paper and read from it.

After reciting briefly the events that led to the Revolution, he read, "They all wanted a king, and abhorred a republic, a kingless republic, that is. They could not think beyond the notion of a monarchical nation. The throne was unoccupied, perilously vacant. Filling it with a special human figure was not so much an obsession, as it was a mental necessity, somewhat like a picture justifying a gilt frame. The throne was the linchpin of constitutional polity; remove it, and society would fly apart. The government was like an elephant. If it lacked the requisite appendages, such as a stately trunk, which could be said to be a sovereign, how could it still be an elephant?

"A republic? Banish the thought! A nation, a government with a graceless executive who was not royal, who had no anointed divinity or hereditary rights or lineage traceable to Adam? Inconceivable! A republic had been tried; the result was a dictatorship — Cromwell! That experience seemed to prove the necessity of a king! James the Second, it was decided after some heated debate between the Tories and Whigs, had abandoned or abdicated the throne. In a juvenile fit of pique, before taking flight, he destroyed the writs for a new Parliament, tossed the Great Seal into the Thames, and ordered the disbandment of the army, hoping that by committing these acts of regal vandalism, the country would fall into turmoil and anarchy, and consequently facilitate his return, on his own terms, by force of arms, or in answer to a plea and an apology. His actions were deemed disgraceful and dangerous behavior.

"The Tories adhered to the principle of hereditary right to the throne as a divine attribute, and absolutely necessary to a stable polity. The Whigs had progressed to the idea of the Crown or throne as a Parliamentary entitlement, a status bestowed by grace and sufferance of both Houses: in the Commons, in the name of the people; in Lords, in the name of the nation, not necessarily the same as the people. The Tories believed that a throne should rule, requiring only tacit recognition by the ruled and deserving obsequious submission to its edicts, imperatives, and pleasures. The Whigs believed that a compact should exist between the king and people, with removal from the throne as a supreme penalty for law-breaking and abuse of that compact.

"The Whig position was an expression of Mr. Locke's theory of the right relationship between government and the governed. But applied to the political knowledge of the time — " Proudlocks paused to interject "and this is Mr. Reisdale's analogy, not my own — this was akin to clothing the elephant in the best haberdashery."

Everyone at the table chuckled at this, except James Brune.

Proudlocks continued. "And these are my queries: The compact between the king and the people sanctions rebellion against a law-breaking king. But is the compact between Parliament and the people so well-founded and inviolate that it forbids rebellion? If Parliament becomes as abusive as a king, what difference should it make to the abused that the abuser is many-headed, and not single? Are not their liberties being violated by one or the other? If our excellent Constitution is so proof against tyranny, why must these questions be asked, in these troubling times?"

Jack Frake remarked, "Parliament believes that rebellion is sanctioned. That is a one-sided compact, clearly evident in its latest actions." He smiled at Proudlocks. "Forgive me the interruption, John. Please, continue."

Proudlocks smiled in answer, then concluded, "Parliament is a legislative body, the king, an executive one. Should that make a difference? Let us consider the charge of treason. If one resists or speaks out against the depredations of royal agents, is that action more or less treasonous than opposing the agents of usurpant Parliamentary legislation? Reason compels me to say they are coequal."

"Excellent, John," said Reisdale. He looked around the table. "I did not assist him in the composition of that dissertation, ladies and gentlemen. It is all of his own effort."

"Bravo, John," said Jack Frake.

"Well done, sir," said Hugh Kenrick.

Proudlocks nodded in acknowledgement with a grin. "Thank you, sirs," he said, and took his seat again next to Reisdale.

The conversation remained on politics, and as it coursed around the table, James Brune sat in speechless shock. He uttered not one word, literally. The nature of the talk left him stunned and blank; he only knew that such talk was unthinkable in London among his own circle.

He glanced at Reverdy; she was sitting and listening to it all with a faint smile. He noted that her eyes lit up somehow when she looked at Hugh. He realized that she and Hugh had reconciled and reunited. What that implied he refused to contemplate.

He choked on his own silence.

"James wished to suborn not only the Constitution and Parliament, but the entire nation," said Hugh. "Well, Sidney said it first: Absolute monarchy, such as James sought, depends on corruption."

"It was seven recalcitrant bishops who refused to order the clergy to recite the Declaration of Indulgence, and an infant boy, James's son, who caused the Revolution of 1688," said Reisdale. "James wanted an heir, and got one at the last moment. And the bishops, tried and acquitted of seditious libel, were hailed as saviors of the nation."

"And a Dutch stadtholder and his designs to contain Louis the Fourteenth, who also made the Revolution possible," said Hugh. "William of Orange was not so much interested in healing English political strife as securing Dutch independence from France. Becoming King of England would obtain that security. Healing the strife was merely a means to his end. A united England would checkmate French designs on the Netherlands. What a piece of statecraft!"

"And the King of France laughed up his sleeve at it all, and did nothing, not even move against the Dutch," said Reisdale. He added with a chuckle, "That was *his* contribution to the Glorious Revolution."

"All important factors of the event," said Hugh, "but none of them fundamental."

"What was fundamental, then?" broached James Brune.

"A lingering memory of liberty," answered Hugh, "and a reluctance to repeat the regicide of the Civil War."

James Brune noticed an object that rested upright in one corner of the supper room, a furled banner on a staff. He ventured to ask his host, "I recognize the stripes there, Mr. Frake. In the midst of all the extraordinary politicking in this county, were they perhaps purloined from a hapless East Indiaman?"

Jack Frake explained the origins of the banner of the Sons of Liberty.

When his friend was finished, Hugh added, "I believe the lieutenant was as discouraged by our banner as he was by our presence, that day."

"Discouraged, and confused," said Reisdale.

Jack addressed the Brunes. "Undoubtedly Hugh has told you of my own origins and my association with a smuggling gang in Cornwall."

"Yes," answered James Brune. "That, also, is an extraordinary story."

"It is the banner that my friends lacked, when they stood up against the Crown."

Etáin said, "I helped sew that banner."

The Brunes were then treated to a second telling of the day that Caxton defied the Crown.

When they were finished with dessert, the men repaired to Jack's library, while Etáin took Reverdy to her music room, which also boasted some shelves of books.

* * *

Etáin asked, "Can you read notes?"

Reverdy replied, "Of course. But you would be surprised at the number of famous singers in London who cannot."

"I have transcribed much for my harp, and the dulcimer over there. Lately, I converted Mr. Handel's 'Dettingen Te Deum,' and I have the words to it, as well. An uncle in London sends music to my mother, who sends it to me."

Reverdy said with enthusiasm, "I have heard it in London. It is enthralling."

"Jack does not care for any of the lyrics to anything I have played. Nor do I. But it is their sense he enjoys, as do I."

Reverdy asked, "Is there a chorus here, or perhaps a private society of singers?"

"None that I know of. Perhaps one exists in Philadelphia. Certainly, none about here. If there were, I would know of it."

Etáin crossed the room to a table on which were stacks of paper bound with string. She showed Reverdy her collection of transcriptions, laboriously studied and written on blank sheets specially printed by the late Wendel Barret. Next to the table was a cabinet that held more music, designed by her husband and built by Moses Topham, Morland's carpenter.

Reverdy glanced through the sheets of Etáin's transcribed Dettingen Te Deum. "Oh, this is wonderful, Etáin!" She turned to face her hostess. "May I call you Etáin?"

Etáin nodded.

"Thank you." Reverdy took the bundle of paper and sat in an armchair, then continued. "I shall never forget the first time I heard the 'Te Deum' at the Opera House. Even when I listen to certain passages of it now, in my head, I experience the same thing, a kind of uplifting — being transported off the earth, not caring if I were thrust back down onto it to my death. Just to have experienced it once is some kind of reward. But you must know that once is not enough. And, then, of course the words to it are irrelevant. One wonders what Mr. Handel felt as he composed it."

Reverdy looked at Etáin again. "Oh, Etáin! I pity you for not ever having heard it as it was meant to be heard! The chorus! The orchestra! The great drums that seem like cannon, beating in time, insisting that one rise, and all of it together propelling one and the music upward to some kind of heaven. Not to the heaven that any minister would preach about in church, but to a glory whose roots are somehow temporal, somehow more immediate, and meaningful, even though one is lifted up from the earth.... Oh, I don't know how else to put it! You see, I have never had a reason to describe it, until now. God forgive me, but what I feel in those moments has little to do with Him."

After a moment, Etáin replied, "I understand. I have listened to it in my head, too, as I do all the music I transcribe. I can only imagine what you have heard, and so must envy you." She smiled tentatively. "And your late husband — did he feel the same thing?"

For a moment, Reverdy wore an expression as though she were trying to remember to whom Etáin was referring. Then she sighed and shook her head. "I don't think so. I quite forgot about him at those times, and never spoke to him about it afterward. I knew he would not understand." She paused. "I don't mind your having asked that. Alex was a good person, but he was not capable of that."

"Hugh is," said Etáin with an unintended emphasis of warning. However, she was smiling at Reverdy with approval, although the object of her scrutiny did not know it.

Reverdy nodded. "Yes, he is. He has been that for as long as I have known him." She laughed and remarked, "Well, George the Second, in whose honor the 'Te Deum' was composed, was a rather dull person, I have read, his victory at Dettingen notwithstanding. I am certain that listening to it must have taxed the ability of the poor dear to stay awake during its performance." She changed the subject by turning again to Etáin's collection of transcriptions. She nodded to the table that held them. "I have only seen so much music in Signori Berlusconi's studio!" She leafed through the collection. "Do you play these often?"

"Not as often as I would like. Only at balls and on other occasions. Mostly at Mr. Vishonn's place, and sometimes at the Palace. There is not much occasion for concerts here, except on the usual holidays."

Reverdy looked at the harp that sat in the corner of Etáin's room. "May I trouble you for a sample of your art? Hugh says you are worthy of the best concert halls in London."

Etáin grinned. "He exaggerates, of course."

"I think not, Etáin," answered Reverdy. "If you understand him in the least, you must know that Hugh does not exaggerate anyone's virtues…or vices."

"That is true." Etáin clasped her hands together. "What would you like to hear?"

"The 'Te Deum.' 'We praise thee.'"

"That is the best part." Etáin rose and went to her harp. She tested its strings to make sure it was in tune, then played the selection. It took her about five minutes to finish it.

But halfway through it, she noticed that Reverdy's eyes had suddenly glistened in an overture to some uncontrollable emotion. Then the woman abruptly looked away, removed a lace handkerchief from her bag, and dabbed the tears that had begun to stream down her face.

With only an imperceptible pause, Etáin continued to play. When she was finished, she rose and went over to Reverdy. She said, "We can be friends."

Reverdy looked up at her hostess. "What do you mean?"

"You love this…and you love Hugh."

"How could you know…?"

Etáin simply smiled, took the handkerchief from her guest, and with it removed the remaining tears from Reverdy's face.

Reverdy did not protest. When Etáin was finished, she took back her handkerchief, and said, "I have never heard the harp played so beautifully, Etáin. Hugh did not exaggerate your abilities." After a pause, she asked, in a solemn, quiet voice, "He was in love with you once, was he not?"

Etáin nodded. "Yes. And I with him, up to a point. I think he would say the same thing about me. But I chose Jack, who has been my future for as long as I have known him. And now he is my present, as well."

"I had...have a similar regard for Hugh. I fought it, but it was useless."

"They are both forces of nature, are they not?"

Reverdy nodded, and smiled weakly. "Yes, they are that. Things and men that seem to be obstacles to them always manage to remove themselves from their path, or surrender, or else be swept aside." She paused. "And, they are...stars," she remarked, remembering what she had told Hugh.

Etáin suddenly reached down, took Reverdy's hands, and brought her to her feet. Then she kissed her on the cheek. "Yes. We can be friends," she repeated.

Reverdy overcame her shock at the gesture, and reciprocated by bussing one of Etáin's cheeks. "Yes. We can be friends."

Etáin's eyes sparkled with delight. "Reverdy...may I call you Reverdy?"

"Yes, of course...Etáin."

"Reverdy, let us imagine that we are to give a concert, and select a program of music!"

Reverdy sat down again in the armchair. "That would be fun! Then we must rehearse together. Are there any other musicians we could perhaps call on?"

"There are a few men near town who can play the violin and the flute. The Kenny brothers, and in Williamsburg, many other persons, as well."

"Wonderful! Do you happen to have the music for Mr. Vivaldi's 'Echo Concerto'?"

* * *

That evening, as they watched Hugh and the Brunes leave Morland, Jack grinned at Etáin. "I have never seen Hugh so composed and happy."

"I am happy for him," said Etáin. "I would have been happy for him had he married Selina Granby. You know that she had her hat set for him, and not all at her parents' urging, either. But Reverdy is different."

"How so?"

"She does not wish to love him. But she does."

Jack was silent for a while. "Do you think they will marry?"

"If she is wise enough, she will marry him. She knows it would be her salvation."

Jack glanced at his wife. "Did you discuss that with her?" he asked, a little astounded that Etáin, so stingily private in social and private matters, would discuss such a subject with another woman.

Etáin shook her head. "No. I have merely seen in her what Hugh has seen."

When the party returned to Meum Hall, James Brune almost immediately begged his retirement, leaving Hugh and Reverdy on the front porch of the great house. Mrs. Vere, alert as always, came out and offered the couple refreshments. Reverdy declined, as did Hugh. "Good night, Mrs. Vere," he said. The housekeeper went back inside the house.

Reverdy and Hugh sat again in the porch chairs. "Did you enjoy the evening, Reverdy?"

"Yes, more than any of the other occasions. Mr. Frake is an unusual man. And Etáin is delightful. We have so many interests in common."

"I expected you both would discover that," said Hugh. "Jack is my dearest friend, and Etáin — Etáin is special to me."

Reverdy looked at him. "I know how special." She paused. "I suppose that when she chose Jack over you, it was not over a 'cargo of virtues.'"

Hugh shook his head. "Quite the contrary, Reverdy. It was because his was greater than my own."

Reverdy folded her arms and looked at the night sky. It had cleared, and stars were visible. "Somehow, since coming here, Hugh, my past life diminishes in my eyes, and I feel ashamed of it."

"Is it shame you feel, or regret?" Hugh reached over and took one of her hands. It was cold from the night air. "Whichever it is, it is time that you forgive yourself. You must contemplate the pedestal again, tell yourself that you are worthy of it, and step back onto it. I know that you are capable of that, my dear, and seeing that capacity, I wish you to stay here, and let James go on by himself."

"Stay here?" whispered Reverdy, confessing to herself that the possibility had often invaded her thoughts for the past two weeks. Sometimes it had been a welcome invasion; at other times, not.

"As my wife, or as my mistress, I care not which. Just so long as you are here." Hugh paused. "You must know how much your presence graces and completes my life, Reverdy. I hope that you may say that about me, now that you know it is not so terrible and burdensome a thing."

Reverdy stared into his eyes. "I can," she whispered again. "And I do know." Then she raised the hand that held hers to her lips. She let it linger there for a moment, then said, "I must think about it, Hugh."

"Of course."

* * *

Chapter 16: The Lieutenant-Governor

In Williamsburg, on a chilly, late November afternoon, Lieutenant-Governor Francis Fauquier found, near the bottom of a pile of important correspondence his secretary had placed on his desk for him to peruse, a letter from Hugh Kenrick of Meum Hall, Caxton, requesting the honor of being married by the Lieutenant-Governor, in his capacity as head of the church in the colony, to Mrs. Reverdy Brune-McDougal, recently widowed, at his earliest convenience.

The Lieutenant-Governor was flattered by the request, but more surprised, for he did not think the young man was either marriageable or the marrying kind of man. He liked the fellow, but considered him too flinty and headstrong. Almost arrogant! What woman could tolerate him? Fauquier pondered the paradox for a moment, then shook his head in amused defeat. He had noted more perplexing unions amongst the populace here. Who was he to judge ideal matrimony? He set the letter aside, and later dictated to his secretary an answer to Mr. Kenrick, setting a date for the ceremony in early December. He was more than curious to meet the woman who would wish to share a life with that rambunctious trouble-maker. He did not know this lady; the name was not familiar to him. Perhaps Mr. Kenrick had met her in Boston or Philadelphia.

Sitting also in the pile of read correspondence were some pleas and many more requests from merchants and ships' captains and masters for Mediterranean passes and special clearances to leave port with "unstamped" cargoes. The undertone in most of these missives varied from desperation to anxiety to restrained surliness, all of them imbued with implicit blame of him for any continued inconvenience, and implying economic disaster if he did not grant permission. He would approve all these requests and had already forwarded to Captain Sterling on the *Rainbow* in Hampton and his officers on other naval vessels bundles of special clearance certificates, which temporarily waived the necessity of stamped papers. The foreman of the *Gazette*, on the Lieutenant-Governor's orders, was still churning them out by the score. The alternative was to have dozens of vessels riding at anchor in the Bay and tied up in so many Tidewater ports, all paralyzed for lack of a piece of paper.

The Lieutenant-Governor thought his wording of those certificates was a spurt of practical genius. "I do hereby certify that George Mercer, Esq.; appointed distributor of the Stamps for this colony, having declined acting in that character until further orders, declared before me, in Council, that he did not bring with him, or was never charged by the Commissioners of the Customs in England with the care of any Stamps...." The onus of responsibility was thus placed directly over Mr. Mercer's head. It was true that Mr. Mercer had not a single stamp on his person when he made that statement, and further, had not signed a receipt for the stamps, which were in fact on the *Rainbow* itself, in Captain Sterling's custody. But the better half-truth was that, for all practical purposes, they had not arrived. The blame-exonerating certificates would have to do until peaceful means were found to introduce the stamps into the colony's course of business. Tempers and passions ought to abate with time, hoped the Lieutenant-Governor.

Peter Randolph, that sly-boots member of his Council and the Surveyor-General for the Western Middle District, had tried to persuade him, during a confidential discussion in this very office a few weeks before, that he ought to allow commerce to continue without the stamps, and to share with him either the blame or credit for such an extralegal action. Otherwise, that man had gently warned, there might be "difficulties" of the sort that other governors and correspondents were reporting in neighboring colonies, unpleasantness that might call for gubernatorial actions of dubious practicality.

Fauquier had agreed then only to allow Randolph to act as he saw fit, but would not agree to split the responsibility with him. Then, it was a grave issue of granting official sanction to flouting the law, and of risking the severest of rebukes from the Board of Trade as a consequence, once that body learned of his action. Fauquier was certain that an absence of specific instructions from the Board to deal with the crisis in such a manner would not have been countenanced by that body as either a legitimate excuse or good governorship.

Now, however, he realized that Randolph's plan was eminently practical. Because, instead of these harmless, inert missives on his desk to answer, there would too likely be, at this very moment, dozens of angry, determined gentlemen besieging the front door of the Palace, demanding assurances that he would do something, and quickly! Perhaps, he mused, the Crown was responsible for those gentlemen's assuming that he had the powers of a wizard.

The Lieutenant-Governor was afraid of Virginians, now. He had witnessed their anger and observed the precipice of violence these men had skirted when the unfortunate Mr. Mercer arrived earlier in the month to assume his appointed duties as stamp distributor. Fauquier thought: *If I had not intervened, Mr. Mercer could have suffered a fate worse than humiliation, one perhaps worse than the roughing up he had received in Hampton.*

He thought again: *Well, I will condone the resumption of business and commerce without the stamps, for they are simply not available. They are indeed here, but consigned to a netherworld. They may as well have never have crossed the ocean with Mr. Mercer!* It was not so incredible a thing, thought Fauquier. After all, London had even neglected to send him a copy of the Act that he was duty-bound to enforce! He knew its particulars only because Mr. Robinson, the Speaker, had deigned to loan him a copy of the Act that had somehow come into the House last May. *Well,* he thought, *they cannot accuse me of being Buridan's ass, that beast of burden that starved to death because it could not decide which haystack to eat!*

In another special pile of paper assembled by his secretary were memorials from dozens of county courts, in which the undersigned justices declared the Stamp Act to be unconstitutional, asserted their unwillingness to admit the stamps into any of their business, and claimed consequently they were unable to perform their functions. What hubris! thought the Lieutenant-Governor. Then there was the memorial from the justices of the court of Queen Anne County, who had made the same declarations and assertions, but had decided to sit in defiance of the Act.

He had received letters from other governors reporting the same phenomena in their own colonies. What would London think when it heard of this universal foolery! Accompanying their reports were details of violence against appointed distributors and of the subsequent resignations of those men. Why, the fools had even destroyed the home and library of the Chief Justice of Massachusetts, Thomas Hutchinson, a kinder, wiser man Fauquier did not know. And the same Boston mob had pillaged the home of the man's brother-in-law, Andrew Oliver, forcing him to resign his commission before he had even received it, and obliging him to repeat his abjuration when he had it in hand!

The Lieutenant-Governor mused darkly on the fact that every one of the appointed distributors had resigned. Not a single one had stood his ground. They had all either resigned or fled, rendering their commissions useless and without power of enforcement. His information came not only from his correspondence, but also in the town's coffeehouses and taverns, in the overheard conversations of other patrons, who talked of the phenomenon with amused, grimly gloating satisfaction.

Even the unfortunate Mr. Mercer, sensing that his life would henceforth be made miserable in Virginia — he very likely shunned, ostracized, and certainly not reelected to his seat in the House by his countrymen — had already left for a return voyage to England, ostensibly to press the claims of the Ohio Company, of which he was a member, but actually because he knew he was now an outcast with a callous future in Virginia. He did not think the man would ever return; during their last interview, he impressed the Lieutenant-Governor as wanting to wish a pox on his fellow Virginians.

Some of the Lieutenant-Governor's correspondents were kind enough to send him newspapers from other colonies. The single item in one of them that gave the Lieutenant-Governor a sense of normality and solace was a report that in July that literary prince, Samuel Johnson, had been made a Doctor of Law by Trinity College in Dublin. The papers were otherwise replete with news of the same outrages and violence. Homes and warehouses owned by the stamp distributors were destroyed, effigies were hanged and burned, noisy parades and all-night vigils were staged, liberty trees and *faux* gallows were erected, loyal recalcitrants were tarred and feathered — all the usual mob violence.

The raw violence frightened the Lieutenant-Governor more than he wished to contemplate, and certainly more than he could allow himself to express angrily in company, for his concern could be interpreted as a sign of doubt and helplessness. He was grateful that this dangerous foolery had not much occurred in Virginia. He resolved to remain stolidly calm, even when he read such things as a broadside forwarded to him by an official in Pennsylvania, in which some caitiff asserted that the violence against the stamp distributors was "the most effectual and decent method of preventing the execution of a statute, because it was an axe that struck into the root of the tree of tyranny."

"Tyranny?" Did these commotions, assaults, and vandalism constitute rebellion, or revolution? the Lieutenant-Governor asked himself. He could

not decide. He wondered: If General Gage sent a regiment or two to any of these venues of anarchy to restore order and Crown authority, would the same roving mobs that preyed on defenseless stamp distributors and chief justices and port officials have the arrogance to confront seasoned, disciplined troops? Fauquier thought they might be reckless and bold enough, their fiery confidence stoked by the example of their late successes and with a fatal sense of righteous omnipotence. He mentally commended the general for staying his martial hand. One such incident might provoke the wrath of the Crown, and Virginia would be among the first colonies to feel *that* particular violence.

After all, it had been his own House's ill-considered resolves from last May, illegally broadcast to the other colonies, that precipitated the anarchy and continuing uproar. The role of those resolves would doubtless be noted by His Majesty, by the Board of Trade, by the Privy Council, by the new ministry. Trials for treason would certainly ensue, either here in the colonies or in London, followed by hangings, imprisonments, and fortune-consuming fines, together with the punishment of lesser ringleaders and offenders.

Fauquier knew, in the deepest part of his political soul, that one such bloody contest of anger and arms anywhere in the colonies between regular troops and colonials would alarm all those powers in London and move them to press vigorously for a complete and explicit reordering of the colonies' subordinate relationship with the mother country. Then there would be no arguable doubts about that subordination. Charters would be rewritten, legislatures emasculated or altogether abolished, and less wise, less patient, and less prudent men appointed to all the governorships. Very likely he himself would be replaced, dismissed from office in disgrace for somehow having allowed it all to happen.

The Lieutenant-Governor paused to reflect sadly: Then, no longer would anyone here be able to proclaim with careless confidence, "*Procul á Jove, procul á fulmine!*" The farther away from Jove, the less to fear his thunder bolts!

But he knew distance was irrelevant to the gods of Whitehall. He was certain that a reordering was in the works, with or without an incident. It had been an occasional subject of discussion and speculation during those endless card games in London among his closest friends and colleagues, and frequently a topic of bellicose ranting in the clubs he had frequented there. Because he was regarded as something of an authority on Crown financial governance, he had even been privileged to read some proposals authored by a number of subministers. The desire to directly control the colonies existed, and had existed long before the late war. Whitehall would deem it lawful administration and proper due deference. But the people here, he knew, would begin to regard it as conquest and enslavement.

The Lieutenant-Governor also knew, in the same depths of his soul, that the colonials would not long brook such a radical reordering without defiance and resistance. Then there would be more bloodshed, and tragedy, the clash of two sets of Constitutional premises. He did not think he would live long enough to witness that certain apocalypse, and was glad of it.

Fauquier read again some of the correspondence, pausing occasionally to take notes for another doleful and obsequious report to the Board of Trade. He could not remember the last time he had composed an optimistic one. *How my veiled complaints must fatigue their lordships!* he thought.

Later that day the Lieutenant-Governor, tired of his labors, pushed back his chair in the diminishing light of fall eventide, and ventured into the chilly air for a late dinner in the Palace with his wife and son. As he passed from the annex to that edifice, a servant rushed from it and intercepted him with the news that Joseph Royle, printer of the *Virginia Gazette* and ill for some time, "was close to passing to his final reward."

Fauquier stopped long enough to frown in dismay. He muttered, "Zounds! They may blame me for that, as well!"

* * *

A more important personage had already gone to his final reward. Or perhaps to his final punishment, for all the maladies and vices that had plagued him in recent years — near-blindness, abscesses, asthma, obesity, and the collective effects of having led a largely dissolute life — seemed to combine to claim their ultimate due in one sudden, unexpected stroke. The Lieutenant-Governor would not receive news of it for some months. The first reports of the summer and fall disorders from General Gage and several colonial governors had only just then reached London and threaded their way up through the various Crown bureaucracies to the desks of first secretaries and Board of Trade members, together with the remonstrances, memorials, addresses, and resolves from other colonies.

Nearly a month before, on October 31st, William Augustus, the Duke of Cumberland — who very likely would have recommended to a vacillating Lord Rockingham and his ministers, and to an uncertain but deferential nephew, George the Third, that the best solution to the seditious turmoil in the American colonies was a military one — died of a heart attack an hour or so before a crucial policymaking meeting at his residence at Windsor Great Lodge, at the age of forty-four.

*   *   *

The Lieutenant-Governor married Hugh Kenrick and Reverdy Brune-McDougal in the regal foyer of the Palace on the afternoon of the first Sunday of winter, well into the Advent season. Present at the ceremony were Reverdy's brother James, Jack and Etáin Frake, and John Proudlocks. The day was cold and overcast, but no snow fell.

It was a simple Anglican ceremony, performed with sonorous dignity by the Lieutenant-Governor, who finished it in ten minutes. In his letter to Hugh, Fauquier had also invited his party to dine with him in the adjoining visitors' parlor. Here was set an elegant and generously laden table in that room befitting the coming holiday season. They were joined by Fauquier's wife, Catherine.

Fauquier was curious about why the couple did not avail themselves of the services of the minister at St. Stepney's parish in Caxton, but settled for private speculation. Animosities, he guessed. Reverend Albert Acland had written him a number of times over the years, complaining about Mr. Kenrick and other Queen Anne planters, but Fauquier had limited his replies to that unhappy man to mere acknowledgements. The clergy here were too bothersome for words, pulling him this way and that in their own campaign for sovereignty over the souls and purses of their flocks. He wished that the matter of establishing an episcopate here in the colonies were not so intimately but irrelevantly tied to political matters. A North American episcopate would save him so much contentious business with William Robinson, the Commissary, and all his allies among the Virginia clergy.

The conversation at the dinner was cordial and sprightly.

"I have heard you are a singer, milady," he said to the bride.

"Yes, your honor," replied Reverdy, "but I am an amateur only, although I have seen notices of my performances in some of the London papers."

"Well, I must envy you on that account. I have not been noticed in the papers at all, except now and then as a devil. Not in London, that is."

Reverdy glanced at Etáin, then said, "We are planning to have a Christmas concert and ball at Mr. Vishonn's place at Enderly on Christmas day, your honor. We would be greatly honored if you and your wife would attend. Mr. Vishonn would be especially honored by your presence."

Fauquier smiled. "Well, milady, I thank you for the thought and the invitation. Regrettably, my family and I had planned to spend a quiet Christmas day here."

Hugh took Reverdy's hand and said, "Music! Had I the knowledge of it, I would compose a concerto and entitle it 'An Ode to Thia.'"

"Thia?" inquired Etáin.

The Lieutenant-Governor answered, "She was a Titan, the mother of Helios, and so, by implication, the mother of light." He addressed Hugh. "You do your bride a great honor."

"You gentlemen flatter me," said Reverdy.

Hugh shook his head. "No flattery, milady. You know I am not capable of it. Of compliments, yes." Then he paused, and added, "For a while, though, we were like Thisbe and Pyramus, and talked through walls for the longest time. But the walls have been surmounted, and now we are together."

"I am not familiar with that legend, Hugh," said Reverdy.

"It is something of a tragedy, milady," said Fauquier, "the reverse of *Romeo and Juliet*." He paused before he continued, and then added ominously, but with muted cheerfulness, "It is one based on an equally sad misunderstanding, if I remember it correctly."

"My beloved and I will rewrite those tragedies," said Hugh.

The Lieutenant-Governor rose and picked up his glass of madeira. "Well, let us toast the groom and his bride, nonetheless."

The dinner concluded two hours later. Jack, Etáin, and Proudlocks prepared to return to Caxton. Hugh and Reverdy had reserved an entire room for themselves at the Raleigh for the next few evenings. Hallam's troupe of actors was in town, with an announced program of two plays, George Lillo's *The London Merchant* and Richard Steele's *The Conscious Lovers*. Jack Frake and Etáin thanked the Lieutenant-Governor for his hospitality. When they had gone outside to wait for Hugh and Reverdy, Fauquier remarked to Hugh, "Mr. Frake is a paragon of reticence, sir. Correct me if I am in error, but I believe he uttered no more than twenty words the whole time. Did I not marry that couple at your request, as well?"

Hugh nodded. "You did, your honor."

"But, I have the distinct impression that he does not like me."

"Perhaps he does not wish to dislike you, your honor. You are, after all, an amiable gentleman, but unfortunately, you are also the Crown." Hugh paused. "The Crown has done him many a disservice. I can make the same complaint. However, in these times, Jack and I are Amys and Amylion."

"There is another tragedy I am presuming you intend to revise the ending of," remarked the Lieutenant-Governor with a chuckle. "Which of you won't die in the end?"

"Neither of us," answered Hugh with exuberance.

"And that Indian chap, Mr. Proudlocks," ventured Fauquier, "he is very well spoken. What is he all about?"

"He is studying with our resident Solon to become a lawyer, your honor," said Hugh. "He has uttered more wisdom than I wager you receive from the Board of Trade."

To this, the Lieutenant-Governor had nothing to say, but he put a hand on Hugh's shoulder, and said, "If you are not otherwise engaged with your bride tomorrow afternoon, sir, please come here and we will take a carriage ride over the grounds here. It is quite a lovely tour, even for all the bare trees. I have some important matters to discuss with you."

Hugh nodded, and he and Reverdy took their leave.

* * *

The next day was bright and cloudless. Hugh and the Lieutenant-Governor rode, not the coach of state, but a less ostentatious landau, the black driver taking them through a back entrance of the Palace yard to a trail that led to Capitol Landing near the York River. The carriage rumbled at a leisurely pace through ranks of bare trees over a narrow road of crushed stone. It was a quiet ride, except for the rattling windows and the crunch of stone beneath wheels and hooves. Hugh was nearly light-headed with happiness. The Lieutenant-Governor was glumly serious, almost morose.

After preliminary exchanges about the weather, marriage, and the extensive preparations for the holiday season in the Palace, the Lieutenant-Governor took a pamphlet from inside his coat and handed it to Hugh. "That was sent to me by a friend in Maryland, Mr. Kenrick. That, and other seditious claptrap. Do you know this fellow?"

It was a copy of Daniel Dulany's *Considerations on the Propriety of imposing Taxes in the British Colonies, for the Purpose of raising a Revenue, by*

Act of Parliament. Hugh smiled and handed it back to Fauquier. "Yes, your honor. Or, rather, I know of him. I own a copy of this very tract. It is widely read. Other tracts are in the works, I understand. Why, I have even heard that our own Mr. Bland here is composing his own fragment on the same subject."

"It will not be printed by the foreman of the *Gazette*, I can assure you of that, sir," replied the Lieutenant-Governor with uncharacteristic conviction.

"Then I imagine that Mr. Bland will need to apply to the printer in Maryland, as well. Have you read this tract, your honor?" asked Hugh.

"Yes, some of it," answered Fauquier. "'Tis the musing screed of a mere pettifogger, written to justify the ingratitude and actions of blood-thirsty factions."

"Hardly a mere pettifogger, your honor," said Hugh. "Mr. Dulany's father studied at Gray's Inn, and the author at the Middle Temple." He paused and grinned at the disgust on his host's face. "I do not entirely agree with Mr. Dulany's arguments in that tract, sir. But he, like many other thoughtful gentlemen, is striving to find a perfect rebuttal to the Crown's assertions."

Fauquier scoffed. "A *rebuttal*? I did not know one had been invited, or even allowed!"

Hugh shrugged. "When one is being told what to do by a complete stranger, and required to pay for the privilege of doing it, as well, the stranger may rightly expect a rebuttal of some kind." He shook his head. "You see, your honor, the ambition now, which was discovered and aroused by our Resolves of last May, is to attain an entelechy of liberty. The present arrangement between the colonies and the mother country is pregnant with that potential, but it also discourages and actively confounds the realization of that ambition."

"How so, sir?'

"To begin with, our trade and commerce are prisoners of the navigation laws. They allow us no freedom to trade on more acceptable terms. As a consequence, the price the colonies must pay is exorbitant and artificial." Hugh paused. "It is much like compelling a pauper to purchase a set of silver table implements for a lord, and as a consequence obliging the pauper to eat with his fingers, unable to find the coin to purchase even a wooden spoon."

"That is too sharp a tale, sir!" objected Fauquier.

"Is it? You have knowledge of economics, your honor. Would you not agree that the monies paid to many of the industries in Britain, who are the beneficiaries of those laws, would be better spent in other industries, which could swim on their own strengths, instead of relying on Danegeld? These industries would be genuinely profitable, and in no need of the protective shield of compulsory colonial requisition."

After a pause, Fauquier cocked his head with interest, but said doubtfully, "It is a novel idea deserving of study." Then he said, "But, Mr. Kenrick, even granting that what you say is true, why, the idea of the colonies securing a better policy from the mother country — well, look at the parties making all the noise! They are like the juries here and in England, composed of drovers, horse jockeys, innkeepers, retailers, and the like. Hardly students of political scholarship! And they are, I suspect, manipulated by merchants, smugglers, and unhappy clergy. At least, that is the case in Boston, to judge from the terrible descriptions of the ruckus that occurs there regularly." He paused to shake a finger at Hugh. "Do not deny that the mobility is ranked and ordered, sir! I also have knowledge of *your* role in a similar affair here, concerning the stamps. I do not believe the good citizens of Queen Anne would have made such a show of unity without direction from *above*."

"Perhaps not, your honor. And I do not deny my role in the affair. But many people not as well schooled as ourselves are like army privates and regular seamen. They need officers to direct their action and skills to the best effect. And, direction or no, they must move themselves, fired by a sense of themselves that no amount of schooling can imbue in any one person."

They were silent for a while as the carriage rumbled on. Presently, on the Lieutenant-Governor's prior instructions, the driver stopped at Capitol Landing. Hugh and Fauquier debouched and strolled along the bank. In the distance they could see the York River and some grayish white spots that were the sails of vessels gliding placidly on it.

Then Fauquier asked, "Why would they allow themselves to be so directed? I confess I simply do not understand the uproar, sir. Do you?"

Hugh shrugged. "The people have had a taste of true liberty, your honor. To borrow an analogy from a friend, they are like the prisoners of Plato's cave, who have seen some light from above and what may be seen with it. They are no longer content to remain chained in the darkness of ignorance and crippled by the palsy of inaction. The Crown, they have realized, no longer needs be a centripetal influence in their lives and minds, nor a justification for their existence."

"Centripetal, you say?" countered the Lieutenant-Governor. "Dear sir, I see nothing but the violent *centrifugal* effects of a people throwing off their allegiances and civility! Anarchy, and destruction, and the extinction of decency!" Fauquier stopped and remarked with a sigh, "You are a man of rational demeanor, sir, a paragon yourself, though of calm logic. I asked to have a word with you with the aim of being reassured that all is not as it seems. But I am not reassured. I agree with you up to a point, about the disturbance those resolves have caused, and will continue to cause. I might even concede the legitimacy of some of your complaints. But I foresee a dire and chaotic future in this dominion, and on all this continent, if passions are not soon reined in." Then he continued walking along the bank.

"It needn't be chaotic, your honor. All the Crown needs do is sever past chains and refrain from forging new ones. Such an action would make Great Britain truly great, and would prosper in the bargain."

"But so many people, high and low, depend on those…well, what you call chains. From lords to lackeys. From merchants to milkmaids."

Again, Hugh shrugged. "Then they, too, can discover true liberty. As for the dependent dross, they will be obliged to find more gainful, honest employment."

The Lieutenant-Governor frowned. "That is a *leveling* notion, sir!" he objected, some color coming to his face. The red contrasted violently with his immaculately white wig. "Altogether radical!"

"Radical? I concede that," replied Hugh with a faint smile. He tried to recall that same remark from somewhere in his past, because the same offense had caused it. "Leveling, your honor? Or just?"

Fauquier stopped again and turned to study his companion. "Well, I expect that, in time, you will produce your own tract, perhaps on that very subject. Please be good enough to send me a copy of it. I will not be shocked by anything you may chance to say in it, and forgive you it. For now, though, enough of this political talk. It is frightening and tiring." He gestured to the landau. "Let us return to the Palace. I must finish some duties, and," he added, permitting himself a smile, "you neglect your bride. Will you attend the theater this evening? My secretary saw some of Mr. Hallam's business last evening, and vouches his troupe is quite as good as any that may be seen in London. I may attend myself."

* * *

Days later, during an afternoon call on Jack Frake at Morland, Hugh reported his private conversation with the Lieutenant-Governor. "He laughed but few times at the theater. I believe that the task of governing a dominion that is in a funk is weighing terribly on him. His loyalty to the Crown clashes with his right reason, paralyzes him, and transforms his soul into mourning blacks."

Jack smiled with indifference. "Perhaps he knows that he has seen the funeral of Crown authority here."

Hugh nodded in agreement. "He also knows of our actions here in stopping the stamps."

"Reverend Acland no doubt wrote him about it."

"He will certainly not report that incident to the Board of Trade. Those gentlemen would doubtless blame him for not being conscious of a conspiracy to circumvent his power."

They talked of the coming concert at Enderly. Hugh had driven Reverdy to Vishonn's place and left her there to rehearse with Etáin, James Vishonn, and the Kenny brothers. "They are planning a special program, and Reverdy won't enlighten me about certain parts of it."

"Neither will Etáin tell me," said Jack with a chuckle.

"Reverdy says that she and Etáin have planned a special piece to perform in my honor. I wonder what it could be."

Jack laughed again. "Etáin claims they are plotting the same for me. I can't imagine what."

*　*　*

Chapter 17: The Concert

When Hugh and Reverdy returned to Meum Hall later that week, they learned that the family merchantman, the *Busy*, had called on Caxton, and then departed for West Point upriver to unship cargo there. Hugh found a packet of letters and a passel of small boxes of household goods he had ordered from his father months ago. One of the letters was from Dogmael Jones, dated mid-October. One evening, shortly after their return, as a light snow fell on the fields beyond in the gathering dusk outside, Hugh read it to Reverdy and James Brune during a late tea in the supper room. His new wife and her brother had expressed curiosity about the man.

"My dear friend:

"The other day I supped with some like-minded members of the House, and in the course of our table talk, one of us employed the epithet 'the good old cause.' I confess that I shuddered when it at last passed through my ears and found a contemplative perch on my pate, allowing me to ruminate on its meaning. The Good Old Cause, indeed! As an epithet for the cause of liberty against tyranny, implying in it the legality of armed resistance against tyrants, I wonder anymore that it is even remembered, never mind revered in that vague, dreamlike manner with which people oft recall it, as though liberty were something, they knew not what, slipping inexorably from their grip, they knew not how or why. Well, the cause of liberty is ever fresh, never old, so long as one man, or group of men, possesses an arbitrary power over other men, that power being tyranny or legislative theft.

"But I must report another memorable supper a few days before, with Dr. Benjamin Franklin and his friend Mr. Richard Jackson, the member for Weymouth and Melcombe Regis, and agent for Massachusetts and Connecticut. Other friends of liberty were also present, including Mr. Richard Price, member for Beaumaris, a voluble opponent of the Stamp Act. My circle of friends and associates in and out of the House grows monthly, so much so that I have informally dubbed it my own Sons of Liberty!

"Dr. Franklin on this occasion was kind enough to describe for the company a plan of union that he and some of his friends proposed to the Albany Congress some years ago, and which that congress of delegates from seven colonies agreed was a good plan, but which their legislatures rebuffed (as did our own wise men). Dr. Franklin is as newly aware of the disturbances in the colonies as are Lord Rocking-horse and the Board of Trade, and asserts that had his plan of union been adopted by the legislatures and by the Crown, all the recent dangerous fuss could have been avoided. He is for empire, my friend, but his notion of it presumes a penchant for reason and justice, allied with an absence of avarice on the part of Parliament and the Board. His notion of it conflicts, naturally, with that of our debtors and special interests here, who are determined to oblige the colonies to pay for the security of their own servitude.

"Dr. Franklin is right about many things, but I fear that in this instance he is off the mark. And I believe that he now realizes that the Stamp Act has forged an altogether different form of union among your adopted countrymen. Why, he even related to me a discussion he had with Justice Pratt, in which the latter opined that once the French had been removed from Canada and North America, the colonies would set their caps for independence. The die is cast, he said to us with some sadness, for Mr. Henry's Resolves from last May — which he agreed with in principle but disapproved of as impolitic and provocative — have set in motion a great machine of logic from which there is no escape. Dr. Franklin's loyalties are with his countrymen, and he confided over supper that he plans a Roman campaign of letters in the newspapers for at least a lessening of the Crown's grip on the colonies.'"

James Brune frowned. "A *Roman* campaign?" he queried. "What the devil is that?"

Hugh answered, "He will sign his letters with ancient Roman names, ones that are famously associated with eloquence and liberty."

The frown did not leave James Brune's countenance. "That seems a cowardly ruse," he commented.

This time Hugh frowned. "Or prudent," he said. "I understand that Dr. Franklin is not altogether welcome in London, and is merely tolerated there, because his business lends itself to the Crown's purposes, which is chiefly to pester the government to convert Pennsylvania from a proprietary to a royal colony. Otherwise, the Grand Caliphs there would not deign to give him the time of day." He paused, then added with a tinge of anger and impatience, directing his words to James Brune alone, "I had a group of friends who employed aliases and *noms de plume* in order to freely speak their minds, but they were persecuted nonetheless."

"Oh," said James Brune, with contrite recollection. "Those Pippin fellows."

"Yes, those Pippin fellows," replied Hugh. He gently snapped the page he was reading from, and continued to read Jones's letter.

"But on to perhaps more important news. I was fortunate to procure from two assiduous members of my stable of agents duplicate copies of an extraordinary document written by Massachusetts governor Francis Bernard, penned by him before the Stamp Act was debated in the House, and while Mr. Grenville was putting on a show of soliciting the opinions of colonial governments about the practicality of a stamp impost. It is entitled *Principles of Law and Polity, Applied to the Government of the British Colonies in North America.* In it, Mr. Bernard very laboriously but thoroughly offers ninety-seven propositions for reforming the colonies.

"Among them are these: Parliamentary representation for the colonies; but, before that gift is bestowed, a complete reorganization of the colonies, viz., the rewriting of all the charters to correct any contentious vagaries and ambiguities; the abandonment of all elective governorships, replacing them with royally appointed ones in every instance; the establishment of an upper house in each colony, composed exclusively of royally appointed permanent members, and therewith a privileged American nobility, much like the Lords here; and a universal recognition of Parliamentary supremacy by all parties in all matters. All to guarantee revenue and obedience to the Crown.

"What is ironic about this document is that it was authored by a chap who protests his sympathies for the colonials and their special problems. It is a pretty ship of state that Mr. Bernard proposes be constructed in the Westminster dockyards, and it might have been taken seriously and perhaps even launched with trumpets and royal blessings in the most gracious and magnanimous manner, had not the Stamp Act sent it to the bottom before it even left paper. It contains many infeasibilities, but I shall dwell on only one, that of colonial representation.

"This act of generosity would be a Greek gift, because you must concede that, even were seats granted to the colonies, and whether or not the North American colonies were reformed from thirteen to ten, as Mr. Bernard proposes, the gentlemen who occupied them would be outnum-

bered and outfoxed at every turn by as many blocs and parties within the
House and ministry as there are keels riding the tide in the Pool of London,
all determined to wring blood from colonial stones. Doubtless such political
alchemy can be performed, but, as you know, popular magic shows depend
on the credulity of a mob for their sustenance and on the peculiar vice of
the credulous to believe in and be entertained by such temporal miracles
and sleights of hand.

"That dire raree show, however, presupposes that the colonial members of the House would be somehow above the temptations of subornation
and chicanery, for they would no sooner take their seats than they would
be approached by the recruiting sergeants of those numberless blocs and
parties, and they would need the constitution and character of sainted mar-
tyrs to rebuff such overtures and stay steady on a course that was nevertheless doomed to disappointment. Need I say that staying that course
would incur the merciless punishment of ostracism? I own I am at a loss to
decide which wrath is worse: that of a woman scorned, or of a conniving
politician who has been shown one's back."

James Brune interrupted again. "This friend of yours likes to hear himself talk, Hugh," he remarked with disapproval.

"Perhaps," said Hugh. "He is a barrister and a member of the House.
Talking is his epée in the law and legislation lists. He must convince himself of the efficacy of his words and thoughts before he will employ them to
skewer his opponents or persuade his auditors."

James Brune shook his head. "Maybe. But he seems to be contemptuous of politics. He nearly reeks of sedition, the way he talks. And then,
he employs spies to gather information that I am certain is not meant to be
shared so freely and publicly."

Hugh smiled. "There is hardly a member in London who does not
engage in the judicious purloining of Crown confidences. Some members
are more successful at it than others." He sighed. "And you are right that
he is contemptuous. But that is a state easily reached when one has
observed, as he has in the Commons — and as I have in Williamsburg —
that many politicians refuse to think, or regard reasoned thought as an
enemy, or have made careers of deceit and complacency."

Reverdy spoke up and chided her brother. "James, please don't inter-
rupt. I am enjoying listening to this man's letter."

James Brune shrugged and sighed in concession. "I beg your pardon,
Hugh, but I own I was not aware that so much dissension existed in any

quarter of England."

Hugh nodded in thanks to his wife, then said to her brother, "The dissension that exists there is proportionately smaller than that which exists here. It is my hope that it grows greater. A general opposition to Parliament's and the King's policies, both here and in London, may prove to be our only salvation and means of redressing the costly abuse heaped upon us." Then he glanced through the rest of the letter. "Fortunately for you, James, there is not much more here to read that you might find disagreeable, except some personal matters I do not think Mr. Jones meant to be shared freely and publicly." He folded the letter and put it aside.

"Mr. Jones sounds like a very interesting man," said Reverdy. "I don't wonder he is a friend of yours and your father. I should like to meet him, if we ever travel to London."

"You shall," said Hugh.

"Sounds like a dangerous and recalcitrant fellow to me," remarked James Brune lightly.

Hugh smiled. "Dangerous? To whom? Besides, that kind of fellow is the best friend to have."

"Like your friend, Mr. Frake?" queried Reverdy.

"Like Mr. Frake, especially," said Hugh.

They talked next of James Brune's planned departure. The captain of the *Busy* had left word for Hugh that he would return from West Point in two weeks, and after taking on new cargo in Caxton and Yorktown — much of it hogsheads of tobacco and other crops from Meum Hall, Morland, and other plantations in Queen Anne County — would call next on Philadelphia, and finally on New York before setting sail for England. James Brune had decided to find passage on the *Busy* and continue his tour after Twelfth Night. Hugh described the two cities to him, and gave him advice on what to see and do in them.

"Hugh and I will write letters to our families for you to deliver, James," said Reverdy. "They will be duplicates of ones we shall send on the mail packet from Hampton. Perhaps you will arrive home before the packet."

James Brune smiled. "Our parents will be surprised with the news of your marriage," he said to her. Then the smile disappeared. "But not altogether pleased. If I recollect correctly, there was quite a row about the pairing of you two before Hugh left Danvers." After a pause, he added, "And, Hugh, I won't essay a prediction of how your parents will receive the news."

Hugh grinned. "They will be surprised, as well. And pleased."

Reverdy said, "James, it is done. Our parents must reconcile themselves to it."

Her brother shook his head in amusement. "More likely would be a reconciliation between King Frederick of Prussia and the Bourbons."

"James," said Reverdy, "you must arrange to have my things sent from home, and from my London residence, as well."

"Yes," said Hugh. "Speak with my father, who can arrange to have her things put on the *Ariadne* or the *Sparrowhawk* if one of them is handy. Mr. Worley will see that they are securely loaded."

James Brune nodded. "I will attend to it immediately upon arrival, but only after Mother Brune has boxed my ears and demanded to know why I did not oppose or foil the marriage!"

His sister smiled in sympathy with him, but said, "You could not have opposed or foiled the marriage, James. And Mother must take some consolation that Hugh and I were married by no less a personage than the governor of Virginia."

James Brune chuckled again. "I will suggest that to her, Reverdy, but she will likely answer that his honor the governor should have instead clapped Hugh in irons and incarcerated him in the town jail."

Reverdy grinned, then glanced at Hugh. "I should like to see anyone try to put my husband in irons and confine him to a bed of straw. The moon will rain honey before that is ever likely to happen."

She rose then and went to a window, and saw the thin coating of white on the bushes outside. "Oh! Look at the snow!" she exclaimed. "It is going to be a pretty Christmas! I hope it lasts at least until the concert at Enderly!"

"Perhaps it will not," said Hugh. "Snow melts fairly quickly here, when one sees it at all."

Later in the evening, when James Brune retired to his room, Hugh took Reverdy to his study and pried open one of the small boxes that Spears had brought in from the *Busy*. After he removed the excelsior and some magazines and newspapers used as packing near the top, he invited his wife to look inside.

Reverdy glanced down, and gasped. She saw sitting in a nest of wadding a mound of gold, silver and copper coins. She looked at Hugh. "I don't understand."

"It is nearly illegal to pay colonials in specie for what they send to England," he explained to her. "Most of what I export is consigned to Mr. Worley at Lion Key in the Pool. You know he is my father's agent. I demanded from the beginning that I should be paid this way, not in credit or drawbacks or paper promises." He paused. "This is why Meum Hall is a success, Reverdy." He smiled. "*My* debts are short-lived."

Reverdy nodded, but seemed confused about her husband's purpose. "Why did you wish me to see this?" she asked.

"So that when you hear Mr. Vishonn and other planters complain about their debts and credit and troubles with their London brokers, you will understand why I do not similarly complain. And you must keep this secret of mine."

"Of course, Hugh."

* * *

The Christmas Day concert at Enderly was one of the finest in Caxton's memory. The snow from a few days before did indeed melt away, but was renewed by a fresh blanket on Christmas Eve. Those who dutifully attended Reverend Acland's service on Christmas morning were happy to escape the drafty, clapboard confines of Stepney Parish Church and to forget their pastor's dour sermon and make their way home to prepare for the journey to Enderly.

The supper room and ballroom of the great house of Enderly were decorated with sprigs of holly and scrub pine bedecked with colored ribbons. The gaming room was stocked with the finest liquors from Reece Vishonn's cellar, and an extra room was set aside for guests' younger children to amuse themselves under the watchful eyes of their governesses. Liveried servants tended to guests' mounts and carriages and treated the horses to water and oats. Vishonn himself greeted his guests at the door and handed each guest a card that contained a printed number. "It is a form of lotto," he explained jovially. "After our supper, I shall draw a card from a silver bowl, and the owner of its mate shall receive a sack full of pineapples I procured from a correspondent in Barbados. They are the sweetest and juiciest I have ever tasted."

Inside the ballroom the guests were served punch by servants and entertained by an ensemble of musicians composed of the Kenny brothers — Jude and Will, corn and bean farmers from the outskirts of Caxton — and some hired musicians from Williamsburg. Vishonn had acquired a

French-made spinet to complement his pianoforte. Jude Kenny had enlarged his musical skills to include the flute and French horn, while his brother remained with the violin. Many guests expressed pleasure when they saw a harp sitting unoccupied among the musicians; Etáin "Angel" Frake was to perform tonight. They saw her standing in a corner of the ballroom talking with her husband and some friends. She was garbed in the familiar green riding suit, and her mobcap sported ribbons and holly berries.

They also noted Hugh Kenrick and his wife, Reverdy, a striking English-woman with black eyes and black hair. She wore a blue gown, no wig, and a mobcap as gaily decorated as Mrs. Frake's. The Kenricks looked as formidable a couple as the Frakes, almost devilish. All kinds of rumors had circulated around Caxton about the captivating newcomer, including stories of a scandalous past and a talent for singing.

Muriel Tippet, wife of Sheriff Cabal Tippet, had seen her shopping in Mr. Rittles's store and Lydia Heathcoate's millinery shop for feminine wares and clothing, and remarked to her husband as they crossed the ball-room at a distance, "Look at the Kenricks, Mr. Tippet! Some marriages are made in heaven, but I swear that one was made in hell."

"Muriel!" admonished the sheriff in a hushed voice. "What a terrible thing to say about anyone! You have not even made their acquaintance! And what language!"

Muriel Tippet's pique was founded on an imagined snubbing she had received from the new Mrs. Kenrick, who, while passing her on Queen Anne Street, mistook her for a servant on an errand and did not return her greeting. She and Louise Rittles, wife of Lucas Rittles, the storekeeper and innkeeper, were responsible for most of the dark rumors about Reverdy Kenrick, lately Reverdy Brune-McDougal, widow. Louise Rittles, famous for her culinary fare, had been hired by Barbara Vishonn, Reece's wife, to help her kitchen staff prepare the Christmas supper.

The whole town seemed to have climbed the gentle slope of Enderly's private, cresset-lit road to celebrate the holiday. Vishonn's guests included the Granbys, the Otways, the Cullises, Thomas Reisdale, the Tippets, the Stannards, Steven Safford, Carver Gramatan and his wife, and other town and county notables. Vishonn's son, James, with his wife, Selina; and his daughter, Annyce, with her husband, Morris Otway, also came from across the river to be here. Reverend Acland even accepted the invitation, though he avoided the company of some guests, and sought out that of others. His known disapproval of the town's opposition to the stamps in November worked against him, and he had to inveigle his way into conversations, which invariably died soon after he joined them.

At one point before supper was announced, Jack Frake took John Proudlocks aside. Jack was dressed in his best finery, as was Proudlocks. The Indian had helped Etáin bring her harp to Enderly and set it up for her in the ballroom. "I have asked Mr. Vishonn to allow you to sit at his table this night. He declined, saying that he would not mind it, but many of his other guests might. I'm sorry."

The Indian shrugged. "I had expected it, Jack. It is Mr. Vishonn and his guests who should be sorry. But I am welcome at your own table, and at Mr. Kenrick's and Mr. Reisdale's, and that more than compensates for the rudeness." He smiled. "Then I shall eat with the servants in the kitchen. They are a good source of information, as well."

The objection was more Barbara Vishonn's than her husband's. She could barely tolerate Proudlocks's presence in her house as a guest, and she harbored a secret disgust for Jack Frake and Hugh Kenrick for their treating the man as a friend and an equal.

At the long, damask-covered table in the supper room, under two chandeliers fixed with the best and brightest-burning candles, the guests were plied with roast goose and beef, chicken, various side dishes, mince pieces and puddings, dry and wet sweetmeats all on exquisite china, and complemented with a variety of wines and ales. The conversation was lively and merry, hardly touching on politics, nor dampened by complaints.

Reverdy and her brother, James, were the special focus of questions about conditions, fads, and fashions in England. Edgar Cullis kept a civil but discreet distance from Hugh Kenrick, his fellow burgess. Carver Gramatan, owner of the Gramatan Inn in Caxton and of farmland throughout the county, and who had resigned from the Sons of Liberty in protest of that organization's plans to resist the stamps and over certain of its members' untoward remarks about the Crown, refrained from venting his anger and opinions at the table. He merely turned a light red when Etáin Frake, in answer to someone's question about what she planned to play this evening, began her answer with "I shall start with 'Brian Boru's March,' which I have taken the liberty to rechristen 'A Meeting at Caxton Pier,' to commemorate our stand against the infamous stamps."

"That is an Irish tune, is it not?" asked Damaris Granby, wife of Ira.

"Yes, and a solemn one, as well. I believe it was inspired by the legend of an ancient Irish king who led his army against the Danes, and died in the battle. The composer is not known."

"Well, I suppose that is appropriate," remarked Mrs. Granby doubtfully. That was the closest the conversation ever came to politics.

"And what else, my dear?" inquired Reece Vishonn.

Etáin said, "Mrs. Kenrick here will sing a cantata on the Nativity by Alessandro Scarlatti, accompanied by all the musicians. I will play a transcription of Mr. Handel's 'See, the conquering hero comes'" — she turned with a smile at her husband, Jack, who looked surprised, adding, "That is in honor of my husband — and a number of other tunes. And I shall introduce a composition of my own, a quadrille, which I call 'Squaring the Circle,' which employs the tempo and movements of the 'Charlotte and Worter,' with which I am certain you are all familiar."

Hugh chuckled and leaned forward to remark to Etáin from across the table, "But a circle cannot be squared."

Thomas Reisdale, who could not in any event dance, asked with some mischief in his words, "Like all quadrilles and contra dances, I am supposing that your own composition could go on forever, *infinitely*, so to speak?"

Most of the guests laughed at this remark.

Etáin looked impish. "This is true. But the number will end abruptly, on a low note, leaving someone without a partner."

"What a novelty!" exclaimed Reece Vishonn.

"A mathematical novelty, at that!" said Reisdale.

"As for some other numbers we shall play," said Etáin, "we lack the requisite trumpets, but hope you will not enjoy the pieces any the less for their absence."

Reece Vishonn said, "And I am certain that Mrs. Kenrick will cause us to forget that she is not accompanied by a choir!" He picked up a glass of wine, then rose and proposed a toast to the newlyweds.

The company rose. Vishonn said, "May you both live long and prosper in this bountiful land and time!"

"Hear, hear!" said Jack Frake.

"Hear, hear!" echoed the company.

Near the end of supper, Reece Vishonn called for the silver bowl and the silk sack of pineapples. A black servant appeared with those items. Vishonn's wife covered his eyes while he picked a card from the bowl, then read out the number on it.

Reverdy rose and waved her card. The company applauded her. "What an auspicious beginning!" remarked the host as he presented her with the sack.

When supper was finished and many of the men made their way to the gaming room for a pipe or cigar before the concert began, Jack steered his wife to the side in the ballroom. Holding her by the elbow, he asked, "How did you know?"

"About 'See, the conquering hero comes'?"

"Yes."

"You told me about it," answered Etáin simply.

Jack shook his head once. "When? I don't remember."

"Before we were married. About a year after Hugh came here."

Jack grinned helplessly. "And you remembered? I am surprised, and pleased. Thank you."

Etáin said, "You said then that when you heard it in the King's Theater in London, you were truly awakened to all the glorious possibilities to you in your life. That is how you described the moment to me. How could I forget that?"

After a moment, Jack said, "You are looking especially lovely tonight."

Etáin bussed her husband on the cheek, as much of an expression of her love as she would allow herself in public. "Now, go and have your pipe before Mr. Vishonn commences the concert, my hero."

Jack passed a loving hand over one side of her face, and obeyed.

In the gaming room, Jack encountered Hugh. As he packed and lit his pipe, he said, "It's a fine Christmas, is it not?"

"It's a fine Christmas," concurred Hugh. "Things have happened so quickly, all I could think to give Reverdy as presents were copies of Elizabeth Carter's translation of Epictetus's *Enchiridion* and her *Sir Isaac Newton's Philosophy Explained for the Ladies*. They were all that was handy on such short notice."

Jack's brow furled in mild disbelief. He asked cautiously, "How were those presents received?"

Hugh smiled. "With more felicity than I had a right to hope for. Miss Carter also writes for *Gentleman's Magazine*, which Reverdy reads. Miss Carter happens to be one of her favorite versifiers and essayists."

After a moment, Jack frowned without losing his grin. "I've read most of the pamphlets you loaned me, Hugh. So has Mr. Reisdale. Perhaps we can talk about them some time soon."

"Why not now?"

Jack shook his head. "No, not tonight. I'm in too pleasant a mood to discuss politics."

"All right." After a pause, Hugh asked, "That Handel piece that Etáin said she would play in your honor — what is its significance?"

"I've heard it only once, long ago, when Redmagne and I went to London. I remember it, now and then. It became a kind of anthem for me."

"I see," said Hugh. "It's curious that you should say that. I have written a fragment on that very subject. Personal anthems, that is."

"More reading for me?"

"If you wish, and only after I have polished it."

They talked of other things for a while, their conversation for once mutually light and airy, in spontaneous conformance to the holiday and as an expression of their own happiness.

Then a servant appeared at the gaming room doors and announced the beginning of the concert. Hugh said, as Jack emptied his pipe in the gaming room fireplace, "Well, let's see what else our wives have in store for us. Reverdy intimated that she has a special present for me, as well."

"You have not heard any of the music?" queried Jack.

"Not a note of it," said Hugh.

"You have not even heard Reverdy sing?"

"No. I am not even familiar with the cantata she is to introduce."

* * *

Beneath the lustre blazing with dozens of candles, servants had set up a semicircle of chairs around the musicians and their instruments. Jack, Hugh, and John Proudlocks sat together in the rear row.

When his guests were seated, and the older children fetched to sit with their parents, Reece Vishonn introduced the musicians, each of whom was given a welcoming applause by the guests. Barbara Vishonn had ordered the curtains of the wall-length windows opened in back of the musicians; the guests could see faint ghosts of snowflakes fall outside.

Etáin indeed opened the concert with "Brian Boru's March," which was a grim, determined melody that spoke of a life-or-death purpose. She reminded the guests that she had renamed it "A Meeting at Caxton Pier" to commemorate the town's foiling of the stamps. It lasted all of two and a half minutes, and received an ovation almost as long.

Next, she and the hired musicians played "See, the conquering hero comes," from Handel's *Judas Maccabaeus*, with James Vishonn on the spinet. During the performance, Jack rose and paced restlessly back and forth behind the last row, and cast glances of loving gratitude at his wife across the room. When they were finished, Etáin and her accompanists received an even more enthusiastic ovation.

James Vishonn sat at the pianoforte and played two Domenico Scarlatti sonatas as a prelude to the "Pastoral Cantata on the Nativity," composed by the son, Alessandro.

Then Reece Vishonn rose and came forward to introduce Reverdy. After some complimentary remarks, he took his seat next to his wife. Reverdy stood up, holding her sheet music. A hush invaded the ballroom, a silence so complete that some guests thought they could hear snowflakes fall outside the window behind her. James Vishonn, the Kenny brothers, and the hired musicians opened with the establishing bars, and Reverdy sang the "Recitativo" that usually preceded the cantata.

When she was finished, there was another pause, and her accompanists played the establishing bars for the aria. And then she sang.

As he listened to Reverdy sing in a flawless soprano voice, Hugh was suddenly overcome with the sense that the music was about him. He could not understand the Italian words that his wife sang, but they seemed nevertheless to beckon him to accept the aria as his own, and to continue his enthralling, guiltless journey through life. The words were irrelevant, he thought, yet words were necessary to accompany the music to convey a joyous, untroubled serenity. The foreign, unknown words seemed to invite him to substitute his own, yet he knew not what words to put in their place. Those words celebrated his every conscious thought and action, his own existence and that of the world. They had the sense of a debut and an end at the same time, and evoked a vista that stretched behind him — the one traveled — and another before him, yet to be traveled. It was an anthem, he thought, one he wished he could somehow project and express. It was as sacred and joyous as any great hymn he had heard in the cathedrals of his past, yet it was somehow addressed to him, and to him alone. He wondered if Reverdy knew this, if she understood him enough to have chosen this cantata for that reason.

Reverdy received a standing ovation from the guests. Hugh was unable to rise, unable even to applaud; he sat immobilized by a benign paralysis. Jack Frake glanced over at him once, and saw a faraway, absorbed look on his friend's face, one that he recognized and understood.

Hugh then rose, walked around the assembly of guests, and approached his wife. He gazed into her eyes with silent thanks, then took one of her hands and raised it to his lips. He was vaguely aware that the guests were still applauding.

Reverdy dipped in an abbreviated curtsy, then leaned closer to her husband and said, knowing she could not be heard in the din by anyone but him, "The song is somehow about you, Hugh, not the Lord, and how you chart your own life. When I first heard another singer perform it in Vauxhall Gardens, I confess I thought of you."

Hugh smiled. "That is markedly sacrilegious, Reverdy, and I am forever grateful," he said with approval. Then the applause became intrusive. Hugh squeezed once the hand he still held, bowed briefly to Reverdy, and stepped away to return to his seat next to Jack Frake.

The guests demanded an encore. Etáin and Reverdy were prepared for this, and had planned and rehearsed another Handel piece, this one sung in English, the words to the first section of the "Dettingen Te Deum." This, too, when the women were finished, received a standing ovation. Some of the guests in the front row of chairs noted that the eyes of their newfound soprano were glassy with tentative tears.

Reverdy bowed, once to the guests, and once to Etáin, then, her part in the concert finished, left the musicians to join Hugh. He rose, took her elbow and walked her to the rear of the last row, out of sight of the assembly.

Etáin sat back in her chair from her harp. James Vishonn put another sheaf of sheet music in front of him on the spinet. Will Kenny stood near him, while Jude Kenny did an odd thing and left the ballroom by one of the double doors, which he left open.

Reverdy linked an arm through one of Hugh's. "I have another surprise for you, my darling. Do you remember the private concert we attended held on the terrace of that merchant friend's of Mr. Worley's in London, when I visited you with James and my mother one summer?"

"Yes."

Reverdy said nothing else. James Vishonn rose to announce, "We are pleased to perform now Mr. Vivaldi's 'Echo' Concerto. Mr. Jude Kenny will serve as the 'echo.'"

Hugh grinned in gratitude throughout the number. Even though the trio played it with a halting tempo and undeniable coarseness, he applauded nonetheless, along with the assembly.

"Thank you," said Hugh to his wife.

Etáin had by now begun playing two other Irish tunes by the composer

Turlough O'Carolan, "Lord Inchiquin" and "Hugh O'Donnell." Hugh and Reverdy stood close together and listened.

"That is a pretty tune," remarked Hugh about the latter.

Reverdy turned to face Hugh. "It is called 'Hugh O'Donnell,'" she said, "but I would call it simply 'Hugh.'"

Hugh smiled at her. They instinctively took each other's hands and, carried away by the melody and the rhythm, began moving together. Soon, they improvised a dance without thinking about it, gently twirling around and rocking back and forth. Hugh thought it a natural thing to hold Reverdy's waist, and was about to, while Reverdy felt a desire to rest her hands on his shoulders, and actually did so. But they stopped in confusion, and separated reluctantly in frustration, because there was no precedent for it. They did not know how else to proceed. But they still smiled at each other, oblivious to the confused or disapproving looks of the few guests and servants who had observed them, because they had together come near to the discovery of something.

The sole dance, at least in the middle and upper classes at that time, that called for a couple, was the minuet, an extremely formal, ritualistic mode that allowed a mere touching of hands by the pair, and then only at a distance. No dancing master then had ever conceived, let alone would have ever approved, of the mutually selfish celebration of a man and woman dancing by themselves. The crude, inappropriate notion of dancing couples was the entertainment only of the *vulgar mobility*.

"Well," said Hugh, "there must be a something like it on the Continent."

"Perhaps, but I did not observe it," said Reverdy.

When the concert was concluded, and the dancing commenced, Reece Vishonn and his wife performed the first dance, the traditional opening minuet, a stately number played by James Vishonn on the spinet and Jude Kenny on the flute. Later, Hugh and Reverdy took part with six other couples and Jack Frake in Etáin's "Squaring the Circle" country-dance, which was well received by the guests and her last solo for the evening. Jack, nominally paired with Selina Vishonn, was the odd man out when the number abruptly ended. As the guests applauded, he retired from the floor, grinning at his wife at the harp, wondering if she had calculated the effect.

A too-bright smile on her face told him that she had.

* * *

Chapter 18: The Clarion

Two days after the concert-ball at Enderly, the snow vanished again, beginning in the morning and disappearing completely by early afternoon. It ebbed steadily under the sun, sped on by some warm western breezes, until little was left of it but a scattering of gray, icy slivers over the vast, brown acreage of Morland Hall.

Jack Frake watched it go. He had traversed his fields that morning and afternoon to decide what would be planted in the spring and where. As the snow receded and revealed the ground beneath it, a certainty grew in his mind, and a revelation of a different kind. The phenomenon fascinated him, and caused him to linger in the bare fields to observe it and to dwell on a conclusion and solution it had triggered in his thoughts. When he returned to the great house, he collected all the Stamp Act literature that Hugh had loaned him, then saddled his favorite mount and rode to Meum Hall.

Mrs. Vere, the housekeeper, answered the door and showed him into his friend's study. Hugh greeted his friend and ordered a pot of tea. Jack said, as he sat down opposite Hugh's desk, "I watched the snow melt today, and more than the ground was bared."

Hugh looked curious.

"The Navigation Act and all its amendments. That is what we should be opposing."

Hugh merely smiled in answer.

Jack leaned forward and put the bundle of pamphlets and fliers on his host's desk, then continued. "In all this literature I have read — narrowly argued, though right as most of it is — I do not see that power questioned or even mentioned as an abuse of colonial trade. The power to regulate our trade implies the power to tax, that regulation ensuring the collection of taxes. For if we were granted the freedom to trade when, where, and with whom we wished, the collection of a tax, if any existed, would become as onerous to its collectors as paying it now under the present system is to us." He smiled in turn. "The absence of that point in this literature is what nagged me for a while. The melting snow caused me to think of it."

"What propinquity," remarked Hugh. "I remarked the same point to Governor Fauquier."

Jack nodded. "Yes. You told me about your meeting with him."

Hugh in turn picked up a sheaf of papers that was in front of him on the desk and handed them over to Jack. "Mr. Talbot in Philadelphia sent me those. They came by post-rider not two hours ago."

Jack reached for the sheaf and read the top page. "A non-importation agreement, signed by Philadelphia merchants?" he queried.

"And copies of similar agreements, signed by merchants in New York, Albany, and Boston. As you will see, Mr. Talbot signed the Philadelphia agreement not to order more goods from Britain as of that date. Exempt from all the agreements are goods ordered before the various covenants."

Jack read through the documents. By the time he was finished, Mrs. Vere returned with the tea tray. When she was finished serving, she left. Jack took a sip of the tea, then remarked, "Still, while this is a good idea, these agreements say nothing against the navigation laws." He put the sheaf back on Hugh's desk.

"Perhaps the men who signed these concur that opposition to them would be either fruitless or counter-productive. Perhaps many of them don't question the rightness of their mercantile captivity, or it has never occurred to them to question it."

"Perhaps," said Jack. "But for as long as the navigation laws are not questioned and identified as another form of servitude, the power of Parliament to regulate us will not be checked." He paused to grimace. "They argue that it is only equitable that we help defray the costs of our own security. But what do they truly mean by our 'security'? That of indentureds? Of captive factotums? Of menials who labor without even the benefit of livery? Is not this style of servitude a sign of conquest?"

Hugh chuckled. "Only servants and horses wear livery," he said with irony. "At least, in London they do."

"What rights of Englishmen may we then boast of, when we have been denied them? If we grant them the power to instruct us what to do with our trade, and where, and with whom, is that not by implication a grant to tax us as well, at their pleasure, for their own ends?"

Hugh said, "You are preaching to the choir, Jack."

Jack nodded to the pamphlets and agreements he had put on Hugh's desk. "One reason I came over was to ask you if you planned to write a pamphlet on that subject."

"You are just as capable of that composition," said Hugh. "You've proven that."

Jack shook his head. "I could not put the argument as finely as you could."

Hugh scoffed. "How rudely would *you* put it?"

Jack did not answer immediately, but sat for a moment, thinking. Then he rose and paced back and forth, hands linked behind his back, as he spoke. He said, "I would say that in the end, the arbitrary direction of my trade to benefit the mother country by means of the navigation laws and their amendments is surely as much a tax on me as a tax levied directly on my purse through a stamp or other instrument. It is as much a...*redirection* of my goods or money as is a direct tax, one also levied without my consent." He stopped to glance at Hugh, who was listening intently.

He continued pacing. "I would say that the authority to tell colonials what may or may not be imported or exported, by what means, and to and from what ports and countries, logically extends to the power to tax as well, for what is a navigation law but a seizure or confiscation of property in favor of an unchosen beneficiary — unchosen by me? What is it but the power of disposal of one's property to the benefit of another? The power to dispose through trade regulations is simply another form of seizure. A tax is a more immediate form of seizure and disposal. That is all."

Jack again glanced at Hugh. His host merely nodded in agreement. Jack said, "I would say further that I predict a greater crisis than what we are witnessing over the stamps. The men in London have no incentive to grant us our liberties. Their palates are accustomed to the taste of power and they will want to retain and perpetuate it. They are determined that we shall be their servants and factotums. To date, we have minded only the taxes and spoken against them — not the means of collecting them. I believe that those men see the contradiction in the arguments made in all this literature, if they even bother to read it. We don't see it. I believe they must celebrate the oversight, or at least breathe easier, when they prepare a rebuttal to colonial resolves and petitions."

Hugh cocked his head in appreciation. "Too blunt by half, but elegant in its brevity. I particularly appreciate your point about the men in London having no incentive to annul what they and their predecessors have wrought." He took a sip of his tea, then put down his cup and leaned forward. "My friend, you are capable of penning that fragment yourself. Your style is not rude at all. It never was. It is refreshingly frank. You should not doubt its potency or efficacy."

Jack nodded in thanks, and sat down again. He gestured briefly with his hands. "But what incentive do the men in London have to acknowledge the rightness of the argument? None. I own that this answer stops me when I contemplate composing such a tract. Whom would I be addressing, but men who do not wish to be addressed by reason? I have not done so in the past in other matters, except when I thought there was half a chance of persuasion." He paused to chuckle in wry amusement. "Do you remember the first night we met, at Enderly, at the victory ball, and the argument in Mr. Vishonn's gaming room?"

"I remember it well," said Hugh. "Do you remember the debates in the House on the Resolves?"

"Of course."

"Well, there you are. Three or four men from that evening at Enderly later sided with us over the stamps. And in the House, more than a dozen burgesses who had earlier objected to my call for stronger language in the memorial and remonstrance, voted for the Resolves. Argumentation is not a futile recourse even in the worst circumstances, when it may seem that one is speaking to an audience of medieval serfs or to the inmates of Bedlam Hospital."

Jack laughed softly. "I remember your relating your nightmare about the medieval serfs."

"The finer one hones its blade, the deeper an argument can cut through all the guff in which otherwise reasonable men clothe themselves." Hugh shrugged. "And constructing a finely drawn argument helps to properly arrange the idea in one's head. Mr. Reisdale, who has had some experience in court, would likely attest to the truth of that."

After a moment, Jack smiled with decision. "I will make the attempt, and compose a pamphlet on this subject. Will you read it?"

"Of course," said Hugh. "It so happens that, while you have been watching melting snow, I have been contemplating chimney swifts."

This time Jack looked baffled.

Hugh said, "The behavior of recent governments in London caused me to recall a day one spring here when I observed the nesting ritual of a flock of swifts. Finding a suitable open hollow oak, they circled round and round it, and when the leader dropped down inside it to begin building its nest, the flock changed the direction of its circling, following the next in seniority until it dropped into the oak. One by one they left the moving ring, the direction of the circle changing each time a swift left the flock. Swifts, of course, cannot build regular nests in tree branches, but construct theirs with their own drool on the sides of walls and inside hollow trees." Hugh's expression changed to one of contented deviltry. "I believe the analogy between swifts and politicians to be strikingly thorough and just."

And this time Jack cocked his head in appreciation. "It's a deserving analogy, Hugh. I look forward to reading it. I have had to clear swifts from my own chimneys." He paused. "It is better than your analogy of epergne and empire," he added.

Hugh looked surprised. "You remember that?"

"There's not much that I forget. Do you still endorse the idea?"

"Yes, I do."

Jack said nothing. He rose and said with excited conviction, "Well, I want to return to Morland and begin my composition."

"Will you stay for dinner?" asked Hugh.

"No, thank you. I don't think I'll have an appetite even for supper until I've put some words on paper." Jack glanced around the study. "How is Reverdy settling in?"

"With difficulty. We both expected it. There aren't as many distractions here as there are in London, or even in Eckley, Surrey." Hugh beamed. "She has set herself to read a number of books. She brought Mr. Rousseau's *Émile* with her, and some paltry novels on the advice of her mother. But she abandoned Rousseau to begin *Hyperborea*." His smile broadened. "She put Mr. Rousseau aside, saying he was too aimlessly pedantic." Hugh left his desk to walk his friend to the study door.

Jack folded his arms. "It will be interesting to hear what she will say about *Hyperborea*." He paused. "Etáin has read it, many times, and claims that it is appropriate that it had something to do with what you and I are."

Hugh laughed and slapped Jack on the back once. "Modesty be damned! I must express agreement with that sentiment! I told Reverdy that you helped to copy it out in a Cornwall cave. That intrigued her, as well as my own recommendation."

Jack sighed. "Well, it seems that now Caxton is obsessed with words. Mr. Reisdale is also composing a fragment, on some obscure religious dispute."

"Yes," said Hugh nodding. "He dropped me a note about it. Obscure? No. He wishes to connect the dispute between Benjamin Hoadley and

Francis Atterbury to the evolution of religious and general liberty. Why, your own Mr. Proudlocks is assisting him in the writing of it — as a copier — just as you once assisted Redmagne."

"Yes. Anymore, John spends almost as much time in Mr. Reisdale's library as he does at Morland. Well, perhaps he will help copy out my own creation."

"I am certain he will. And when you have finished it, I will send a copy of it to Mr. Jones in London. He may readily agree to employ it in the House, when it convenes again, though not ascribe its reasoning to a former felon and smuggler. I am certain that should Mr. Pannell be in the House that day and hear your name, he will recognize it after all this time, and pelt Mr. Jones with distracting and grand-sounding irrelevancies for the delectation of the Commons."

They were standing on the porch of Meum Hall now. Jack asked, "Speaking of copies, how are we to have these printed, now that Mr. Barret is gone?"

Hugh said, "We will need to send them to an Annapolis printer, I suppose. Or to Mr. Talbot in Philadelphia, who knows some printers there. I am sure that neither ailing Mr. Royle nor his foreman, Mr. Hunter, will agree to print anything we may submit to the *Gazette*'s office, not even for ready money. But let us first give them something to spurn!"

Jack untied his horse's reins, which he had secured to the balustrade of the porch steps, mounted, waved Hugh good day, and rode off.

When Hugh went back inside, he found Reverdy standing halfway down the central staircase in the breezeway. She held his copy of *Hyperborea* in one hand. "What did Mr. Frake want?" she asked.

"My advice," said Hugh. "He is going to compose a pamphlet on the current troubles. His first."

Reverdy gestured with the book. "I am surprised that it will be his first effort."

"He did not write that, but was fired by it. As was I." Hugh added, "In anything that matters to him, he says little. For all his sociability, Jack is still very much the solitary man. He suffers fools nought, and has little to say to them. I have seen him silence them with his dismissive quiescence many times."

"I had observed that effect myself." Reverdy glanced at the book in her hand. "I wonder how many fools have read this, and not been similarly fired, but remained indifferent or dead to it."

"Undoubtedly, countless fools, as numerous as once were the kings of ancient Mercia and Wessex. But they do not matter. Only those capable of being moved by the work will want to bring to life in their own actions the spirit of Drury Trantham."

"Yes," replied Reverdy gravely. Then she grinned. "I have not yet finished it, but I know now why you were moved by it. I know now why you chose to stay here." Her smile tempered. "This land is your Hyperborea."

"I am happy that you understand that, Reverdy," said Hugh with solemnity. "And grateful."

She nodded once, then turned to ascend the stairs again to her room.

"Reverdy," Hugh called after her.

She paused and turned on the landing above to look inquiringly down on her husband.

"I am quite proud of you, my dear," said Hugh.

With a faint nod of her head, she answered, "And I of you."

* * *

When he returned to Morland, Jack went immediately to his study and sat down at his desk. He found a few sheets of paper, and drew forward the inkwell. Then he changed his mind, pushed the inkwell aside, and picked up a pencil. He wrote rapidly, remembering everything he had said to Hugh at Meum Hall.

Etáin knocked on the door and came in. "How are Hugh and Reverdy?" she asked.

"They are well," Jack answered with unintended curtness.

Etáin then saw a look in her husband's face that she knew so well, one of a purpose that would not be denied, even for her. She smiled and said, "I will leave you alone. Will you have dinner?"

"No," said Jack. "But ask Mrs. Beck to prepare me some tea."

"Yes." Etáin turned and left the study.

For the next few hours, Jack wrote feverishly, propelled by the momentum of the possible. The thoughts now crowded into his mind and spilled out onto the paper, thoughts marshaled by years of perceptiveness, foresight, and commitment to truth. Sheet after sheet became filled with words, sentences, and paragraphs. He was so obsessed by the effort that when he chanced to look up and out his window, he was startled to notice a tea service sitting on his desk; he vaguely remembered Ruth Dakin bringing it in. Later, when he was nearly finished, he glanced again out his window, and saw that dusk was beginning to darken the fields beyond.

He reached a point in his effort when only a conclusion remained to be composed. He poured himself some tea from the earthenware pot; it was cold, but he drank it. Then he lit a pipe, sat back, and read without pause.

He argued in his "fragment" that a repeal of the navigation laws would effectively end Britain's legal and legislative authority over the colonies in all matters, and that the North American colonies would consequently become either thirteen independent nations, or unite under one central government to become a single large nation. They might even acknowledge the authority of the king and Parliament, but, in practice, exist as sovereign nations, or as one sovereign nation, in their own right.

Britain, he explained, would never allow such a thing to occur, not even under the most sympathetic, friendly ministry. "The alternatives to repeal of the navigation laws and subsequent legislation will be war and independence, or war and conquest," he had written.

The abolition of this political and economic connexion with Britain, he continued, is precisely what many colonials will not yet concede; or rather, they will not admit its necessity in order to regain the "liberties" they claim Britain to be infringing upon. "They must know that it would be the end of a British North America." They do not, or cannot, perceive themselves as men first, and Britons second.

What are the alternatives? he asked in the fragment. In the best scenario, the abolition of all navigation and manufacturing acts and laws, the abolition of taxes on colonial goods to and from Britain, and a recognition of the freedom to trade with nations other than Britain without penalty or harassment, must also be accompanied by Parliamentary representation for the thirteen colonies, which might henceforth be deemed "counties" divided into "boroughs." This representation would imply the supremacy of the British legislative and judicial branches of government over those of the colonies. Colonial assemblies would either be abolished or severely delimited in their legislative powers. British judicial decisions would override colonial ones. The colonies would need to conform to a multitude of British political practices and customs, including a universal union of church and state. Special legislation would likely be enacted that would enable the Crown to pay the new lieutenant-governors, their councils, and the judiciary directly, allowing them complete independence from colonial influence.

Thus, the former colonies would lose their tacit independence as surely as if they were conquered by arms, and become the object of royal and Parliamentary caprice and scheming.

But, he warned, further into the fragment, such a scenario is a fantasy. The politicians would oppose it, for it would mean an end of revenue and authority. They would be obliged to take seriously the "rights of Englishmen," and moved to cavort around the Constitution as best they could to wring some larcenous advantage from the arrangement. They had that power now, and would not surrender it.

British merchants would oppose it, for it would mean the end of a captive market for their goods and the drying up of artificially cheap raw materials for their manufactures. They would not surrender that statutory boon, and would call for a tighter regulatory grip on colonial trade.

The entire system of sinecures, placemen, and other ministerial and royal appointees, if colonial revenue due the Crown should abruptly evaporate, would in a short time become bankrupt and destitute. These persons would know it, and realize, too, that raising taxes in Britain to compensate for lost colonial revenue to ensure their lucrative entitlements, could cause a crisis and perhaps even revolt in England itself. They would be among the most stubborn and vocal opponents of American "independence" or of the notion of America becoming "separate from but equal to" Britain.

However, wrote Jack, the worst scenario, and the more likely one, would be the wholesale introduction of the most sinister and obnoxious element of British politics, unprincipled party competition for power and place, together with the inevitable corruption and politicking that are both offensive to colonials, and the subjects of grave satire even in British drama. Exceptions would eventually be made to everything granted in the name of liberty and equity to the colonials, who would find themselves in the same or worse circumstances as they endured now, except that then they would be under a firmer and more confident hand than they are at present. And when that realization occurred to them, the colonials must decide to fight for their liberties as Englishmen, or as Americans for an independence that would better secure those liberties and not leave them to the invidious mercies of legislators across an ocean.

"They must decide to fight, or to submit; and if to submit, then ignobly, bitterly, shamefully, after all the stirring, defiant words they had spoken."

That was where the fragment stopped.

Unbidden, the proud, serene face of Augustus Skelly on the Falmouth gallows came to his mind, together with the man's words that were addressed directly to him that day long ago: "This Briton will never be a slave."

And the boy who was now a man answered, more than fifteen years later: *But, I am no longer a Briton.*

The question came to him then: *Was I ever?*

Perhaps. Perhaps not, he mused. It had never been an issue to him of what he was or was not. But he could not think of the words that answered that paradoxical question with ineluctable finality.

He looked at the steady hand that held the sheet of paper, the hand that had written all those words. He felt proud of that hand. It was his, as were the words. The answer to that question lay somewhere in that hand, he thought.

Jack put down the sheet of paper. A stern smile bent his mouth at this moment. He was satisfied that he had said everything that needed to be said. All that remained to write was a conclusion.

The floor clock in a corner chimed nine. Unconsciously, at some point, perhaps hours ago, he had paused to light his desk lamp. He saw now that blackness had enveloped the fields beyond the window. A few lonely snowflakes, lit faintly by the circle of light from his desk, swirled briefly against the window glass, then flew away on the wind into the night.

Jack glanced once more at the last sentence, and decided that it was a proper conclusion.

* * *

On January 1, 1766, the Frakes and Kenricks exchanged visits and New Years' presents, and even traveled together to Williamsburg to see a pair of comedies and a pair of Shakespeare's tragedies at the theater near the Capitol Building. Morland and Meum Halls settled into an involuntary lassitude governed by the early winter months. There was little work to do except repairs and planning.

In early February, Hugh received a bundle of copies of his fragment, "The Chimney Swifts of Chicanery," from the Annapolis printer, as well as several numbers of the *Pennsylvania Gazette* from Otis Talbot in Philadelphia. In one of the *Gazettes* he encountered an item that reported the death of the Duke of Cumberland on October 31st. He read the item and was surprised that he read it with indifference. His failure to bow to the Duke many years ago, he thought, ought to be regarded as a tidemark in his life. Strangely, he felt nothing at all. He showed the item to Reverdy. She read it, and only after a moment seemed to remember the role the late Duke had played in her husband's life.

"Oh, him," she remarked. "Well, I suppose he's gone now." She smiled at her husband and handed the newspaper back to him without further interest.

In early March, another passel of *Pennsylvania Gazette*s and copies of the *New York Journal* arrived at Meum Hall. One item reported the death of Prince Frederick William, the King's youngest brother, at the age of fifteen, on December 19th. On the next day, the Dauphin of France died, at age thirty-seven.

In another of the New York papers was an item reporting that on January 1st, James Francis Edward Stuart, the "Old Pretender," had died in Rome. His eldest son, Charles Edward Louis Philip Casimir Stuart, the "Young Pretender" to the English throne, had led the Jacobite Rebellion in 1745. He immediately adopted the title "Henry the Ninth." Pope Clement the Thirteenth, however, refused to acknowledge "Bonnie Prince Charlie" as king of any nation, even though the father and the heir-presumptive son had campaigned partly in the name of Catholicism and lost England, and even though Charles's younger brother, Henry, was a cardinal. It was suggested that Clement's refusal stemmed from knowledge of Charles's furtive adoption of the Protestant faith during a secret visit to London in 1750, in an attempt to raise the Stuart banner again.

After an itinerant and stormy life on the Continent, Charles would eventually retire to Florence, Italy, where he was taken care of by a bastard daughter. He would die there, wracked by asthma, the dropsy, and the effects of alcoholism, nearly a century after his father precipitated the Glorious Revolution of 1688.

* * *

Chapter 19: The Strategists

A year before his victory at Quebec, Brigadier-General James Wolfe wrote his mother from Louisbourg about North America: "...This will, some time hence, be a vast empire, the seat of power and learning.... There will grow a people out of our little spot, England, that will fill this vast space...."

Five years before the Declaration of Independence, Horace Walpole, novelist, letter-writer, and stalwart Whig, would write: "The tocsin seems to be sounded in America. I have many visions about that country, and fancy I see twenty empires and republics forming upon vast scales over all that continent, which is growing too mighty to be kept in subjection to half a dozen exhausted nations in Europe."

Wolfe and Walpole foresaw the future of America without benefit of pamphlets, governors' reports, military appraisals, or ministerial conferences at Whitehall. They judged the continent and its inhabitants, and resigned themselves to an inevitability that was as tangible as it was abstract. In this sense, they were more honest and perceptive than those who charged themselves with the task of securing that continent in the name of *Magna Britannica*.

Instances of the hopelessness of administering a continent for the exclusive benefit of the mother country began when the collector of customs for Rhode Island in late November 1765 followed Virginia's lead and issued clearance certificates without stamped papers. That colony was followed by New York, Pennsylvania, and New Jersey, even though the Surveyor Generals could not indemnify subordinate collectors against penalties for taking such extralegal actions. The collectors in Connecticut, Maryland, and the Carolinas were the last to issue the certificates.

In all the northern colonial ports, officials were moved by the twin nemeses of numerous merchant vessels, many loaded with perishable cargoes, being potentially immobilized an entire winter in ice-locked harbors; and of countless idle sailors seeking diversion and liable to mischief, a sit-

uation that could lead to roving mobs and property destruction, for which
the collectors could be blamed and also sued. In more than one port town
the tension abated when sailors gladly returned to their vessels and hoisted
sail for departure, unstamped clearance papers safely in their captains'
pockets.

In 1766 there appeared in the colonies many pamphlets that disputed Parliamentary authority in the loftiest terms, one after another, for the price
of a few pence. They were read by countless individuals, and by tavern
keepers to their patrons, by dissenting pastors to their congregations, by
lawyers to their fellows, by representatives to their legislatures. A great
number of letters also appeared in colonial newspapers, penned by dis-
puters and loyalists, over their own names or Roman pen names. These
either argued that Parliament had usurped the King's authority and pledge
to protect the colonies from Parliamentary abuse, or defended the Stamp
Act in the name of civil society and fairness.

Jack Frake's, Hugh Kenrick's, and Thomas Reisdale's "fragments"
were printed, with their own names on the title pages, by a printer in
Annapolis and subsequently offered for sale in various locales throughout
the colonies. Otis Talbot agreed to distribute them to his merchant correspondents and to newspapers in most of the other colonies. There was a
large and impatient market for such political tracts, which sold well in colonial bookshops, printers' shops, and over newspaper counters.

Jack's fared the worst, in terms of both sales and reaction. Most men
who read it through liked it not, because it foresaw the means and consequences of Parliamentary supremacy, and in plain language projected a dire
but logical course of events. Many secretly, privately conceded its arguments, but refused to think clearly about them. Unable to counter them,
they looked for other reasons to disagree with the pamphlet. Its style was
too harsh, or too bare, or inelegant. In all its irrefutable assertions, there
was not to be detected one instance of a regard for the King and Parliament.
It was vain, because it did not cite a single revered authority or historic
precedent, but relied exclusively on the author's own reason and certitude.
Further, it hardly dwelt on the glories of English liberty. It was neither
apologetic, nor humble, nor conciliatory. It offered neither consolation nor
hope nor a salve for its perceived doom.

Jack received many letters accusing him of these things, and also of
proposing regicide, assassination, or treason. One correspondent claimed

that the pamphlet must have been written by a drunken Irishman. Another opined that it was an article adapted from Diderot's *Encyclopédie*.

Another letter-writer wrote: "You point to the tree of liberties which we enjoy and repose under, thanks to our most excellent Constitution, and claim that lightning is sure to strike it and all who seek refuge under it from the storm of Parliamentary abuse. But, sir, it is the only tree we have knowledge of, and the only one that offers us protection. Your imprudent insinuation that we abandon it is reckless, radical, and nearly heinous. If your position is of the heady style that our resistance to the stamps will provoke, then I fear for all our safety and security."

Jack Frake replied to none of the letters. He had said what he thought needed to be said.

Hugh's fragment on the chimney swifts sold well. It mocked the ministers of the government in London and the governors and councilmen in various colonial establishments. It read more like a fable than a critique of Parliament and past and current ministries, although in it he expended little effort to disguise the identities of the men whose characters, careers, and beliefs he lambasted. His fragment was frequently excerpted in other colonial newspapers.

Thomas Reisdale's fragment on the conflict between Bishops Hoadley and Atterbury also did well. It was an eloquent, if somewhat pedantic and scholarly, history of the co-evolution of religious tolerance and freedom of thought, supported by numerous footnotes and citations.

"A concession to Bishop Hoadley by Atterbury and his High Tory allies in the Church that religion was a matter of private judgment and personal belief, would have robbed the adherents of ecclesiastical authority and proscribed ritual of the principal pillars of a state church and its exercise of political power. Such a concession would also have led to the eventual denial that the Crown had a legitimate, demonstrable interest in maintaining a say in what men may hold office and what men may not, founded on its notion of a proper creed. Perhaps it might have led even to a repeal of the Test Act of 1673, which would most assuredly have in turn led to a revolutionary reorganization of the Commons, whose members now must once a year declare their loyalty to the state church in order to retain their seats and privileges."

Appended to the end of Reisdale's essay, and ostensibly linked to the Hoadley-Atterbury controversy, was John Proudlocks's shorter, unsigned "fragment" on the English Civil War of the 1640's and the Glorious Revo-

lution of 1688, in which he asked whether or not the conflict over the
Stamp Act was a continuation of those conflicts. He ended his disquisition
with: "The accession of William and Mary, and their assent to the Bill of
Rights in 1689, did not settle the questions raised and debated in this
period of English history. Their contemplation and resolution were
bequeathed to our own time. We cannot gainsay the men of that period for
not having answered or resolved those questions, for men of this period are
likewise struggling to grasp them. But chief among those questions is:
Whence liberty?"

One evening after supper in February, as they stood on the porch of the
great house, Jack confided to Proudlocks, "I liked yours best, John. You ask
a question I have striven to answer all my life."

Proudlocks acknowledged the compliment with a nod of his head. He
looked thoughtful for a while, then said, "I do not think the answer to my
last question will concern mere politics, Jack. I believe the answer, which I
do not know, is somewhere else, in some greater subject."

Jack nodded in agreement. "I believe we have the answer now. And we
use the words every day." He smiled with reassurance at his friend; his
smile was almost the answer itself.

"Whatever it is, Jack, the answer will come to you first," said Proudlocks.

"Perhaps," answered Jack. As he looked away, he recalled Proudlocks
when he first met him, when they were both boys, and contrasted the
young Indian with the man who stood at his side now. Then his head
jerked up, because, in that instant, the shadow of an answer to the question
seemed to swoop through his mind, too quickly for him to perceive its
cause.

Hugh Kenrick praised both his friends' pamphlets. Of Jack's, he said,
"You are right, but let us hope that men grow wiser before they contemplate
war." To Proudlocks, he said, "True enough."

* * *

In London, Bristol, Birmingham, Leeds, Coventry, Glasgow, Manchester,
and Liverpool, and the textile towns of Frome, Taunton, Minehead, Brad-
ford, and Macclesfield, merchants and manufacturers formed committees
and alliances to draw up petitions to be submitted to the Commons, petitions that either complained of reduced trade with the colonies, or pleaded
for repeal of the Stamp Act. They knew that while trade was expected to

recover from the post-war recession, that recovery would be impeded, if not permanently stalled, if that Act were enforced on the colonials. Remittances for goods would instead be frittered away in the money spent submitting to the Act. Jamaica, whose planters had been paying a stamp tax since 1760, also submitted a petition for repeal, for the sugar colony received most of its lumber, building materials, foodstuffs, and dry goods from the North American colonies, many of which now refused to supply the island until the Act was repealed.

British newspapers began to report more and more incidents of rioting and chaos in the colonies over the Stamp Act, and the correspondence columns filled quickly with letters from subscribers who expressed bafflement over, hostility to, or support for the colonials over the matter.

Dogmael Jones and Baron Garnet Kenrick, before the new session of Parliament met in mid-December 1765, emulated the Society of Merchant Venturers in Bristol and other mercantile associations, and made a project of persuading a number of London tradesmen to sign a petition in which the signatories claimed that their businesses had declined after the peace and would suffer more from enforcement of the Stamp Act. In November and December they trudged from door to door in the chilly, damp weather of the city to speak with the print sellers of Pall Mall, the wine merchants in Wapping, the clockmakers and watchmakers on Fleet Street, the carpenters and carriage makers on Swallow Street, the shoemakers and leather goods artisans on Maiden Lane, and to numerous investors, bankers, and brokers in the Great Piazza and Royal Exchange.

With Benjamin Worley's assistance, for he was acquainted with the denizens and could introduce Jones and the Baron, they also accosted the insurers and brokers at Lloyd's Coffeehouse, the traders at the Baltic Coffeehouse on Threadneedle Street, and the merchant buyers of auctioned goods at Garraway's Coffeehouse. They invaded the Corn and Coal Exchanges, bullied the factors into an audience, and nearly talked themselves hoarse in their quest for signatures; colonial corn was becoming scarce, while sea-coal was exported to the colonies, and could not move until either the Crown or the colonials relented. They collected many signatures and arranged meetings of tradesmen, manufacturers, and factors to discuss the consequences of the Act's continuation, amendment, and repeal.

All their signatories were convinced by Jones and the Baron that they faced a bleak future if the colonials dug in their heels, refused to pay the tax, and pledged to boycott British products until the Act was abandoned. Several showed Jones and the Baron letters they had received from colonial factors and loyal customers requesting that no further goods be sent them until the Act was repealed; the authors of a few strident letters even stated they would refuse to pay their debts until that event occurred.

The tradesmen also concurred that their future was dismal should the colonials submit to the Act, for the profit of a few pounds and pence that might permit the continued existence of their individual enterprises would likely be consumed instead by colonial customsmen and stamp distributors.

Neither Jones nor the Baron was amused when, in most instances, the eyes of their petitioners lit up with interest when the arguments turned from the rights of Englishmen to the effects of taxes and boycotts on their trades. They gathered names enough for the petition to repeal, but it was a bittersweet victory. Instead of being heartened by their successes, Jones went away every time muttering imprecations.

"Don't blame them much, Mr. Jones," counseled Garnet Kenrick as they walked through a light rain up the Strand. "They are ignorant."

"But think themselves wise," replied Jones with irony.

"According to their lights."

"Which cast a stingy nimbus over a miserly collection of concerns."

They were quiet for a moment as they strode up the bustling thoroughfare. Then Garnet Kenrick asked, "Is there anything to this argument I hear being bandied about, that the colonies cannot be taxed, for they are not represented in your House? I mean, is it an admissible contention?"

"Yes and no," answered Jones. "If not admissible, then one must logically concede that the colonies constitute an extension of this island, and that lawfully, the internal taxes the colonists distinguish from external ones stand no better than the cider and stamp taxes imposed here. If admissible, then the colonies exist outside the pale of the Constitution, all Crown law, and Parliamentary authority." He paused. "If repeal is achieved — and there is certainly no guarantee of that — we may be sure that both Houses will insist on some form of declaration concerning Crown authority. Mr. Grenville will demand that sop to our nation's wounded pride, and to his own. If repeal advances to a hope, renunciation will not."

Jones's next great task was to persuade a Commons committee to accept the petition as evidence meriting the House's serious attention, to be incorporated with all the other "American papers" that might be collated. He did not savor the task, for he knew that he would be in competition with other members of the Commons who were preparing petitions for submission, and that his and the Baron's document could be rejected for the most specious of reasons.

Checking confidence in a Grenville victory was the ugly, exasperating term *conciliation*, which floated about to infect deliberations both public and private. Curbing it also was the question of what William Pitt, ill in Bath, would say when he attended Parliament, or whether he would attend at all, his illness and mood permitting. Would he defend the colonists in their rebellion, and so sway all the fence-sitters? Would he argue for conciliation? Would he deign to join the Rockingham ministry and give it direction? No one knew.

Not even Pitt himself, as some observant wits remarked in private.

Basil Kenrick, the Earl of Danvers, was likewise busy, and had kept in close correspondence with his peers in Lords and his allies in the Commons. To his angry disgust, no unanimity existed in Lords that the Stamp Act should be retained in all its particulars and strictly enforced, militarily, if necessary. Like the Earl, half the peers maintained this position with vociferous contempt, while the other half of them seemed to drift in a tenaciously clinging fog of uncertainty and irresolution. Sir Henoch Pannell and Crispin Hillier, his chief men in the Commons, however, reported well before Parliament convened that they had succeeded in forging a solid bloc in favor of retention and enforcement. And, shortly after Parliament opened on December 17th, they assured the Earl, during tea in his study at Windridge Court, that this bloc would work closely and loyally with the larger Grenville party, which would oppose every attempt at repeal and conciliation.

"If the Commons rejects repeal and conciliation, your lordship," reported Hillier one evening to the Earl over supper, "and sends over a resolution to Lords consistent with that finding, I am certain that your House will concur with it, regardless of a division amongst your number there."

"It is hoped, your lordship," added Sir Henoch, "that the business will be dealt with and disposed of swiftly, before the Christmas recess. As you know, attendance in the Commons especially is markedly spare before the holiday. Mr. Grenville is counting on that truancy to push through the terms of debate and consideration in that short time, so that should debate on the colonial crisis ensue next month, our party — or, rather, his party — will have the House in strong harness."

The Earl looked dour, bored, and unconvinced. "There is an informal cockfight in your House now over whether or not to admit the American petitions, reports, and letters into such a debate," he said. "And, if they are admitted, whether or not they ought to be printed for distribution amongst your own number for their edification. No doubt the same pecking and slashing will occur in Lords. You should know that I intend to speak against their admittance, and, failing in that, against their printing."

Pannell smiled weakly. "Doubtless, Mr. Hillier is not surprised that you have kept such a close watch on matters," he said. "Nor am I."

The Earl ignored the gratuitous compliment. "What about Mr. Pitt?" he asked. "No matter what barriers Mr. Grenville succeeds in erecting, Mr. Pitt is certain to blast them to blazes, if he chooses to."

"Overtures are being tendered to the gentleman, your lordship," said Hillier, "and with His Majesty's leave and encouragement, no less. But we cannot predict what he will choose to do," he conceded with a sigh.

"This I knew," confessed the Earl, satisfied that his and his guests' intelligence agreed. He continued. "I have it from private conversations that His Majesty's preferred, ideal ministry would consist of Lord Northington, who would accept the seals of the Treasury, with Lord Egmont and Mr. Townshend as Secretaries of State. Mr. Pitt, Lord Rockingham, and even Mr. Grenville would be retired from politics, perhaps forever. Lord Northington's solution to the crisis would be the rod applied vigorously to the colonial rear. *Repeal*? An obscene term to him — and to me! *Conciliation*? An appropriate bargaining between nations, and parties, not between the Crown and renegades! What the weak-spirited in Lord Rockingham's party mean, when they speak of conciliation with the colonies, is *clemency*! An equally obscene term! We do not shower clemency upon our lawbreakers and thieves here! Why should we bestow clemency upon criminals when they commit their perfidies out of our sight, across an ocean?" He paused in his tirade, then spoke more calmly. "Lord Chancellor Northington, if he held the Treasury seals, I am certain could convince both Houses of the efficacy, rightness, and economy of such a strict policy."

"Unfortunately, His Majesty's overtures in that direction came to naught," remarked Pannell with muted smugness, for he wished the Earl to know that he, too, had a close watch on the comings and goings of lords and commoners at St. James's Palace. "It is unfortunate, too, that the Duke of Cumberland chose a difficult moment to exit this mortal coil. Mr. Hillier and I are certain that he could have persuaded Lord Rockingham to follow just such a policy."

"Or Lord Northington could have persuaded the both of them of it," replied the Earl. After a moment of silence, he asked, "Is there any credence to this nonsense about colonial representation and taxes? Will it cause any uproar?"

Pannell shook his head. "Mr. Grenville does not grant it any, your lordship. Nor do Lord Mansfield and Mr. Yorke, and all of the Duke of Bedford's party. Not even the colonial agents and their friends in the House give it much weight, one way or the other. There has been some talk about it, but no uproar." He paused. "I addressed this issue some years ago, your lordship, at the beginning of the late war. Now it is a question of virtual versus actual representation. But the question will not absorb much of the House's time, I am certain of that. Unless Mr. Pitt makes a meal of it."

Hillier chimed in, "The ministry's party is averse to discussion of it. Colonial representation in the House is a vain, impractical, absurd, and foolish notion. Everyone knows that. Even its advocates."

"Of course," agreed the Earl. "It is all those things."

The conversation reached a pause. Henoch Pannell was uneasy when men sat around a table in silence. He felt awkward and exposed. He preferred momentum in social intercourse. So he remarked, "I think it is ironic, your lordship, and the stuff of jest, that Lord Northington was once a member for Bath, and that he was immediately succeeded in that seat by his anathema, Mr. Pitt."

Hillier nodded in agreement. "Yes, that is truly ironic."

Basil Kenrick saw neither the irony, nor any grounds for humor. He admonished his guests with mild severity, "Let us hope that our little campaign to elevate Mr. Pitt succeeds, sirs. If the gentleman abandons Bath for my House, then we shall witness another cockfight, and hopefully the end of Mr. Pitt."

Pannell forgot his place for a moment and allowed himself a chuckle. Casually, he remarked to Hillier, "That will be honest entertainment, indeed! Two hobbled, gouty old lords, limping around each other like a pair of three-legged cats, whacking away at each other with their canes, injuring only the air between 'em, hissing drunken insults, like a pair of foppish wags on Mr. Garrick's stage!"

Crispin Hillier thought a discreet silence was the better part of manners; he sat with a blank expression that was almost a frown, and did not acknowledge the jest. The Earl simply stared in amazement at Pannell, who with a start realized his *faux pas* and rushed to qualify it. "Of course, it would be the subject of some caricature or other, your lordship, in some damned newspaper. We must anticipate such folderol. *I* would never subject your ancient house to gross levity!"

"Of course not, Mr. Pannell," answered the Earl with flinty eyes. "But in future, you will respect the dignity of this house by leaving your jollity at the door, or with the servant who admits you."

* * *

Chapter 20: The Session

On the inauguration of the Rockingham ministry in July 1765, the Earl of Chesterfield wrote his son from London: "Here is a new political arch almost built, but of materials of so different a nature, and without a keystone, that it does not, in my opinion, indicate either strength or duration. It will certainly require repairs, and a keystone next winter; and that keystone will, and must necessarily be, Mr. Pitt." A month later, he warned in another letter about Parliament: "The next session will be not only a warm, but a violent one, if you look over the names of the IN and the OUT."

He reiterated that evaluation to Sir Dogmael Jones and Baron Garnet Kenrick one evening over supper in early January 1766 at his Greenwich residence. They discussed the likely character and direction of both Houses over the Stamp Act when Parliament sat again on the 14th after the holiday recess. "The 'outs,' led by Mr. Grenville," opined Chesterfield, "wish to be back in, while those who are 'in,' I suspect, wish they were not." He grinned mischievously, and added, "And, of course, there is the Duke of Newcastle, an ageless meddler whom all parties wish to be 'out.'"

At one point in their conversation, which included speculation on the lines of succession since the death in December of Prince Frederick William, the king's youngest brother, and of the Dauphin of France, Jones inadvertently referred to Lord Rockingham as "Lord Rocking-horse," as he had in private conversation and in many letters to the newspapers.

Jones had launched a letter-writing campaign in the newspapers for repeal, adopting a Roman name, "Cicero Cygneus," and did battle with a number of other correspondents who demanded enforcement of the Stamp Act and reparations from the colonies as punishment for their defiance of the Act. Jones was especially critical of "Anti-Sejanus," the name under which the chaplain for the Earl of Sandwich voiced his and the Earl's anti-repeal sentiments. "The parallels between that ancient Roman conflict and our own are not quite true," wrote Jones in an early letter. "The gentleman who writes under the name Anti-Sejanus might have taken more care in choosing his allegiances, as well as his aliases, for Tiberius, too, was a tyrant. Both the emperor and his ambitious, presumptuous co-consul met violently ignominious ends."

The Earl blinked once, then smiled. "What perfect disrespect, sir!" he exclaimed. "I like that appellation! 'Lord Rocking-horse'!" He laughed once, and then his face brightened for a different reason. He turned to address Jones. "Ah! So you must have been the fellow responsible for that wonderful caricature I noticed in the *Weekly Journal* a while ago! The 'Westminster Fair'! 'Mr. and Mrs. Mumpsimus'!" He paused. "Or, rather, was it your inspiration?"

Garnet Kenrick confessed boastfully, "Sir Dogmael and I are both responsible for it, your lordship. He conceived it, and I paid for its publication."

Sir Dogmael added, "The Duke of Richmond also thought the caricature a deserving comment, your lordship."

"Yes, *he* would," Chesterfield said. "Well, I must have some fun with this! Let me think! Ah! Continuing on the same theme, I would say that Lord Rocking-horse's desire to have Mr. Pitt join his ministry is much like the horse calling to the man for assistance!"

"Very good, your lordship," remarked the Baron.

Jones smiled and nodded in agreement. "Why, that could be the subject for another caricature, your lordship."

The Earl waved a hand. "I make a gift of it to you." His expression brightened even more. "But wait! Here's better, sirs! Lord Rocking-horse's ministry labors at the oars of state, succeeding only in describing a circle through discontented waters, which threaten to swamp their vessel of policy. Or: No one is satisfied with the Grand Jockey's captaincy, not even his stable. A repeal, though coupled with a peevish declaratory bill, will doubtless cost him the saddle of office. Or: His weathercock inconstancy is regretted by Lord Grafton, and keeps Mr. Pitt at a distance, for they cannot tell which way the wind is blowing." He paused to look expectantly at his guests. "Well, admittedly the imagery is confusingly mixed, but I trust something may be salvaged from it."

Jones smiled. "We shall labor at the oars of clarity and precision, your lordship, to contrive a memorable caricature or two."

"Clarity and precision, you say?" queried Chesterfield. "Well, Lord Rocking-horse lacks those qualities in speech, as well as in mind. An inarticulate soul, I dare say." After a moment, the Earl nodded to a trio of gold-rimmed rococo vases that sat in a niche in the supper room. "However, I must say that his pottery works in Swinton turn out the prettiest wares. Those, for example. If he follows Mr. Grenville's example, his pottery, at least, will sustain him in his political bereavement. "

The Baron and Jones glanced at the vases and uttered compliments on their workmanship.

"Speaking of His Grace the Duke," said Chesterfield, "it is my opinion that Lord Rocking-horse committed a grave error by appointing him ambassador to Paris. I know the timbre of Lords, and I can assure you that the Duke would do him far greater service in that chamber than practicing the art of genteel verbal skirmishing at the Tuileries among the *bonne compagnie.*"

"We are agreed on that point, your lordship," Jones sighed. "However, Baron Kenrick and I also concur that Lord Rocking-horse is somewhat skittish of the Duke, which might explain why he wished to put some water between himself and His Grace."

"His Grace confided in me, your lordship," added the Baron, "before he departed, that he may return to speak in the House in any event. He said it was rather useless to send ambassadors to Paris, for the French will always hate us, no matter how civil and prudent our tongues. But you are right. His Grace may have been able to recruit support from Lord Bedford's faction, before the Lords take up the Stamp Act business that doubtless will be sent them by the Commons."

"Poor Lord Rocking-horse," the Earl remarked in mock lament. "One must pity a man who is afraid of those who cast longer shadows than he." He paused, and lifted a finger. "And a greater shadow approaches now. Mr. Pitt. I do believe that Lord Rocking-horse will find refuge and salvation in that particular umbrage." Chesterfield paused to take a sip of his precious French wine, then asked, "I have heard some rumor that Lord Rocking-horse intends to entertain the Commons with a masque of misery."

Jones nodded. "Yes, your lordship. He was approached by Mr. Barlow Trecothick, a London alderman and merchant with part-interests in several East Indiamen. Mr. Trecothick has persuaded a number of merchants and manufacturers here and in the outports and towns to compose petitions that beg for repeal or modification of the Stamp Act and cite dire trade consequences if the Act is continued. These petitions have already been submitted to the House. And if the House sits in a committee of the whole, many of these fellows may be called as witnesses by the ministry and asked to sing a chorus of calamity. A very enterprising fellow, is Mr. Trecothick."

Garnet Kenrick said, "Sir Dogmael and I also canvassed a number of tradesmen and merchants in London, and persuaded them to sign a petition of protest against the Act. Sir Dogmael will submit it to the House for consideration at first opportunity."

Chesterfield hummed in thought, then remarked, "I see. Well, I am certain that Lord Rocking-horse's *modus vivendi* will rest on the peril of certain economic catastrophe, rather than on the injustice of taxing the colonies, and will discourage discussion of the latter. Messrs. Grenville and Bedford will show the opposite side of that coin, and assert Parliamentary authority in taxation regardless of the cost here or in the colonies." He paused to grin. "But be warned, good sirs. Mr. Pitt may scuttle both fire-ships and exceed everyone's expectations and fears. When he is not morose, he is brilliantly mad!"

* * *

Jollity was left at the door of the Commons on the 14th of January and for weeks thereafter. The session resumed in a mood as cloyingly grim as the gray winter skies over London. Strangers and visitors had been barred from the House galleries from the beginning, and would be until the American crisis was resolved. Baron Garnet Kenrick, brother of a peer, could audit the proceedings from the galleries, together with others who had special connections to the ministry or the peers. Rockingham, as a peer from Lords, could not address the Commons, only observe it; he had to rely on his ministers, such as Secretary of State Henry Conway and others, to advance or defend his policies.

The House wasted little time turning to the crisis. Spoiling for a fight, the party whips of repeal and enforcement marshaled their hostile armies across the floor from each other to trade volleys of acerbic, blame-assigning speeches, contemptuous character assassinations, and taunting rebuttals.

Before many members of the Commons trooped into the House to take their seats for the resumed session, they milled about in the Westminster Yard around the burning barrels to keep themselves warm in the cold January air, or huddled together by faction or alliance for comfort and reassurance. Jones and the Baron strolled together leisurely, exchanging greetings with their allies for repeal and wondering with others if William Pitt would appear in the House.

It was known he was in town, dividing his residence between a house on Bond Street, rented from his political ally, the Duke of Grafton, and his former residence, Hayes House in Kent. Some members allowed their trepidation to get the best of them and wildly predicted that John Wilkes would also make a dramatic reappearance in the House, and worried lest the Sergeant-at-Arms had it not in his means to eject and arrest the renegade.

They nearly encountered George Pitt, member for Dorset, Groom of the Bedchamber, and a colonel in the Dorset militia, but succeeded in avoiding him. Garnet Kenrick knew him, as did his brother, Basil Kenrick, the Earl. But neither of them solicited his alliance. Lately, their mutual dislike of the man was one of the few ties that held the siblings of Danvers together. The Baron pointed out the member to Jones, remarking, "He has pestered a number of ministries for a title, and even His Majesty, I have heard, and will continue to pester until he is given satisfaction. Under Mr. Grenville, he voted for the Act, and met no success. Now he has pledged his vote to Lord Rockingham and possible repeal, in hopes of cajoling a title in that manner. He is more interested in securing robes than right."

"Surely, then," Jones said, "such a base scamp is in your brother's pocket!"

The Baron shook his head. "No, sir, not at all. Even my brother has spurned him, after *that* Mr. Pitt wrote him a number of pleas requesting his assistance in his quest. My brother has little tolerance for made peers, although he will stoop to associate with the likes of Sir Henoch, as we both know. He rightly judged *that* Mr. Pitt a useless, roguish man, whose obsession for a title will drive him to ally himself with whatever eminence promises to procure him six pearls and two rows of gold lace. It is not so different from the hope and promise of a place or appointment."

Jones could only agree with his sponsor.

Then they chanced upon Colonel Isaac Barré and William Beckford, member for London, with whom they had consulted and dined in the past, and exchanged news. "Have you met Lord Rockingham's protégé, Mr. Burke?" asked Barré at length. "He has quite a style of speaking, and will surely administer some bruises on Mr. Grenville's party."

Jones answered that he had not met Edmund Burke, and asked why his skill in oratory should matter today.

"Haven't you heard?" asked Beckford. "Lord Rockingham arranged for him the seat for Wendover. He will speak for Rockingham in the Commons, it is assumed."

"I see." Jones demurred an opinion on Burke. He had heard him converse with Dr. Johnson and other lights during literary gatherings in coffeehouses, and thought that the young man, while he championed liberty, had a way with words that was not entirely sincere. He suspected that Burke was simply a stubborn pragmatist, and would argue that the foundation and value of liberty was fundamentally a practical one, as a policy, and not a matter of principle.

Colonel Barré was laughing. "I must tell you this, as well! I encountered Mr. James Marriott, a king's advocate, at a rout the other evening," he said. "He has cast his lot with the Grenville people, and says he has an argument that is the equal of Mr. Blackstone's and Lord Mansfield's, concerning the colonies. In my mind, it is a most farcical argument, and I plan to laugh in the House should anyone advance it!"

"And what is that argument, sir?" Garnet Kenrick asked. He and Jones were familiar with the name Marriott. They had both read his pamphlet, *Political Considerations*, published some years before, in which the king's advocate argued for a reconciliation between the Duke of Newcastle and Lord Bute.

"He avers that the colonies' objection, that they cannot be taxed because they are not represented in the House, is airy, because it is specified in their various charters that they are to be regarded as attached to the manor of Greenwich, and so are indeed represented by the members for Kent. And if that moonshine is objected to as well by our cousins, the ingenious Mr. Marriott insists, too, that the colonies should be consoled in the flummery that they are of equal status with the East India Company, which is likewise represented in the House by the manor of East Greenwich by way of the Governor's Mansion in Bombay!" Barré laughed again. "I own I could not compose a better lullaby!"

News had recently reached London that in August 1765 the East India Company had assumed control of revenues of the Indian states of Bengal, Bihar, and Orissa with the approval of the Mughal emperor, and to the utter delight of the Crown, for it was certain that both the emperor and the Crown would reap a growing portion of those revenues in taxes on the Company's trade. It was the transition of the Company from being a strictly trading entity to a political one, as well.

"What folderol!" Jones exclaimed. "I have heard such nonsense only in Drury Lane satire! I promise to join you in laughter!"

A House factotum appeared outside the doors to the Commons and rang a bell to call the tardy members to their seats. Jones took his leave of Garnet Kenrick and joined the throng as it filed inside St. Stephen's Chapel and upstairs to the chamber. The Baron followed, making his way to the gallery stairs.

Sitting in the galleries, or standing at the bar at the head of the House, and gathered on the stairs that led to the upper floor chamber, were many lords and privileged interested parties.

Jones glanced up at the gallery across from him and above the other tiers of seats, and saw Garnet Kenrick and his brother, Basil Kenrick, the Earl of Danvers, sitting at opposite ends of a front row. On one side of the Earl sat Viscount Temple, brother of the author of the Stamp Act; on the other, the Duke of Bedford and the Earl of Northington, the Lord Chancellor. Next to him sat William Murray, Baron Mansfield, chief justice of the King's Bench. Jones also espied Bevill Grainger, now Viscount Wooten, retired Master of the Rolls, the King's Bench and the judge who had condemned his clients the Pippins years ago. He sat next to Norbonne Berkeley, until recently the member for Gloucestershire for twenty years. Since last year or so ago he was Baron Botetourt, and was among other peers known to Jones to be adamantly hostile to repeal, modification, or conciliation.

Also in the gallery were Benjamin Franklin and other colonial agents, including James Abercromby and Edward Montagu, the agents for Virginia. Barlow Trecothick and many London merchants, who were scheduled to testify as witnesses to Britain's economic woes later in the session, had also secured seats in the gallery. Franklin, guessed Jones, had been admitted to the gallery on the recommendation of his friend, Richard Price, member for Beaumaris.

The Marquis of Rockingham sat near the bar with his new secretary. Directly opposite them sat Sir Fletcher Norton, member for Wigan and of the Admiralty Board, and a staunch opponent of repeal.

Jones that first day did not seek a chance to speak. He bided his time to observe how the debates shaped up and what direction they would take. However, he complained to Barré, who sat next to him on an upper tier, "The manner in which the American petitions are received and rejected is vindictiveness posing as mulish formality. The petition containing the resolves of the so-called Stamp Act Congress of last October has been deemed the pronouncement of an illegal political assembly, and therefore inadmissible for recognition and discussion."

"Indeed?" answered Barré. "I had heard it was because especially the Stamp Act Congress petition had not been signed by the petitioners. A rather petty excuse, I must say!"

"I swear, this House grants a greater ear and more credence to the pleadings of visiting aborigine delegations from North America than it does to legitimate political complaints!"

During the debates on how to word the House's Address to the King, Sir Henoch Pannell, member for Canovan, was able to deliver one of the opening speeches. This time he sat on a tier behind the Grenville opposition party. "The honor of Parliament has been injured by the colonials, who have again subjected us to gently versed grievances, and we who oppose repeal and likewise any modification of the existing Act, we reply to all parties that the Crown requires a redress of *its* grievance! This ministry sails with the shredded, torn sails of vacillating *conciliation*! Damn that word! Let it be stricken from our dictionaries, from our tongues! Further, great mountains of verbiage are expended here and by the colonials on *principles*. Forgotten in all that blather is the long-standing and revered principle of the sovereignty and authority of this House, established with great wisdom, courage, and justice during the travails of the late century! The principles broadcast by the colonials and their tactless, undutiful friends here are but a gossamer web of fantasy, spun by a nest of jealous, spiteful, *tiny* creatures, while the principle of authority and power that resides in this House is as tangible as the shoes on our feet!"

Colonel Barré rose and was recognized by Speaker Sir John Cust. The war veteran winked once at Jones, then turned and said, "Speaking of boots and the gout they will not accommodate, it would seem that the gentleman across the way there has neglected to mention another aspect of that power and authority, namely that the late ministry under Mr. Grenville was afflicted by a severe episode of Turkish gout when it persuaded this House to serve the Stamp Act upon the colonies. I refer to the gout of a usurpation of the liberties of English subjects abroad, aggravated by the *spirited* inebriation of avarice. I can assure the gentlemen there that the malady may be tolerated only at the risk of amputating the offending limb. In this instance, it may not be merely the aching foot that is amputated, but the pate and the purse, as well." Then he sat down. A murmur of agreement coursed through the bloc of pro-repeal members around him.

Jones leaned over and remarked to Barré, "Fine words, sir, but you know as well as I do that Mr. Pitt, who is afflicted with the gout, when he appears here, will instead likely offer his shoulder to limping Lord Rockingham."

Barré chuckled in agreement.

Another member from across the floor rose and was recognized. "If the gentleman there alludes to the possibility of the colonies severing political ties with their mother country over the Act in question, I wish to inform him that the likelihood is inconceivable. The colonies must be retained by means of medicinal curative or military campaign. The power and authority of the Crown must be proclaimed, asserted, and perpetuated, as gently or belligerently as necessary, at whatever cost is necessary. The action this Parliament takes will be determined by the behavior and words of the colonies."

"Hear! Hear!" muttered the fuming former First Lord of the Treasury, George Grenville, present now only as the member for Buckingham Borough. He insisted from beginning to end on the right of Parliament to regulate and tax the colonies. He would continue to dispute any distinction between external and internal taxes, as well as any limitations on the taxing and legislative powers of Parliament.

Attorney-General Charles Yorke, member for Reigate, also rose to speak, insisting that if repeal were adopted by the House, it must be accompanied by a second resolution that affirmed the authority of Parliament, and that such a declaratory resolution must state that to deny Parliamentary sovereignty by word spoken or written should constitute treason, and further, that the colonial assemblies should be required to expunge from their resolutions all denials of that sovereignty.

Alexander Wedderburn, another king's advocate, a bencher at the Inner Temple, and member for Ayrburghs, rose to propose a clause in such a declaratory act that would make it illegal to dispute Parliamentary right in books and pamphlets.

Jones remarked to Colonel Barré about Wedderburn, "There's man of ambidextrous principle!"

"He is a man to watch — like a cat," remarked John Sargent, member for West Looe, who sat on the other side of Jones. James Hewitt, member for Coventry and sergeant-at-law at the Middle Temple, sat below Jones. He glanced up and nodded in agreement. Both members were in the pro-repeal bloc.

Further on in the day's session, after the House had moved into a Committee of the whole House, these severe measures were endorsed by

William Blackstone, the eminent legal historian and member for Hindon, who cited the opinions of Lord Mansfield, chief justice of the King's Bench, a privy councilor, and the king's Sergeant-at-Law. Mansfield had last year provided Grenville, at the latter's request, with a legal rationalization for the Stamp Act.

Henry Seymour, member for Totnes, then rose to deliver a tirade for the strict enforcement of the Stamp Act, by military and naval means if necessary. He was followed by Bamber Gascoyne, barrister at Lincoln's Inn and member for Midhurst, and Robert Nugent, member for Bristol, who urged the same action. George Cooke, member for Middlesex, rose to declare that the Stamp Act was illegal, and questioned Parliament's right to tax the colonies. He was answered by Hans Stanley, a Grenvillite and member for Southampton Borough, who emphasized the need for an American revenue, no matter how small, in order to reaffirm Parliament's sovereignty. "That sovereignty must be maintained and proclaimed to the colonies, and to the inhabitants of this land, as well. We must all ask ourselves this question: *When were the colonies emancipated from that sovereignty?* The royal charters do not emancipate them! Neither did Cromwell, nor did the criminal family of the late Pretender!"

Stanley was well into his speech, when William Pitt, who had been lingering at the door of the Speaker's Room, listening, chose to make his entrance into the House.

Hans Stanley finished his speech, chagrinned that the hush that suddenly quieted the restless House now was not caused by his own oratory or points, but by the abrupt presence of the man whose words he knew would set the terms of further debate and the course of the rest of the session. He finished his speech on a humble note, his words diminishing in volume and sureness, and resumed his seat with a knowledge of their momentous irrelevancy. The silence was so absolute that members could hear the clop of horse hooves on Whitehall and two ferrymen arguing over a fare at the Parliament stairs.

His gout arresting his progress, Pitt hobbled painfully to a seat reserved for him by Edmund Burke and others of the ministry. He handed Burke some papers, and sat down. If he was conscious of the four hundred pairs of eyes on him, he did not show it. He sat back, as though steeling himself for the effort, then rose and faced Rose Fuller, member for Maidstone, and chair of the Committee. That man seemed to point a somber finger of death at the Great Commoner in recognition.

Even from his upper tier vantage point, Jones could see Pitt's ghastly visage, a pale mask that Jones associated only with the embalmed dead. It turned pink only when he reached certain parts of his oration, and later when he traded salvos of near invective with George Grenville, but then faded again to ash. Jones recalled Chesterfield's remark from a week ago, and could not decide whether he was listening to a great orator speaking profundities, or to a man driven by pain to utter delirious ravings.

This was the man who, with Lord Camden, later opposed general warrants, especially if they violated Parliamentary privilege; who wanted declared illegal searches by authorities of homes on suspicion of violation of the new cider tax; who wanted declared illegal the arbitrary seizure of personal papers, except in cases of treason and capital crimes.

* * *

Chapter 21: The Keystone

As was his custom when the whole House moved into Committee, Jones placed sheets of paper atop the satchel on his knees, and readied his pencil above them to record now what one auditor later in a pamphlet would dub "The Celebrated Speech by a Celebrated Commoner." Jones noticed that many others in the seats and in the gallery opposite him were doing the same.

Pitt advanced to the Speaker's table, glanced around him, and began his oration. "I hope a day may soon be appointed to consider the state of the nation with respect to America," he said in a conversational tone. "I hope gentlemen will come to this debate with all the temper and impartiality that His Majesty recommends and the importance of the subject requires; a subject of greater importance than ever engaged the attention of this House, that subject only excepted when, near a century ago, it was the question of whether you yourselves were to be bound or free. In the meantime, as I cannot depend upon my health for any future day — such is the nature of my infirmities — I will beg to say a few words at present, leaving the justice, the equity, the policy, the expediency of the Act to another time.

"I will only speak to one point — a point which seems not to have been generally understood. I mean to the *right*. Some gentlemen seem to have considered it as a point of honor. If gentlemen consider it in this light, they leave all measures of right and wrong, to follow a delusion that may lead to destruction. It is my opinion that this kingdom has no right to lay a tax upon the colonies. At the same time, I assert the authority of this kingdom over the colonies to be sovereign and supreme, in every circumstance of government and legislation whatsoever. They are the subjects of this kingdom, equally entitled with yourselves to all the natural rights of mankind and the peculiar privileges of Englishmen; equally bound by its laws and equally participating in the Constitution of this free country."

Sir Henoch Pannell, seated next to Crispin Hillier, frowned and remarked, "Well, if they are subjects, they may and must be taxed like any others! Sir, make up your mind, please!!"

Crispin Hillier turned to him and put a finger to his lips. "Please, sir! The man will not need your assistance to dig his own grave! I see where he is going with this!"

"The Americans are the sons, not the bastards, of England!" proclaimed Pitt with indignation. "Taxation is no part of the governing or legislative power!"

"What??" whispered many members to themselves or to their mates on the seats on both sides of the House. Pannell snorted once and gave his partner a supercilious look of satisfaction.

"The taxes are a voluntary *gift* and *grant* of the Commons alone. In legislation the three estates of the realm are alike concerned; but the concurrence of the peers and the Crown to a tax is only necessary to clothe it with the form of a law. The gift and grant is of the Commons alone.

"In ancient days, the Crown, the barons, and the clergy possessed the lands. In those days, the barons and the clergy gave and granted to the Crown. They gave and granted what was *their own*! At present, since the discovery of America, and other circumstances permitting, the Commons are become the proprietors of the land. The Church — God bless it! — has but a pittance. The property of the Lords, compared with that of the Commons, is as a drop of water in the ocean; and this House represents those Commons, the proprietors of the lands; and those proprietors virtually represent the rest of the inhabitants. When, therefore, in this House we give and grant, we give and grant what is our own. But in an American tax, what do we do? 'We, your Majesty's commons for Great Britain, give and grant to Your Majesty' — what? Our *own* property? No! 'We give and grant to Your Majesty the property of your Majesty's Commons of America!'" Pitt scoffed with a flick of a hand. "It is an absurdity in terms!"

"Your reasoning is absurd, sir!" murmured the Earl of Danvers to himself. "Then there is no fault in granting the property of the colonies, of which the Crown is the proprietor, as well, in the King's name! *We* are the proprietors!"

Lord Temple, who overheard and agreed, remarked in a whisper to the Earl, "There's a novelty I have not heard before, your lordship, and we have Mr. Pitt to thank for it! The Commons as *steward* of all property in the dominions, here and abroad? We ought to pursue that notion in our own House."

"The distinction between legislation and taxation," said Pitt, "is essentially necessary to liberty. The Crown and the peers are equally legislative powers with the Commons. If taxation be a part of simple *legislation*, then the Crown and the peers have rights in taxation as well as yourselves; rights which they *will* claim, which they *will* exercise, whenever the principle can be supported by power.

"There is an idea in some that the colonies are *virtually* represented in the House," said Pitt with a wryness that almost produced a grin on his face. "I would fain know *by whom* an American is represented here." With turned up hands, Pitt paused and glanced expectantly around him.

"By the members for Kent and Greenwich! That is *by whom*, sir!" said James Marriott to his bench mate. "It's in the charters!"

"Is he represented by any knight of the shire, in any county in this kingdom?" asked Pitt. "Would to God that respectable representation was augmented to a greater number! Or will you tell him that he is represented by any representative of a borough? — a borough which, perhaps, its own representatives never saw!" Pitt laughed once in dismissal of the idea. "*This* is what is called the rotten part of the Constitution! It cannot continue a century!"

There's a treasonous notion, if I've ever heard one! thought Attorney-General Charles Yorke. *I shall certainly take him to task for that statement!*

"If it does not drop, it must be amputated." Pitt looked grim. "The idea of a *virtual* representation of America in this House is the most contemptible idea that ever entered into the head of a man. It does not deserve a *serious* refutation."

George Grenville snorted at this personal slight. He thought: *Dear sir, if it were represented in this House, it could be taxed with impunity, without inciting altercation or rebellion!*

"The Commons of America, represented in their several assemblies, have ever been in possession of the exercise of this their constitutional right of giving and granting their own money. They would have been slaves if they had not enjoyed it! At the same time, this kingdom, as the supreme governing and legislative power, has always bound the colonies by her laws, by her regulations, and restrictions in trade, in navigation, in manufactures, in everything, except that of taking their money out of their pockets without their consent."

"Sir!" sighed Grenville to Thomas Whateley, member for Ludgershall, next to him. "This man teases us with all the arts of a courtesan! Either they are bound by our legislation, or they are not!"

"A very unskillful exposition of principles, I must say," agreed Whateley with less emotion.

"Gentlemen, sir, have been charged with giving birth to *sedition* in America. They have spoken their sentiments with freedom against this unhappy Act, and that freedom has become their crime. Sorry I am to hear the liberty of speech in this House imputed as a crime. But the imputation shall not discourage me. It is a liberty I mean to exercise. No gentleman ought to be afraid to exercise it." Pitt turned a stern face to Grenville in the opposition seats. "It is a liberty by which the gentleman who calumniates it might have profited. He ought to have desisted from his project. The gentleman tells us America is obstinate; America is almost in open rebellion. Well, I rejoice that America has resisted!" he shouted to the House at large. "Three mllions of people, so dead to all the feelings of liberty as voluntarily to submit to be slaves, would have been fit instruments to makes slaves of the rest!"

George Grenville averted his eyes from Pitt's glance with frosty insouciance. Whateley's eyes were focused on a scuff on one of his shoes.

"Since the accession of King William," continued Pitt, "many ministers, some of great, others of more moderate abilities, have taken the lead of government. None of these thought, or even dreamed, of robbing the colonies of their constitutional rights. That was reserved to mark the era of the *late* administration. Not that there were wanting some, when I had the honor to serve His Majesty, to propose to me to burn my fingers with an American stamp act. With the enemy at their back, with our bayonets at their breasts, in the day of their distress, perhaps the Americans would have submitted to the imposition; but it would have been taking an ungenerous, an unjust advantage."

Members on both sides of the repeal question gasped. Clearly, the member for Bath had just indirectly criticized the Proclamation of 1763, and, by implication, the king himself. John Wilkes had been expelled from the House for a more circumspect insult to St. James's Palace.

Pitt turned another stern face to Grenville. "The gentleman boasts of these bounties to America! Are not these bounties intended finally for the benefit of this kingdom? If not, he has misapplied the national treasures!"

Grenville simply stared back brazenly at his accuser with a defiant expression that was almost comical, as though he were daring Pitt to punch him in the face. In the gallery, Lord Mansfield leaned closer to the Duke of Bedford and remarked, "Poor Mr. Grenville! He is taking it on the chin over and over today!"

The Duke shook his head. "Not to worry, your lordship. Look at him! That fellow has a soul of chain mail! He is proof against all charges, real or imagined! He will not be shamed!"

"I am no courtier of America," protested Pitt, sounding, however, as though he were one. "I stand up for this kingdom. I maintain that the Parliament has a right to bind, to restrain America! Our legislative power over the colonies is sovereign and supreme. When it ceases to be sovereign and supreme, I would advise every gentleman here to sell his lands, if he can, and embark for that country. When two countries are connected together like England and her colonies, without being incorporated, the one must necessarily govern. The greater must rule the less. But she must so rule as not to contradict the fundamental principles that are common to both."

Jones paused in his transcription, surprised by Pitt's words. He remembered his own, when, early last year, he stood in this chamber and argued against the Stamp Act, when he suggested that perhaps America was indeed another kingdom. "By God!" he thought. "Then I am not the only one here who suspects that the colonies are already lost! They are as great, if not greater!"

"If the gentleman does not understand the difference between external and internal taxes," said Pitt with a casual glance at Grenville, "I cannot help it. There is a plain distinction between taxes levied for the purposes of raising a revenue and duties imposed for the regulation of trade, for the accommodation of the subject; although, in the consequences, some revenue may incidentally arise from the latter."

Grenville sniffed at this statement, thinking: *Dear sir, in the end, there is no distinction between their purposes and consequences. Taxes are revenue and revenue is taxes! What babbling naiveté!*

Pitt looked around and found the attentive face of Hans Stanley. "The gentleman asks, when were the colonies *emancipated*? I desire to know, when were they made *slaves*?"

"They make themselves slaves by being *there*, and not *here*," grumbled Sir Henoch Pannell.

"A great deal has been said without doors of the power, of the strength of America," continued Pitt. "It is a topic that ought to be cautiously meddled with. In a good cause, on a sound bottom, the force of this country can crush America to atoms."

In the gallery, young Thomas Howard, third Earl of Effingham and a

major in the army, leaned closer to Charles Pratt, Lord Camden, chief jus-
tice of the Common Pleas, and said, "That, milord, has convinced me that
I should resign my commission rather than be instructed to fight fellow
Britons, wherever they may reside, if their cause be just."

"It is a just sentiment, your lordship," answered Camden. "Indeed, it
is. I commend you for it."

Below them, old General Sir George Howard, member for Lostwithiel
and veteran of Fontenoy, Culloden, and Rochefort, sniffed in amazement,
and thought: *Not with the mere five thousand troops there, good sir!* They
*would be crushed to atoms by an angry militia twenty-fold in number, who
would be fighting for their liberty!*

"I know the valor of your troops," said Pitt. "I know the skill of your
officers. There is not a company of foot that has served in America out of
which you may not pick a man of sufficient knowledge and experience to
make a governor of a colony there. But on this ground, on the Stamp Act,
which so many here will think a crying injustice, I am one who will lift up
my hands against it!

"In such a cause, your success would be hazardous. America, if she fell,
would fall like the strong man; she would embrace the pillars of the state,
and pull down the Constitution along with her. Is this your boasted peace
— not to sheathe the sword in its scabbard, but to sheathe it in the bowels
of your countrymen? Will you quarrel with yourselves, now the whole
house of Bourbon is united against you; while France disturbs your fish-
eries in Newfoundland, embarrasses your slave trade to Africa, and with-
holds from your subjects in Canada their property stipulated by treaty;
while the ransom for the Manilas is denied by Spain, and its gallant con-
queror basely traduced into a mean plunderer — a gentleman whose noble
and generous spirit would do honor to the proudest grandee of that
country?"

Lord Mansfield chuckled and remarked to Bedford, "Methinks the
chap's mind is wandering now." The Duke nodded his head in silent agreement.

"The Americans have not acted in all things with prudence and
temper; they have been wronged; they have been driven to madness by
injustice. Will you punish them for the madness you have occasioned?
Rather let prudence and temper come first from *this* side. I will undertake
for America that she will follow the example. There are two lines in a
ballad of Prior's, of a man's behavior to his wife, so applicable to you and

your colonies, that I cannot help repeating them:

"Be to her virtues very kind.

Be to her faults a little blind."

Jones, from his seat, scowled and muttered to himself the next lines of the ballad: *"Let all her ways be unconfined, and clap your padlock on her mind."*

William Pitt glanced around the House, and uttered his summation. "Upon the whole, I will beg leave to tell the House what is my opinion. It is that the Stamp Act be repealed *absolutely, totally, and immediately!* And that the reason for the repeal be assigned — because it was founded on an erroneous principle. At the same time, let the sovereign authority of this country over the colonies be asserted in as strong terms as can be devised, and be made to extend to every point of legislation whatsoever; that we may bind their trade, confine their manufactures, and exercise every power whatsoever, except that of taking money from their pockets without consent."

All through Pitt's oration, Jones's hopes, and those of many others, were dashed, raised, and dashed again. The member for Swansditch had closed his eyes in despair each time the Great Commoner uttered a baffling, reason-defying contradiction. He gasped imprecations as his pencil hurried across the paper on his lap. Wanting to rise and correct Pitt, he fidgeted to the distraction of the members who sat next to him. As Pitt hobbled back to his seat, Jones finished his transcription, then dropped his pencil on the paper. He resisted hanging his head in despair, remarking plaintively instead to Colonel Barré, "There goes the father of another kingdom. The die is cast, and we shall be conquerors of our own citizens."

Colonel Barré glanced at his colleague, wanting to ask what he meant by that, but George Grenville had risen and was recognized by Rose Fuller from the Chair. Grenville and Pitt then commenced an exchange of vitriolic remarks on policy and constitutional matters that lasted two hours. Pitt, at one point, walked out as his brother-in-law addressed the House.

Emboldened by Pitt's assertion of Parliament's authority and supremacy, and by a realization now that certain defeat need not be risked by questioning or denying that power, William Beckford and George Cooke delivered their own arguments for repeal of the Stamp Act. They were joined by John Huske, member for Malden, a former colonist and Boston merchant who had voted for the Act last year, and as a consequence had been burned in effigy by his former countrymen. He was one of a handful of American-born members of the House.

Sir Dogmael Jones did not rise to speak. For the first time in his career, he was at a loss for words.

The House did not adjourn until close to midnight. The next day, the wording and resolutions of the Address to the King from the Commons on the American crisis were reported from the Committee to the House and approved. The only speaker was James Harris, member for Christchurch and a close friend of Grenville's. On the premise that the colonies were truly in rebellion, and not merely in a state of tumult and riot, as Beckford before him had claimed, he opined that the Address was imbued with "too much delicacy and tenderness."

*   *   *

Chapter 22: The Rivals

"Whatsoever! Whatsoever! Whatsoever!" Jones exclaimed furiously that next evening over supper at Cricklegate, Garnet Kenrick's Chelsea home. "That single word has exploded the whole edifice of his principles! It gives Lord Rocking-horse a three-sparred sail and the wind to propel it!"

"I don't understand why you are so disturbed, Mr. Jones," said Effncy Kenrick, who regarded her other guest with worry. "He defended the colonies, did he not?'

"Oh, yes! He defended them!" answered Jones. "But one cannot decide whether he opposed internal taxation of the colonies and likewise our right to impose it or not. One cannot decide whether he asserted that the colonies, in terms of 'internal' taxation, are beyond the realm of our legislative authority or within it. His memorable assertions on the matter are to the contrary notwithstanding. One cannot determine where he stands at all, for he obfuscated the encompassed issue, so that it is no longer a clean, round circle, but a mere blur. This phenomenon, I predict, will be Lord Rocking-horse's salvation, for while that man was unable to navigate his policy aided by the sun of clarity, he has been made a gift of the means of finding port in a miserable fog! Mr. Pitt? It must be said that he is checked by a worse infirmity than mere gout."

"By what, Uncle Dog?" asked Alice Kenrick shyly. The Kenricks' daughter was approaching her late teens, and blossoming into a beauty with gray eyes, nearly perfect features, and black hair made blacker by the immaculately laundered mobcap atop her head. She was not as a rule present during these political discussions — which were often spiced with Jones's coarse language — but tonight was special, chiefly because of the presence of the second guest.

"By a discomposed mind, milady," answered Jones.

Effney Kenrick ventured, "Perhaps he spoke that way just to spite his brother-in-law, Mr. Grenville." She paused to glance at her husband. "It is not beyond modern politics that I can see, not so unlike the division between Garnet and his brother, the Earl." She turned to address her husband. "Basil's politics are half animosity for you, my dear. I cannot be dissuaded from that observation."

Garnet Kenrick simply nodded in agreement.

Jones shook his head. "Begging your pardon, milady, but that is hardly the case. Mr. Pitt simply detests Mr. Grenville's politics. He can only hate them the more, now, because his other brother-in-law, Lord Temple, heard Mr. Pitt's speech yesterday, and it is rumored that that eminence has sided with his luckless sibling and this morning has made a present to him of one thousand pounds! That is the word I heard in the Yard this afternoon. It is a moot point whether he was motivated by spite or politics."

"'Whatsoever'?" mused Garnet Kenrick. "I don't agree that it explodes his principles. Would you not say, rather, that his contrary notions *are* the keystone to his edifice?"

Jones smiled at his patron and friend. "My apologies, milord. You are right." He shook his head again. "*Whatsoever*," he mused with a sigh. "With that single, innocuous word, he has granted Parliament unlimited powers, which are incompatible with the liberty he defends. One or the other must yield. In such a union, the greater must absorb the less, rendering the less a nullity."

Effney Kenrick remarked, "And then it is a union no more."

Jones laughed in bitter triumph. "A deduction, milady, lost on Mr. Pitt himself! My compliments."

Garnet Kenrick smiled and attempted to bring some levity to the conversation. "Well, perhaps, accounting for all that, it is well the colonials have named a fort and several towns after Mr. Pitt."

Jones sighed. "True, milord. But what an insidious luxury they have now, to indulge his fondness for liberty, yet neglect to fault his confusion!"

"No doubt you plan to send my son a transcript of Mr. Pitt's speech."

"Yes, of course. Of his, and a précis of some of the other speeches."

"To judge by the quality of many of the pamphlets Hugh has sent us, I am certain that many colonials will be sharp enough to detect the contraries in Mr. Pitt's mare's nest," remarked Garnet Kenrick. "And Hugh will make the same observations as you have."

"I am certain he will."

Alice Kenrick ventured, "What about the king? Surely he has some role in this affair."

Jones chuckled. "Oh, His Majesty? Well, our royal papadendrion of the colonies bends this way and that, like a sapling in a stiff breeze."

The second guest, Roger Tallmadge, who sat next to Alice at the table, grinned in amusement. "Well, here is one sapling that will not bend," he said. "I shall also vote for repeal, if such a resolution is reported to the House."

Jones grinned at the other guest. "In all modesty, sir, I must say that, as you have benefited from a close association with wisdom, so may the nation."

"Your modesty in this house and in the House is notoriously *legend*, Sir Dogmael," replied the newcomer. "I now quite appreciate the appellation that milord Kenrick said was your *nom de guerre* in the House — the Demosthenes of the demimonde!" The company laughed, including the object of the jest.

The House would not sit again for three days. When Jones journeyed up to Chelsea the day after Pitt's momentous speech, he was surprised to encounter another guest of the Kenricks', an army lieutenant on half-pay and a member for Bromhead, a borough on the outskirts of Sheffield, a manufacturing town that did not itself have representation in the Commons. He recognized the young man from among all the other members he saw in the House, but until now had had no reason to mark him for special attention as either friend or foe.

Roger Tallmadge was a close childhood friend of his host's son, he learned after introductions were made shortly after his own arrival. The officer had arrived at Cricklegate the day before, and was to stay there for the duration of the session. At the moment, Tallmadge was an occasional artillery instructor at Woolwich down the river and was awaiting an appointment to a regiment. He had recently returned from Prussia, where he spent a year as an attaché in the court of King Frederick. He had traveled the Continent on similar postings for two years, and had also seen action in the late war.

This tall, blondish, handsome young man, neatly garbed in a gentleman's attire, blessed with a seraphic face, sat next to Alice Kenrick. Jones noted that a special rapport existed between him and the Kenricks' daughter. Jones, who was in love with the girl, had not yet made his affections known to her or to her parents. His observation of the pair's behavior this evening caused him to curse both his age and his duties at the Inns of Court and in the Commons, important distractions which had not given him enough time to consider a proper, inoffensive way to broach the subject.

He was certain that her parents, usually sensitive to such things, were unaware of his affections, but were markedly, and approvingly, conscious of the wordless regard their daughter and Lieutenant Tallmadge had for each other. The young people sat comfortably together, shoulders nearly touching, like a married couple whose sense of propriety would not permit them outlandish public displays of affection for each other. Doubtless many letters had been exchanged between them. Now, he thought, it was too late for him to pen his own.

And, doubtless, Alice's brother Hugh would welcome such a union, thought Jones. But he himself would not. He managed to repress a bitter sigh and continued the conversation. He asked, "How did you come by your seat, Mr. Tallmadge?"

"Through no ambition or fault of my own, I can assure you! My father wished me to preserve my hearing, and thought that I might by listening to the babble of a hundred voices in the House. He served with a Sheffield alderman in the 'Forty-five, and this fellow arranged for my election opposite another chap who fell out of favor with his constituents for having voted for the cider tax against their express wishes. That was two years ago. I was at the Prussian court last year, and only took my seat this last December. Until yesterday, I had been dividing my time between the House and my duties at Woolwich." Tallmadge paused. "I must say, auditing the House's business is every bit as horrific as a cannonade, deafening to the ears, and numbing to the mind!"

Jones grinned in agreement, then asked, "Would you vote for repeal at the risk of your commission, Mr. Tallmadge?"

Tallmadge blinked once and frowned. "How would I risk my commission by voting with my conscience?"

"Surely you must know that during the last ministry, a number of officers lost their appointments for having voted against Mr. Grenville's schemes, or were pressed to resign them. Colonel Barré, for instance, and old General Howard, to name a few of the more prominent officers, were dismissed from their ministerial appointments, as well."

"I was not aware of that. How naïve I have been! What villainy!"

"It's quite true, Mr. Tallmadge, what Sir Dogmael says," said Garnet Kenrick. "Lords of vengeance haunt both Houses and smite mere innocent mortals on the slightest offense."

"Oh," Tallmadge said in wonder. He leaned forward and asked, "But, who would be responsible for such a contemptible action?"

"Everyone, and no one," answered Jones. "Mr. Charles Townshend, for instance, is Army Paymaster, and a friend of Mr. Grenville and his policies. He could easily arrange the demise of your career, but you could never prove it, never file a suit against him, for he would simply plead economy or budget. Then there is Viscount Barrington, Lord Rocking-horse's Secretary at War, also a staunch advocate of strict enforcement of the Act. Our Great Jockey's government, after all, is half composed of its enemies. A wise man would have stuffed his stockings with friends."

Effney Kenrick remarked, "Barrington is an Irish lord, which counts for nothing here, allowing him to sit for Plymouth."

"I did not know that, either, milady," Tallmadge said. "Why, I made his acquaintance yesterday, and we sat together in the House. He seemed an affable and jovial fellow. We shared ale afterward, at the Cocoa Tree."

"Nonetheless, he is influential," Jones said. He shook his head. "His pointed smiles may conceal daggers of deceit. And, the Cocoa Tree is a den of Tory iniquity, although I must concede the place serves the best coffee, cakes, and ale to be found in Whitehall."

Tallmadge looked grim, and after a moment answered with angry defiance, "I should still vote for repeal!"

Jones smiled, but not in answer to Tallmadge's assertion. "If repeal is not attained, and it is decided to discard practical reason and enforce the Act, would you accept a commission to go to America and help to oppress the colonials? Perhaps to draw your sword, and command your troops to fire on them, as though they were a nation of smugglers and pirates?"

"Goodness, no, Sir Dogmael!" protested Tallmadge with genuine anger. "They are not merely colonials! They are Englishmen, like us! But, to hear some of the talk in the House, you would think we were judging the fate of upstart colonial Frenchmen!"

Jones remarked, "Well, they may as well be Frenchmen, for all that it matters to many in either House. And there is a difference between the arrogance of a Frenchman and that of an Englishmen."

Garnet Kenrick, who had been looking pensive, said, "I have just had an original realization, and it is not irrelevant to this matter of voting for or against repeal. It is this: For the first time in my memory, at least, the Commons has been made divisive. So many members who owe their places to the ministry will refuse to vote with it. A remarkable phenomenon! It may augur well for the future of liberty!"

"Indeed, milord," agreed Jones somberly, as though he doubted it. "A remarkable phenomenon, worthy, perhaps, of a treatise." But then his face brightened, and he picked up his glass of wine. Holding it aloft, he said, "A toast to Mr. Tallmadge's role in that phenomenon, and to his unmitigated conscience and principles, as well!"

"Hear, hear!" answered Garnet Kenrick, emulating Jones.

His wife and daughter raised their glasses, too, and exclaimed together, "Hear, hear!"

Roger Tallmadge, blushing at the attention, nodded in silent acknowledgement.

In part payment for the tribute, Tallmadge regaled the company with stories from the late war, and from the courts of Prussia, Hanover, and Denmark.

That evening, after the Kenricks had retired, Jones invited the lieutenant out for a stroll along Cheyne Walk. As they passed beneath the lampposts, they talked of many things — Parliament, the French, the Prussians, the colonies, and Hugh.

"You are a fellow of granite principle," said Tallmadge to the barrister at one point, "and I would not deny that, tonight, I have benefited from your wisdom. I think I shall count you among my closest friends."

Jones waved the compliment away with his silver-capped cane. "I will accept admission into that company only if you include me with your friend, Hugh."

"I do, sir. I haven't many friends, Sir Dogmael, but he is one of them. I am indebted to him for so much. You see, he was my first true mentor." Tallmadge chuckled. "He once adopted me as his younger brother."

"A mentor? In what subject?"

Tallmadge said, "It was not so much what he taught me, as in what he was. What he is. I correspond with him, and know that he has not changed a whit."

Jones smiled with irony. "On that point, I must own he has been something of a mentor to me, as well, in some respects." He paused to brave the next question. "A brother, you say? Would I be correct to suppose you would both welcome the chance to become brothers-in-law?"

Tallmadge grinned, and said without special emphasis, "In a few years, yes. I suppose we will both welcome the chance. The prospect absolutely enthralls Alice, and me." The lieutenant glanced at his companion, and remarked, "Speaking of wisdom, I enjoyed your remarks about Mr. Pitt's speech. I think you are right that it contains so many contraries, as Alice's father called them, and those contraries do form a keystone."

Jones stopped to light a pipe, saying, "What I deemed his keystone would establish a benevolent despotism of the Commons, that is all. But if we are to learn anything from the histories of ancient Greece and Rome, it is that such a benign despotism must by its nature and without exception sour into a malevolent one. It is a historical law."

Tallmadge exclaimed with renewed astonishment, "Well, it seems that Mr. Pitt defends the colonials' pockets, at the expense of their purses! Why, that single point of his muddles the mind!"

"Quite true, sir," Jones said. "And in that muddle of contraries nests the destiny of the empire."

Jones was wrought up by a frustrating impotence. In the last session, he had tried to introduce resolutions in the appropriate committees' bills to open Parliament to public reporting; to allow private persons and members to criticize the king, the Crown, and Parliament without risk of penalty or charges of seditious libel; to abolish the duties on imported corn and tobacco. In every instance, he was rebuffed. Often, he had been advised not to pursue these subjects by wary members, barristers and sergeants-at-law like himself, who considered themselves advocates of British liberty.

Now, after Pitt's speech, he felt honor bound to rise in the House at some important stage of the session to point out the contradictions in the Great Commoner's address. This, he knew, would mean contradicting a powerful man, and possibly alienating himself from his allies. It would mean going counter to the direction he was certain the House was going. It was a guarantee of isolation and solitude.

Over the next two months, Jones would sleep little while the future of the Stamp Act was being decided in the Commons and Lords. He would watch the proceedings, powerless to alter the course of the debates, and could only observe a phenomenon he could not yet name. At one point in them, he remarked to Garnet Kenrick, "It is said that a watched pot never boils. This one fairly seethes with scalding water."

He resigned himself early to defeat — in the Commons, even if repeal were passed, and at Cricklegate, in the company of Roger Tallmadge and Alice Kenrick. He resigned himself to defeat in the Commons, and to being no more to his beloved Alice than her "Uncle Dog."

* * *

That same evening, at Windridge Court in Whitehall downriver, another supper was held, presided over by Basil Kenrick, the Earl of Danvers, convened on the advice of his key men in the Commons, Crispin Hillier, member for Onyxcombe, and Sir Henoch Pannell, member for Canovan. In the morning he had consulted with them and confirmed his understanding of the faults and contradictions that he, too, had noted in Pitt's speech. He decided to call a parley of his bloc in the Commons, in order to instruct its members to emphasize those contradictions in their speeches and conversations, and to attempt to refute all pretensions of limitations on Parliament's power.

From the head of the table, he said to the company before dessert was served, "We may lose the argument against repeal — Mr. Pitt has seen to that — but win the day on the subject of supremacy. Not even Mr. Pitt contests the legislative supremacy of the Crown. Thrice he confirmed it, by my count."

"Why do you say that, your lordship?" asked Captain James Holets of the Foot Guards, and member for Oakhead Abbas, Essex.

"Because it is felt by certain individuals in both Houses that if repeal is adopted, some form of assertion, in the form of a declaratory resolution, must accompany it, necessarily and absolutely." The Earl seemed to smile. "That is the opinion of no less an eminence than Lord Rockingham himself."

"If I may add, your lordship," said Crispin Hillier, "since Mr. Pitt has unarguably set the terms of debate, the dispute will now be chiefly over the wordings of the resolutions for repeal and declaration."

Henoch Pannell glanced at the Earl, who with a nod gave him leave to speak. The member for Canovan said gruffly, "And Mr. Pitt has given us a word to use as a weapon in that dispute!"

"Which word is that, Sir Henoch?" asked Sir Fulke Treverlyn, member for Old Boothby, Cheshire, knighted in recognition of his successful prosecution of the ringleaders of the Skelly gang in Falmouth years ago. He now practiced law at the Court of Common Pleas. Sir Henoch, who had captured the ringleaders, renewed his acquaintance with the attorney shortly after his own entrance into the House.

"*Whatsoever!*" exclaimed Sir Henoch. "What fulminating folly!"

"An evil and encompassing term," mused Sir Fulke to himself. "It may be employed to good purpose."

Sir Henoch, who sat next to him at the table, remarked to him, "It will prove to serve as salve for those who argue strenuously for repeal, sir."

"Those with pudding for guts!" interjected Captain Holets contemptuously. He sat across from Sir Henoch. Holets was a veteran of the late war, and regarded the violence in the colonies against Crown officials and the stamp distributors as a justification for military reprisal. In hopes of securing a promotion to major, he had bombarded the late Duke of Cumberland, Lord Northington, and other policy "hawks" with many letters detailing the logistics, number of regiments, ships required, and timetables for an "offensive" against the colonies in the coming spring. "I still say that the Address from the House should advise His Majesty that the colonies are in a state of rebellion."

On the Earl's right sat Bevill Grainger, now Viscount of Wooten and Clarence, and retired Master of the Rolls at the King's Bench. He ventured, "It was expected that Mr. Pitt would set the Commons and Lords on their ears, when he deigned to attend. I agree with his lordship the Earl that to argue against repeal from this point forward would be laudatory, though futile. Mr. Grenville doubtless will continue to argue that line. We may sympathize with him in that regard. After all, it is his child that will certainly be slandered in both Houses and libeled in the newspapers, and possibly even abandoned. However, it is said that while good winds too often bring bad news, bad winds may bring good news. Yesterday, Mr. Pitt was all that."

"Yes, he was all that," concurred Norbonne Berkeley, fourth Baron Botetourt, Lord of the Bedchamber and Lord Lieutenant of Gloucestershire, and, until he was raised to the peerage two years ago, member in the Commons for that county for over twenty years. He sat on the Earl's left, and was the newest member of the Earl's bloc. Attending Parliament was, for him, simply an excuse to come down to London to frequent its many gambling dens. He had voted in Lords for the Stamp Act, and now opposed repeal of it in a civil, suave, non-belligerent manner.

"Instead of debating repeal and a declaratory act," he said calmly, "both Houses ought to reject every blasted petition from merchants and colonials, dismiss all the witnesses we will be painfully obliged to hear, and discuss instead the rewriting of every colonial charter. Repeal would become a moot point, if Parliament were made co-protector and -sponsor of the colonies with His Majesty. The colonies have a point there, concerning their charters, but it is a point that could be easily nullified, and ought to have been after the Act of Settlement ages ago. Then there would be no question of Parliamentary supremacy and authority." He glanced around the table in search of agreement.

He found it in the intrigued expressions of Sir Henoch and Sir Fulke, but Lord Wooten cautioned, "I am not certain His Majesty could be persuaded to share that power, milord Berkeley. It is unlikely he would relinquish any portion of it, even though he does not now exercise it, as some colonials seem to claim with odd bitterness."

"There would be constitutional questions, milord, as well" added Hillier. "And Lord Camden would be sure to oppose it with more fervor than that with which he opposes general warrants."

"I must concur with Lord Wooten and Mr. Hillier," volunteered Sir Fulke. "Speaking as a lawyer, I understand that Lord Mansfield has ruled privately on the speciousness of most colonial charters."

"Oh," replied Botetourt, "Lord Camden would need to answer Lord Mansfield's points of endorsement of the idea. And I am certain that some diligent under-secretaries in the Privy Council or Board of Trade could be found to study the problem and draft proposals amicable to His Majesty. Mr. Grenville employed a company of them to compose and refine the Stamp Act."

The Earl said, almost in the manner of a command, "His Majesty cannot now decide whether he is for repeal or enforcement or modification of the Act, so it is unlikely he will fix his mind one way or another on that question any time soon."

Lord Wooten frowned and clucked his tongue in admonition. "Why would you say that about His Majesty, your lordship? The poor fellow is beset by opinions and advice from such a multitude of quarters, I can't imagine he knows where to turn or what to think."

"He will not fix his mind until he knows which way the cards are dealt." He glanced around the supper table. "Baron Berkeley, and you others here who are wedded to games, surely you should know better than I that His Majesty will not reveal his true hand until he is sure of the contents of his fellow players' hands, and that it will take him some time to decide. His Majesty, after all, is a paragon of caution." His guests could not decide whether their host was complimenting the king or mocking him. But that was the end of discussion of that matter.

Crispin Hillier remarked in the resulting conversational vacuum, "Word is that His Majesty will now seek to persuade Mr. Pitt to join the ministry."

Baron Berkeley laughed once. "There is another doomed project, sir. France is more likely to cede us the Aquitaine and Calais than is Mr. Pitt to join any ministry he does not govern."

Sir Henoch glanced at the Earl. "Your lordship, may I propose a toast of gratitude to Mr. Pitt? I think we are all agreed here that he has rescued us from a bothersome conundrum!"

The Earl seemed to smile again, and nodded in appreciation of the ironic suggestion.

Sir Henoch held up his glass of brandy and proclaimed, "To William Pitt, the Great Commoner, whom we may now also call the Great *Confabulator*! Here's to *repeal*!"

The company laughed with him, and raised glasses in answer and agreement. Basil Kenrick joined in silent approval of the toast, and drank with the rest of his bloc.

Later in the evening, when the most of the guests had departed, Hillier and Pannell lingered on, although going through the motions of departure. Sir Henoch addressed his host. "Your lordship, I had the honor of breakfasting with the Bishop of London today, and he brought these to my attention. He and I thought you might be interested in them, as well." He took from his frock coat two pamphlets and presented them to the Earl. "They were sent to him by a correspondent and colleague of the cloth in Virginia. You may keep these, of course. Bishop Terrick was sent two sets of them and had copies made. One in particular interests me, and the other may particularly interest your lordship."

The Earl took the pamphlets and glanced at the title pages. One contained the name "Jack Frake." It meant nothing to him. On the other, he saw the title, *The Chimney Swifts of Chicanery*, "by Hugh Kenrick, Esq., Virginia Gentleman." He grunted once in surprise, then glanced at Sir Henoch. "Thank you, Sir Henoch, for the courtesy. But what caused you to believe I would be interested in these?"

Sir Henoch braved, "You have your devils, your lordship, and I have mine." When the Earl did not reply, he added, "In the letter to Reverend Terrick that accompanied these pamphlets, his correspondent related that my devil, Mr. Frake, whom I sent to the colonies as a felon many years ago, and your nephew, were directly responsible for obstructing Crown officers in their duties regarding the stamps. Successfully, I might add. Reverend Terrick, I am sure, would be happy to share with you those and other details of the incident, your lordship." After another pause, he added, "I think you will see that they are both tracts of treason."

"I am certain they are. Thank you for the information, Sir Henoch," sighed the Earl. "I will peruse them." He nodded to Pannell, and then to Crispin Hillier. "And good night to you both."

When they were gone, Basil Kenrick wandered down the hall and into his study. Here he tugged on a bell-pull to signal Claybourne, his valet, that he wished to retire soon. He lit a pump lamp on his desk, sat down, and glanced through his nephew's pamphlet for a moment. His face grew progressively redder as he absorbed and grasped his nephew's prescient characterization of not only Parliament's conduct concerning the Stamp Act matter, but his own and his guests' parley this evening. He was frankly dumbfounded by his nephew's ability to foretell such things.

Most assuredly, his nephew had sent copies of the pamphlet to his brother in Chelsea, and to that annoying lackey of his, Sir Dogmael Jones, and they both had had a good laugh.

When Claybourne appeared in the study, the Earl angrily tossed the pamphlet onto his desk. Scowling petulantly up at the man, he exclaimed, "A devil indeed! A thousand leagues away, yet he still manages to provoke me!"

The valet, ignorant of the cause of his employer's fury, merely blinked in surprise, but limited his reply to a practiced expression of mute contrition.

* * *

Chapter 23: The Summons

If purblind consistency is the hobgoblin of little minds, then the terms of the debates over repeal and enforcement of the Stamp Act were set by one outstanding mind whose errors were seized upon and exploited by a passel of vicious little ones. They were all, if nothing else, consistent and uncompromising. The Grenvillites in the Commons and the Bedfordites in Lords hammered away at the idea of repeal. But, if resigned to repeal, they demanded that it be accompanied by a declaration that would essentially render it meaningless. They were certain that victory could be had even in defeat.

Pitt was openly contemptuous of both Houses and the motives of their members who demanded enforcement of the Stamp Act. He detected a species of fear in most of his colleagues which he sensed went beyond mere practical politics. He was too much of a gentleman to name it in private conversation or public address, but was haughtily determined to confound and defeat it. Perhaps it was his knowledge of and association with such fearful men that contributed to his chronic bouts of melancholy depression.

Those who opposed repeal were also contemptuous of the politics and even of each other, but their livelihoods depended on the range of authority wielded by Parliament and on the lucre derived from such authority in all the Crown's purviews. It was more desperation than commitment to any higher, disinterested end that moved them to argue for the preservation of that authority.

And during the debates, they did not disguise their desire to obstruct Pitt. Here was a great man, they saw, greater than anyone in either House; they knew this and wished him to acknowledge his own folly and just how impractical and obstinate he was being. He was an affront to all their pretensions of nobility, dignity, and concern for the Crown's solvency. If they could not be rid of him, they wished to reduce him in stature, to make him more manageable and familiar, and consequently less to be feared.

So, despite the advice of Benjamin Franklin to Lord Dartmouth, president of the Board of Trade, that enforcement of the Act might cause "more mischief than it was worth"; despite the observation of General Thomas

Gage on the Stamp Act Congress that "the question is not of the inexpediency of the Stamp Act, or of the inability of the colonies to pay the tax, but
that it is unconstitutional and contrary to their rights"; despite the
repressed suspicion that the colonies were not protesting merely a shilling
tax on a pack of playing cards or a sixpence tax on a copy of a will; and
despite a growing miasma of doubt in both Houses about the wisdom of the
Act and its expected windfall in revenues, a miasma that clouded the character of their debates, the reigning policy in the Commons and Lords was a
flat refusal to question the right *whatsoever* of Parliament to impose any tax
or control on the colonies.

This refusal assumed the outward character of incorruptible principle,
and allowed many members of the Commons to oppose repeal with righteous anger, such as Colonel Thomas Molyneux, member for Haslemere,
who at one point assailed an "ungrateful America. Shall we stay 'til some
Oliver rises up amongst them? Four sorts of people appear among them:
hypocrites, agitators, preachers, and levelers!"

"Also, patriots and men of honor and industry," said Jones to
Molyneux in the coffee room of the House later that day.

"Excuse me, sir?" asked the member for Haslemere, turning with surprise to him.

"Very few of *those* to be found in this other hospital for invalids," said
Jones. He paid the servant at the bar for the beverage, and gave the man a
halfpenny gratuity. It was seven o'clock in the evening. The room was
filling up with members seeking refreshments and respite from the debates
in the chamber.

Molyneux, after he too had paid the servant, turned to Jones and
replied, with tentative frost allayed by doubt, "You have lost me, sir," for he
was unsure whether or not he was being insulted.

"I refer to your speech today and the prisoners you name in the dock
of treason. If you believe that the colonials are being shepherded in their
outrage by hypocrites and agitators, then you underestimate them and you
will lose the colonies. But I have heard that preachers there command more
attention than ours do here — when they preach liberty, which they often
do these times. As for the levelers, I am certain they would object to a
grasping Cromwell with more fury than they would for a mere stamp distributor. And surely you have heard of the misfortunes of some of those
chaps."

Molyneux frowned in genuine confusion and replied with some irritation, "God's truth, sir, I don't know whether to agree with you or take offense!" Then he narrowed his eyes, and said, "I know *you*, sir! You are the fellow who insulted the House last session!"

"And I may find it necessary to insult it again."

"If you do, sir, you may find your cheeks smarting from several pairs of gloves!" Molyneux sniffed in dismissal, then turned and strode to another part of the crowded room to join some cronies.

Jones smiled in amusement and sipped his coffee. "Doubtless, yours will be the first."

A familiar, mellifluous voice behind him remarked, "Collecting friends again, Sir Dogmael?"

Jones turned to face the great bulk of Sir Henoch Pannell. "I love thee not. Therefore, pursue me not," he answered. By mutual agreement and animosity, the two had conspicuously avoided each other since passage of the Stamp Act in the last session of Parliament.

Pannell chuckled and shook his head. "Doubtless, you plagiarize another bard unknown to me."

"No. Just the usual one."

"Why, I half expected you to have risen across the aisle by now to assail us with half a dozen bardish gems, steeped in your own novel notions," Pannell said. "I am gravely disappointed. We do need our entertainment in such grave affairs as this, you know." Henoch Pannell waved a hand to indicate the coffee room and the chamber beyond the closed oaken doors, through which a speaker could still be heard. Pannell exuded a genuine air of jollity the whole two months of debates, in sharp contrast to the humorless determination of other members on both sides of the question. He was one of the few who were certain that victory could be had in defeat. The Crown would have a revenue from its British "flora" in North America, by hook or by crook. A declaratory act, he had been privately assuring allies in the House, would guarantee it, backed, if necessary, by an increase in the garrisons there and a more vigorous prosecution of the myriad strictures of the navigation laws.

"I am biding my time, and will strike at a moment of my choosing," Jones said.

"You know," said Pannell, "you really oughtn't to burden military fellows like Colonel Molyneux with such high-flying talk. Most of them sport walnuts for brains. They may take it as abuse, and call you out to pistols. You heard the dear Colonel." The member for Canovan sipped his tea.

Jones shrugged and tasted his coffee. "I face my mortality every day, Sir Henoch, as I search for a proof against stealthy eavesdroppers."

"Yes, of course. So do we all. But you would face expulsion from the House only once, if you insult it, as you promised the Colonel you would. You know the rules."

"I will speak my mind, nevertheless."

"So said Mr. Wilkes. You know what happened to him." Pannell laughed. "He is not *here*."

"He will be back. The rogue has champions here. I will be one of them."

"Why, that fellow is a worse bounder than I believe you think I am, sir! And you propose to enter the lists in his cause? That is most confabulating indeed, as confabulating as Mr. Pitt's speech, wouldn't you agree?" When Jones did not reply to his question, he shook his head. "It is beyond my ken!"

Jones smiled pointedly. "Much is," he remarked.

"There you go again, chiding me for my ignorance," laughed Pannell, indifferent to the slight. Then he frowned in mock seriousness. "Speaking of books, lately I have been reading Lord Wooten's book on collateral justice. Fascinating stuff. I hear it's got all the benches in a dither. Have you read it?"

Jones remembered Sir Bevill Grainger's remarks on the subject from years ago when the former Master of the Rolls presided over the Pippins' trial. "Yes, I have perused a few of its pages. I was present when he took his first notes on the subject." He paused. "It surprises me that you would bother to tackle something as difficult as a judicial theory, even one as disturbingly degenerate as Lord Wooten's."

"Well, there you are, sir! It pleases me that I have shocked you, for once! Degenerate, you say? Rather, revolutionary! Try a man for his charged crimes, find him guilty of all the others he weren't tried for, or was suspected of, and toss in a few more years or even the noose, if the judge and jury have a mind to!" Pannell grinned. "It was *my* idea, you know, though I could never have worked out the details. Never had the time! However, I have written Lord Wooten about how his notion could be applied to the colonial problem. Round up all the upstarts there and hang them for treason! Or at least sentence them to a turn in Jamaica or the Barbados to harvest cane, where they would meet much the same end, with the sun as their hangman." Pannell's broad face brightened. "Here's a notion, sir! Have supper with me tonight at my place in Canovan, and you can explain to me why you now sport such a sour phiz!"

"Thank you, Sir Henoch," answered Jones, shaking his head, "but wisdom would be wasted on you, just as it might have been on Judge Jeffreys." He saw that Pannell did not grasp his allusion to the Bloody Assizes, and finished his coffee. "Or, shall I say, the labor would be lost? So, before I return to my seat, I leave you with an appropriate bardish gem to contemplate: 'A world of torments though I should endure, I would not yield to be our house's guest, so much I hate the breaking cause to be of heavenly oaths, vowed with integrity.'"

Pannell grinned with an appreciation that startled even himself. "That's pretty, sir! It almost rhymes, it does! What fellow is credited with that?"

"Not a fellow," sighed Jones, surprised that Pannell did not ask what it meant, "but a Princess of France." With a slight nod of his head, he turned, handed his cup to a passing factotum, and made for the oaken doors and the chamber beyond.

Pannell trailed behind him across the room. "You know, Sir Dogmael, there's no reason why we can't be friends. We have such diverting chats. I own that each time we trade insults, I walk away a little wiser. I mean, we know each other well enough that our politics oughtn't to interfere at all. "

Jones paused to turn and answer, "Well, you must also own that, from my perspective, it would hardly be a fair trade, something akin to the relationship between the colonies and the Crown. So, I must say of you what I have heard has been said of the late Duke of Cumberland, and urge you to adopt it as your own rule, as well."

"What is that?"

"Those who knew him best, liked him least, or not at all. Good night to you, sir." Jones turned and left the noise of the coffee room for the noise of the House chamber.

Pannell grimaced sadly and shook his head. "Difficult fellow, that Jones."

Jones slept irregularly those two months, for the debates in the Commons usually began in mid-afternoon and often lasted until the early hours of the next day. He attended the Commons daily, not wanting to miss an important speech or motion, dividing his resting times between his rooms near the Inns of Court and Cricklegate in Chelsea. He was particularly interested in hearing the testimony of the witnesses. Benjamin Franklin was scheduled to be questioned — or rather interrogated by a hostile House, he warned the Pennsylvanian during a supper at William Meredith's house one evening — and he wanted to put some questions to that man when he was called. Also, Colonel George Mercer of Virginia was scheduled to testify, and he had some particular questions to put to that man, as well.

Often he would appear at two o'clock in the morning at the Kenricks' house in Chelsea, bleary-eyed, unshaven, unkempt, to be admitted by one of the servants. In the mornings, while Owen Runcorn shaved him, he would report the previous day's events in the House to Garnet Kenrick, then break-fast with the Kenricks and Roger Tallmadge before departing with the lieu-tenant by carriage for another round of debates or his barrister obligations at the King's Bench in Westminster Hall adjacent to the Commons.

When he returned to his rooms on Chancery Lane near the Serjeants' Inn, he would gaze wistfully at the mass of unorganized papers that was his own book on the subject of property and public places, hoping that after this session of Parliament he would find more time to devote to its further progress. His occasional secretary and amanuensis, Winslow LeGrand, was assisting him with the research for that book and also with his correspon-dence.

One morning in mid-February at Cricklegate, he was awakened by one of the Kenricks' servants and informed that his sponsor had been sum-moned by his brother the Earl to Windridge Court. The Baron wished him to accompany him to London. He hurriedly dressed, shaved himself, and joined his friend downstairs for a quick breakfast. Then, as the carriage made its way to Westminster through the chilly, charcoal gray fog, Jones asked, "Why does he want to see you?"

"I don't know, Mr. Jones," said Garnet Kenrick as the carriage rumbled over the road. "The footman who delivered the note could or would not say. Bridgette, who received the note, said he did not tarry long enough for a reply, but remounted and rode away before she could even close the door." After a moment, he mused, "It can't be about estate business. I sent him the accounts and his draft a month ago, and I should have heard from him sooner if something had been amiss."

Jones merely drummed his fingers on the top of the satchel on his lap. He had never voiced an opinion about his sponsor's brother, although he was certain the Baron knew what he thought of the Earl. The Baron had often railed against his brother in his presence, but Jones did not presume to criticize the Earl himself. It was a rule he vowed never to break, if only for decorum's sake. He had never related to the Baron the Earl's ruse last year with the false invitation to the Duke of Bedford's residence.

They did not talk much during the ride. They had too often discussed, as the debates ground on, a phenomenon they had both observed, which was the gradual whittling down of the arguments of those who argued for repeal to a pathetic concession by them of Parliamentary supremacy. Only a few other members saw the contradiction and conflict between repeal and a declaration of blanket authority. Almost to a man, taking Pitt's lead, even though he at the time denied it, the most ardent advocates of repeal began to surrender the high ground to the opposition.

Jones and the Baron stoically endured the debates and the desertion of the high ground, certain of the outcome. Neither of them knew how to persuade their allies of the poisonous contradiction. Only a few prominent members, such as Pitt, were opposed to a declaratory act, and they would not be able to influence the crucial vote against it.

Jones, wanting to distract his friend, who seemed anxious about his first meeting with his brother in over a year, said, "Lord Camden granted me a moment yesterday, milord. He deigned to join me in the Purgatory Tavern near the Yard. He plans to argue that since both Houses refuse to recognize or even debate the rights of the colonials as Englishmen, they affirm those rights, and so nullify the legality of the Stamp Act. 'If I contradict not, then I affirm,' he said. He will also maintain that taxation and representation are inseparable. God has united them, and no British Parliament can separate them. That is his contention." He added, with sour irony, "I believe he hopes that his fellow peers are not so full of themselves that they would attempt to substitute their own design and will for the Almighty's."

Garnet Kenrick scoffed in amazement. "What has God got to do with it? I am not so familiar with the Bible, but I am certain there are no books in it devoted exclusively to the limitations of Crown authority over the internal business of Virginia and Massachusetts!"

Jones shrugged. "Doubtless, he will call on Mr. Locke's authority." After a pause, he grinned. "You've hit upon an interesting notion, milord. Material for another caricature! The Book of Mansfield in the Old Testament, versus the Book of Camden in the New, each lordly justice holding a pair of stone tablets. I can imagine now the holy hell such a caricature would raise, if we could find a newspaper with bottom enough to publish it."

"And you wouldn't, Mr. Jones! Don't you even think of it!" snapped the Baron immediately. "Holy hell it would be! I would not want to see you tried and hanged for heresy, as well! It is one thing to portray bishops and churchmen as packs of vultures. It is quite another to ascribe Godly omniscience to mortals, even though it may flatter them! You would be sued and persecuted nonetheless! Remember what happened to your clients, the Pippins!"

"How could I forget?" After a pause, Jones asked, out of curiosity, "As well as what, milord?"

"For being yourself, you incorrigible rascal!" answered the Baron with angry affection.

"Thank you, milord." A moment passed, the silence broken only by the rattle of the carriage windows. Then Jones said, "I must say that Lord Camden's proposed argument is a rather specious and dilatory advocacy of the colonials' cause. Even so, I doubt that anyone in Lords or the Commons will take the bait. In any event, it does not address the issue of rights."

"That is true," said the Baron.

They said no more until they reached Windridge Court.

* * *

Alden Curle appeared at the door of Windridge Court when the carriage stopped in the flagstone courtyard. As its passengers debouched, he was surprised to see his employer's brother accompanied by a stranger. He doubted this would please the Earl. When the pair was before him, he bowed slightly with the greeting, "Milord Kenrick, it is so nice to see you again." He did not glance at Jones.

The Baron nodded curtly to Curle; he had never liked the man. The major domo preceded him and Jones into the mansion, and showed them to the Earl's study. "His lordship will be with you shortly, milord," Curle said as he bowed and began to leave the room.

"Mr. Curle," called Garnet Kenrick.

Curle stopped and turned. "Yes, milord?"

"It was a damp ride, and we would appreciate some tea to warm our bones, thank you."

"Of course, milord," answered the servant, seeming surprised that anyone should make such a request. "This instant." He bowed again and left them alone.

"Basil will make us wait," remarked Garnet Kenrick to Jones as they removed their overcoats and sat down in a pair of chairs in front of the desk. "And, properly, a tea service should have been prepared and laid out here already. That it was not is an omen of what I can expect from my dear brother."

"How will you explain my presence?" asked Jones. "I am certain he will not be pleased to see me. To judge by your reception, I'm wagering that he's as dismal as the day."

"I shall say you are my bodyguard. He can take that as he wishes."

"Or your legal counsel, milord," Jones suggested. "Much the same thing."

Garnet Kenrick chuckled. "That's right. You are a lawyer. I am always forgetting that."

The tea service presently arrived, brought by one of Curle's underlings, who left without offering to assist. Jones poured their cups. The tea was cold. Jones nodded to the bell-pull behind the Earl's desk. "Shall I ring for hot?" he asked the Baron.

Garnet Kenrick shook his head. "No, Mr. Jones. Don't bother."

Half an hour later Basil Kenrick came through the door. "Good morning, dear brother," he said with a nod to the Baron. "I trust you are well."

Garnet Kenrick rose. "Good morning, Basil," he also said with a nod. "Yes, I am well. And, you?"

"Well enough." He glanced at Jones, who had also risen. "And who is this gentleman?"

"Sir Dogmael Jones, member for Swansditch, and my friend and ally."

The Earl took his seat behind the desk. He studiously ignored Jones the rest of the interview, his glance flitting between his brother and a framed Furber print on the wall near him. "Is his presence necessary?"

"In politics and in social occasions, we are often inseparable," answered the Baron in a conversational tone. He sat down. Jones followed suit. "Sir Dogmael has business at the Inns, and then he will attend today's sitting in the Commons."

"A new batch of witnesses is scheduled today, your lordship," volunteered Jones.

The Earl did not acknowledge that Jones had addressed him.

A moment passed. The Baron said, "The tea ordered by Mr. Curle was tepid, Basil." He waited for his brother to reply.

"Oh, I am so sorry. The kitchen must have served you the remnants from breakfast. Shall I order more?"

"No, thank you." Garnet Kenrick waited another moment, then asked, "What did you wish to see me about, Basil? I assumed there was some urgency." He paused. "Was there something amiss in the accounts?'

"No," said the Earl, shaking his head. "No, the accounts were perfect, as usual." After a single sharp glance at Jones, he continued. "Our business is of a private nature, dear brother. I really cannot discuss it in the presence of a stranger."

The Baron sighed with impatience. "If the business concerns the debates, Basil, then Sir Dogmael's presence is unfortunately necessary." His tone made it clear that if Jones were obliged to make his excuses and leave the study, so would he.

The Earl understood this and grimaced. "All right. It is this. I am hoping that this gentleman will not speak for repeal or against a declaratory act."

The Baron frowned in amazement. "Not that it is within your right or privilege to make such an improper request, Basil, but why do you so hope?"

"Because I do not wish our family to be associated with anyone or any party that defies His Majesty and Crown authority. Everyone knows that this gentleman speaks for you."

Jones's face was almost livid. Before the Baron could caution him, he rose to say, "Your lordship, your request is improper, and if you insist on making it, I shall be compelled to report this incident to the House. You propose to impinge on the right of a member of the Commons to speak as he sees fit, and that is a more serious violation of the independence of the Commons from Lords than lords purchasing blocs of votes in the House. I might also remind his lordship that both Houses are populated with riven families. It is nothing unusual."

The Earl's response to this outburst was to turn his back on Jones. The Baron sat mute, doubly stupefied by his brother's request and Jones's words.

Gathering more breath, Jones went on to say, "And, begging your pardon, your lordship, but when I speak, I speak for myself, of my own mind. If it seems that I speak for your brother the Baron, you may put it down to a propinquity of ideals and ends."

The Earl's features, too, had grown scarlet. Without turning his head, he said to his brother, "Tell the gentleman that if he is calling me a liar, there will be consequences, in the courts, or elsewhere."

Garnet Kenrick glanced stonily up at Jones. The barrister's mouth was gnarled in disgust. He turned, picked up his overcoat and satchel, and said to the Baron, "I am more a burden than a help to you here, milord. I will await you outside."

The Baron nodded. Without another look at the Earl, Jones left the room.

When the door had closed behind Jones, the Earl said, "He has the manners and insolence of your son, dear brother, to speak to me like that!"

"You should have expected it, after the insults you paid him. *Your* manners are inexcusable."

"I paid him the courtesy he deserved!" The Earl jerked open a desk drawer, seized a pamphlet, and tossed it across the space at his brother. "And that is the courtesy I must pay you, dear brother, for raising a son who would write such treasonous rubbish, a son who would defy the Crown with a cocked pistol and a rabble behind him!"

Garnet Kenrick bent to pick up the pamphlet, which had fallen at his feet. It was a copy of Hugh's *The Chimney Swifts of Chicanery*. He smiled. "Oh, this? One of Hugh's finest efforts. I am surprised that he would send *you* a copy, as well."

"He did not," growled the Earl. "It came to me by way of the Bishop of London. He was quite scandalized by it, as well!" He stood up and paced behind his desk. "Copies of that filth have been read by other members of *my* House. It is a subject of jest, as now am I." He leaned over his desk and shook a finger at his brother. "I was being considered for an appointment to the Privy Council or to the Board of Trade, dear brother. That discussion has now ceased, thanks to your son!"

The Baron chuckled. "Well, someone must think highly of you," he remarked, "if no one else does."

The Earl seemed not to hear. "How could I be trusted with such an office, when my own nephew is a traitorous Whig puppy who champions blasphemous freethinkers and sides with rebels??"

Garnet Kenrick feigned indifference, and mused, "I suppose no one could. You know, Hugh once thought he would write a parable about sheep, to make the same points, nearly." He waved the pamphlet once and tossed it back onto his brother's desk. "That is infinitely better, but not as to the point as his friend Mr. Frake's pamphlet on the same subject." He paused. "Also, your account of the incident is erroneous. Hugh and his fellow citizens simply foiled a scheme to smuggle stamps into a country where they were not wanted, without benefit of arms of any kind. He wrote me about it. Apparently the naval officer charged with the task decided that discretion was the better part of judgment." The Baron shrugged. "But if you would rather believe that Hugh is some kind of pirate or highwayman, so be it." He rose and collected his overcoat. "Is that all, Basil?"

"Yes. I simply wanted to warn you that if your son continues his treason, I will be forced to take appropriate measures, legal or extraordinary." He waited for his brother to respond.

"Meaning?"

"I leave the meaning to your imagination and grief. Now you know why this was to be a private meeting, and I could not tolerate the presence of a stranger, particularly not *that* one."

Garnet Kenrick stared at his brother. "What an evil modesty! What a dubious virtue!" he scoffed in the manner of an abstract observation. Then his eyes narrowed, and he said softly, "Damn you, Basil." He approached the desk and put a finger on his brother's shimmering satin neck-cloth. "Do not threaten my son, Basil. Or Mr. Jones. If anything *extraordinary* ever happens to either of them, you will need to answer to me. That is *my* warning." He draped his coat over an arm. "Good day to you, *your lordship*." He turned and strode out of the study.

Basil Kenrick raised a clenched fist, shook it at the closing door, and shouted. "I will *not* be disgraced!"

* * *

Chapter 24: The Questions

One afternoon, the Kenricks and Roger Tallmadge accompanied Jones to a dinner party of repeal advocates at the home of William Beckford, member for London and former lord mayor of it. Here he introduced them also to Colonel Isaac Barré, William Meredith, Benjamin Franklin, and Edward Montagu, the agent for Virginia and member for Huntingdon, and his wife, Elizabeth, a social and literary light. Politics, the colonies, and speculation about the debates in Lords, of course, were the chief topics of lively conversation, together with Franklin's voluminous and pseudonymous letters in several London newspapers that promoted and argued the colonial position against the Stamp Act.

Franklin was the center of attention and the object of adulation throughout the occasion. His host and several guests employed every guile at their command to coax an admission from him that he was the true author of the letters, but he would only confess responsibility for a caricature, "Magna Britannia: Her Colonies Reduced," which depicted Britannia's colonies as dismembered limbs and Britain's merchant vessels sitting idle in a harbor, their masts stripped of yards and sails. He had printed hundreds of cards of the caricature, and distributed them to as many merchants, members of the Commons, and government officials as were willing to take them.

"*I* found it gruesomely offensive," remarked Beckford half seriously at one point in the conversation. "Britannia looks as though she had been chewed on by a shark."

"Or the subject of the ministrations of a diligent surgeon who could not make up his mind," quipped Elizabeth Montagu. "But gruesomely offensive, nonetheless."

"Offensive?" asked Franklin in reply. "If you find it so, then I have succeeded in convincing you of the gruesome consequences of the Stamp Act, if it is not repealed."

"Oh, we are all here persuaded of those consequences, Mr. Franklin," said Beckford. "You needn't worry us further on that matter. Only a block-head would fail to see the lesson in your caricature."

Roger Tallmadge, sitting in between Alice Kenrick and Jones, had only just been presented with a copy of the caricature by Franklin himself. He spoke up and addressed Franklin. "Well, here is a blockhead, sir. I cannot decide on its imputation. Is Britannia's condition meant to convey the con-sequences of enforcing the Act, or of the colonies having withdrawn from the Empire? Forgive me the confusion, but you must own it could be con-strued either way."

Franklin's eyes sparkled with mischief. "Either way, sir. I must com-pliment you for the inquiry."

At one point during the dinner, Jones said to the Pennsylvanian, "Mr. Franklin, when you are called to testify, and if the chance presents itself, I shall ask you some inconvenient questions."

Franklin replied, "And I shall give you inconvenient answers." He looked inquiringly at the member for Swansditch, who sat next to Roger Tallmadge.

Jones grinned and shook his head. "No, sir. I shall not prompt you. But I can assure you that our questions and answers will be more inconvenient for the House than for either of us."

Alice Kenrick, who sat opposite Franklin, asked him, "How can ques-tions and answers be inconvenient, Mr. Franklin? I confess that when I hear men talk of politics, it is in English but still in a language cryptic to me."

Franklin bestowed a smile on the girl. "Dear child, what Sir Dogmael and I meant by that was that his questions and my answers may not be wel-come by so many gentlemen in Parliament, who may decide to inconve-nience him in some manner. A very brave friend sits next to you there."

Alice Kenrick beamed at Jones and touched his arm. "Oh, you needn't convince me of my Uncle Dog's bravery, sir! We often talk about it behind his back, Roger and I and my parents."

Franklin looked confused, and glanced down the table to Garnet and Effney Kenrick. "Oh?" he said. "Is the Baron your brother, Sir Dogmael?"

"In honor only, Mr. Franklin," said Jones, "and in the frequency with which I dun his abode for *gratis* meals and a place to rest my leaden head after a long day in the House."

"You may as well be my true uncle," said Alice, smiling up at Jones again. "I have disowned his lordship the Earl, and am resolved to be cold to him if ever we should meet again." She grasped his hand and squeezed it. "You *are* a member of our family, Uncle Dog, and we shall always love you."

Jones repressed a bitter thought, and said, "Well, do not be disappointed if on that occasion your true uncle does not break down and weep on his knees at your cruelty. I fancy the Earl is quite accustomed to being shown arctic airs. I myself have shown him my back."

In the carriage ride back to Chelsea that evening, Effney Kenrick remarked, "Mr. Franklin seems to be a completely honest and dedicated person, Mr. Jones. We should not fear for him when he is called to the bar of the House. I wish I could witness it. He is as wily as a French courtier. He will confound and shame his enemies."

"Wily, milady?" answered Jones. "Oh, no, he is not wily at all! And let us not insult his character by comparing him with a French courtier! Rather, when he is called to the bar, think of the contest in terms of a pack of mad squirrels attempting to bait a buffalo! Their numbers will be quite irrelevant."

Jones was certain that he would know when he had the right information to ask those inconvenient questions. It was the next day in the House, when he heard two prominent merchants' trade and debt figures — "a trade volume of between two and a half to three millions of pounds per annum, and a colonial debt to our merchants amounting to some four millions, which, if it were not repaid, would have catastrophic consequences for our merchants and the nation" — that Jones knew he had found his means. These figures and other relevant information were already in his satchel of papers, but until he heard the merchants pronounce the figures, they had been mere data of no useful value.

On February 12th, Colonel George Mercer of Virginia was called a second time. He stood as other witnesses had, at the bar at the head of the House, flanked by two sergeants-at-arms. In the course of his questioning he confirmed another witness's contention that Virginia alone could raise fifty-two thousand militiamen if necessary. The cause of their being called to arms remained unspoken, as no one dared imagine it; there were only five thousand British regulars to oppose them. One member asked him if the Stamp Act could wring £35,000 from that colony, considered the richest in North America. Mercer's answer was evasively ambiguous. William Meredith rose to ask him if he was certain of that figure. Mercer again wavered, but then conceded that by his own calculations it was closer to £12,000.

Unbidden, he went on to relate his treatment by the "drunken rabble" in Hampton and Williamsburg, and that, had he been allowed to fulfill his appointment as stamp distributor, he would have employed twenty-five under-distributors to serve the colonies of Virginia and Maryland. He claimed that he had had to resign his commission in England, because the Lieutenant-Governor refused to oblige him in Williamsburg. He ended his unsolicited speech with, "I have heard that the naval commander there attempted to deliver the stamps to me in the capital, but that the attempt failed."

Meredith put on an expression of sympathetic concern. "Did you journey all the way to England to resign your commission, sir?" He already knew the answer, but wanted to soften the witness up for his next questions.

"Not entirely, sir. I am here principally as a representative of a land company with patents west of the transmontane. There is some conflict between those patents and Crown policies."

Jones, sitting next to the member from Liverpool, pulled on Meredith's cuff. Meredith bent down and Jones whispered something in his ear. Meredith nodded and turned again to Mercer and asked, "Well, sir, we may settle on one figure or the other, but would you venture that £35,000 or even £12,000 in specie circulate in Virginia?"

Mercer blinked once, then remarked, "What an odd question, sir. Of course not. I would say there are scarce a thousand pounds in the whole colony, lost amongst a ton of Virginia notes and Spanish pistoles and other foreign coin." Wishing to sound important, he added, with a dismissive snort, "I rather doubt that either amount could be scraped together from all the colonies together at any one time."

"You fool!" grumbled George Grenville, who all through the debates was steadfast in his assertion that the colonies could easily pay his stamp taxes. "You were *not* to digress or opine!"

"Quite," commented Meredith. "But it is not so odd a question, sir. As a stamp distributor, you must have known that the Act stipulates that the tax must be paid in sterling. So how then could any honest man, or even an addled spendthrift, expect that colony to pay the greater or lesser figure?"

Mercer blinked and stuttered, "I don't know, sir," but it was inaudible under a rush of sound in the House that was an uneasy mixture of astonishment and disapproval. It was unclear to him whether Meredith's points or his answers were the object of the astonishment and disapproval. When the hubbub had subsided, Mercer peevishly asked the House whether or not repeal might encourage Virginians and other colonists to resist other revenue acts. The question was regarded by most as merely rhetorical, but George Grenville took the opportunity to rise and answer ominously in the affirmative.

The next day, Benjamin Franklin was at last called to testify. Over a grueling four-hour period, he answered one hundred and seventy-four questions from the members, more than half of them put to him by hostile Grenvillites. Jones was correct in his assessment: It was not a fair contest. Franklin easily disposed of questions designed to embarrass him, impugn the character of the colonials and their cause, or refute the colonial view of legislation. The questions ranged from the capabilities of the militia to the distinction between internal and external taxation. No matter what leading question he was asked by Grenvillites, his answer only served to buttress the quest of the ministry, which was repeal of the Act.

His answers at some points in his interrogation stood out like sores that the House did not wish to contemplate. He warned that a military enforcement of the Act would be pointless, for bayonets could not force a man to purchase stamps; and possibly counter-productive, for he warned further that while the Army and Navy "will not find a rebellion, they may indeed make one," if they were employed in enforcement. As deputy post-master-general for the colonies, he countered Grenville's glib contention that the colonists were willing to pay the tax on mail, by stating that the tax on mail was not truly a tax, but payment for a service. He asserted that the last two wars in America against the French were prosecuted for predominantly British purposes, not American.

His most unsettling statement was that if the Crown continued to make no distinction in its policies between internal and external taxation, the colonies might likely follow suit, and deny Parliament's right to impose external taxes, as well.

"You damned fox!" muttered Grenville to himself. "You would have to make *that* point!"

"The point is made, and all is lost," sighed Thomas Whateley next to him.

Toward the end of Franklin's questioning, Jones rose, managed to catch Rose Fuller's attention, and was permitted to question the witness next.

He began, "Sir, we have heard in this chamber the dramatic numbers

in trade and debt between Britain and her colonies, cited by Messrs. Trecothick and Hanbury. And we have also read the petitions and heard the
testimony of many of our merchants here concerning their plight as a consequence of reduced trade with the colonies. That reduction may be attrib-
uted to a combination of a falling off of trade after the late war — a chronic
and perhaps natural occurrence — with a determined spurning of our manufactures by the colonies in protest of the Act under discussion. But, would
you contest those numbers, sir?"

"No, sir, I would not. I am sure that, whether they are exact or approx-
imate, those numbers represent a true state of the trade and debt."

"Doubtless, you have also heard expressed in this chamber the wish to
perpetuate dependence of the colonies on their mother country, by one
means or another."

"Yes, sir. I have." Franklin leaned on the bar with both hands, partly
from exhaustion, partly from curiosity about where Jones's line of questioning was leading.

"Now, taking into account the numbers between this isle and the
North American continent, would you not agree that this dependency in
trade is a fiction, that in fact, this isle is dependent for her solvency and
prosperity on the continent — artificially dependent, I might add, thanks
in no small part to the navigation and other constraining laws which
govern that trade?"

The House stirred at this question. Franklin smiled. He thought: *This
must be the overture to an inconvenient question!* He answered, "Reasoning
would lead one to that conclusion."

"And that the colonies' own solvency and prosperity would be
increased if they were able to trade freely with other nations, with each
other, and even with Britain and her other dominions?"

"That is true, sir. The complaint that they cannot festers into smuggling and much other unfortunate law-breaking."

"So, the odd, intractable desire of our merchants to perpetuate their
own dependence on the colonies, could be and has been met only by constraining those colonies with statute and legislation — with volley and
salvo, if necessary — irrespective of the sovereignty of their various governments and the dictates of our excellent constitution." He added, "That
is not a question, sir, but a considered observation."

The brows of William Pitt and other pro-repeal members wrinkled at
this choice of words. Jones heard a rumble of disapproval sweep through

the benches on both sides of the House, like the warning growl of an agitated mastiff. He continued. "The question is this: If you agree with that observation, does it not describe a dreadfully cyclopean form of indentured servitude, or, perhaps…of slavery?"

Franklin nearly laughed, but only modified his previous answer. "Reasoning would lead to one or the other appraisal, sir."

A second after Franklin pronounced the last syllable of his reply, the murmur burst into an uproar. Several members stood to shout at the chair, pointing at Jones, not Franklin, and angrily object, "Expel that man!" "Insult to the House!" "Take down his words!" "Silence that fellow!"

Jones removed his hat and waved it in the air in the direction of his assailants, and exclaimed in answer, "*Fiat lux! Fiat lux!*" Then he turned to Rose Fuller. "I have asked my questions, sir," and sat down. Roger Tallmadge, who sat next to him, stared at him with incredulity.

The House at length quieted down. Rose Fuller, a repeal advocate, dismissed the objections, saying that the allegedly offensive comments of the member were made while the House was sitting in committee, and so did not constitute a formal offense. He ignored the protests of the objectors and recognized the next questioner.

Jones was satisfied. He had raised the issue, which all the others could ignore at their own peril.

Garnet Kenrick, sitting in the gallery, said to the figure below, "'Let there be light!' Bravo, Mr. Jones. You never fail to surprise me."

Winslow LeGrand, who sat next to him taking notes in shorthand, glanced up and remarked, "He is well named, Sir Dogmael is, milord."

"How do you mean, sir?"

"He once told me the meaning of his name. 'Bringer of light to children.'"

"I did not know that. I agree. He is well named." The Baron sighed. "But would that he were tutoring mere children," he added with sadness.

Basil Kenrick, sitting on the opposite end of the gallery with some other peers, muttered, "Let there be light, indeed! There's a candle that must be snuffed!"

"Too many candles burn too brightly here today," remarked the Duke of Bedford in idle agreement. "That Franklin fellow has them all running to ground like frightened rabbits."

Viscount Wooten shook his head and said, "One's answers are only as good as the questions asked one, your grace. You may take that advice on the authority of the bench. That Jones knows how to ask questions. Together with Mr. Franklin, he has damaged Mr. Grenville's cause beyond repair."

When Jones left the Commons that evening, he was humming a tune he had heard in a tavern, and twirling his cane in a state of mild contentment. In the lobby and then in the Yard, he encountered other members who gave him looks of disgust or apprehension. He smiled in answer. Henoch Pannell greeted him with a mere nod, regarding Jones as he would a skilled magician or a felon who had survived a hanging at Tyburn Tree.

Rose Fuller had intercepted Jones in the lobby. "Fine questioning, Sir Dogmael. Stunning points you made, truly. I do believe they have helped clinch repeal."

"Thank you, Mr. Fuller."

"However, I must caution you to be more judicious in your choice of words. I was very nearly obliged to call you to the bar. You may thank the weariness of the opposition that I did not."

Jones replied, "Thank you, Mr. Fuller. I shall take care with my words."

Fuller nodded once, bid him good night, and returned to the chamber.

While waiting with Roger Tallmadge in the lobby for Garnet Kenrick, he happened to have encountered Benjamin Franklin emerging with his sponsor from the stairs that led to the gallery. "Thank you for the questions, Sir Dogmael. I could not help but notice the effect they had on the House. Your questions have furthered our cause."

"And your answers, as well. Thank you, sir," Jones replied.

Then Franklin glanced around him. Other members lingering in the lobby glowered at them from a distance. In a lower voice, he said, "But, sir, a caution. Your powers of persuasion are not welcome in many quarters. They will not protect you from brute harm. I have heard…comments."

Jones nodded in thanks for the advice. But he was feeling light-headed, and replied, "Thank you for your concern, Mr. Franklin. But if the colonies are willing to place themselves in jeopardy by speaking their minds, I can do no less."

When Franklin had left them, Roger Tallmadge remarked, "I must agree with him, Sir Dogmael. I, too, have heard, well…suggestions."

Garnet Kenrick nodded in agreement. "You know, of course, there are several gentlemen here who have a taste for dueling." He had already told Jones about his brother's words at Windridge Court.

Jones shrugged. "My friends, I have given myself the task of trooping the colors of liberty in this House, to see who rallies to them and who shoots at them. It is a necessary risk. War is not friendly game of whist, as *you*, Mr. Tallmadge, should well know."

Outside, Jones bid the Baron and the lieutenant good night, and with Winslow LeGrand took a hackney to his rooms on Chancery Lane, where he slept soundly for the first time in weeks.

The next day, Secretary of State Conway accused Grenville of having concealed American information from the House when the Act was proposed and debated a year ago. Grenville denied the charge, claiming that the Board of Trade, contrary to instructions in an Order in Council, had been lax in forwarding the American papers to the House. This excuse did little to allay the suspicion that he did not during his ministry much solicit colonial advice on the feasibility of a stamp tax. General Howard and other members rose to state that had they known about these papers, they would have more vigorously opposed the Act.

Over the next two days, the House heard Grenville's own witnesses, who related lurid stories of the rioting and violence in the colonies, and of the humiliation and property losses of several distributors and government officials. A West India merchant detailed the scope of smuggling in the North American colonies. Other witnesses described the finances of some of the colonial governments, and revealed, much to Grenville's chagrin, that over sixty percent of the colonial share of the war debt had been paid.

The day ended when Conway announced that on the 21st he would move for repeal of the Stamp Act, as opposed to its modification or enforcement. Another member rose to state that he would on that date move for some form of declaratory resolution.

Late afternoon on that day, William Pitt arrived at the House on crutches and fell immediately into a seat reserved for him in the front benches by Edmund Burke. Tickets were pinned to hundreds of the green cushions by members hours before the opening to guarantee themselves seats for what they all knew would be a crucial sitting. In the slush-covered Yard and adjacent surroundings milled hundreds of spectators in the gray February cold. Some one hundred pro-repeal merchants dined in the King's Arms Tavern nearby before going to the Commons to find a place in the galleries, on the stairs, or in the lobby.

Jones arrived with Roger Tallmadge, William Beckford, and William Meredith and secured seats in the top tier of benches. Garnet Kenrick had already ascended to the gallery opposite him and claimed front row chairs for himself and Winslow LeGrand.

Jones had drafted a short speech he planned to make on the chance he would be recognized by Fuller. As the Grenvillites were resigned to repeal, he and other advocates of it were resigned to a declaratory resolution. He knew that such a resolution would be proof against persuasion; that its obvious contradiction to repeal would be acknowledged, ignored, and accepted by so many of his allies. He would not inveigh against it. He would let the colonies make that argument.

As the members arrived in talkative clots and noisily filled up the chamber, Jones read again the speech he hoped to make today. In his satchel were two pamphlets: *The Chimney Swifts of Chicanery*, by Hugh Kenrick, and *Reconciliation or Revolution*, by Jack Frake. He had sat up the night before, pondering which Virginian would speak in the House today, and for whom he would be a mere messenger. He had not discussed his speech with Garnet Kenrick, Tallmadge, or with any of his allies.

These Virginians would have a representative in Parliament, after all, he thought. There had been so much discussion about the necessity or impracticality of colonial representation here. Ironically, he thought, many who argued for colonial representation did so from larcenous motives, for taxation with representation would end all the endless bickering over charters and constitutions and supremacy. The colonies would then have no grounds to object. These men argued from necessity.

Those who argued against the idea did not want to grant the colonies equal political status and did not wish them to have a say in their fortunes. And, they alleged, it would be unfair to the rest of the nation if legislative business were slowed to a crawl so that colonial members could communicate with their constituents in North America about this bill or that resolution. These men argued from impracticality.

But, Jones thought, all that was so irrelevant.

Members who chanced to glance at Jones in his seat that day were startled to see a man whose eyes burned brightly, because his mind was on fire. They did not know that they were seeing a man who was about to make a perilous leap from precipice to precipice across a chasm of contradiction.

The sitting began with George Grenville claiming that it was too soon to think of repeal, as he had news that some southern colonies had agreed to submit to the Act. Pitt immediately opposed postponement, while Secretary Conway stated that no such news had reached the government. At four-thirty Conway moved to adopt repeal, and argued from pragmatic reasons why it was desirable to adopt it. He was seconded by Grey Cooper, Under-Secretary of the Treasury and member for Rochester.

Charles Yorke, Attorney-General and member for Reigate, also argued for repeal from a pragmatist position, asserting the right of Parliament to tax the colonies. But this particular exercise of it was unwise, he said, for if enforcement of the Act produced the opposite of what was intended, the authority, if not the right, to tax the colonies in America might be irretrievably lost.

Edmund Burke, recognizing the distinction between internal and external taxation, agreed nonetheless with Yorke, Pitt, and other prominent members that the colonies ought to be coerced into "perfect obedience," but that the Act was not the ideal instrument for that purpose, being neither friendly nor fair to the colonials.

At one point, a member moved for a declaratory resolution, its wording to be debated and decided another day once the repeal issue had been voted on in the full House. The House in Committee passed it by an overwhelming majority. When Jones was canvassed, he voted "Nay." Its adoption surprised no one, least of all the member for Swansditch.

A series of speakers rose to argue for and against repeal. Charles Jenkinson, member for Cockermouth, a career placeholder and a "king's friend," rose to reiterate the warning that repeal might lead the colonists to believe that they could resist other Parliamentary taxes and regulations, as well. Repeal, he concluded, would only serve to exacerbate the conflict between Parliament and the colonies. When he was finished, Jones rose before anyone else thought to, and captured Rose Fuller's attention. That man, his curiosity getting the better of his knowledge of Jones, nodded to him.

Jones handed Roger Tallmadge his hat and cane. He glanced around the chamber and saw that all eyes were on him. In one hand he held his speech, which he looked down at now and then, almost in awe that the words in it were being spoken for all present to hear.

He had planned to open his remarks with: "It is thought here that to adopt repeal would be tantamount to this House, this Parliament, swallowing its pride and admitting that it was wrong. But it has no pride to swallow, and it will admit no wrong." He thought, however, that it would be a clear aspersion of the House, and, as much as he wanted to say it, as much as he thought the House deserved to hear itself so judged, he knew he would be shouted down and silenced, and Virginia would not be heard.

Instead, he began, "It is the anxious concurrence among the advocates of repeal and the defenders of the colonies here that some form of declaration of supremacy must accompany any act of repeal, for otherwise it is imagined, and not entirely without truth in the notion, that it would appear that the Crown, in such an act, would implicitly grant the colonies a unique state of political and economic independence not enjoyed by other Crown dominions.

"I join in that concurrence. For if the colonies are exempted from 'internal' legislative authority by Parliament, in little time it is supposed, also not entirely without justification, that they would begin to chafe under the proscriptions of the navigation laws and other constraints, and subsequently question that authority as well, and press for the immediate removal of those fetters.

"This is a true fear which I have often heard spoken in hushed words or delicate insinuations amongst both friends and foes of the colonies in this chamber. This fear may be credited, I am sorry to say, not to honest foresight, but to the natural apprehensions of frustrated and foiled political ambition and avarice.

"But what have these gentlemen and lords to fear? I do not believe that the consequences of repeal by itself have occurred yet even to the most eloquent colonials, for, if the reports and testimony in this chamber are any guide, the most vocal and robust opposers of the Sugar and Stamp Acts there do not have political independence in mind so much as a fair and just regard by the Crown for their rights under our excellent constitution. An accompanying declaration of Parliamentary authority, if it comes to pass, will not much be noted by our fellow Britons over there. Only a few of them, and fewer of us, will see in such a sibling act the foundation of a more ruinous and angry contention than they believe the Crown is capable of handling, except in the manner of Turks."

Jones paused for a moment to look around the chamber, almost surprised that no one had risen to object to his remarks. But, in the back of his mind, he knew that no one ever would. He knew that there was no answer to his words. He continued. "So, rather than seek to defend the temple of liberty, as many here purport to do, we will instead decide to prop up a moldy, half-collapsed, vine-smothered gazebo, which is infested with vermin and home to numerous rude and spiteful insects.

"Bind and confine the colonials?" he asked, glancing down at the top

· of William Pitt's hat in the front row of benches. "Should we not be honest about what this House intends to do? It is to bind and confine the colonials as captive felons, but take niggling, fussy care not to invade their pockets and appropriate what pittance is left to them after we have charged them the costs of their binding and confinement! What generosity! What kindness! What fairness! We propose to grant them the sanctity and liberty of their pockets, but not of their lives! But, should anyone in this House ever call this mode of supremacy 'tyranny,' would he then be accused of treason?"

There was no answer. Only the muffled babble of spectators in the lobby could be heard.

With some satisfaction, Jones looked down at George Grenville, who sat in a front row across the aisle with his protégé, Thomas Whateley, who had drafted the Stamp Act. The former first minister sat studying his shoe. "I wish to dwell for a moment on the unacknowledged, unspoken, but common premise among all the speakers here, pro-repeal and anti-repeal alike, past and present, that the colonies are already 'another kingdom,' and that the alternatives open to them are mutually grim. Be warned: When that realization has occurred to our colonial brethren, the logic of their binding and confining circumstance must lead them inexorably to a choice, which is to decide whether to fight for their liberties as Englishmen, or as Americans for an independence that will better secure them those liberties, and not leave them to the invidious mercies of legislators across an ocean, as we propose to do here.

"I say again: For the Americans, the alternatives to repeal of the navigation laws, as well, beginning with repeal of the Stamp Act, ultimately will be war and independence, or war and conquest. Then the Americans must decide to fight, or to submit. If to fight, and possibly to win, this nation should feel no shame in having lost, for it will be credited with having birthed a giant. If to fight and be conquered by us, then they will simply rise up in another decade. And if to submit, then they will do so ignobly, bitterly, and shamefully, after all the stirring, memorable, and defiant words they had spoken. Then we will have won by default, we will have the colonies in thrall, and we will have a dubious revenue from them, but we should feel no pride *whatsoever* in that triumph."

Jones braced himself for a unanimous, vitriolic counter-rebuke, led by Pitt, whose own words he had employed, but only then realized how much he had the House in his grip. Except for the sounds of voices of spectators in the lobby beyond the chamber's closed doors, and the sputter of candles in the great candelabrum over the Speaker's chair, the space was, for a moment, silent.

On impulse, for the pleasure of hearing the words spoken in the chamber and not drowned out by protests, he said, "*Fiat lux.*" The words resonated across the space, and he wondered if any he had spoken would find a home in the minds of some of his auditors.

He nodded once in thanks to the Chair, and sat down. He looked up at the gallery opposite him, and saw Garnet Kenrick. He knew by the Baron's expression that his sponsor had recognized the words of Jack Frake. The Baron merely smiled in forgiveness of Jones for not having used his son's pamphlet to make the speech. Most of the other faces in the gallery were cold, opaque masks of aversion, as were most of the faces in the benches across the aisle.

The silence that followed was the kind accorded a condemned man. Whether its object was the House or the speaker, no one cared to dwell on, beyond knowing that it was a righteous pouting. Rose Fuller stared at the floor for a moment, then surveyed the House in search of another speaker to break that silence. He saw that George Grenville had risen, and eagerly acknowledged the former first minister, even though he was weary of listening to him harp on the ingratitude of the colonies.

To everyone's relief, Grenville did not answer Jones, but launched into a tirade that the colonies could afford to pay the tax. After him, others rose to agree or rebut. The debates continued on that note, descending at times into a riotous pandemonium. Jones's words were not forgotten, but conveniently and mercifully belayed by a more familiar and comfortable obsession with minutiae.

A little after midnight, a motion was made for a final vote on the resolution for repeal. Rose Fuller seconded it. When he was canvassed, Jones rose to say "Aye." At 1:45 a.m., the House divided to retain repeal, 275 to 167. When the tally was shortly thereafter announced by a member to the spectators in the lobby, a nearly deafening cheer was heard beyond the doors of the chamber, making it difficult for the House to conclude the business of the day. The cheer wound its way outside through the clogged piazzas and byways around St. Stephen's Chapel and seemed to rattle the chamber's icy windows.

As they made their way out of the chamber into the lobby and then out into the cold night air, Pitt, Conway, and members of the ministry were greeted by a hundred flambeaux and by throngs of jubilant spectators who applauded, huzzaed, and doffed their hats. George Grenville and his allies were greeted with derision, insults, and some roughing up.

Jones witnessed it all with detached interest. It was all so irrelevant. Nothing was settled. "Nothing whatsoever," he said to himself as he made his way through the jostling crowds.

The next day, church bells throughout London rang for hours in celebration of the victory, and on the day after, throughout the land.

*   *   *

Chapter 25: The Repeal

As the bells rang in London, Sheffield, Birmingham, Leeds, and other towns, and as victory bonfires blazed from coast to coast, thousands of letters were posted by merchants placing orders for the colonies with factors and manufacturers, who reemployed thousands of idled artisans and mechanics, while over two dozen merchantmen in the Pool of London were instructed to lade cargo and prepare to make sail for America.

A victory supper was held at the home of William Meredith, attended by Barré, Edward Montagu, William Beckford, and other pro-repeal advocates. Jones elected not to attend.

"It was your finest address, Mr. Jones," said Garnet Kenrick the next afternoon when they met at Shakespeare's Head tavern in Covent Garden. They had dined here often, and sat at their favorite table.

"If it is that, I must credit Mr. Frake of Virginia," answered Jones, lighting a pipe.

"Will you write him and Hugh about it?"

"Mr. LeGrand is busy making copies of it as we speak."

The Baron sipped his ale. "And there has been no hint of a move to censure you?"

"None at all." Jones paused. "That does not surprise me."

"It surprises *me*, Mr. Jones. Yours was a most condemnatory address. Mr. Wilkes was persecuted for a lesser offence, and he did not even make his remarks in the House."

"It depends on the scale of one's perspective. Mr. Wilkes aspersed His Majesty, which was a particular offense, comprehensible to even a village idiot. I aspersed the House in the most biting way, by the crack lay of the indisputable identification of the character of the House and the means of its ways. That was not graspable by an idiot, but was by all present, especially by the rude and spiteful insects."

"Have any of those creatures approached you?"

"No, not as yet."

"But dare you return to the House? I am certain that many there would like to put your head on display above the Temple Bar Gate."

"I won't be kept away from it, come what may." Jones paused. "You must know, milord, that Mr. Frake and your son must ultimately come to conflict on some of these matters. As you know, I am fond of Hugh, but I believe now I am closer in some respect to his friend there on the York River, whom I have never met. Some day, I hope I may." He shook his head. "I could not help but beggar his words. They were timely, and in harmony with the occasion."

"Time will tell, Mr. Jones," said Garnet Kenrick with a smile. He wagged an admonishing finger at his friend. "And don't you forget, sir, that it was my son who had a hand in the Resolves that caused all this trouble and speechmaking of late. If Hugh is lagging behind Mr. Frake, it cannot be by far."

"That glorious responsibility has never left my mind, milord."

"Sir, you are inflexibly serious, and I've always found that to be your chief virtue." The Baron checked his pocket watch. It was two o'clock "Well, let us take a carriage to Lion Key and see how busy Mr. Worley has become. He is likely happy with distraction, now that repeal is a certainty." The pair finished their ales and early dinner, then hired a passing hackney to take them to the Pool of London.

Jones did continue to attend the House, but more as a spectator than as a member of it, for everything that followed was, to him, a mere post-script to repeal. He could have no influence on the course of events; he had little to do with them. He did not attempt to speak; did not wish to address the House, for he had said all that needed to be said. Indeed, he knew that he would not be allowed to speak, neither by Rose Fuller, acting as Chair of the Committee, nor by John Cust, Speaker of the House, when it was not sitting in Committee. His presence was noted but studiously ignored. While the House snubbed him, he snubbed the House. It was as though he had never spoken, and the House had never heard him.

On February 24th the resolutions of the 21st were reported from Com-mittee to the House by Rose Fuller. James Oswald, member for the Dysart burghs, a naval commander and friend of Adam Smith, proposed that the Stamp Act be enforced, but the revenues from its enforcement not be used for the army until colonial debts had been paid. Colonel Barré repeated his opposition to the Act, but modified his stand by stating that further colonial resistance should be in turn resisted, even if it meant using military force. When Jones stared at him in amazement from several places down the bench, Barré averted his eyes. Richard Hussey, member for East Looe and Attorney-General to Queen Charlotte, also excoriated the Stamp Act, but claimed that rioters ought to be punished, and also that if the colonies refused to make the requisitions through their own legislatures to meet necessary revenues, they should be taxed.

William Blackstone, in an effort to modify Alexander Wedderburn's earlier proposal to censure any colonial protestation of Parliamentary supremacy, made a motion to limit repeal to those colonies whose assemblies expunged from their records all resolutions contrary to that supremacy. Grenville rose to second the motion. Edmund Burke countered by claiming that such a requirement would surely be resented by the colonials and result in a delay in the resumption of trade, and that, in any event, the physical erasure of such colonial resolutions would not erase them from colonial minds. Blackstone's motion was voted on and defeated.

The repeal and declaratory bills thus went through several readings in the full House. Jones merely sat back and listened, took occasional notes, and did not interfere. He smiled in irony when a few members, on March 4th, pointed out the contradictory nature of the declaratory bill. Pitt opposed a declaratory bill, but seeing that the House was determined to pass one, subsequently limited his opposition to one of its clauses, "in all cases whatsoever," perhaps forgetting that it was he who introduced it early in the session. Grenville and others objected to its omission, claiming that without such a clause, the colonists might assume the Parliament had surrendered its supremacy. Some twenty speeches were made for and against Pitt's proposal, which was defeated. Pitt contented himself with the warning that enforcement of the Stamp Act could cause a civil war, and that His Majesty would be compelled "to dip the royal ermine in the blood of his British subjects in America."

As everyone expected him to, George Grenville rose for a last time to insist that the Americans could pay the tax. Jones yawned, as did many other members.

The wording of the declaratory bill was voted on and passed. At 11 p.m. on March 4th, the repeal bill passed a divided House, 250 to 122.

The Stamp Act, proclaimed the bill, was "repealed and made void to all intents and purposes whatsoever" as of May 1st. The declaratory bill sustained the power of the sovereign, on the "advice and consent" of both

Houses, to "have full power and authority to make laws and statutes of sufficient force and validity to bind the colonies and people of America...in all
cases whatsoever." In addition, it declared all colonial resolutions and
assertions to the contrary to be "utterly null and void to all intents and purposes whatsoever."

Speaker John Cust ordered the bills prepared for Lords. On the next
day, nearly two hundred members escorted the bills as they were formally
committed to the House of Lords. Jones secured copies of both bills and
showed them to Garnet Kenrick in Chelsea. "*Whatsoever*," sighed the
Baron after he had finished reading them. "You were right to rail against
the notion, Mr. Jones."

"I've a good mind to propose to the gentleman that he make it his epi-
taph. Think how it would perplex the pilgrims to his graveyard or Westminster Abbey, where he is sure to be interred."

After the Commons committed the bills to Lords, Jones barely took
notice of what other immediate but delayed business was taken up by the
House, which was budget and private bills unrelated to the Stamp Act. He
was not privileged to observe the proceedings in Lords, which lasted a mere
week and a half, but relied on reports from Chesterfield, the Duke of Richmond, and other peers friendly to repeal. The peers were also conscious of
the contradictory nature of the bills, but, like the Commons, regarded it as
irrelevant.

The Duke of Bedford's bloc in Lords was as stubborn in its disapproval
of repeal as Grenville's was in the Commons. Lord Suffolk, echoing Lord
Mansfield, saw repeal as encouragement to the colonists to free themselves
of other "acts more disagreeable and detrimental to them." Lord Halifax
defended the Stamp Act, claiming it would enforce itself, if given a chance.
Lord Temple defended not only the Act, but the wisdom of his brother,
George Grenville, for having authored and championed it. Lord Northington warned that repeal would sanction rebellion.

Lord Camden, in a series of acrimonious exchanges with Mansfield,
privately declared both the Stamp Act and the declaratory bill unconstitutional, then in the House that the Act would cause hardship in the colonies
to the detriment of trade, and caught Mansfield citing two nonexistent laws
in support of his argument. Camden on March 10th heatedly debated
Mansfield again, asserting that it was a waste of time to debate the details
of the declaratory bill since it was "illegal, absolutely illegal, contrary to the
fundamental laws of nature, contrary to the fundamental laws of this con-

stitution." After midnight on March 11th, the peers approved the repeal bill by 105 to 71. The Bedford and Bute blocs signed a protest against the motion. Over the next few days, the bills went in and out of committee, until, on the evening of March 17th, both bills were passed in Lords by comfortable margins. That day, Chesterfield wrote his son in Baden, "The repeal of the Stamp Act is at last carried through. I am glad of it, and gave my proxy for it, because I saw many more inconveniences from the enforcing than from the repealing of it."

George the Third attended Lords the next day to give his royal assent to the bills, and they became Acts. Throngs cheered him as he left Westminster, and as he returned to St. James's Palace. Jones studiously boycotted the ceremony and the jubilant crowds. Lord Chancellor Northington ordered official copies of the Acts prepared for the Board of Trade, the Privy Council, and colonial governors.

As church bells rang again, post office couriers placed hundreds of letters aboard mail packets and dozens of merchant vessels preparing to sail again for America, letters to friends, relatives, and merchant correspondents, all excitedly reporting the passage of repeal.

The Marquis of Rockingham had preserved the Empire.

* * *

The following day, Colonel Thomas Molyneux appeared with two other army officers at the door of Jones's rooms on Chancery Lane. Winslow LeGrand, who was assisting Jones with a King's Bench case, answered the knock, and returned to report the colonel's presence. Jones rose from his labors and went to the door.

Without preface, Molyneux exclaimed to him, "If the House will not bother itself to censure you, sir, I will!" Whereupon he produced a silk glove and whipped it across Jones's face.

"It was so kind of you to wait until all was said and done," answered Jones with humor. "Unfortunately for you, sir, I will not oblige you with swords or pistols. I spoke a truth that night in the House. You must accustom yourself to it."

Stunned by this rejoinder, Molyneux glanced at his companions, then boomed, "I *will* have satisfaction, you cad!" Again he slapped Jones with the glove. "Name your weapon! Pistols or swords!"

Jones grinned again. "Then you must satisfy your honor by penning a pamphlet, sir, one that will explicate your position vis-à-vis my own. Refute me, if you can. I promise to read it. That is the only kind of duel I recognize. Good day to you, sir." He then gently closed the door in the colonel's face. Returning to his desk, he instructed an amazed LeGrand to ignore the pounding on the door.

Over the next few days, a succession of members — officers, country squires, even another barrister from the Common Pleas — climbed the narrow stairs to his rooms and appeared at Jones's door to offer the same challenge. He would not admit them, and rejected their challenges with the same verve.

He remarked to the Kenricks and Roger Tallmadge over supper one evening in Chelsea, "If I were able to keep all the gloves that have so violently warmed my cheek, I should be able to open a shop on the Strand. They have been of the very best quality, I have noted."

"Take care, Mr. Jones," cautioned Effney Kenrick. "These men are not to be trifled with."

"Yes," said Roger Tallmadge. "Your notions of courage and honor are foreign to them."

"Their notion of courage is but a trifle," Jones replied. "Some of them may have fought battles in Germany and burglars at home, but none of them has faced judge and jury at the King's Bench!"

Alice Kenrick ventured, "These men are a mean sort! Uncle Dog is courageous and honorable! Why, did he not smart the cheek of the whole House, and did they not deny *him* any satisfaction?"

Jones smiled lovingly at her. "My compliments to you, milady. You alone have grasped my experiment in reciprocal justice."

"This is true, my girl." Garnet Kenrick raised a glass and beamed proudly at his wife, Effney. "My paladin of liberty sits there." They went on to discuss new mischief brewing in the House, a revenue bill that would contradict repeal in turn and assert the intent of the Declaratory Act.

"Has he not accepted *any* of their challenges, Mr. Hunt?" asked the Earl one afternoon.

"No, sir. He has laughed at the gentlemen. They are all somewhat bollixed by his behavior."

Basil Kenrick had heard from Crispin Hillier and Sir Henoch Pannell of a cabal in the Commons among some members to challenge Sir Dogmael Jones to a duel of honor, even though dueling had been outlawed years ago.

He subsequently assigned his secretary the task of witnessing the certain demise of his brother's protégé. "Mr. Hunt" — the alias of Jared Turley, the Earl's bastard son by a servant girl — had just returned from Chancery Lane after observing the furious departure of the latest challenger. He stood before his father's desk in the study at Windridge Court, waiting.

The ornate ebony Tompion bracket clock that sat atop the fireplace ticked away in the long silence, causing Mr. Hunt to count the seconds before his master responded to his information. He risked a glance at the annoying machine, and found himself entranced by how beautifully the flames below it reflected off the clock's gold and brass facing and mounts.

At length, the Earl said, "I see. That is unfortunate. I was certain we would soon be rid of him by cut or ball."

"He *would* be bested in such a contest, sir," volunteered Mr. Hunt, "as I do not think he is easy with sword or pistol. Books and words are his preferred weapons, it would seem."

"A nice observation, Mr. Hunt," mused the Earl in a mocking compliment. "Well, I think some men can be found who are easy with swords and pistols and even cudgels. I am not alone in thinking that the honor of Parliament and of the Crown cannot — must not — remain disgraced and besmirched. I am sure one of those bollixed gentlemen will see to justice, if not in the light of day, in some chilly wood, then in the dark of night in a street or alley. That would be fair. Fairer still, my brother would lose his voice in the Commons. How unfortunate! I am certain that he put Sir Dogmael up to it! To insult the House by proxy! Yes, fairer still!" The Earl shook his head, not having meant to digress on that subject. His private thoughts were not for other ears. "What do you think, sir? Price would be no object to such a person, of course, though discretion would be advisable and necessary. And, anonymity, needless to say."

Mr. Hunt gulped, and understood what his next task was to be. He had known for years that something like it would be asked of him. "Yes, sir. I have heard of such things being done, when satisfaction was not to be had in the courts."

"How many gentlemen did you say have visited Sir Dogmael?"

"By this afternoon? Seven, sir."

"Of course, all those unsatisfied gentlemen were wise to wait until Parliament had done with the business to pursue their honor. Some time has passed. Perchance, if Sir Dogmael wounded or killed one of them, that gentleman may not have been able to enjoy the Crown's victory, and Sir Dogmael would live to speak and offend another day. Yes, some time has passed since he slighted the Crown."

Mr. Hunt did not understand the relevance of these remarks, and said nothing.

The Earl reached over and toyed with the gold-coated tassels of the bell-pull. "Seven, you say? Well, I imagine that a determined man could find seven capable rogues in Whitefriars or Southwark for ready money who could administer a thorough thrashing."

"They are as plentiful as sand on a beach, sir," replied Mr. Hunt with a sigh, wishing now that he was back in Lyme Regis. "And as cheaply purchased, I would say," he added, knowing that his father would wish to hear it.

"What do you think are the chances of that kind of incident coming to pass, Mr. Hunt?"

Mr. Hunt paused to swallow some spit. "Very good, sir, if he dunned Parliament as you say he did and if nobody's been able to get him to feel bare knuckles for it, nobody would be surprised if he got turned off hasty like." As he spoke, he was surprised to hear his usually impeccable grammar disintegrate into the patois of beggars and criminals. Nerves, he thought. Even more surprising to him, the Earl did not seem to notice it. *No nerves*, he mused; *my father possesses a bloodless soul. It's a wonder I was begotten.*

"Well, let us hope that justice is done to Sir Dogmael, and that we may soon read of his desserts in the newspapers. *Very* soon." The Earl paused to look at his son with unmistakable meaning. "That is all, Mr. Hunt. Thank you for the information." Before his son could turn to leave, he added, "Oh, yes, Mr. Hunt. Your services to me these last few years will not go without some special reward. I have been thinking of signing over to you a few of my shares in the East India Company. They are better than consols, as you might imagine. Remind me of that in a few days, would you?"

Mr. Hunt blinked in astonishment. "Yes, sir. Thank you. Good night, sir." Mr. Hunt nodded once and took his leave.

The Earl congratulated himself on his own patience and discretion for having, like all those offended gentlemen, waited until the crisis had passed before acting. He tugged on the bell-pull for Claybourne to signal the valet his wish to retire.

"Cold-blooded bastard, he is," mumbled Mr. Hunt to himself as he made his way to his room. He would see to this latest task tomorrow morning, when it was light. In his nocturnal wanderings around London in search of diversions, he had met some men who would do the job for a bumper of gin, or men who knew others who would. When he entered his room, warm from the blaze in the fireplace, he felt an unnatural heat coating his face. He went to the washbowl for a handful of water to splash on himself. In the looking glass over it, he saw that he was sweating. He snorted once in self-reproach. Well, he thought, when those East India shares are in your hands, you won't remember the sweat. Not a drop of it.

A few evenings later, after a hearty supper with Winslow LeGrand at a tavern near the Inns of Court, Dogmael Jones bid the young man goodnight and strolled home, humming a melody that had suddenly come into his head. He was not a man to recall music of any kind, but the consumption of the right number of glasses of wine, when he was in the right mood, could trigger the recollection of something that had in the past struck his discriminating esthetic. After he had hummed the melody for a while, he recognized it, together with some words — some lines from Handel's *Messiah*. He smiled. Alice Kenrick had sung some portions of it weeks ago during a family music party at Cricklegate, her mother at the pianoforte, her father and Lieutenant Tallmadge and some neighbor guests listening appreciatively from a semicircle of chairs.

"Of course, I will sing!" he said to himself, for he saw a means of sharing something with the girl. He would not sing in private company, for he knew he could not sing, not well, at least. A duet with her, he knew, was out of the question. So, it would need to be a solo duet! He would sing in public tonight! So he raised his voice and sang the words as best and loudly as he could, to address and entertain the unseen occupants of the dark forms of the buildings around him:

"To break our bonds asunder,
And to cast away our yokes!
Break them with rods of iron,
And dash them to pieces like a potter's vessel!
Our sound goes out to all the lands!"

He stopped and laughed quietly to himself. "Or, words to that effect," he said. "An oratorio," he announced to the darkness, "composed by the greater George, as amended by Serjeant-at-Law Sir Dogmael Jones, member for Swansditch, for the delectation and edification of a sleeping populace!" He glanced around in the near darkness, up at the darkened windows, twirled his cane once, then swept it in the air above him. "Hey, you sheep who safely graze on the innards of your brothers across an ocean! Wake up and listen as I serenade your House! *Double entendre* there, if you've the wits to catch it!"

And he sang the words again, this time with more gusto than harmony. And stopped to listen for any response. Nothing, he noted. Silence. Not even a curse. "Since when was deafness a virtue?" he asked the buildings. "That was your call to liberty! Must I bang a pot? Sound a trumpet?"

Silence, he noted. He sighed and walked on. Well, that was the story of his life: Eloquence answered by Morpheus. In the House, in the King's Bench, and in public places. But, he thought, I have solved the riddle of them all! It is confusion, abetted by fear and avarice and a penchant for a proper remuneration to salve the sin of voluntary servitude. "'Oh, mighty God!' you slaves pray on your knees!" he shouted at the window shutters closed to the winter air. "'Let me remain ignorant, for I know that a knowledge of true liberty would be a reproach, and so I would be a harsher judge of myself than would you of me, Lord! Forgive me my weaknesses, oh Lord, but let me indulge them! I know that the meek and the humble shall inherit the earth, and cowards made saints! Let me be saintly! Is that not your *plan?*'" Jones paused. "Why, Lord! You dishonest rascal! You know very well you snitched it from Parliament!"

Jones stopped again. Still a silence answered him. He shouted to the houses at the top of his voice, "I have just insulted you! Have you no souls to offend? Are you so destitute of pride?"

A shutter somewhere did slam open then. A rough voice shouted down, "You, down there! Be quiet, or I shall call the watch on you!" The shutter slammed closed.

Jones tipped his hat to the unseen person. "Thank you, sir, for being my gallery. I have made you conscious." He walked on. An interval of warm weather had melted all the snow; the streets were dry.

"I might have been a noted actor, if I had so chosen," he mused to himself. "I shall write a play — *The New Hudibras, or No Laughing Matter*, I shall call it — and submit it to Garrick for consideration." Then he stopped again to whip the back of his hand across his forehead. *What ramblings!* he thought. He could not decide whether he was happy or sad or merely drunk. *Surely, not drunk. I have been drunk before, but never like this! But, the answer is irrelevant*, he thought. He felt alive and invincible. Even for all the failures over the course of his career. In the courts, in the House. In love.

With Alice. Lovely, innocent Alice! Smitten with a man in a uniform!

How like a woman, to fall for glitter, mistaking it for substance! No, no! thought Jones. *I will not insult her! There is more to her than that! After all, she grasped my experiment in reciprocal justice, and in so doing, even enlightened her own father! I must settle for remaining her Uncle Dog. That is at least a measure of something.*

A measure of something? He could not forget, either, the aria she sang in halting Italian at the same recital, Bononcini's "The Glory of Loving You," from his *Griselda*. Of course, she had sung it with discreet glances at Lieutenant Tallmadge. But, no matter, he thought. One does not stop admiring the moon because one cannot reach it, or touch it. One merely suffers the inconvenience.

He glanced up at the clear winter sky, whose stars were occasionally dimmed by passing billows of smoke. But it was more sky than usually canopied London in winter. He glanced around, raised his arms, and bent them to encompass the city and the sky to his bosom. Even for all my failures, he thought, the earth and my life on it are mine. Dear Hugh Kenrick, dear Judge Grainger! *That* is the solution to public places! He thought: *I shall write Mr. Kenrick about it, but not Lord Wooten. That great felon, indentured to his pearls and ermine, may stew in his own farrago of fallacies! Wisdom would be wasted on* him!

He walked on. Then the joyful solemnity of his soul was abruptly disturbed by a sound. A kicked pebble. Up until now, he had been conscious of his lone footsteps on the cobblestones and the frozen dirt as he trod his earth. Now he became aware of a tribe of stealthy footsteps behind him. He became alert.

Ahead of him at the corner were a lamppost and Chancery Lane. He was a block away from his rooms. There he had a pistol and a sword, and a door. He thought that if he ran, he could reach the safety of that fortress. But the footsteps were moving closer. If he ran, he was certain to be overtaken. Besides, he was not inclined to run. After all, he had stood and defied five hundred.

He turned and peered into the darkness. The lamplight behind him allowed him to perceive the forms of six or seven men. As they moved closer into the light he could see their faces, which were uniformly taut with purpose and grimly blank. They did not look like Mohocks, but like denizens of Alsatia, the most notorious of London's disheveled slums, a community of thieves, murderers, and prostitutes, recently cleared to make way for the north end of the Blackfriars Bridge. They were dressed in ragged cast-offs or in coats and hats too new and rich-looking to have been acquired by honest work. And they carried a variety of implements for subduing a man. He recognized one of the men, whom he had noticed loitering outside of the tavern earlier in the evening. He seemed to be the leader. This man stopped, and the others stopped with him.

Jones felt the mahogany cane in his hand. He could defend himself with it. Once, on the Pall Mall months ago, it had foiled, with a single whack on the head, a lone man who had leapt from the bushes and tried to rob him. But what could it do now? He doubted its adequacy here, against so many heads.

"We're the night watch, guvna'," said the leader, "and we heard you disturbin' the peace with your catterwailin'. We're here to put a stop to it, you see."

"Caterwauling," corrected Jones almost without thinking. He raised his cane and held it leisurely in both hands before him. "I require that my murderers at least be familiar with the King's English. You are not, so you may go home and acquaint yourself with Mr. Johnson's dictionary, if you have been discriminating enough to steal one."

The gang laughed in unison. "We'll be home afore you, guvna'," said the leader.

A burning fear of death shot up through Jones's chest, then fell to the pit of his stomach. He shut his eyes in brief regret. This was not how he wanted it to end, in the dead of a cold night, anonymously, at the hands of a band of common cutthroats. Rather, to die on a pillory, or by a noose, for having disturbed a greater peace. "Who sent you? Colonel Molyneux? The Earl of Danvers? George Grenville?"

"Don't know any such gents, guvna'," said the leader as he moved forward again, tapping a short truncheon in the palm of his other hand. His companions followed him, all menacingly waving their implements.

Well, no matter who sent them, thought Jones. It was not so bad to die like any of the Pippins. Yes, he was a Pippin. He remembered then what Hugh Kenrick had once told him, about how he had met the Pippins by rescuing Glorious Swain in similar circumstances in another dark byway. "Koshes and cudgels it is, gentlemen! Against my brave cane? Then you will have the privilege of dispatching the last Pippin in London! Ah, what a glorious exit! Mr. Garrick would envy me!"

He raised his cane and shouted, "Charge your bayonets, sons of liberty, close ranks, and follow me! Long live Lady Liberty!" and rushed headlong at the gang. Startled, the men scattered, reformed to encircle him, then swiftly closed in on him and did the deed for which they had been paid a pound a piece to do. Koshes, cudgels, and staves whipped up in the frigid air and flailed away. Thumps and grunts broke the silence. Lamplight glinted faintly off a knife blade as it rose and fell. A man bellowed in pain when mahogany met his skull. It was not the member for Swansditch.

When it was done, and the body moved no more, it was relieved of its cane, hat, cloak, watch, and shoes. And money. More would have been taken, but at that moment a lamp on a pole rounded the corner, the light of a pair of watchmen. The gang rose from its feast of loot and ran.

A lone witness, wrapped in a cloak and scarf so that only the eyes were visible, huddled in the shadow of a doorway. When the watchmen became distracted by the sight of a body in the middle of the street, and cautiously brought their light closer to see, the figure slunk quietly away in the wake of the fleeing gang.

* * *

Chapter 26: The Victory

"What do you think of this?" asked the Earl of Danvers of John Montagu, fourth Earl of Sandwich, some days later over coffee in the Cocoa Tree near Westminster Hall. He pointed to an item in the *London Weekly Journal*, and handed the newspaper to Sandwich.

Sandwich, who had contemptuously declaimed in a speech in Lords against both repeal and the Commons as an anarchical instance of "that democratic interest which this House was constituted to restrain," read the item, which briefly reported the murder of Sir Dogmael Jones, member for Swansditch, by persons unknown. He immediately handed the paper back to his companion. "What do I think of it? *Ought* I to think of it? Not at all, Lord Danvers! But, I will tell you this: It ought to be the *common* fate of half the *lower* House!" He frowned when his peer failed to acknowledge the jest with so much as a grin. Sandwich was known for his good humor, and few were immune to it. Disappointed, he then asked, "Why do you inquire? How could such a trifle concern you? Why should it concern anyone?"

Basil Kenrick shrugged in turn. "The chap was my brother's man in that lower House. He made a particularly offensive address there, and was subsequently challenged, I have heard, by a number of members there, whom he rebuffed in an equally offensive and cowardly manner. Or, so it is said."

"Would that had happened to that knave, John Wilkes," remarked Sandwich. "Then we should be spared the worry that he might return to bedevil us." He shook his head and grumbled, "But, no, Mr. Martin merely knacked him in the arm in that duel, on the second exchange. Poor shots, these commoners." Samuel Martin, member for Camelford and a friend of Lord Bute, had called Wilkes a "cowardly scoundrel" over remarks about him in *The North Briton*. Following the duel, Wilkes fled to Paris to escape the courts.

"Well," said Basil Kenrick, "at least Mr. Wilkes attempted to defend his honor. Sir Dogmael, it seems, had none that he cared to defend." He did not pursue the subject. He was satisfied that no one of consequence suspected his role in the matter. He had already asked Bedford and Halifax.

Nor did he pursue the subject when Crispin Hillier and Sir Henoch Pannell made circumspect inquiries about the murder. "You are as much informed of the matter as am I," he said to them with bluntness. "He was set upon by a band of rakehells. It appears the man was foolhardy, as well as *radical*. The two phenomena often occur in pairs, as you yourself, Sir Henoch, once pointed out to me."

"So I did, your lordship," conceded Pannell, recalling the occasion, and not a little flattered that the Earl would remember.

The two members were reluctant to entertain the possibility that the Earl was in some way complicit. Pannell limited his comments to, "Well, I shall miss him, for he was good for an occasional verbal joust."

"Many in the House will not miss him," Hillier added. "His verbal indiscretions are likely what led to his demise. A blustery and provocative sort, he was." He cast a last inquiring glance at the Earl. But the Earl's face was set in stone. The subject, therefore, was closed. He could not decide whether the Earl was uncomfortable with the subject or bored.

He and Pannell, having discarded their repressed suspicions, satisfied themselves with the more credible possibilities that Jones's death was either a consequence of an unfortunate encounter with criminals, or of an intrigue by members whom they knew had challenged him to a duel.

In the Commons, the would-be duelists, seven in all, exchanged furtive glances, wondering who among them had resorted to the ruse. But none of them was brave enough to raise the subject.

The night watchmen had known Jones, who had often paid them a kindness with civil banter and an occasional shilling for a draught of warming ale in a nearby tavern. One of them went to fetch Winslow LeGrand at his parents' tobacconist's shop on Fleet Street. LeGrand immediately hired a hackney to take him to Chelsea to break the news to the Kenricks.

Jones had no immediate family, at least none that Garnet Kenrick knew of, nor did he know where in Wales he had come from. He bought a plot for Jones in St. Giles in the Fields, paid for the casket and a tombstone, and grieved with the rest of his family. The news affected Alice Kenrick so much that she was bedridden for three days. Indeed, the entire household grieved. Owen Runcorn, Bridgette, and many on the staff at Cricklegate had frequently been the object of Jones's generosity.

Garnet Kenrick told his wife at the funeral, "When we can return to Danvers, I will have him removed to the family vault there."

"Your brother would not permit it, Garnet," warned Effney Kenrick.

"He will have nothing to say about it, by then."

Roger Tallmadge volunteered to "take up the spy" in the Commons in hopes of learning who had arranged Jones's ambush. After several days of discreet enquiries, he could report nothing. With disgust he told the Baron, "They must have sworn to an oath of silence that I cannot breach, sir, on pain of excommunication from their club, if they broke it, or on pain of perhaps the same fate."

In his study at Cricklegate, the Baron sat reading through the papers and documents he had retrieved from Jones's rooms. Among the papers was a draft of the speech he had made in the Commons that drew on Jack Frake's pamphlet, with acknowledgements in the margins of the author for many of the points Jones made in the address.

Some irony occurred to him then. He happened to glance up at the Italian bronze statue of Hermes on his desk that he had brought from Danvers. Around Hermes's neck was the black satin mourning ribbon he had attached to it years ago, after he read the accounts then of the executions of the leaders of the Skelly gang in Falmouth. The ribbon represented a paradox to him, a mystery to be solved. Now, things seemed to be clear to him. Jack Frake had been a member of that gang. Through Jones, he had spoken in the Commons.

He reached over and untied the ribbon. A son of Hermes had spoken, he thought. Another had listened, and had spoken in turn. And now was dead. He agreed with Dogmael Jones and Jack Frake. In time, all the sons of Hermes across an ocean would refuse to deal with the mortals of England.

He gently retied the ribbon to Hermes's caduceus, in memory of Jones's warning of war. Or was it Jack Frake's? He decided that they were both messengers.

He made his own enquiries in the Commons about the men who had challenged Jones. Every member he spoke to denied any knowledge of a cabal to force the late member into a duel. The denials uniformly exuded the character of lying. He forgave Roger Tallmadge his youth for not having been sensible to it. He very nearly was tempted to challenge Colonel

Thomas Molyneux, who at first retorted, "The cad bolted from me, and I'm sure he got thirty paces before his assailants caught up with him that night. Typical behavior of a chap who has more mouth than manhood, wouldn't you say?"

Garnet Kenrick was not wearing gloves. He slapped the colonel hard across the face. That man gasped in surprise, as did many members in the lobby who witnessed the incident. The Baron said, "He was a friend, sir, and more man than you could ever dream of being. One does not judge a man's character by the number or method of his murderers — wouldn't you say?"

The colonel sputtered an incoherent reply.

The Baron scoffed. "There's the speech more to your character, sir." He paused. "You know my name, Colonel Molyneux, " he said calmly. "Challenge *me*, if you dare." When there was no reply, he turned and walked out of the lobby.

At Windridge Court, he met a man who was coming out just as he was climbing down from the hackney. The man looked familiar, but he could not remember where he had seen him before. The stranger glanced away guiltily, hastily wound a scarf around his neck and mouth, and hurried at a quick walk through the slush out of the courtyard to Whitehall. The Baron asked Alden Curle, who admitted him, "Who was that who just left?"

"His lordship's secretary, milord. Mr. Hunt."

"How long has he acted in that capacity?"

Curle looked genuinely astonished by the question. "For years, milord. He is an extension of his lordship's will, so to speak, and has resided here for as long."

"I see," mused the Baron. "You may announce me." Curle escorted him to the Earl's study.

"I know why you are here, dear brother," said Basil Kenrick immediately as he entered the room moments later. "And, before you begin to make regrettable insinuations and threats, I will state once and for all, that I had nothing to do with Sir Dogmael's...end." He sniffed once. "If I had wanted to teach him a lesson for having disgraced his House, I should have arranged it long before."

Garnet Kenrick narrowed his eyes. "I am not inclined to believe you, Basil."

"That is your privilege."

"Perhaps you did not arrange it. Perhaps it was Mr. Hunt. I saw him departing as I arrived. He looks more callidish than does Mr. Curle."

"Think what you wish of him, dear brother," snapped the Earl, surprised to hear his son's alias mentioned by his brother. "Mr. Hunt is a loyal and capable servant of impeccable character. As is Mr. Curle," he added. "Your constant disapproval of my staff grows tiresome." He paused. "Did Mr. Hunt introduce himself?"

"No, he did not. He rushed off looking as though he had just taken some of your silver. I inquired of Mr. Curle."

"What did Mr. Curle tell you about him?"

"That he is your secretary, and, in his own words, an extension of your will." The Baron paused, remembering his brother's threat in this room on his last visit. "Would that extension perhaps include arranging *extraordinary* measures against Mr. Jones?"

The Earl stiffened and his eyes narrowed. "If you were not my brother, I would challenge you to a duel for that remark." He turned his back on the Baron. "Having made it, you have overstayed your welcome."

Garnet Kenrick did not know what to think, only what to suspect. He had no proof. Aggravating his uncertainty was his knowledge of all the challenges to Jones. A cabal could have existed, he thought. His brother doubtless would have been told about it, and perhaps exploited it somehow. He stood up. "I leave now, Basil, dismayed, I must emphasize, not relieved, by your assurances. You remain as you have always been to me, a caitiff and a menace. Good day to you."

Watching from his study window as the Baron boarded the waiting hackney in the courtyard, Basil Kenrick managed to convince himself that his brother had no cause to despise him. He had gotten away with a lie. His brother could be so unjust and cruel in his ignorance.

Two weeks later, the Kenrick household journeyed from Chelsea back to Milgram House in Dorset for the balance of the season. Garnet Kenrick had no further business in the Commons.

* * *

In the last week of April, the *Sparrowhawk* arrived in Caxton on the York River. John Ramshaw found the town in a bustling state, and also in a state of expectation. Out of habit, for he had done it for years, he climbed the hill from River Road to Queen Anne Street and began to make his way to the

Caxton *Courier*. He found that building occupied by another establishment, a cabinetmaking shop. *René Jalbert, Proprietor*, read the signboard. Then he remembered the fate of the *Courier*. Stopping off at Safford's King's Arms Tavern to leave bundles of mail, he then hired a horse from the Gramatan Inn and made his way under the warm spring sun to Morland Hall. At the great house he was directed by a servant to the fields and Jack Frake, who was busy in them supervising the new plantings.

In Queen Anne County, tobacco seedlings were beginning to sprout, and planters waited for the right day to move the plants from the seedbeds to the fields. Corn was being planted, and oats, and many growers were experimenting with English common red wheat. Barley and rye were also being sown.

Ramshaw hailed his friend, who greeted him in turn and rode toward him. "It was a fair crossing, Jack, and I bring some news." He reached into a saddlebag and waved a bundle of correspondence and London newspapers wrapped in twine. "Good news, and bad."

"What?" Jack asked. He took the bundle from Ramshaw.

"Repeal is certain. But so is a spoiler or two." He paused, however, to grin at Jack Frake. "You have a missive there from Mr. Kenrick's friend here, as well. From Sir Dogmael Jones."

Jack frowned. "What could he have to say to me?"

"It isn't so much what he has to say to you, sir. It is what *you* said in the Commons."

The owner of Morland Hall looked baffled. He knew that Hugh Kenrick had sent his father a copy of his pamphlet, *Reconciliation or Revolution*, and could not grasp the connection. He could not imagine the man using any portion of his pamphlet in the Commons without incurring its wrath. "We had better have some tea first, Mr. Ramshaw. Let's go to the house."

"Send a man to fetch Mr. Kenrick. He'll want to be here. And I have brought his mail."

When Hugh Kenrick arrived shortly thereafter on horseback, Jack Frake had already read Jones's Commons speech, and the thank you note that was appended to it. He was still mildly incredulous.

When Hugh had read them, he grinned at Jack Frake. "My compliments, sir. You have beaten me to the chamber." He turned to Ramshaw. "My God, Mr. Ramshaw! How did the House receive it?"

"I can't say, sir. I was not present. Your father happened to catch me at Mr. Worley's and he told me about it. I was obliged to weigh anchor and leave London the next day, when I believe the bills were taken up to Lords. But the day after the Commons voted the resolutions for debate, bells rang all day throughout the city. All over England, I'm told. And the Pool was as mad as Bedlam." He added with irony, "Even the customs men were in a jolly state."

"They would be," remarked Jack Frake. Etáin came in then. He gave her his copy of Jones's speech. "I've been heard in Parliament." It was her turn to look baffled. She sat down at the table to read.

They were gathered in the supper room. Hugh also sat down and opened his own mail. In addition to a copy of Jones's speech, there was a long letter from Jones on the conduct of the Commons. "He writes that the House will probably pass a declaratory bill, as well, one that would assert Parliament's authority over every matter whatsoever." "*Whatsoever*," Hugh mused. He looked up from the letter. "He writes that this term will negate repeal, if it is passed."

"That's the spoiler I mentioned," commented Ramshaw.

Hugh impatiently put the letter aside and stood up excitedly. "Still, can you imagine hearing Jones's speech in the House? Mr. Grenville's soul must have curdled! And all those 'rude and spiteful insects' must have clicked and buzzed furiously! And think of it, Jack!" he said, laughing. "He cadged *you*! He doesn't even mention my silly pamphlet on chimney swifts!"

Jack Frake chuckled, "Your friend there is my friend, on that point alone."

Etáin had finished the speech. She rose and bussed her husband. "He is a remarkably brave man, to have used your words in Parliament," she said. Her face brightened. "Why, this Mr. Jones spoke for Virginia! He spoke for us. In Parliament!"

"One could look at it that way," agreed Hugh. "What a triumph!"

Etáin clapped her hands together. "Jack, let us celebrate your maiden speech in Parliament with a grand supper! Tomorrow! We'll invite all our friends. I will entertain with music, and I am sure Reverdy will volunteer her voice, as well." She glanced at Hugh, who said he would ask his wife.

Jack Frake laughed. "If you insist. We will celebrate." He glanced at Ramshaw. "You will stay here, sir, if your business allows it."

"It does, and I will, thank you."

Hugh Kenrick rode back to Meum Hall and to Reverdy. In his study, he told her the news, and gave her Jones's papers to read. "I remember him," she said to him when she was finished, "from the time he spoke against the

Stamp Act." She shook her head in disbelief. "I cannot believe he was allowed to say these things in the House without giving many in it the vapors. It is such a churlish place that I am sure some members would have called for his expulsion."

Hugh shrugged, and nodded to the letter on his wife's lap. "He does not mention any recriminations for having said them." He scoffed. "Perhaps the House was so stunned, it was at a loss to devise a penalty."

Reverdy put the speech and letter aside and studied her husband for a moment. "Do you envy Mr. Frake for having been favored by him on such an occasion?"

"Not at all. Well, yes, I do envy him. But, not in any malicious way. He wrote the better essay. I must credit Mr. Jones with the judgment." Hugh looked pensive. "Strange sentiment, envy. It is almost synonymous with bitterness. But I am not bitter." He told her about Etáin's proposed grand supper to celebrate the speech and the possibility of repeal. Reverdy eagerly agreed to sing.

Reece Vishonn had also received mail, delivered to him by a servant from the King's Arms tavern. His agent in London sent him a statement of accounts and a report on the debates in Parliament, in which his agent said that repeal was very close to passage. The news so excited him that he rode to Morland Hall. "Haven't I said it all along?" he laughed. "They would see reason!"

"Have they?" queried Jack Frake.

Vishonn waved the caution away. "Oh, you are always looking under tree stumps for possums, Mr. Frake!" He paused to sip the sherry his host had served him. "Although my agent does caution that, if repeal passes, we should not consider it a victory over Parliament, lest the ministry hear of our jubilation, and look darkly on our behavior."

"If repeal passes, it won't be a victory, Mr. Vishonn, and there will be little cause for jubilation."

The master of Enderly stuck out his lower lip in thought. "Reconciliation, then?"

Jack Frake shook his head. "Not even that. You have read my pamphlet. You would be wise to consult it again."

In town, Vishonn called on Arthur Stannard, the tobacco agent, and apprised him of the news. Stannard, too, had received a letter from his superiors in London, reporting on the progress of the debates on repeal. Vishonn related to him Jack Frake's comments. "What do you think, sir? If it is not a victory, and if it is not reconciliation, what could it be?"

Stannard laughed as though it should have been obvious. "Mr. Frake is right, for once. It is neither. What it is, is a truce, an acknowledgement of an inexpediency. We have not heard the last of it, sir. The declaratory bill that may pass with repeal will set accounts straight. Parliament will not let the colonies go. You may count on it."

The next evening's supper at Morland Hall was attended by the Kenricks, Thomas Reisdale, John Proudlocks, Jock Frazer, Ramshaw, and Steven Safford. Jack Frake endured two rounds of toasts to him.

In addition to speculation about repeal, they discussed Richard Bland's own pamphlet, published in March, *An Inquiry into the Rights of the British Colonies.* Neither Jack Frake nor Hugh Kenrick thought much of it. John Proudlocks commented, "In it, he goes up and down tedious hills in circles of logic, never coming to rest, never reaching a conclusion, because I believe he is afraid of the end to which his logic leads him."

Thomas Reisdale nodded agreement, "It would be interesting to hear him discourse on Mr. Frake's pamphlet. But probably he would be so outraged by it that, instead, he would call for Mr. Frake to be put into the stocks."

"Very true," agreed Hugh. "He does not care for the conclusions." He scoffed. "Well, he was among the objectors to Mr. Henry's resolves last session, and Mr. Henry and I and our party correctly predicted that he and others would attempt to take credit for having discovered our rights."

They discussed the General Assembly. In early February Lieutenant-Governor Fauquier announced in the *Virginia Gazette* its proroguement from March until May. Hugh said, "Very likely he will delay the Assembly until he is certain there is no cause for trouble. I do not expect to see a new sitting until the fall."

"He and their nabs on the Council tremble," said Jock Frazer.

Hugh noted, "There has been talk in Williamsburg that some burgesses will invite a Maryland printer to begin a new *Gazette*, to answer the Governor's *Gazette*. That ought to be interesting. The Governor would not then have a monopoly on the news."

News, thought Jack Frake, as the company turned to other subjects. The next few years will bring us much news, and little of it will be cause for celebration.

Etáin glanced at her husband at that moment, and guessed his thoughts.

* * *

The news came.

News of repeal began filtering into the colonies as early as late April, and throughout May. Early in June Lieutenant-Governor Fauquier received a packet of correspondence from the Board of Trade. In it were copies of the Repeal and Declaratory Acts. On June 13th, in the *Virginia Gazette,* he formally announced repeal, and the Act was reprinted in that paper. It was also reprinted in the new competing *Gazette,* published independently by William Rind of Maryland. Its masthead boasted, "Open to all Parties, but Influenced by None." It was the first free press in the colony's history.

A ball was held in the Capitol to celebrate the news. Reece Vishonn and his family, and other prominent families from Caxton, attended. Hugh Kenrick agreed to attend, knowing that Reverdy was hungry for such an event. He noted that, despite the Lieutenant-Governor's best efforts and strenuous cautions, most attendees treated repeal as a victory.

Repeal was celebrated in all the colonies with balls, fireworks, and parades. Countless toasts were made to George the Third and his family, to Parliament, to Rockingham and his ministers, to all the friends of the colonies in London who had a hand in repeal. Few men paid attention to the accompanying Declaratory Act. Jack Frake and Hugh Kenrick observed this neglect, and knew that Sir Dogmael Jones was right to say in the Commons, that only "a few of them, and fewer of us, will see in such a sibling act the foundation of a more ruinous and angry contention than they believe the Crown is capable of handling, except in the manner of Turks."

On May 10th, John Robinson, Speaker of the House of Burgesses and Treasurer, died. His death was, of course, reported by both *Gazettes.* The late Treasurer's books were finally examined, and it was discovered that he had loaned many prominent planters the notes he was required by law to have destroyed years before, leaving his own and the colony's accounts in debt for over £100,000. Fauquier, whose friend he was, could no longer postpone the separation of the Speaker and Treasurer's offices.

On May 16th, Fauquier prorogued the General Assembly to July.

That summer, Robinson's father-in-law, Colonel John Chiswell, whom Hugh had dueled on horseback in Caxton, got into a drunken argument with a Scottish merchant, Robert Routledge, in a tavern near the Cumberland County courthouse, and ran him through with a sword, killing him. He was arrested for murder by the sheriff and was to be imprisoned in Williamsburg to await trial in the General Court. Three judges of that court — who were also members of the Governor's Council — intervened and arranged for Chiswell's bail. This extralegal action was also reported in both *Gazettes*, revealing to Virginians the scope of the Old Guard's influence throughout the colony. In his Williamsburg home, Chiswell, not long afterward, put a pistol to his head and committed suicide.

Shortly after the *Sparrowhawk* left Caxton in early May for West Point to unload and load cargo, the *Busy* arrived. Its new captain, George Requardt, inquired at Richard Ivy's tobacco inspection office after the residence of Hugh Kenrick, and was given directions. Requardt hired a mount at the Gramatan Inn and rode to Meum Hall. After he had introduced himself to Hugh, he conveyed his family's regards, and handed him a parcel of mail. Hugh invited him to stay at Meum Hall for the duration of his business in Caxton, and introduced him to Reverdy. Requardt accepted the invitation, and asked his host to send one of his servants for his baggage.

One of the letters was from Hugh's father. It was short, and dwelt on two pieces of news: repeal of the Stamp Act, and the murder of Dogmael Jones.

"Oh!" cried Hugh, and the pain of his exclamation was so loud that Reverdy rushed into his study, alarmed and frightened, for she had never before heard him in such agony. "Hugh! What is it? Some terrible news of your family?"

Hugh stood over his desk, resting on his arms, his head bowed. "My darling, they have killed him! They have murdered Mr. Jones!" He looked up at her. There were tears in his eyes. "You were right. There *were* recriminations. The bastards!"

Some days later, Hugh sat on the veranda of his porch, sketching, first in pencil, then in crayon, a portrait of Dogmael Jones, member for Swansditch, sergeant-at-law at the King's Bench, as he remembered him. When he was satisfied with the likeness, he said quietly, "*Fiat lux*, my friend." He had the cooper frame the portrait, and placed it on the wall at the end of his collective sketches of the Society of the Pippin.

On June 6th, Parliament passed a new revenue act that was more pernicious than was the Stamp Act. No one, not Hugh Kenrick, not Jack Frake, nor even the House of Burgesses and Lieutenant-Governor Fauquier, would learn of it until the end of July. In that month, William Pitt was elevated to the peerage as the Earl of Chatham. He left the Commons, where he wielded the most influence, for Lords, where he wielded none. In August he acceded to the request of the king and formed a ministry to replace Lord Rockingham's. Pitt's ministry, which lasted a year and a half, was more a

mongrel government than was Rockingham's, composed as it was of antag-
onistic parties and personalities. And it was a greater disaster, for Pitt was
absent for most of its duration. His ministry was thus steered, not by him,
but by those who wished to put teeth in the Declaratory Act in all colonial
matters whatsoever.

It was the beginning of the end.